# Acknowled

This is the third aspect of who attention should be paid. Over I have spent considerable time and altered our lives accordingly, adapting to a fresh set of tenets. It is how these books and this story was born, evolved and grew into the almost self-aware entity it has now become, summoning me to do it's bidding when new aspects of the story are imparted to me or inspire me or however the imagination and the mind interprets what takes place in there. Invariably, like any summation of three decades, there are too many to mention individually but to highlight some of the stand out moments for us; New Mexico and Arizona, the incredible people we met out there and the generous of spirit Native Americans we traded with and who helped formulate OUT OF THIS WORLD, our (primarily Sue's) business and the shops we have had and the fantastic shows we have attended - both locally and during our short lived time in the West Country - and as stall holders at a variety of shows and festivals, great times were had at Greenwich, Crayford, the USAF Bazaar held by the officers and enlisted wives of the USAF locally to us here at Woodbridge and Bentwaters, Lakenheath and Mildenhall. To our Xifu, D; where we learnt quite likely more than was good for us then, but in light of the decades passing we understand so much better those lessons now. All these things take their share of eating away at your pathway. Narrowing your options as you traverse it, with every choice (we are 34 year now vegetarians) removing another paver until instead of the landscape either side, you're faced with sheer drops. Nature is generous but demanding, nurturing but cruel and does not suffer fools – it's called natural selection for a reason. All these differing cultures and belief systems we enveloped, studied and incorporated highlight the interconnectedness of everything. A great Native American Chief likened it to a web, the web of life where by sitting in the middle, you are connected to 360 degrees of the universe. If you want…and you do need to want; answers are provided. We may not always like them but there they are all the same, act or don't act. The more you act, like a riddle or a puzzle or a labyrinth, more answers are revealed. Pieces of a picture most rarely see or understand. A picture that inspires and saddens in equal measure. For like I said about Nature being nurturing but cruel, the duality is always at play. Many who know me know I've spoken of this

1

often. It pervades everything everywhere but missed by the majority. There are millions of options to recognise duality but here are a few to demonstrate, up and down, in and out, black and white, on and off, good and evil, light and dark, male and female, wet and dry, cold and hot etc. etc. You see how this could go forever? Try it yourself, pick anything and find its opposite – there will be one. A balance must be struck, a middle ground, that narrow line that separates yin from yang. The Navajo call it the Beauty Way, a harmony. Science recognise these fulcrums too, after all for one example, it's called the PH balance for a reason. In this instalment, we acknowledge that which nature has given us and humanity tries desperately to destroy, master or dominate. We have left the middle ground in our constant and never ending consumption. The balance has been lost in favour of destruction and devastation on unprecedented levels. Humanity had become unplugged from the Earth. Recall the last time you walked barefoot upon the soil, consider how shoes insulate us away from our world, clothing from the life giving sun and even our time in the symbiotic waters of the world is diminished in favour of staying indoors and absorbing virtual tech instead of nature. Here, in this volume, we acknowledge Nature and all that is associated to her in a way you may have not considered before dear reader, enjoy and look for that pathway, it is waiting for you.

theseraphimcollective.com

# Seraphim Collective Chronicles

## Book 3

# Trinity

James R. Bowman

Published by New Generation Publishing in 2021

Copyright © James R. Bowman 2021

First Edition

Paperback ISBN: 978-1-80369-084-1
Ebook ISBN: 978-1-80369-085-8


**www.newgeneration-publishing.com**

New Generation Publishing

# CONTENTS

# Introduction

In the vein of duality, what sleeps must, at some point awaken. Since before the Kalithine Empire, there have been areas around the world of powerful significance, where the life force of this planet flows close to the surface and occasionally spills out. When sentient life learnt of these wells, these sacred pools of mystical power, they subsequently learnt how to tap into them to draw upon that power and enhance themselves. The Kalithine Empire exploited these sites to their benefit and to the detriment of those they ruled over. After the war that saw these creatures deposed with extreme prejudice, many of the wells and sacred pools and surface points vanished into myth and history. When humanity rose, they slowly learnt of these conduits and over time began to utilise them in much the same way. Empires come and go, and they rise and fall. History does not always give the account of why, only the account of whoever writes it. The fall of the Egyptian Dynasties, the collapse of the Holy Roman Empire, Alexander's downfall and many others right up to present day can be attributed to many things that cumulatively laid them low, but there are a few elements that run true through all of them were the dots to be joined. Nobody now believes in magic and few believe it was ever employed by anyone other than tall tales, but magic has been an influential factor through every Empire and gradually, like dominoes these cultures collapsed and with them went their magic and those who employed it. Without use it grows dormant, the longer the inactivity the deeper the sleep. But human existence has been running an exponential curve and our discoveries and leaps in technology have been getting faster, the gaps closer, the innovations almost over-lapping as we rise once more and as we rise, we grow careless in our arrogance. This arrogance has allowed for a power to grow in strength and bring a war to this world the likes it has never seen and one to dwarf every one that has come before it. This power brings magic and that is enough to waken the dormant, unused conduits. What slumbered for a thousand years now stirs and the unwitting and unaware humanity is about to discover how the world operated before it came along as these wells and sacred pools flicker and grumble, exuding power as they awaken and randomly discharging that power like a sleeper muttering in his sleep before sitting up and going to war. The world is about to shift and it has no idea…but that's all about to change.

# ΛCT 1

## Chapter 1

## Conjunction

The lights turned green and a hundred pedestrians flooded the 3 way crosswalk at 5<sup>th</sup> Avenue on the Museum mile, desperate to reach their respective destinations, converging momentarily as they had a mutual goal, but upon reaching the opposite sidewalk they then scattered like cockroaches with the lights turned on, each intent upon their own business. Being one way traffic, it was at least for the most part predictable as to what direction it was hurtling at during the five pm rush, there were fortunately no buses to avoid this time; luckily enough as they often believed they had right of way just because they had a lane of their own and all that the crosswalk lights did was to serve no other purpose than to change colour; instead today it was simply a lot of impatient yellow cab drivers, keen to be about their particular agendas. Gwen wasn't in the same rush as the denizens of the City That Never Sleeps, she was still functioning on California time even after arriving from sunnier climes several months prior. The frenetic New York existence hadn't infected her yet, though she suspected if she stayed there long enough it probably would eventually. She could feel it in the air, with every deep lengthy breath she took she could see others taking three to her one. As though time and oxygen were limited and they had to get as much and as many in as they could, just in case. Gwen often wondered about 'in case'. In case of what? She heard in case said frequently but why? Was everything always suddenly ending? A cosmic whistle blown where everyone had to put their pencils down and be judged there and then for what they were about and where they were at? A great apocalyptic exam? Gwen shook her loose, shoulder length blonde curls in mock dismay and smiled to herself, secretly with her head down lest she draw attention from someone demanding to know why she was smiling to herself; she'd encountered their New York, big city paranoia already and she didn't care for it. Constantly suspicious, perpetually on guard, invariably self-absorbed and many narcissistic, believing that the world orbited them and their concerns instead of the other way around.

5

This was the curse of city living and Gwen was feeling more oppressed with each passing day. Gwen put the hustle and bustle of others from her mind and refocused on what she was doing, sloughing the claustrocityphobia as she called it and focused once more upon the park, her escape, her oasis in a concrete desert. A dozen deep breaths, meditation style and she was ready to go once more.

A day off was precious and Gwen wanted to make the most of hers. Since arriving in New York from Los Angeles over half a year earlier, Gwen had secured herself three little jobs to keep her solvent and occupied. The one she had just finished was at Hannigan's Bar and Grill where she washed up, tended bar and was getting to grips with waiting the tables, she liked that place as it reminded her a little of home. That ran from eleven until four thirty, but before that Gwen had secured an early morning gig helping distribute food at the Mount Sinai Hospital. Preparing and delivering breakfasts to patients; that was a tougher one as it was from six am through to ten am and Gwen really wasn't a morning girl. It didn't leave her long though to grab breakfast herself and get to Hannigan's for her shift. Every third day however, Gwen helped at a local gallery and this was by far the most helpful as Gwen was something of an artist herself and after demonstrating her sketching to the owner, he offered her a position that came with a remarkably small apartment above the gallery. Otherwise there was no way on earth Gwen could afford to live on the Upper East Side, walking distance to Central Park, her current destination. They kept her busy but she was happy enough. Enough cash to live comfortably and slap bang in the heart of the Big Apple.

'Ha, if they could see me now.' Gwen muttered to herself as she thought about her teachers and school chums and her wasted time at school and latterly from art school, though any time at school was something of a giggle to Gwen as she spent more time not being at school than actually attending. Much to her parent's dismay and nearly all her teacher's consternation. Gwen didn't care for either and spent her time in town with her few friends who for the time back then, thought similar. The first real chance Gwen got to leave it all behind, she did. Being lithe and somewhat athletic even as child, not tall but well proportioned, Gwen was a natural dancer, loving it before she could even walk, pursuing more as she grew and even into her early twenties as she kicked art college into touch, she was good enough to have had a career dancing. Gwen hooked up with a small troop she had met whilst at college and who - as it turned out - needed one more before they could enrol in a once in a lifetime opportunity, world support tour and Gwen grabbed it by the throat. One year and several months as well as several countries later and it all began to fall apart, as three of the girls managed to get themselves pregnant and the manager himself arrested. That was Las Vegas. Gwen gravitated north to LA and had several months there but a spate of sudden deaths in her neighbourhood where she was staying spooked her. Gwen saw that as a sign, grabbed her stuff, as much cash as she could manage, hopped on a Greyhound and headed out of town. It wasn't until she hit the ground running at the Greyhound station at the Port Authority Midtown Bus Terminal New York City did she take a breath and decide to stop for a bit longer than her impromptu road trip cross country. Choices up until that moment had both saved her life and subsequently now Gwen had stopped once more, put it in jeopardy again, but Gwen knew nothing of this.

## TRINITY

'Hi Gwen, where you off to?' The female voice with a distinctive New York twang to it caused Gwen to spin, suddenly alert – having been caught dreaming in her own world and it made her jump – and with relief only to see a familiar face. One of the Doctors at Mount Sinai but she couldn't quite recall her name and Gwen hated that and was mentally embarrassed. Her mind went off in search of it, and it would let her know when it found it.

'Oh Hi doc…' Gwen improvised 'you startled me there, daydreaming still and it's nearly over.' Gwen rolled her eyes skyward and pulled a face to show her as scatter-brained 'If I wasn't careful I could just wander off some days.' The doctor smiled wistfully 'Hmm, I know what you mean.' The doctor replied 'It's either too much on my mind or too little, I swear I just work so hard just to keep my mind focused on something.' 'I know right.' Gwen agreed, placing a friendly hand upon the doctors fore arm 'I've three jobs and I'm still here trying to catch the early evening light to create a bit of art for the gallery this coming weekend.' The doctor with long silvery hair who Gwen mentally placed at her early thirties, mid-thirties tops as she had vividly blue eyes, almost flawless skin but for the subtle laughter lines at the corner of her eyes, full lips barely made up. Just enough makeup to accentuate those eyes and lips. Yet she seemed older and wiser than she looked – maybe it was those eyes – eyes that became instantly animated at the subject of art. Gwen didn't know it but it was an interest of hers too. 'Ooh, what are you looking to do?' Silver hair asked and Gwen was happy to talk about it even as she glanced wistfully in the direction she was intending to go as if hearing a distant

7

voice beckon her and she was unsure what to do, reply or be drawn away towards it. The Doctor caught the look and offered to walk with Gwen for a bit, taking two birds with one step. Linking arms then, Gwen started to talk about her plan as they headed into the park. 'Well, I was sort of going to try the Obelisk in charcoals with a pastel backdrop.' Gwen explained 'Guy has a small exhibition coming from an Egyptian artist and he wanted something to gift her, I said I'd do him something exotic but local.' Doctor silver hair nodded her agreement, citing it as a terrific idea. 'I know the very thing' she said 'I often spend time sitting there myself. It is fascinating isn't it?' Gwen had to agree as she had been spending a lot of her time in the park lately and nearly always found herself by the Obelisk. Suddenly the doctors name came to mind as though she were inwardly scrolling through a rolodex of names and it sprang out quite suddenly.

'Doctor Beldane I...' Gwen was interrupted by Doctor Beldane herself who laid a long, delicate fingered hand upon her arm – which stopped Gwen talking immediately, quite the feat too – before the Doctor spoke softly. 'I know you moonlight at the hospital Gwen, bringing meals and such so we're as good as work colleagues so please, Doctor Beldane is so formal, my name is Rebecca but most who know me just call me Bex and as a fellow artist, truth be told, I prefer that.' Gwen smiled, both in relief to have slipped past an uncomfortable moment of forgetfulness and in perhaps getting to know another side of the highly respected and much spoken of Cardiothoracic Doctor Rebecca Beldane. 'Bex it is then.' Gwen stated and it was so.

Neither woman noticed they were the object of intense scrutiny by more random passers-by, they would stop and watch the progress of the duo as they made their way into the park then slowly as if uncertain why, they hesitantly and quite spasmodically, followed them in.

## TRINITY

Gwen and Bex were sitting on one of the many benches arrayed before the Obelisk, Gwen had phoned for pizza and wine and a slightly steaming box sat between them as Gwen, with her legs crossed and folder resting on one knee fussed and muttered as she moved her charcoal expertly on the large pad. Smudging here, rubbing a bit out there and cocking her head from time to time to better understand the light as it failed and cast its shadows across and around the ancient monument, placing the hieroglyphics in staggering relief.

'Were going to lose the light before you're done I think.' Bex observed as she leant across and tried to see what Gwen saw, appreciating the apparent skill of the little English blonde woman beside her as she worked furiously. 'I know' Gwen answered absently 'but I think I'll have what I need to finish back at the apartment anyway. I could have taken loads of photos but I like seeing things for myself first if I can. Plus I like it here, there's something about home with these red brick pavers all around, I don't know.'

'I've not been to England for some time,' Bex whispered in a remembering sort of hushed tone 'my work has held me here for too long I suppose. I'd like to go back someday.' Gwen studied the woman beside her briefly as she spoke, a note of almost forlorn longing in her voice and wondering not for the first time her actual age, she didn't like to ask but she had spoken of many places she'd been and spent time while Gwen sketched and if Gwen gave it any serious thought, her time spent in all those places should make her at least three times the age she appeared to be. *I'd like some of her genes if she is actually that old.* Gwen thought enviously although her own looks defied aging and had been the curse of her school years as her friends aged progressively each year as though were living in dog years and she seemingly didn't. Neither woman however saw the three people from further down the viewing area snarl, tear at their eyes and start to run towards them. Suddenly there was a blur and a rush of wind and they were just gone. Gwen happened to look up curiously just in time to see a young man, blonde hair as unruly as hers walking into the viewing area, he was wearing a vintage leather flying jacket, tan slacks and Gwen took for construction boots, slightly darker than his pants but dusty and scuffed walking casually, almost too casually. He sat himself down several benches along and waved a cheery hello and started to stare at the Obelisk as though studying it. Seb hoped it didn't look too contrived but he was intrigued now, why were there three revenants here and why did it look like they were about to attack those two women? He'd been in New York a few months himself – having been sent there as part of their ongoing investigation which Harry was working on still in New England - and he'd noticed an increase in revenant activity straight away almost and although it was not unheard of, it was rare, especially in the short time he'd been there. Ted liked to be kept appraised of any sudden influx as it often heralded something more serious. Seb had left Harry in Boston and followed the trail of some particularly nasty and far too sentient revenants as they headed south, here as it happened; they appeared to be searching for something but gave no clue as to what and Seb had been unable to fathom their motives as they seemed vague themselves. Revenants, or possessed if called by their common name were always drawn to power, be it people, places or objects they gravitated like orbiting moons until they determined if it was either what they were after or if it could benefit them or their master whoever that might be, but they were nearly always after something. It just depended on what. Seb knew it wasn't him for a Hound of both his age now and origins could conceal their auric signature, remain undetected from even the keenest senses excepting a much older Hound or something more powerful still, Corben claimed to sense him occasionally when their paths crossed but he was a rarity. Chances were it was either someone who wasn't doing a good enough job of disguising themselves or someone who didn't know they had to. These were often strange folk, fey of mind and a little detached from everyone else's reality. The Collective had scrolls apparently that implied people such as this were escapees from the world labyrinth, souls that had been so close to power for so long and so detached, they were like a pin drawn over a magnet, simply empowered with no knowledge or control. Many medical institutions were filled with humans like this, where occasionally the medication kept them hidden, others were not so lucky. Seb recalled his map back at his apartment that was fast showing a pattern emerging of revenant activity all around the park where there were no such institutions so it was unlikely a fey, and more sightings these last weeks at this end, it made him doubly curious, was it this Obelisk? It certainly had…presence. But they weren't looking at that when they started to transform. They were looking at the little blonde lass with the easel further down or maybe her companion, the one with the silver hair. He'd have to watch and see what more he could discover. Clearly there was power at play and it was increasing. So watch Seb did and it was a disturbing discovery he made, for Revenant activity was definitely up and there were more around the park, on all sides. Some he had seen and tracked from Manhattan, Greenwich and even two from New Jersey. All were methodically making their way towards the park. Seb was a dab hand at disposing of them for there were few possessed who could stand toe to toe with a hound of Seb's capability but doing it discreetly was getting harder and what made things worse was that the petite blonde woman - who he had learnt was called Gwen and curated a small gallery off 5th - was somehow a focal point for them. Whether it was her, the area where she lived or simply that she was where they gravitated was yet to be seen and was no more than just coincidental for Seb and his highly distrustful nature.

The afternoon, six weeks later and Seb was sitting in the park wondering if Gwen would show today as she had fairly frequently the last few weeks, sometimes alone other times with the silver haired doctor Beldane, but after a couple of hours neither had made an appearance. Seb felt it was time for a drink, maybe grab some food before starting his evening patrol. So he wandered off and eventually hailed a cab, feeling the need to save his legs for five minutes and gain a different perspective. Eyes, ears and nose never really turned off, Seb startled the cabbie who was chatting inanely about something by yelling 'Stop...sorry about that, stop here, that'll do fine.' Seb tossed some bills at the cabbie and all bar jumped from the cab before it had entirely stopped moving. He soon caught sight of that which prompted his bizarre behaviour, six Revenants – together. This was a rare thing as they usually avoided each other as a rule. Seb knew it was selfishly about power and mission success – they didn't like sharing. Something powerful must be drawing them and he needed to find out what. Checking where he was, Seb looked up to a green neon sign above the door which read Hannigan's Bar and Grill. 'Two birds, one stone at least.' Seb said to the sign and stepped into the smokey gloom. His golden eyes quickly adjusted and he stopped short, surprised by two things straight away. The first was that Gwen was behind the bar and the second was the doctor she had been with the first time he saw her was sitting at that bar and the two were laughing. Doctor Rebecca Beldane Seb had learnt after following her one afternoon to verify who she was, a cardiologist by all accounts from Mount Sinai. Seb did a quick recce of the bar before finding a booth, flashing his golden eyes at the couple who were sitting there and in a growled voice almost below human hearing – though the menace felt behind it was very palpable – told them to leave, which they very promptly did, Seb sat himself down and summoned the waitress. There appeared to be no-one else of significance inside and if there were, they were hiding it well.

'Damn I wish Harry was here.' Seb bemoaned to himself not for the first time. They worked well as a hunting duo and two heads were always better than one when confronted with a mystery like what was unfolding here in New York. Seb had free reign to run his investigations pretty much how he chose, but eventually he would have to report in to Ted and the office and he really wanted more to offer than a couple of names and a coincidence. Suddenly the doctor stopped talking and casually turned to stare in Seb's direction, then her eyes fixed on him and there was no disguising it, it was direct, intense and very, very serious. Silver hair spoke briefly to Gwen, making an excuse it seemed as she hopped neatly off her stool and made her way through to Seb's booth with an uncanny directness that saw people simply move from her path, with no reason why they moved apparent. 'Mind if I sit?' She asked lightly but it wasn't really a question and Seb was expected to answer only one way. 'Please.' He stood and gestured to the other seat. 'Manners?' Bex noted dryly, 'That makes a change from one such as you, and I have to say I've not encountered one of your kind for many, many years. They tend to avoid the built up cities mostly, unless on extreme occasions. Why are you following me?' Seb absorbed all she said and was busy reading between the lines when it occurred to him. 'You? Why am I following you?'

'That is what I said, maybe you're not as bright as I thought.' Seb laughed then, turning on his full charm offensive, sitting back into his booth and holding a hand up again for the passing waitress who deviated immediately from what she was doing to tend to Seb.

'What'll it be?' Seb sniffed 'Wait, don't tell me golden Margarita…' Seb sniffed again then continued '…with that top shelf tequila, triple sec and Grand Marnier…no salt. For me, I'll take a Guinness, it's as close to real beer as I'll get I suspect, so thank-you …Danica.' Seb smiled one more reading her name badge, all teeth and tan and she spun away efficiently, glowing warmly inside, pleased to fetch the drinks.

'Very good, so you're not a basic mongrel then.' Bex noted 'Too much control, what are you exactly? And you can call me Rebecca...Sebastian?' Seb weighed up her assessment of him and was genuinely curious how she knew his name, things were getting complicated real fast and there were still Revenants outside who could burst in any moment and create havoc as was usually their intent and modus operandi. 'No, I'm not. Nor are you a mere doctor Doctor, so how did you know my name?' Bex shook her head and smiled 'You first hound, you're on my turf here so I get to ask the questions first.' Seb hesitated for a moment before making his decision. 'Well, you are a doctor after all so people trust you and you're accountable somewhere which makes it unlikely you're willing to burn your cover just to quiz me, so I'll trust you…I can't I?' Bex smiled and took her drink as Danica returned with them. Sipping, nodding her approval and putting it down Bex waited for Seb.

'You're right, my name is Sebastian, Captain Sebastian Mortimer, well formerly Captain as that was a some time ago now, but you can call me Seb. I work for an organisation that has a vested interest in…shall we say beings and items of power the general public has no business knowing

12

about. I've been tracking an increase in their numbers in this city and it seems more than a coincidence that they gather in numbers whenever you and Gwen are together, why is that I wonder? Who are you?' Bex leant back considered how to answer as it wasn't something she had had to do for many centuries now, she would have to be careful as clearly Seb had done some homework. He knew who Gwen was too. 'What I am is probably above your pay grade Seb, no offence but who I am might be closer. I am actually a healer, so me being a doctor is quite natural but I have many other gifts, mostly of the mind allowing me to perform certain…tasks.' Seb frowned at her evasive answer, a little put out at her assessment of his status too but he dug for a bit more. 'Like what? What sort of tasks?'

'Reading your mind for one, it is harder and not normally possible with your kind but you have an ancient clarity, you have control the vast majority do not. Why is that? What are you to Fenris?' Seb was stunned she even knew that name and floundered briefly in his train of thought and inadvertently allowing Bex to read a little deeper. 'My god, the ring itself?' Bex whispered, stunned for the first time in a long time 'Where is it now?' There was a certain urgency verging on panic in that question. 'Safe, it is with the Collective. Little short of the Apocalypse will it see the light of day, maybe even not then, so don't worry. Clearly you possess enough power to draw a revenant but I would have thought with that much, you would have a better handle on it and not attract the attentions you seem to be.' Bex frowned and looked back to the bar where Gwen was laughing with some of the locals, she caught the glance and waved cheerily. 'Maybe it isn't all me.' Bex whispered in hushed tones that no-one but Seb heard. 'What do you mean?' Seb asked looking over to Gwen as well whereupon Gwen cocked her head quizzically silently asking why Bex and her new friend were both looking at her so intently. 'Have you read her?' Seb asked breaking the moment and looking away, Bex quickly did the same. Bex looked at Seb with concern then. 'I can't say I've intentionally pushed but when we first started to talk there was nothing, which does happen from time to time but it stayed nothing and although it was refreshing to not be rummaging through someone's head now you mention it, there has been nothing for weeks now. I didn't feel any hostility or malignancy on an emotional level so thought no more of it. Taking the relief for what it was' Suddenly Seb sat alert, scenting the air towards the rear of the building, then turning his attention to the front door. 'They're here, Revenants, and there are more of them than when I came in, how effective in a fight are you as I'm not sure I can get all them both front and back at the same time.' Bex was not happy at all at this sudden turn, she had avoided this problem for numerous decades bordering on centuries, keeping her low profile had been her first and foremost priority. She had nearly been discovered at the twin towers that fateful September. She was only one and wished her sororitas was with her that day. She had saved who she could but the devastation was even too much for one of her kind alone. 'I'll take those at the rear.' Bex said resignedly 'If you can clear them from the front and join me when you can back there, it's been a while and I'm not sure how I'll hold up, your strength will be handy I suspect.' Seb nodded and before the next heartbeat, Seb was over the table and moving like a blur towards the front door. Bex moved with a swiftness of her own to the backdoor that was almost as fast but where Seb was pure supernatural speed, Bex uttered a word and she was simply there and from her silvery hair she withdrew a metallic object the size of a toothpick and with another word it expanded in her hand to a fantastically carved and ornate silvery quarter staff. Pushing the emergency exit bar Bex stepped through into the crisp New York evening air. Five brutalised faces spun as one to lock on her as she pushed her back to the door, ensuring it was closed and without taking her eyes from the things before her, Bex placed her hand upon the door and uttered two more words. The door glowed orange for a split second then the glow was gone, so too was the door but it would take a hundred humans to open that door from the inside now until Bex dispelled it. 'You shouldn't be here you know.' Bex said calmly, slowly spinning the quarterstaff. 'This world is forbidden to your kind and has been for millennia, but that has not stopped you has it.' They ignored Bex's rhetorical question and thrust out their arms with fingers stripped bare back to the bone and as one mind they howled and charged the lone woman. Seb had taken many, many years to master his affliction, at first it was unclear if he ever would and the condition would overwhelm him but with Harry's help they both turned a corner and could now manifest as needed or partial manifest. Seb burst out of the front door, praying there were no incoming patrons or too many general public present and he was relieved when there were neither. There were however seven revenants, in various states of mutilation but all had savaged the eyes, bloody sockets giving them away. Seb bulked nominally, drawing on his now superhuman strength and talons for hands, then moving at eye watering speed, he body slammed into the group, holding his arms wide to scoop as many as he could into his embrace, lifting their mortal shelled bodies off the ground, Seb made for the side alley who at the other end

Bex was battering revenants with a skill they did not expect. The quarterstaff looked like helicopter rotors as it spun deftly in her hands, one end or the other connecting solidly with head and limb of a revenant, sending it staggering, broken and battered. Three were never rising again but the last two pressed her and she had to fight desperately, calling upon skills she hadn't used in years both physical and mental. Her telekinesis sent one revenant cartwheeling across the alley to impale upon a broken pipe just as Seb came roaring around the corner and smashed his group into the wall to stun them long enough to step back and make a full transformation. Within seconds, a massive pale wolf, standing on hind legs with muscles rippling beneath blonde fur rose up to its full eight feet in height and a mere few seconds more and the revenants ceased to be a problem. The human shells spattered up the walls and too many smaller pieces littered the alley to be reanimated. Bex dispatched her two in time to witness the savagery of the hound that was Sebastion Mortimer, Hound of Fenris and even she felt a twinge of fear at his raw power. Golden eyes slowly turned and his fang filled slavering maw faced Bex. Their eyes locked and for a split second Bex wondered if the creature had over ridden his mind and she was next for a grizzly fate, but then she saw something in those golden eyes, intelligence; Seb strode down to where Bex stood and she had to look up at the wolf man who in turn looked down and spoke to her. 'You did well Bex, I'll take it from here. The Collective granted me the ability to best dispose of possessed so as to leave little evidence to panic the world. Go back and see to Gwen, I fear she is more than even she knows and you must try to ascertain what that is and keep her safe in case more have infiltrated the bar. I'll be in shortly.' Bex was amazed at the encounter and she hesitated a few seconds before dispelling the locked door and reducing the quarterstaff once more, long enough to catch a glimpse of green fire and burning, vanishing bodies.

## TRINITY

'Where did you and the hot blonde guy go then, hmmm?' Gwen asked smiling and winking as Bex retook her seat at the bar, Gwen brought another drink over automatically without Bex having to ask. 'Seb? Oh no it wasn't friends with benefits if that's what you're implying?' Bex and Gwen then smirked like school girls at the image both conjured for themselves at that prospect until Bex took the upper hand and the more serious high ground and insisted then it was so, they weren't a thing of any kind by any stretch of the imagination and it would be a stretch, Bex

15

made that quite clear. 'Whatever you say Bex' Gwen sniggered finally, absently wiping the bar and wandered off to serve another patron. This just as Seb came back in through the front, timing not really adding credence to Bex's insistence on no funny business, also not helped by Seb adjusting his jacket. Gwen saw this and smirked all the more whereas Bex just shook her head sadly. But over the forthcoming weeks, Bex, Seb and Gwen learnt a bit more about each other as during one of Gwen's days off they all met up. Bex had tried surreptitiously to find out more about Gwen and why she might be special and attracting revenants but Gwen gave nothing away that would give any reason for such behaviour. Seb on the other hand had been somewhat forced to report in. The use of magics and the increase of revenant activity and of course Bex herself warranted more info than he could muster if indeed she was above his pay grade, he needed to know how far. Uploading a picture of both Bex and Gwen he hoped the Collective database would provide more answers. It certainly provided one he wasn't expecting. One of their own elite Collective assets, one Major Tomas John Arthur 'Morningstar' Walker was the brother of Gwen, or Gwendoline Mary Sabella Walker as her file listed it though she hadn't mentioned once she had a brother. Ted had added a note to keep her safe at all costs. Seb didn't need asking twice about that as he instantly felt protective, as she was the daughter of his friend Tobias who Seb hadn't seen since they parted company that fateful night his and Harry's life started anew in the Dorset countryside shortly after WW 2. Tobias was a younger man then, Seb – who looked no different - would have liked to have seen him again older and as a father; maybe after this mission, he'd track him down. It had been a long time – too long perhaps - since he had visited his native England. Gwen however was the easy part, she was capable and easy on the eye and definitely no child. Seb may be a Hound of Fenris but he was still a male and Gwen ticked all the boxes red blooded males have when first looking at a woman. That aside and Seb shook that train of thought away quickly, maybe a little too quickly as her face kept resurfacing in his mind despite his best efforts - it was Bex who was the conundrum. Any and all records for her appeared some twenty plus years ago and started at Bex's 18$^{th}$ year. Before that there was nothing, not just nothing but a nothing that implied she just sprang into existence. No siblings, no parents, no fingerprints, no record of any kind. No educational record they could verify. Clearly she must have had something to validate her status at the hospital. Were they forgeries? Who was this woman or certainly not a human woman but a supernatural being as she clearly wasn't what she claimed, that much by her own admission. Above his pay-grade? Apparently above Ted's too as Bex came up blank on anything they had. What was she then? Seb left it with Ted to speculate and let him know if and when the Collective found anything, Seb assured he would do the same if he came up with any revelations. Seb knew Ted would have to take it further up the food chain, likely involving Lady Clare and the archivists. Seb was curious what can of worms this might open.

So the trio hung out often. When Gwen was at the bar, Seb would hang around, Bex would join them when she could, when she wasn't elbows deep in some poor soul having his heart sorted out. Bex frequently caught up with Gwen in the mornings as Gwen did her breakfast rounds and both Seb and Bex hung out at the gallery and Gwen's apartment above when she was curating there. Which was looking to start commanding more of her time as Guy – her sort of boss and landlord – so loved her charcoal and pastel rendering of the Obelisk had commissioned her for several more pieces and now Gwen had a small exhibition in a corner of the gallery. Ancient monuments, taken from the many pictures Gwen had taken during her brief spell dancing across the world. So now in her mid-twenties and with something of a comfortable life unfolding before her, a few dollars in the bank Gwen was feeling the familiar sensation of itchy feet and new horizons beckoned insidiously and whispered to her from the back of her mind. Gwen knew she was the primary saboteur of her own life, unsure of what she wanted, where she wanted it, interested in greener grass as long as it was elsewhere, grass that was in fact rarely greener, merely different and full of its own issues and stinging weeds. If she analysed it a bit deeper, Gwen knew it was the proximity to the park that kept her here really. She wasn't a city girl, she'd ascertained that much already but to have such a natural oasis, in such a city and one so accessible was what kept her sane she felt and if she did move, such space would have to be paramount in her choice of locale.

## HALF A WORLD AWAY

Tomas hadn't expected the helicopter to crash so soon. He had hoped his escape from the General's compound would at least see him back to his pre organised exfil site. No such luck and Tomas cursed and swore all the way down as he fought the helicopter to try and land it with at least a hope of his survival. It was falling now more than flying and the lack of engine heat was causing the infernal machine to freeze faster too. Tomas aimed for a clump of trees intending the foliage to break some, if not all the fall to the very frozen and very hard ground looming towards him at a lethal speed. 'Holy shit, this is going to hurt!' Tomas yelled as adrenaline and speed both ramped up seconds before the helicopter smashed into the tree tops. What followed was equivalent to tossing a machine, some trees and a few rock into a blender, tossing in a lot of ice and snow and flicking the switch on. Tomas was strapped to the seat and all he could do was close his eyes and wait for the chaos to stop moving and see if he could open them again once the maelstrom ceased. Fortune often favours the bold or stupid, occasionally the brave though fortune maybe believes if you knew what you were doing, you had more luck than maybe you deserved. Tomas had been known to bemoan his lot, citing that if it wasn't for bad luck he wouldn't have any at all. Today however, the fates mocked him by amazingly unbolting the whole seat and throwing it clear of the wreckage as it cartwheeled though the trees at breakneck speed. Leaving a trail of itself along with broken and burning foliage a hundred yards long. Tomas opened his eyes to see the fruits of his expert landing and was frankly stunned. There wasn't enough helicopter left intact to fill a grocery bag and he was still strapped into the seat half buried in a drift of snow and ice. Tomas mentally worked out, albeit a bit slowly as his head was still ringing that he was somewhere near the base of the Urals, or so he hoped. The blizzard he had subsequently taken off in didn't do a lot for his visibility but thankfully that had subsided and it was now just white and cold, in fact a bone chilling cold that would finish what the crash started if he didn't get his arse in motion. Easier said than done as Tomas wasn't feeling much use in his limbs from chest down. One arm was broken he knew but the disturbing thought he had suffered more fundamental breaks cheered him not at all. 'What an ignoble end, frozen to death, paralyzed and probably eaten by bloody wolves, you have shit luck Tom.' Glancing skyward more by accident than design, Tomas saw dark clouds forming above and knew that when they dumped their payload he would be as good as dead and buried. 'Maybe archaeologists will find me in a hundred years, stuck in this bloody chair. I knew this was a shit job the moment I took it, just one bad …' it started to snow…again. '…bollocks.' Tomas struggled as best he could to free himself but he was both wedged and limited mobility wise and neither gave him any ground. Inch by inch the snow rose around him and as his face lost sensation through icy wind chill, Tomas drifted slowly into oblivion.

'Wake up Tomas!' The voice cut through his torpid slumber like a band-saw through a banana. 'WAKE UP!' That did it and Tomas jerked awake, eyes panicked and rolling in his head as looked around for the danger, quickly recalling there was little he could do about it anyway but as he took in the vaguely familiar crash site which was now mostly buried under snow his eyes locked on to the figure hunched over the small fire burning not ten feet away. The figure was hard to define, in one instance looking just like a rock until he moved and the shadows gave him away, he wore something archaic it seemed, long coat or robe even with a voluminous hood drawn up over his head and face. 'Who are you? Are you Death?' The figure stopped what it was doing and sat back laughing, deep and rich and genuinely amused.

'Good grief no. But we have met once or twice, he does leave an impression I must say.' The figure looked away thoughtful before continuing. 'Anyway, good to see you awake. It doesn't help to sleep when you're buried in snow, that'll kill you. Tomas looked at the figure with almost disbelief before realising he was no longer actually buried in snow, nor attached to the chair and he was in fact propped up against a rock, one arm in a sling and a fur thrown across his legs. Tomas wiggled his toes and breathed a sigh of such relief, the figure rose and came to see what was up with his charge now.

'I have too many questions, how I'm alive, who you are, why you're even here, why you're helping, who you are...' The figure regarded Tomas 'You know you asked who I was twice?' Tomas chuckled 'I did. I'm pretty keen to know who my apparent saviour is and really keen to know your motives.' The figure paced the small area around the fire. Silent except for the crunching of snow underfoot. He threw an occasional glance to Tomas as though considering him amongst many other things. He seemed to reach a conclusion and stopped, turning with both hands behind his back but with his face still concealed with the gloom of the hood. He spoke calmly. 'You died Tomas, just for a moment or two before I could reach you. The cold got you, like it gets everything eventually but I was waiting for you which kept your death to a minimum, sadly not before the damage was done.' Tomas was on instant alert. 'What damage? What happened?' Tomas began an inventory on himself looking for something he had missed maybe, internal damage perhaps?

'Don't panic, you're fine now. The shoulder was only dislocated, it'll be weak and susceptible to that in the future now but it'll be fine in a few hours, I've seen to that. No, the damage is much more esoteric in nature. You don't know me but I know you, I know your family. In fact I know your lineage right back to its source. We're related you know.' Tomas was agog, what was this loon raving about? How could he know what he was stating quite lucidly before him? Tomas stayed quiet to hear him out though, curiosity always did get the better of him. 'That's nice bro, how about some more detail to this family get together.'

'Ah, if only we had the time, our window of communication is closing and I must be somewhere else very shortly, suffice to say we are truly related. You can call me Reaver for that is simplest. I tell you this not because you'll remember this conversation but it'll be locked into your DNA for future use when you'll need that knowledge. I'll tell you this now because I fear an ending is near, of what I'm not sure. My divinatory capabilities haven't been as reliable as before but that I suspect is due to THE ADVERSARY interfering where he shouldn't be and disrupting what he has no right to disrupt. I tell you this because this death of yours puts not only you in danger but your sister too. Sadly her I cannot reach and it will fall to others to assist her. I can reach you because of the river nearby.'

'What load of old bollocks are you babbling on about? You left me behind with you talking to my DNA...' The figure grew animated and clearly annoyed. Tomas had that effect.

'Be still your flapping lips and I'll try to tell you. Your blood goes back a long way, before the Covenant, as do I and we are hid from celestial view by a powerful spell, that is the easiest way to describe it but it has hidden all your line from those that sought its annihilation. But you died. Your death however brief fractures the spell, creating slivers of opportunity for those that seek your kind...' Tomas was losing what little patience he had.

'My kind? What kind is that? English?' The figure stood abruptly from the crouched position it had settled in as it spoke to Tomas. 'No you fool, your destiny. It is not yours to control and it may come to pass you will be called, the same for her but your death disrupts the pattern and puts you both in increasing harm. You must stay alive at all costs. Every near death experience you suffer fractures the spell more and more until one death too many and it will sunder. Exposing you both to horrors even your imaginations will shy away from.'

'Dude, how much more harm can I be in right now? And while you're at it, what is it about the river? Do you have a boat? I really need to be somewhere else...fast. So if you've a bo ...what the...' The figure looked down at Tomas then and something in the hood stopped Tomas talking immediately. 'You can call me by my more recent name if that helps you understand, history may confuse you more but you'll get the gist.' Tomas wasn't so sure now that he wanted to know after glimpsing what he thought he saw. 'Tell me anyway, this can't get any more surreal.'

'Don't bet upon that mortal. You can call me Charon, The Ferryman.'

Tomas was fuzzy on what happened after that revelation. Charon or The Reaver or whatever he wanted to be called spoke to Tomas of dire events, of possible futures and even some of the consequences. He reiterated to Tomas that he was telling him this so his future self would be more inclined to believe what was happening when it happened for events were at an irreversible state of play and many aspects of what Charon told Tomas were inevitable. Once done, Charon helped Tomas up, made sure he was healthy enough to survive his trials ahead, helped him gather his weapons then with barely a touch to Tomas's forehead, he rendered Tomas unconscious once more and wiped his memory almost clear of their encounter. Tomas would simply believe he had survived the crash and had to make his way on foot. Charon knew he would make it for he had seen as much. The line was long and convoluted but Charon summarised hundreds of generations as he took his first steps back to the river, glancing back to the sleeping Tomas he whispered to the breeze 'Farewell grand-son.'

## TRINITY

'Any increase in revenant activity?' the voice asked down the end of the phone. Seb sat reclined in Hannigan's, early afternoon mid-week and the place was comparatively quiet. Just how Seb liked it when he needed to make a call, one that needed a beer chaser. Ted could interrogate anything even down a phone and Seb had almost forgotten how intense he could be. Thirty years as a Hound of Fenris, doing his own thing mostly will push more than a few human made memories to a dark recess. It was only the last five years that Seb and Harry had reached out to Ted and the Collective and were working with them on a loose basis.

'There has been, both the rabid kind and the sneaky sentient kind. It tells me there is something more going on here than meets the eye and to cap it all, the NYPD are starting to get a little tetchy and poking around. Seems some of the victims were people other people might miss.' The silence down the phone from Ted wasn't reassuring as it meant Ted was thinking. If he had to think, then matters were truly off the chart and this did little to settle Seb. 'What news on Bex? Any idea who she might be yet?' But he was met with more silence. 'That's not good Ted, our boffins come up short? Thought we knew all there was to know about everything the public knew nothing about.' Seb added glibly.

'Don't be flippant Sebastian.' Seb knew Ted was rattled now by the mere fact of using his full name Seb felt the level of importance rise dramatically.

'She really has you all baffled doesn't she?' Seb had tried several times to get Bex to reveal more than she was letting on but she just smiled and kept mum much to Seb's increasing frustration. 'How is Gwen?' Ted suddenly asked and Seb was about to reply when Ted added 'She doesn't know what is going on I take it?' Seb answered in reverse order 'No, she has no clue amazingly, as for her health, she's tip top. So Lady Clare no help then?' Seb tossed that one in as Ted kept his friendship to the Lady Clare St John on the down low, citing optics. It didn't do for the upper management to be seen too frequently together as tongues wag and Ted was nothing if not discreet, Seb knew it as a throwback from their younger days and what different days they were, Seb had a brief moment of reminiscence before |Ted answered. 'She has her suspicions but even if she is right, Doctor Beldane may be even beyond Clare's remit. Best we can do now is observe, if she helps fine but if she shows the slightest inclination of harm towards Gwen you'll have to take her out…or try to anyway.'

'You're not a lot of help boss you know that? Its beer O'clock and I have a few here with my name upon them so if you've nothing useful for me, I'll be getting amongst it.' Ted didn't hang up as Seb expected instead he gave Seb a warning. 'One thing Clare did ascertain by the increase in Revenant activity is that there is probably a… still doesn't come easy saying this but there is probably a demon behind it. Something powerful has to be opening the portals letting the deminions through in order to possess so many. Watch out for this one Seb, we have nothing concrete but Clare has a bad feeling and I've learnt to trust them.' Seb sighed, as if things weren't complicated enough. 'A demon? Really? You actually think one of them broke the Covenant and is actually here?' Seb could almost hear Ted nodding 'We do but we aren't sure who. Ever since I took the Shard and we learnt of Drakel, Drakul and Drakareth I've learnt to take nothing for granted on the power stakes these days. Our basic sorcery may be as nothing against these beings whose every fibre is wrought with arcane magicks, humanity once thought of them as our gods after all once upon a time.' Seb didn't need reminding, he hadn't believed in werewolves either once upon a time, now he thought differently. 'A demon, luvly. Cheers boss, I'll keep you in the loop as and when.'

'Roger that. Be careful Seb.' This time Ted did hang up and Seb pocketed his phone.

'Danica? Can I get two more of those and two whiskey chasers darlin' as soon as you like.' Danica was happy to comply and was right on it, returning swiftly 'You expecting someone?' she asked inquisitively and Seb shook his head ruefully 'I hope not, these are for me, hoping they'll dull the news I just got.' Danica framed an expression of horror swiftly followed by sympathy 'Nothing too dreadful I hope' Seb smiled as he thought about it. 'Actually it is pretty dreadful, in fact dreadful doesn't even do it justice. What it does do is give me headache and I'm hoping these will dull it for five minutes.' A sudden thought flitted across Seb's mind. 'What time do you get off here?' Danica's face began to light up and Seb had to quash that thought 'I ask as I'm suddenly concerned for your safety. Do you drive? Cab or tube?' It had the right effect and Danica looked both crestfallen and nervous now. 'I take the subway if that's what you mean?' Seb nodded 'Do you go alone or with someone?' Now Danica was properly nervous 'A...alone, why?' Seb wasn't sure what to tell her, he couldn't say his paranoia was getting the better of him or that gangs of possessed were roaming the streets or that a demon – which was actually a thing, very real – was also probably on the loose and as she worked at the place where Seb, Bex and Gwen hung out, anyone working there was a potential target for a fate worse than death. 'Okay, so that won't do. Not for the near future anyway. I'll see you home each night from here on in. Nothing creepy I promise, but I want to see you safe...at least until I can resolve what's going on.' Danica now wasn't as giddy as she was before and the fear in her eyes Seb considered a good thing, maybe it would stop her doing something foolish and getting killed or worse. 'What's going on then?' she asked cautiously, not entirely sure she wanted to know but Seb had embroiled her somehow and she felt she needed to know more. 'There is a gang war going on and NYPD are struggling to get a handle on it that's all, but there has been some innocent collateral damage and we don't want you being part of that.' That did the trick, Danica had heard about gang wars and she relaxed a bit, enough to go about her shift anyway. Seb finished his drinks which with his supernatural constitution barely affected him at all, much to his disappointment and waited for Danica to finish her shift. He knew Bex was with Gwen this night as she was helping Gwen at the gallery with her exhibition. Whilst Gwen had some VIPs to show around on a private viewing and after party. That should keep them busy until after he had seen Danica home and he could turn up for the last hours or so he figured.

23

# TRINITY

'So what time are your guests arriving Gwen?' Bex asked as she poured Champagne into glasses and set them upon a series of trays. 'They should start filtering in about eight, the eager ones but the fashionably late ones won't rock up until at least eleven, it's gonna be a long night.' Gwen groaned and pulled a face as Bex settled in to long shift mode. 'It's like being at work' she drawled but Gwen nudged her playfully, nearly sending champagne everywhere 'But you can't drink at work, you rarely eat, or so I've heard and there is a lot less blood here.' This time Bex pulled the face. There was copious tables of finger food and Bex had collared a few interns from the hospital to help distribute and keep things topped up and handed out. Guy had thrown a small fortune at the caterer to ensure the finest quality everything and it showed. Guy had recently expanded his gallery by buying out the building next door and he had workmen work night and day to knock through and make good so he could expand his exhibitions. All had gone to plan, which Gwen was glad about as the noise of the construction workers meant she had to check into a hotel for a week just to get some sleep. Bex and Seb went loopy when she told them after the fact, both insisted she could have stayed with them and she had put herself in unnecessary danger by doing this without telling them. Gwen laughed it off but was both pleased by their consideration and equally disturbed by it. She had been living alone for quite some time, she knew how to take care of herself so what was the problem she asked. Both Seb and Bex just looked at each other and then at Gwen as they had just been explaining to a child about the dangers of getting in vans with strangers just after Gwen admitted getting out of a strangers van only last week. There had been no words, just incredulous stares which Gwen just laughed off.

The event was soon underway as Gwen predicted, the eager and early guests arrived and mingling escalated. There were faces Gwen recognized and yet more she didn't, it was a security nightmare if she was honest but Seb had helped there and the two slabs of protein at the door – although actually polite and eloquent – did look like they could prevent a vehicle getting in let alone an irksome guest. Though so far, everyone was behaving themselves and even conferring differing opinions on the art, not just freeloading the booze and food as Gwen feared might happen. As her photo and bio was attached to her own exhibition, she did garner some curious looks every once in a while as though they put two and two together for the first time. She was in fact the only artist exhibiting this night actually present and her nerves were surprisingly – it was a surprise to her anyway - increasing as it drew nearer and nearer to the VIPs arriving. Gwen didn't even know who they were. She had their booking name but not who the individuals were. It was the Heremus Society, Gwen knew that much though she had never heard of it personally, their CEO was supposedly some big wig in reclamation of the desert for the underprivileged or some such and that person had a plus twelve invite apparently. What made her palms sweat all the more was before Guy abandoned her to deal with this, he said they were coming to see her exhibit especially as much of their work was around North Africa and Egypt. 'Great, typical. I hope Seb gets here before they do, I could use a buffer between them and me and he does make a good one.' Gwen smiled to herself as she hadn't even confided in Bex just how much she appreciated Seb being around. 'Crikey, hope I'm not getting all nesty.' Gwen shuddered at the thought of kids, especially her own. She barely tolerated anyone else's. Taking her mind of it, Gwen mingled once more, smiled and chatted and even sold four pieces, three of the gallery and even one of her own, Bex was dealing with for her but Gwen was secretly giddy, barely containing herself as Guy had priced the piece at a touch over four grand. That was the night covered at least, Guy would be ecstatic. But once that excitement died down and the clock struck eleven, all Gwen's dread came flooding back though her mood immediately lightened as Seb strode in through the doors, exchanging brief words with his employees? Gwen didn't really know what Seb did and it had rarely come up or when it did he swiftly changed the subject. Gwen decided to broach the subject soon and get to the bottom of the big blonde mystery man, for now she was content to watch him weave gracefully through the crowd like a lion, mocha coloured suit, crisp white shirt open at the neck and impeccable shoes, he truly looked the only one who belonged there. Gwen smiled smugly as watched the women's eyes follow him as he made a bee line for her. Stopping before her, grabbing her hand and raising it to kiss the top softly. 'You look stunning Gwen, positively aglow.' Gwen blushed. She tried not to but she was beyond self-control at that moment. 'I've just sold my first piece of art.' Gwen giggled like a school girl then stopped abruptly and looked around, barely containing herself like bottled lightning. 'Well done.' Seb was effusive and praised her long and loud, loud enough to carry to the other guests and make them wonder what they were missing out on. Seb the salesman. 'Are your VIP's here yet?' Seb looked around for the extraordinary 'the guys reckon they've not seen anyone note-worthy yet, they are coming I take it?'

Gwen shrugged 'I hope so, be a shame after all this, they are supposed to be the highlight.' At that moment there was a commotion at the door and around twenty people flooded into the gallery. They were immaculately dressed, mostly in vary hues of white, slashed with one colour for accent. Red. It was either make up, nails, shoes jewellery or hair colour. They came into the rooms like a whirlwind and immediately oppressed everyone already there. They got up close, right into their air space, some even sniffed the guests quite deliberately making a spectacle of it. 'Seb!' Gwen, whisper shouted. She didn't know what to do, things were going from good to bad and bad to worse as she watched. Gwen looked to the door hoping the guards there would come in and start grabbing these reprobates but they were nowhere to be seen. Gwen started to panic. Surely these aren't her VIP's, this was scandalous. A woman strode into the gallery then as ethereal and regal as any goddess. Tall, lithe dressed in pure white head to foot, but what made it worse or complete was the fact she was albino. Her skin was whiter than her clothes and her eyes were more than pink, they were crimson. Long red nails and lips so red it looked like she had been kissing razor blades. Her eyes had been locked on Gwen the moment she stepped into the gallery behind her entourage but she quite suddenly halted and barked a word that sounded either Latin or Hebrew, Gwen wasn't sure but it had the effect of stopping her follower's dead in their tracks. Gwen didn't know she commanded that sort of effect until from behind Gwen Seb stepped level one side and Bex the other.

'To me!' That bit Gwen did understand and her flock swarmed around her like dogs to heel. She glided forward to stand mere feet before Gwen, Seb and Bex. 'I must apologise for the rudeness of my…people.' She spoke and her voice was like warm red wine, heavy and accented, one Gwen couldn't place but certainly no origin on this continent. 'They are…enthusiastic. You are Gwendoline?' Gwen found her voice suddenly as Seb nudged her slyly, she hadn't realised it but she was quite mesmerized by this strange white woman. 'Ah Yes, yes I am and may I welcome you to The Guy Beacham Gallery Ms…?' The woman looked at Gwen like a praying mantis eyes up a cricket 'Yes of course, you may call me Shiraz Azelea and I am the founder of the Heremus Society. We have many famous members you know but that is for another time, you must show me your work…now.' All the time she had been speaking, though brief it felt like an age to Gwen who hung on every word as though she was tasting something rare and limited; Shiraz had eyes only for Bex

26

and Seb though, glancing only at Gwen Shiraz couldn't take her gaze from Gwen's companions.

'Yes of course the exhibit…'Gwen found her voice then her manner '…but first allow me to introduce you to my associates, Captain Sebastian Mortimer and world renowned Doctor Rebecca Beldane. Seb went to take the hand of Shiraz the same as he had done with Gwen but she pulled it back faster than a scorched cat 'Please do not touch…' Shiraz snapped 'I have shall we say… sensitivities.' Her tone immediately softened as she forgot Seb and turned her attention to Bex 'you doctor I have heard of, though I expected you to be older, not the ravishing beauty before me.' Bex never batted an eyelash at the compliment and Gwen was bemused as she looked between them, it was almost as if they knew each other. 'Shiraz you say?' Bex started 'That's an unusual name, did your parents give it to you?' Shiraz and Bex locked gaze for what seemed an eternity until Shiraz broke the stalemate by smiling, a cold affair as the red lips stretched to reveal feral, but equally very white, possibly paid for even teeth. 'They did not sadly, they granted me a name of function, although had I known them longer maybe they would have chosen something equally exotic to proceed through life with. For a long time, I did not know myself, but the more I learnt the more I understood and as we know names have power, a resonance if you will it behoves us to name ourselves with something complimentary. But enough of me doctor, where are your kin? Who knows you are here?' Bex's eyes darkened then and she gave the impression of either deepest sadness or imminent violence, Gwen had not seen this look on her face before. It was nearly always so open and benevolent but it seemed Shiraz whoever she was knew how to push her buttons. 'It matters not who knows or your futile provocations of what you think you know darkling, I'm more surprised by your overwhelming arrogance walking in here as brazen as you like, clearly with an agenda otherwise you wouldn't have brought your toadies with you. What do you intend… Shiraz.' Bex laughed at the pointed declaration of the woman before hers name as though she knew something very different.

'I came to investigate a surge in power that has defied my deminions for weeks, causing many of them to mysteriously vanish without a trace, that will not do by the way…' Shiraz looked pointedly at Seb then '…but what I did not expect to find was the reason for this surge was the culmination of three such as yourselves. We assumed it was just one but you all amplify each other very conveniently and here you all are…together.' Gwen watched this by play with absolutely no understanding of what was really happening; she definitely felt the atmosphere change and not for the better. From the corner of her eye she could see the white clad entourage had somehow herded her patrons into various corners where they either huddled fearfully or for a few, railed indignantly until they were silenced by a brutal slap or worse and Gwen felt the rising need to do something before things went squirly any more than they already had.

'Look here Shiraz or whoever the hell you are, you're guests here apparently and based on your actions I'd say under false pretences and I'd like you to leave, right now and take your rabble with you before I call the police.' It sounded okay to Gwen but what she was not expecting was laughter. From both Shiraz and the pack who had been listening.

'Now you wait a moment…' Seb started, interposing himself between Gwen and pending carnage that his heightened senses told him was imminent. '…You all have seconds to leave before I throw you out.' A glance from Seb to the door where he expected a modicum of back up to be clarified his fears as the door men were gone, no doubt dead by now he sighed inwardly. Someone would pay dearly and it looked like it was going to be these clowns. He never saw the back handed blow from Shiraz that lifted Seb off his feet and propelled him across the room to smash into the wall. That was the cue for the entourage Shiraz had brought with her to commence their frenzy. The screams were the first thing Gwen heard but she didn't get to see as Bex grabbed her and swung her clear of the reach of Shiraz and she too got some air time as Bex sent her flying backwards. It didn't seem like relative safety at the time but Bex had been quite accurate and Gwen crashed through the small door that led to the back room and kitchen area where she smacked her head against the wall and saw stars, tried to stand on reflex but she had clearly hit her head harder than she realised and slumped back down again feeling suddenly nauseous. This meant she didn't see however the next few moments out front. Seb recovered like a rubber ball hitting a wall and with his recovery came the transformation into the master hound he was. Eight foot of blond muscular werewolf, razor talons and fang filled maw clearly displayed. The feral snarl he issued he had barely left his throat when he launched himself across the gallery. He expected to slam into Shiraz and overwhelm her but she was so much more than she appeared and it was like hitting a concrete post. She absorbed the impact and using Seb's momentum, kept him airborne and tossed him away like a rag doll. Bex took a back step and incanted several words whereupon the room seemed to slow and the white dressed followers who came in with Shiraz slowed to an almost crawl as the golden orb Bex conjured expanded to fill the gallery, it was like moving through thick molasses. It bought her and Seb the time they needed, even Shiraz had slowed though not as much as Bex hoped nor as slow as her entourage. Seb turned with a supernatural agility in mid-air and almost ran around the wall to regain his footing. Raking and destroying several followers as he did so. The wild eyed guests – those that still lived anyway – were as caught in the spell as those trying to kill them and where one couldn't get to them, they in turn couldn't get away either and this just ramped their fear and terror to all new heights.

'You cannot defeat me dog!' Shiraz projected her voice through the spell but it was no longer her voice, it was a sound of a hundred voices in torment, coming together as one horrendous sound and Seb rolled his lips back from his teeth in that canine way and affected the hounds equivalent of laughter 'Creature, you have no idea what I am, nor what I can do so let's see about that claim.' Seb smashed three more followers as he strode towards Shiraz. His talons ensuring they would not get up again. Shiraz mouthed words now herself and the air shimmered around her and her features melted away to reveal something else entirely. Her form grew as her flesh dropped away leaving scaly hide, like that of a rhino and from her shoulder grew another head even as the first head morphed. Both became goat like, horned and massive golden eyes with vertical slit pupils but the heads were scaled also as though some deranged scientist had crossed a komodo dragon with a goat. Wings began to manifest behind her appearing as though there were at least twelve. 'As I said dog, you cannot defeat me.' This time it was roared at Seb and he was buffeted by unseen winds though that barely slowed and he leapt at Shiraz. The impact was felt a whole block away as he smashed into the creature and both crashed out through the gallery window into the street. Bex took the opportunity to deal with the followers and instead of a staff this time, Bex withdrew a sword. A long wickedly curved yet thin blade that was a creamy in colour as though it was made from horn but when she sliced through the snarling, slavering followers, it cut like razor steel and they feel like weeds. Seb and Shiraz were rolling across the sidewalk and people began to scream outside. 'This is not good.' Bex would have laughed at the understatement of the century if she wasn't rattling her brain for how to limit the damage being wrought by this supernatural spectacle. Seb in the meantime was raining blows down upon the creature and as fast as he opened up gaping wounds upon it they closed and Shiraz repaid the compliment, both beings were beating each other to ribbons and healing as they fought. Shiraz was indeed surprised by the power Seb

29

demonstrated, he was indeed more than a mere hound, she had underestimated him; it was a mistake she was paying for. With a herculean effort, Shiraz broke the hold Seb had upon and she put some much needed space between her and the mighty hound Seb was. Those seconds were not lost on the public who had the misfortune of gazing upon the demon and the huge werewolf. Some would never regain their sanity and the image would be etched forever in the forefront of their minds, others would never sleep properly again. A lucky few passed out while others prudently ran as fast as they could the opposite direction. Then the fight was on again and Seb took the offensive, bunching powerful legs, he body slammed the demon so hard they cleared the road and the sidewalk and smashed into a wall opposite. Bex stepped out through the now smashed front window and ran towards the scrambling duo, incanting as she did so. Bex had no idea if the offensive spell she prepared would even work on a demon of her power but it was all she had. Bex was feet away when she raised the sword and delivered the final word of her spell. Every single light for ten square block went out and all that light poured into the raised sword Bex held aloft and once it reached its maximum Bex could hold, she levelled the blade at Shiraz and with the command word released to light. It left the tip of the sword like a laser beam of pure white light. If Bex had pointed it upwards, it would have punched a hole clean through the moon, instead it hit the demon full on in the chest and Seb was knocked back by the concussive force it generated. Shiraz screamed was instantly aflame like a small sun, all incandescent and searing. Bex knew that not even dragon flame could match this for intensity but for all it was explosive, even she could see inside the inferno to determine the result. Seconds passed and with a concussive shockwave, the fire went out. There was nothing there except molten sidewalk and a crater of liquid concrete. Of Shiraz there was no sign. Bex hoped for annihilation but doubted it. Demons were always covered in charms and defensive spells to protect them if things went sideways. Bex suspected a wily demon like Shiraz was no exception. But she couldn't think any more about her, it was now all about damage control and explanations as with their impeccable timing, the NYPD were hurtling down the street towards them. Seb had sped off the moment Bex lit up Shiraz and he was now back in human form, clothed in a hastily grabbed ensemble and was checking on Gwen. She was fine, still breathing but very groggy from the hit to her head. Seb whispered a few words of power, words of suggestion and coercion. Gwen would hopefully wake up believing an explosion from a blown gas main outside had taken out the window and caused the few casualties. Seb placed Gwen in her room upstairs and then rushed back down to dispose of the very dead and too sentient revenants Shiraz had brought with her. Not enough for him or Bex but she hadn't counted on them. Green fire quickly consumed the bodies and Seb knew that he had to do the same for the victims, better they be missing than subject to a forensic exam that would raise way too many questions about the manner of their death. Gwen had to be kept safe at all costs, the public were second to that as it was what the Collective did. Did well up until recently but there were more and more incursions with increased severity. There was seriously more taking place than he was privy to for sure. He would have to let Ted know about this though, it was unprecedented. It was also the first demon Seb had encountered and he was more than a little disturbed. Very little walked the earth he wasn't a match for but this thing threw him about like a rag doll and took all he threw back at it. If all demons were anything like this one, they were in deep shit if they came in numbers. Seb was seriously concerned.

The next few days were a boring series of questions and paperwork filling out as the NYPD were not wholly convinced of the hastily constructed lie but there was little alternative to it they could find. Seb, Bex and the freshly risen Gwen were adamant and played the victim to the fullest. Seb applied all the coercive magic he could muster to whoever he spoke to, getting them all on the same weak gas leak page. What the people saw was simply pieces of exhibits blown outside, they were archaic representations of ancient creatures of mythology as was the exhibit. 'How could creatures like that be real detective?' Seb reasoned for all he was worth 'Surely you don't believe such nonsense?' And the police, sceptical as they were, eventually went away as satisfied as they were going to get, for now. Bex and Gwen arranged clean up, glass replacement and by the end of the week – other than the crater which was still there – there was no sign anything untoward had happened at all. People were missing but this was New York and people went missing all the time for no end of reasons. Bex and Seb kept up their subtle magics upon Gwen and by the following week she was as convinced as everyone else and normality resumed once more with Gwen none the wiser.

## CRINICY

'We did that.' Seb had gone to the hospital one afternoon a couple of weeks later to talk to Bex in private. He had kept a steady vigil until he was as sure as he could be there were no repercussions or follow up attacks by the bizarre Shiraz Azelea 'We gave off enough combined energy that with Gwen there, she became the centre of attention.' Bex sat in the doctors rest room, leaning on the table their and cradling a mediocre coffee dispensed from an uncaring vending machine. It didn't care what it spat out, nothing about its taste, condition, warmth or value for two dollars. This day, neither did Bex. She tasted nothing as she hadn't the last several days after the attack. It played over and over in her mind and something was desperately wrong with it all. Shiraz hadn't turned up for Bex or Seb, she had appeared mob handed for Gwen, Bex was sure of it. That meant there was something special about the little English woman above and beyond mere artistic talent and old world charm. But she had no idea what it could be; Seb had nothing sage to add either except her brother was an asset for the organisation he worked for. Bex had heard of the Seraphim Collective from centuries past but kept that knowledge to herself, it didn't do to muddy the waters any further with how that was possible, Seb had settled to the fact she was off limits and his bosses hadn't deemed it necessary to pursue or reveal what or if they knew anything. Gwen was the mystery here and that being said, she was increasing in danger here in New York exponentially as Revenants and full on demons were now coming after her, brazen and in full view and disregard for the mortal public. Gwen needed to leave and she needed to believe it was her idea. The trick now was how to make that happen without her getting suspicious or blowing anything else up; the NYPD were still hanging around long after they should have moved on to the next. She had noted the same detective watching, hanging out at the park, visiting Hannigan's so much so it went beyond coincidence. Seb had taken to following her following Gwen but she reported to no-one nefarious it seemed, just her being too damned suspicious for her own good, she would bear watching. Bex had seen it in hospital cases where the female detectives were often as not more intuitive and more tenacious than many of their male counterparts. There it was good but here it was nothing but a nuisance.

## TRINITY

Detective first grade Elspeth Farrow sat at the end of the bar in Hannigan's and watched the petite blonde woman behind the sweeping counter, mixing cocktails and chatting like it was just another day. For many though it was just that, but Elspeth had been first on the scene that

32

night when literally all hell broke loose on 5$^{th}$ Avenue. Some of the statements she had taken and read over and over since gave her chills and even random nightmares. There was something wholly wrong about the entire incident. There had then been a record number of statement retractions the days following it and to the untrained observer, it was like someone was going very far out of their way to make this all go away, to downplay events and turn something catastrophic and heinous into something virtually non-existent, harmless and uneventful but Elspeth was having none of it. She had moved to New York from Albuquerque some years previous, more by accident than design for she had been following a murderer. It had been a complex case and she refused to give up on it. Luck threw her a bone – quite literally – for it was during an exhibition at the Natural History Museum where the local news anchor was reporting on the forthcoming exhibits, Elspeth saw her killer in the background. Why Elspeth was even watching was only for the fact the exhibition was full of Southwestern artefacts and she knew the people involved in taking it to New York. Elspeth wangled herself an undercover role as an intern and went along for the trip. It took three months more, liaising with NYPD and their homicide detectives to finally nail her killer. Yet three months in the city had been enough to get under her skin and entice her away from the sleepy desert to the Big Apple where everything happened all the time 24/7. Elspeth was something of an insomniac so being up and busy at all hours suited her down to the ground. But aside from all the city lights and never ending torrent of human wrought crime, Elspeth was a creature of the desert and had been raised on stories of legends and creatures of myth, skinwalkers and wendigo. Though that was a more northern creature, the equivalent was everywhere and what she saw spill out onto the street that night fitted her version of what a wendigo was. Though the huge hairy beast didn't sport the usual antlers associated to them it ticked enough boxes for Elspeth to be concerned. Of course she knew of werewolves and such - how could she - not and in all likelihood that fitted the description better, but she had a start to work from. Of course, her rational mind told neither were actually real and she didn't see what she thought she did and neither did the thirty seven witnesses she initially had which had whittled down to two as of that morning. Elspeth had little doubt that by the time she found her desk once more, they would have retracted too. Her case was fast dissolving before her very eyes until soon, there would be no case to even speak of. That irritated Elspeth as she knew there was something here, her intuition told her so. 'There's definitely something going down.' She would say to herself as her mind sought clues or connections to whatever was troubling her. In fact she said it so often, her colleagues back at the precinct had started to emulate her, many shouting it out across the squad room before she could say it during daily briefings. They thought it funny but in an endearing sort of way because her arrest record spoke volumes for her and her uncanny success solving the seemingly unsolvable.

'Did you see what actually happened that night?' Elspeth casually asked as Gwen drifted into her orbit. 'Sorry what?' Gwen was all innocence 'What night was that?' Elspeth looked at Gwen and tilted her head sideways birdlike as though trying to see through smudged glass. Her view of Gwen and her shock at the sheer denial were at odds with how Elspeth thought she should be responding so she elaborated. 'You know, the night the gallery exploded and those two things were seen tangling in the street and where all those people disappeared…that night. Surely you've not forgotten? It was your gallery and you were exhibiting there were you not?' Gwen stopped dead then and turned her gaze upon the woman at the bar as though truly seeing her for the first time. 'You're police aren't you?'

'Is that a problem? Aren't police allowed to drink?' Gwen smiled and the fencing began.

'Of course they are, what can I get you?' Elspeth noticed she had no drink already and that was odd enough, giving her away in hindsight. Elspeth mentally kicked herself for letting Gwen notice it. 'Beer is fine.' Gwen looked calmly back over her shoulder at the six under counter refrigerators full of varying craft beers. 'Any preference, we have a few.' Gwen added smoothly, making the most of the detective's discomfort. Elspeth craned over the bar to try to see what was available and quickly spotted one she knew. 'Amber Bock please.' Gwen went to the requisite fridge and pulled the Michelob out. Popping the top and pausing Gwen added 'Glass or as she comes?' Elspeth was desert raised, hanging around cowboys had left her with few lady like tendencies. 'As it comes is fine.' Gwen stood the bottle down on the counter, ignoring Elspeth's outstretched hand intentionally. Noting too that the detective was reaching for money and Gwen stopped her. 'Oh no, the first one is free for police in here.' Gwen said it just loud enough that several heads turned to regard Elspeth.

'Thanks.' She replied sardonically 'No really, nicely done. I'm getting you don't want to talk about it…' Gwen jumped into the pause with a look of curiosity 'about what?' Elspeth was about to respond but Gwen wasn't finished. 'I saw you there that night, we all did. You've been in here several times and I've seen you at the hospital. I have friends who look out for me and one of them is very good at spotting people who behave suspiciously. Thanks to him that night didn't happen, not as you think and with each passing day, not at all. There is no mystery for you to solve here detective, I don't know what to tell you beyond that.'

'I want you to tell me what I really saw. I don't care at this rate that every witness we have is in greater denial than you are here and their story matches yours almost perfectly that nothing occurred out of the ordinary. A utilities hiccup and that was that. You and I both know I'm not buying that. I know what I saw…well I don't actually know what I saw, but I did see something and we both know that wasn't your every day run of the mill utilities hiccup.'

Gwen looked at Elspeth carefully then leaning on the bar she asked 'What do *you* think you saw? Then tell me out loud and ask yourself how that sounds.'

'Don't you think I've been doing that?' Elspeth breathed 'I know how crazy it sounds even now but what I really want I suppose is to hear it from someone else, to know that I'm not the only one left who has that image burned into their mind, a fight between two things I can barely bring myself to think about let alone speak aloud.' Gwen looked at her sympathetically before answering. In a recess in Gwen's mind she thought she felt something similar, a memory of horror and carnage but after speaking with Seb and Bex, that memory was fading by the day, to the point she couldn't now even recall what day it had been or what actually happened. Gwen had been asked these questions repeatedly the days following the event but as each day passed the questions became fewer and her memory became hazier. She knew deep within what the detective wanted and it irked her still to be questioned - but truth be told, she couldn't remember enough to answer even if she was inclined to. Each day her memory faded with the nights events until reminded of it, when a hazy recollection resurfaced but so vague as to be almost dreamlike. Of course Gwen was blissfully unaware of such things as magic and any sort of supernatural persuasion, both of which had been gently applied to Gwen to force the incident clear from her mind. Bex and Sebastion had each applied their abilities a little at a time, not only to Gwen but to the many involved that fateful night. Luckily there had been no recurrence of Shiraz or as Bex reluctantly told Seb, her real name had been Azazel and the fact a full on demon had breached the Covenant and come directly after Gwen like that meant nothing good.

'Who are you really?' Seb had asked Bex that night after her revelation of demons and the Covenant. Seb was barely aware of such things as was Ted and it was only due to the circles Seb moved in he had heard stories of both, he was unsure how much Ted knew though for that matter, most people who knew Ted were unsure how much he knew now, but he gave up little about Bex so Seb was forced to push a little harder in person. He was happy to try now after knowing her now for a while, familiarity made those harder questions easier to ask and as she knew more of him too, maybe she would find it easier to answer. 'I'm still not sure you need to know Seb…' Seb on the other hand felt he did and said so. 'Look Bex, I fought a demon out there and I think it's only because of how I became what I am that I survived. The fact I survived at all kinda warrants some answers. You know what I am, that I work with the Collective and how you know them could use an answer or two too. I don't get that same smell of Drakul from you, yet you move similar to them, you employ magics and I'm curious as to how powerful you are on that front. The Collective aren't giving much away either but they aren't here on the ground with an increasing amount of shit hitting our fan. The number of Revenants I've disposed of is unprecedented and I don't know why. They seem to follow Gwen not you or me otherwise your hospital would have been overrun long ago but when we are in proximity to Gwen she becomes very popular as though we light her up somehow more than she would normally alone, so I know what I am by knowing you that's two out of our three taken care of then we can figure out why Gwen is so special.' Seb sat back and folded his arms and waited, his expression and demeanour brooked no more obfuscation.

'Very well.' Seb noted the tone of her voice, laden with reluctance and defeat, even her scent had changed but Seb held his ground and waited to see what Bex would say.

'I am Unc' Anharaphim.' She said it like that explained everything and Seb just shrugged and shook his blonde head none the wiser. 'You've not heard of us?' The incredulity in her voice made Seb curious 'Should I have done? It doesn't sound like something on the school curriculum and I've never heard it at the SC, so you'll have to elaborate I'm afraid.'

'Oh dear, I was hoping that would be sufficient.' Bex looked nervous and her scent reflected that which made Seb all the more concerned for who she was though in the same breath he recognised the scent of fear of betrayal, of someone in hiding. He was used to that scent.

'Look Bex, I know it's taking you a lot to speak about this and trust me, your secret could not be any safer but I'll tell you now I will share it with one other.' Bex's eyes widened in horror but Seb placated her by taking her hands and explaining 'Don't worry Bex. That one other is my brother in fur, Harry. He is like me, we were turned together by the same artefact and we've been partners for decades now, changing the world and working with the Collective. We have no secrets and you can trust him like you trust me – like I hope you trust me?' Bex didn't look so sure but her scent changed and Seb was relieved enough to let on what he had gleaned to perhaps reassure her further. 'I know you're in hiding, on the run so to speak and you have been here a while so you've kept this secret tightly under wraps for a long time, with mine and Gwen's arrival I bet you've used more of your abilities than you have a very long time, am I right?' Bex relaxed then as Seb was spot on. 'It's true and thank you for not pressing earlier, this isn't easy for me. I've been in hiding for centuries, truth be told. I've moved across the world and lived in many lands until it gets suspicious so I then move on. My kind were hunted to almost extinction millennia ago and the few that remain are all so deeply hidden even I don't where they are. I feel them occasionally especially if they are working powerful magics but that's about it.' Seb knew there was more and encouraged Bex to go on 'You've heard of Drakel?' Seb had and told her of Corben. 'Ah Aeneas, yes I've heard of him though never had the pleasure of meeting, anyway he is only part Drakarim, the other part could be mortal or celestial depending on who his mother mated with either way he is a hybrid, his mother however would have been full Drakareth I suspect, one of the exiled.' Seb was keeping a straight face amidst names he was unfamiliar with so not to sway Bex's explanation, he'd figure it out after. 'The exiled were Drakareth because they were afflicted with Reversion, a disease you really do not want to mess with, come into contact with and definitely not contract - there is no known cure anywhere in the galaxy.' Seb raised his eyebrows at that, feigning horror and shock. He was immune to most things now and knew little enough about Reversion to be worried but he wanted her to continue. 'Anyway, the Drakareth come from Esolaria, my long lost home-world and the beings who flourish there now are my kin. Imagine if here on earth there were only two races of sentient human, let's say Africa and here in America. Let's say also that for the sake of my analogy, the two races had never met, never left their own shores; you would still be kin for all your differences as you would both be human. We are the same, the Drak and my kind are both kin yet we are so very different. You know of the Drak as they have been here, your species call the dragons. My kind has been here too but we chose another form and your legends depict us as equine, well sort of but the distinction of note is the single horn prominent upon our forehead.'

'You're a unicorn?' Seb blurted before he could reign in his enthusiasm and utter excitement as well as astonishment but that took third place in his emotions right then as the sheer bewilderment of what he was hearing overwhelmed him momentarily/ 'Sorry about that, but that was NOT what I was expecting, threw me there for a second, sorry.' But Bex wasn't concerned at all, she was instead almost laughing at Seb's reaction. 'Now you know why we don't tell people very often about us.' Seb got up, walked over to Bex's drinks cabinet - as they were at her place – poured two large glasses of a particularly pleasant single malt, brought one to Bex and he sat cradling his. A few long seconds later as he was clearly processing, Seb then downed his in one swallow, blinked slowly then took a deep breath.

'I'm fine now, holy legends and all that. Wow.' Seb and Bex talked then for the rest of the night, finishing off the scotch as the sun came up.

Elspeth was however still sitting at the bar word fencing with Gwen whenever she came by to see if she wanted another beer. Though it turned out Elspeth was a font of knowledge about many subjects and as the night wore on, the two women spoke less and less of the events she had originally intended and after Gwen finished her shift, they retired to a booth and talked long into the night too. Six am rolled around and the sun came up reluctantly. A fact Gwen only noticed as the stained glass window above the door lit up and cast blue and green shadows across their table. Gwen looked up and suggested breakfast.

'I really should be getting back…' Gwen was in no mood for excuses now 'Back where? The office? Hubby? Home? All of which require explanations better delivered on a full stomach and mine is definitely protesting…it'll help my head too as there was probably one too many tequilas in that conversation.' Elspeth assimilated Gwen's reasoning and found it sound and quickly agreed, being reluctant to be apart from the quirky English woman who as it turned out had wicked sense of humour much akin to her own and Elspeth thought that was rare on its own. But familial similarities bound her a little tighter also, an estranged elder brother, parents not seen for probably too many years, a love of the outside and the wild places. Elspeth had started to describe some of the parks and trails of Arizona and New Mexico she had hiked as a girl before moving to the city by accident. In fact much to Elspeth's surprise, she found herself actually homesick for the first time since moving to New York. She missed Albuquerque, Taos, Santa Fe, hiking around all the national parks, climbing the Sangre de Cristo Mountains just so many things lost to her since becoming a city girl. Gwen brought all this out in her throughout the course of their all-nighter and as they sat devouring breakfast – both unaware just how hungry they really were – Elspeth began to forget about the frenzied attack and concentrate more on how many vacation days she had left and where she should spend them – and who with. Gwen mopped up the last of the blueberry syrup with the last piece of buttermilk pancake one handed, the other hand was twiddling the new crystal pendant Bex had given her. Gwen had a thing for the semi-precious gems and loved the jewellery in its many complex and colourful varieties, owning a fair bit herself. Bex had told her it was a Herkimer Diamond, hewn from Dolomite actually from Herkimer County, close to the Mohawk River. Bex explained that now she was a New York gal, she should have one. Bex knew also that was the easier sell to make Gwen wear the gentle memory erasing charm, targeted specifically to memories of that night only. Little did Bex also know that its arcane radius would work equally well upon any in Gwen's immediate vicinity.

Seb was still busy though and no time for breakfast this day as even though some weeks had passed since Azazel had made an open attack, Revenants were still gravitating to Gwen and the gallery, even to start focusing upon Bex and the really daring – or really stupid ones – targeting Seb. It was taking all his supernatural skills in covert behaviour and equally as much coercive skills to eradicate these creatures both physically and mentally from the minds of those they attacked with little care as Revenants didn't bat an eye for collateral damage – if they had an eye to bat that is. Seb had just followed a group of six into an alley and he had started to transform when he heard the familiar sound of flesh tearing and the curses of Revenants just before they died. Seb was baffled as he hadn't even reached them yet and at full speed he rounded the corner only to be met with an incongruous sight, leaning against the wall, standing nearly nine feet tall, bristling black fur and muscle, flicking pieces of bone from beneath talons big enough to open a car like a sardine can a figure looked up at Seb's arrival and it said in a deep growling baritone 'You're getting slower you know.'

Seb just looked on bewildered and after several seconds just burst out laughing. Both figures then began to shimmer, reducing in size and transforming to something more recognizable and Seb was the first to speak when he had regained his human form 'Hi Harry, what took you so long to get here?' Harry grimaced in involuntarily touched his side 'Had a bit of witch trouble. Sorted now though so I thought I'd see what kind of mischief you were getting up to and the moment I hit the city, all I could smell was Revenant. What have you been doing?' Seb brought Harry up to date over drinks at Hannigan's. Knowing Gwen was at the gallery this day having worked last night. She would sleep best part of the day and open the gallery at four until midnight so he knew he would be undisturbed there. Seb did indeed tell Harry everything, including what he had learnt about Bex and as he did so, Seb called the Doctor and recommended she meet them at the bar ASAP.

'Hi Bex, this is Harry or should I say Captain Harrison Gill…' Harry stood and took Bex's hand and kissed the back 'you can call me Harry though, any friend of Seb's and all that.' And he sat back down dramatically and lounged back, feet up on the booth beside Bex and arms wide across the booth he was in, one behind Seb and the other grabbing his Guinness. Bex regarded Harry with something born from amusement, curiosity and disbelief.

'This is Harry? The Harry you share all your secrets with?' Seb looked confused and asked why she seemed concerned 'Well, he looks like you just found him behind a dumpster and his aura is not the same as yours…' Harry held up a hand and sat a bit more upright as Bex looked at him. 'Hold yee hard good lady, before you make any snap judgements, Seb has told me what you are too and I'm inclined to say that although you're pretty, it's a bit anticlimactic…I was expecting…well, you know…a horn? Anyway…' Harry breezed on before Bex could respond 'I'm a little off colour as you so eloquently put it due to a bit of witch trouble surprisingly enough in New England…I know, you couldn't make it up could you. Anyway, things got a bit…shall we say messy and I got myself stuck with a particularly nasty iron spike. She clearly had preparations for my kind but another young lady, one not quite so homicidal treated my wound, otherwise I'd have been here sooner. I'm not quite myself yet although give it a few days more I should be right as rain once more. Benefit of Hound healing, were I not me I'd be dead as post right now. I got careless and paid the penalty for it, as for these rags, well mine are still in Boston. The witch I was with had a sudden premonition that sounded fairly catastrophic the way she put it, so I made all haste and ran most of the way in lupine form.' Bex frowned 'Wouldn't a plane have been quicker?' Harry smiled as did Seb. 'Normally I'd say yes, but after going through all the motions of boarding etc. etc., I take it you've never seen a hound at full speed?' Bex shook her head. She had seen many things over her long life but admitted that wasn't one of them, citing perspective as the handicap. 'Unless he ran with a built in camera I'd have no way of knowing and I've never had to out run one.' Harry shrugged at that last comment 'Never say never my dear, the witch I had to put down was working with the Revenants and they in turn were summoning hounds as she opened gateways.' Seb was stunned, Harry had missed that little detail. 'A witch was opening gateways? Straight to the Domain?' Seb blurted and Harry nodded emphatically 'Oh yeah, gave me the shivers for days that very thought.' Seb grew silent and troubled and Bex asked what was wrong.

'If a witch, here and now is capable of opening gates to the Domain and we have had an up close and personal encounter with a denizen of said hell hole, namely Shiraz or Azazel or whatever her name was then more could be on the way and something bigger is happening that this is only a puzzle piece for something far nastier.' They all looked back and forth between each other, their own thoughts racing as Seb summarised 'And, if she wasn't the only one capable of this then we have an even bigger problem than just a few Revenants.' Seb turned to Harry and asked 'I presume you've told Ted?' Harry spread his hands wide and raised his shoulders 'What do you take me for? A pup? Of course I told him and I'm not repeating the words that an old man of his age and breeding should be repeating, certainly not in the company of ladies.' Seb smiled as he knew what Bex was capable of and had heard her let loose a string of obscenities herself one evening as a few of the patrons of Hannigan's got a bit beyond their capabilities and touched where they shouldn't. Being evicted by Seb from the premises probably saved their lives, Bex was not happy that night and was eloquent in voicing her displeasure. That seemed like an age ago now to Seb as the gravity of what could be settled upon them like a wet concrete blanket had just been tossed over their mood.

'We need to get Gwen out of here, somehow she is pivotal in these incursions and just being Tomas's sister can't be the only connection, can it?' Harry looked dubious and shook his unruly head 'I don't think so. I've only met him once, Tomas that is. Couldn't resist it being Toby's kid, looking forward to meeting this one too. I had to take a look you understand and other than being a cold hearted bastard, The Collectives top covert agent for missions off the chart I didn't notice anything that would attract anything from the Domain other than a job offer.' Seb looked thoughtful as though he were reorganising those pieces in his mind, reconfiguring, trying to find anything to link anything together but he came up blank. 'She isn't going to like it you know.' Bex suddenly said and both Seb and Harry turned to regard her. Harry with no idea what she meant and Seb the complete opposite. In fact he grimaced at the prospect of raising the subject with the little fiery English artist he had come to know and care for. Then he had a sudden idea 'You tell her.' He said to Bex and smiled his most charming, tooth filled smile which promptly earnt him a brutal kick to the shins from beneath the table. Now supernatural creature or not, that still stung. 'Ow' Seb moaned, rubbing the welt but he was still smiling as pieces of the plan fell into place and he added then to alleviate the fury in Bex's eyes. 'We'll have to approach this like a WITSEC event. She has to disappear from here with no trace or trail and enough time to cover her tracks from those bloody revenants hanging around stinking up the place.' Seb felt the edges of the plan knitting together like a wound that looked serious at first, but after cleaning up, would heal well 'How messy is that going to be?' Harry asked looking between them, not knowing Gwen's life like they did. Both Bex and Seb looked at each other for several silent minutes then said at the same time 'Very.' Then Bex asked 'What is WITSEC anyway?' Seb's and Harry's laughter alleviated the moment and earnt Seb another kick from Bex as she was definitely not laughing, thinking it a perfectly reasonable question.

'Witness security or witness protection by any other name, depends what governmental department is employing it and who they're trying to hide. They're not as good as us though, we have… attributes they don't possess. The reason the rich and powerful built secret chambers and tunnels and pyramids we're only now finding was the simple fact that they could hide that secret by killing all the builders and anyone else who might have known…' Bex's expression spoke volumes.

'You're not going to kill a load of people are you?' Bex was horrified and Harry diffused the moment by vehemently waving his hands before him in mock horror – Bex need not know he was quite happy to do so if required – but he mollified her by adding details 'No, no, no. We have as you may have noticed with Sebastion here, a certain charm that opens people to suggestibility. With our gifts we can be very… persuasive when required. We will leave no trail a human can follow.' Bex pulled a face that said she wasn't really worried about humans and Seb translated that. 'I know what you're thinking Bex but limiting it to supernatural creatures only and as much as I dislike the idea, separating her from us, whatever we trigger may diminish and as we know where and how, we can monitor that easily, leave magical booby traps if you will. Our only problem is where.' Little did they know, but that problem was being solved, albeit on a temporary basis as they spoke.

'I can't just up sticks and take off any more than you can El.' Gwen tried to explain to her new shadow who had just suggested a hiking vacation in and around New Mexico way quite spontaneously and thrown Gwen a sideways curve ball she hadn't expected or seen coming.

'Why not?' Elspeth pushed 'What's pressing here so much someone else can't cover it?' Gwen did actually have to think about that for a convincing argument because the only problematic one was the gallery and Bex had already volunteered to cover that several times if Gwen needed to get away. She had said that the break from the hospital would do her good too, the slower pace might be pleasant. She would look after the apartment and open the gallery for her as she did. 'I'm sure Guy will be happy enough for a fine upstanding cardiothoracic surgeon of international renown looking after his gallery for a couple of weeks.' Bex reasoned and had seemed quite genuine. Covering her morning stint delivering food to the patients had a waiting list the agency could call upon as it was a role people came and went in. Even her shifts at Hannigan's had earnt her some vacation time and any of the other girls there would be glad of the overtime covering her. Gwen knew she really didn't have too many excuses beyond not really knowing the attractive detective with the disarming smile though relationships had been formed on less than a 24 hour drinking and talking session. Gwen wondered about the intense brunette opposite her who had been all business when they first met at the bar but since then she had become an almost different person, a darker haired version of herself and Gwen found that oddly comfortable and not at all alien. For having travelled as extensively as she had, Gwen had experienced the intimacy of both men and women and found she could enjoy either just as emotionally invested as any relationship can be. She had even lived with a girl for a bit in LA until she left to go back home to Colorado, after that it was six months with a firefighter she had met when the apartment next door caught light strangely. He was too clingy though and wanted a whole football team of kids, this sent Gwen running. Bouncing through various lovers as she felt the need or attraction though she hadn't been in anything serious since arriving in New York. The closest friends she had made were now Bex and Seb and although Seb was definitely Chippendale material, Gwen didn't think of him quite that way. He was more like the Tomas she had hoped for but never got. Bex on the other hand was more like a big sister or matriarchal teacher slightly older than herself, someone to aspire to maybe but Gwen abhorred the hours Bex put in at the hospital citing one afternoon to the good doctor that it was way too much like hard work. Elspeth on the other hand was breath of floral air and Gwen felt a connection forming she hadn't anticipated and a warmth inside that made her cheeks flush slightly if she pondered too long on the idea. For all the sweet sensations and burgeoning companionship Elspeth and her offer promised, a grain of caution irritated her soul like a grain of sand nestled inside an oyster. Sure it turned into a beautiful pearl eventually, but in this case Gwen wanted the support of the only family she had in this neck of the world, Gwen wanted the support of both Bex and Seb. Somehow their approval would make or break her decision and that would have to happen before she upheaved her life once more, even temporarily. That decided, Gwen gave Elspeth an answer 'I have a couple of people I'd like you to meet first.'

It didn't take too long and a few phone calls later all five were seated at Hannigan's. Gwen had taken the introduction of Harry a lot easier than Seb thought but the way he stared at her, like she was a walking talking exhibit from her own gallery was a touch disconcerting to say the least. 'Why does he do that?' Gwen finally asked Seb after Harry had excused himself for a restroom stop. 'He knows your father and your brother, you make the ensemble complete for him. Harry is big on family, more so never having one of his own.' Gwen was curious as Harry was much younger than her father and she couldn't place how Harry would know him, certainly enough to be concerned about the welfare of his kids. 'Trust him Gwen, he's a good guy, more so than me even. I'll bend the odd rule to achieve my goals but Harry hates that and even gives me a hard time about it, still after all the years we've worked together.' A fact that was also niggling Gwen as neither of them could have reached their forties yet, barely even late thirties by the looks of them; fit, agile, moving with the economy of movement of a predator or athlete yet they spoke of events and time like they had been around decades. Gwen tried to reason to herself it was because the life was so intense, it felt like a lot longer to those who worked on the edgy fringe of society that Seb frequently implied was his normal habitat. Even Bex gave off that older than looks vibe from time to time, eyes that had seen far too much and secrets the world would never know buried behind them. Then life intervened and the moment would pass and Gwen would consign it to later on memory. Until Harry turned up and it all came flooding back. Gwen sat between Elspeth and Bex opposite Harry and Seb and when Harry returned, Gwen made the introductions and put forward the idea of a small vacation, change of scenery, grab a bit of head space from her hectic and eclectic life. Maybe even get some art done, Elspeth had told Gwen of the incredible colours and enchanted light that lit up the canyons and desert like nothing on earth. Bizarrely – certainly to Gwen who was expecting more objections – Bex, Seb and Harry looked between them and seconds later they almost all said at once what a wonderful idea it was and they thanked Elspeth for coming up with such a brilliant idea. They treated Elspeth like one of the family almost instantly and it was several hours later and a few too many pitchers of beer that Bex and Seb were escorting a sleepy Gwen and Elspeth back to Gwen's apartment above the gallery whereupon a slight magical nudge from Bex and the two girls were curled up fast asleep on the Cali king in Gwen's bedroom.

'Well that was easy. We've got her out of the state but how do we dismantle her life here and leave no trace in a few days so she doesn't have to return here and can stay out west?' Bex asked and Seb smiled and just shook his surfers head and told Bex he knew people, it wouldn't be a problem.' Bex wasn't so sure, it had been a long time since she had to switch identities and it had only been for her, not for someone else who didn't know it was happening to her. 'Trust me Bex, the Collective are very good at this. The hardest part will be removing us from her memory, implanting new ones that cover why she would have left here in the first place without raising any supernatural suspicions. She can't know what's been going on, if she did we both know she'd pick at like a scab until she put herself back in harm's way again and it would have been a wasted exercise.' Bex agreed and said she would have to craft a more sophisticated enchantment to make New York like a dream. 'What do we do about Elspeth?' Bex asked having been reluctant to raise that loose end but knowing it would eventually have to be addressed as she had a life here, a job, friends who might miss her. They couldn't enchant all of them. 'I agree but let's see where they go with this, she may just come back leaving Gwen there. It would be easier to make her forget Gwen then and believe she had been away alone, guess it depends on how close they get and how strong those bonds become. The stronger they bond, the harder that'll be.' Bex stretched out, kicking her trainers off and wiggling her toes to relax them as she put them up on the small coffee table. 'How did my simple life get so complicated all of a sudden Seb? Rhetorical as you know it's your fault.' Seb feigned indignation 'Mine? How do you work that out?' Bex leant back into the soft chair and laid out her theory 'I've spent millennia dampening my aura to avoid detection from anyone and anything – quite successfully I'll have you know – I meet Gwen at the Obelisk – a powerful object in its own right - her aura was brighter than normal I grant you but not supernatural, though there is something about it even I can't fathom, maybe it's that that attracts the Revenants as you call them, possessed by any other name but you, you turn up and you all bar glow like a magnesium flare. I didn't notice at first having turned down my abilities, but once you had me attack possessed and utilise magic, my perception has grown stronger and I suspect my aura has too so between us we just throb power now on the various planes that are monitored by those we'd rather not attract the attention of, now Harry is here glowing like a small sun and he's your friend, therefore your fault.' Seb processed what Bex had said and realised she was quite right in a convoluted kind of way. Had they not all come together, Gwen might have stayed below the radar; then again may be not. As he'd suggested, events were in play that defied simple coincidence and if something bigger was afoot then all this may have been foreordained and destined to happen and Seb was determined to get to the bottom of it. To do that, he had to make sure Gwen was safe first, Ted had been more than just insistent he had used the words *your hide and rug* in his instructions to Seb and the possible results of his failure to do so.

By the time dawn had rolled around, Seb had gone. He had left around four in the morning to do a sweep of the area, make sure there were no possessed hanging around then on to liaise with Harry who would set the Collective to work cleaning up accounts and pulling identities from all known databases and transplanting them elsewhere. Seb had suggested Santa Fe as the best option, a little more out of the way than the larger Albuquerque but it would suit Gwen's sensibilities. In the meantime Bex went around the apartment, quieter than a church mouse and warded every wall and window with ancient *astray* runes. Should anybody scry the city, they would simply slide past this building like it was magically Teflon coated. Bex did a last check on Gwen and Elspeth before leaving herself, they had gravitated in their sleep towards each other and Elspeth had one arm and one leg lightly draped over Gwen's recumbent form like a couple of BFF's on a sleepover. 'Sleep well girls,' Bex whispered 'your big adventure starts all too soon and it's an uncertain future we're all heading into, rest while you can.' Bex left then, inscribing sigils on all the doors as she closed them behind her. It was probably the safest apartment in the whole city now but there was always the exception.

Azazel didn't become a powerful, high ranking demon by being stupid. She was crafty and conniving, nefarious and extremely dangerous. Few were deadlier than her, except perhaps Lillith who had been on

Nescaria as long as Lucifer himself had and ruled alongside him. But Azazel gave the absent Queen of the Night little thought as she was applying her mind this night to locating those who had escaped her clutches once already, they would not be so fortunate a second time as she would bring greater numbers and they would pay dearly for her humiliation. 'I have no doubt they will attempt to hide her from me, possibly with magic as you have that creature protecting you.' Azazel spoke to no-one in particular, merely liking the sound of her own voice as she talked it out 'There is little magic left in this human infested, concrete termite mound, so I will look simply where I *cannot* see.' Azazel knew it would be like looking at a map with a small area rubbed out, that absence would be the human's likely whereabouts and after only a few moments searching, she couldn't believe her fortune when she found it was at the very same place she had found Gwen at before, as the gallery no longer appeared upon her map or in her thoughts. 'This is too simple.' The demoness laughed as she began her preparations, dismissing any sort of trap believing humans too simple for such deceit. 'Adax!' Azazel raised her voice in summons and a pale thing, skin as white as bone glided into the chamber Azazel had taken as her own and it abased itself before her, pressing her damp, colourless face wetly to the floor. 'Adax, rise' Azazel commanded almost as an afterthought 'and summon the witches, I wish to converse with their high priestess.' The figure dressed in layered, cowled robes rose smoothly as though its bones were fluid and as Adax looked upon its mistress with adoration. Huge dark eyes, larger than mortal kind and darker than apache tears, unblinking fixed upon Azazel. It was hard to determine gender but it moved with a feline, feminine grace and its voice had an effeminate quality and pitch. Slender and white fingers attached to arms scant of flesh protruded from slits in the sides of the robe and they soon began to move in a spasmodic rhythm, repeating gestures and then Adax moved to the fire against the wall whereupon an oversized, globular iron pot hung over flames and embers. Its contents bubbled with an unnatural viscosity and it was a foul looking, oily concoction but Adax thrust her overly long fingers into the mix and stirred the contents oblivious to the evident heat. Seconds passed and the previously bubbling gloop within began to smooth out until it was as glass upon the surface. Adax looked down upon it and another face looked back. 'Why do you summon us this way?' The face demanded 'You are fortunate one of the sisterhood was attending the flame and recognized the spell forming. We are opening gates as fast as we can, no amount of persuasion will make it happen any faster.' The face in the cauldron brooked no argument to its declaration. It didn't expect the serene face of Azazel to loom into view and regard the woman with such contempt and disdain it would have caused kings and queens to take a step back in fear they had overstepped. 'It is not the reason my maid summons you Lysandreth,' Azazel hissed 'I want your sisterhood here in New York by the moons rise tomorrow; I want every gateway you can open to be ready to open here upon my command.' Lysandreth said nothing but listened raptly 'I want carnage and chaos, blood and destruction for which your kavern has a penchant for and bring the harpies, I want terror as much as I want bloodshed.' Lysandreth regarded Azazel through veiled eyes and wondered what insanity the demoness was about now, but wisely kept her thoughts to herself and simply answered 'Your will Azazel, where would you like us?' Azazel thought for a moment then knew. 'Use the Obelisk in the park here as your focal point, its own power will unwillingly assist you as it is a portal device in itself though unused for millennia.' The demoness instructed and Lysandreth nodded her understanding and stirred the waters, breaking the connection. Azazel took no umbrage at the poor manners of the witch, she had proven herself time and time again to earn her recalcitrant behaviour and besides, it amused the demoness. 'Adax, go now to the place they call Central Park and commence a summoning, I want every possessed in this infernal city here by the setting of the sun tomorrow, have no care for the mortals nor however many we lose getting them here. I've had enough of hiding in shadows until our great lord's plan has reached the point he considers it time to rise, I say now and I say here. This human has a powerful secret I cannot divine yet the power she emanates would grant me enough power to challenge even Lilith for her role in the Domain.' Adax looked on, torn as to her next move, be about her task as set her just now by her mistress or stay and answer her possibly rhetorical, certainly narcissistic musings but Azazel soon cleared that up. 'Why are you still here? Do you not have something to do?' 'Yes mistress' Adax quickly hissed and swiftly slid from the room.

## TRNITY

'Coffee?' Gwen asked Elspeth as she stumbled from the bedroom rubbing her eyes and stretching languidly. 'Hell yeah, can you do it in a pitcher sized mug?' Gwen smiled at the image 'Sorry, just regular sized ones here but there is no limit on how many you can have.' Elspeth slumped into the sofa across from the kitchenette where Gwen was multi-tasking, pouring steaming coffee into mugs with one hand and stirring eggs in a pan with the other. 'Got any hot sauce for those?' Gwen looked at Elspeth askance with an expression that asked why 'Remember, I'm from Albuquerque, we have hot sauce with everything. Santa Fe does some amazing things with Chilies that would curl your toes. So I chuck it into most things I eat as it reminds me of home a bit.' Just at that moment, mid breakfast thoughts, the door flew open and Seb came charging in as though the zombie apocalypse were right behind him and his expression did little to detract from the fact it wasn't. 'Pack now!' Gwen didn't move, neither did Elspeth but they just looked at Seb and each other as if it were some joke and they were waiting for the punch line. 'Did you not hear me? Gwen, put that down and go pack. Elspeth get dressed, Bex is at your place right now doing the same for you and she'll meet us at the station when she's done.'

'Slow down Seb, you're not making any sense and I'm not going anywhere just like that.' Gwen snapped her fingers demonstrably. 'Not being funny but who the hell do you think you are? Busting in here and dishing out orders that will screw my life up, especially when I'm not ready. You are aware of letting people know, preparations, finding cover etc. etc?' Seb took a breath then and looked between the two unmoving girls and wondered how much to tell them about the end of their lives here in New York as they knew them. Neither would take that well and based on Harry's report, they really didn't have time for debate. The witches were massing for something in New England and Harry had left eyes and ears there in case this very thing happened. Knowing they worked in league with Azazel it was obvious the demoness wanted revenge or at least round two and this time she was coming mob handed, they were out of time. Seb was conflicted as neither option would end well, don't tell and feel like they were kidnapped until Bex could wipe their memories or tell them, freak them out and wipe them all the same. He chose. Hobsons choice was to tell them and at least they would be galvanised for a time. So he did. He told them then and there what was hunting them and how their lives were now forfeit to creatures both ancient and evil. A fight was coming and it was one even Seb with his larger than life confidence was unsure they could win without help. The last thing they needed was to have to protect them in the midst of battle. They needed to leave now. Everything here was taken care of, every legality Gwen was attached to had been erased and relocated, the same

49

for Elspeth. The NYPD were sorry to see her go but understood once Harry and the Collective had politely explained it to them.

'You're serious?' was about all Gwen could say once Seb had finished covering the high points 'You're making this crap up?' Elspeth was dumbfounded but was soon jumping around the room poking Seb in his chest and making demands of him and how dare he shut her life down and many other very loud, very pokey expletives until even Seb could take no more and grabbed her wrist mid poke. 'Please stop!' Seb put as much of his natural coercive power into the quietly spoken command as possible and brought the ranting Gwen and almost screaming Elspeth to a stunned and silent halt. The girls looked wide eyed at each other as neither moved, their bodies obeying the hushed command of Seb as though they were mere spectators in their own bodies. 'Now sit down.' Equally hushed and measured but both girls sat. Like scared children they sat upon the sofa and stared at Seb. 'I didn't want you to see this and I don't want you so scared you can't function but clearly all I've just told you seems to have not done the trick so I'll have to show you. With that, Seb transformed to his full Hound of Fenris form, full height – which meant he had to stoop else concuss himself upon the ceiling – he reached out swiftly and with Taloned hands big enough to grab a girl in each around the waist he lifted them off their feet and held them before him as he pulled his lips back and snarled his most fang filled and ferocious right at them. Harry walked in right at that moment and took one look at the sight and shook his head. Moving behind Seb and the now loudly screaming Gwen and Elspeth, Harry walked round to the coffee and slugged one mug full before refilling it and slugging another. 'I told you they wouldn't believe you. You've done too good a job keeping all this shit from them, probably should have come clean ages ago.' Seb put both girls back down as Elspeth as feinted and Gwen had calmed. Seb balanced and used a hind foot to reach out and close the door Harry had left open in case someone bolted for it or someone outside looked in inadvertently, that would take some resolving. Shifting form back to his own form Gwen just stared at him, wide eyed with her mouth open a little, breathing erratically both Seb and Harry could almost see her mind processing, accepting then disregarding it, back to disbelief then back again. Her eyes told her emphatically what had happened but her mind was questioning it like a defence attorney desperate to get their client off the hook by any means possible. 'You're a…' she started and Seb answered, saving her the trouble and pain of saying it 'Yes I am, so is Harry here. Just like I told you, we've been doing this for a lot of years, some of it with your dad some of it on our own with the people your brother work for as well as who your dad once worked for. All of which will be academic shortly unless you and Elspeth pack and do as we tell you. Some really nasty things are coming and it's going to get messy. Trust us, we've got you but you need to go…' Harry piped up and butted in then 'half an hour ago to be honest.' We let you sleep last night as we were busy and you were safer here but that's over now; you are most definitely not safe here now and like Seb says, something wicked this comes and it doesn't care who it has to kill to get its own way. For some reason none of us can fathom, it wants you Gwen. It will kill Elspeth simply for knowing you and anyone else for being between you and it. Seb did mention it was a demon?' Gwen nodded dumbly, her mind registering what her body couldn't quite fathom so it automated her as best it could.

'All this time. All those times you Bex and I stayed up here drinking and talking and laughing, you were one of those…' Seb nodded sadly '…those…I really don't know what you are…I can't form the words to say it.' Seb knew how she felt. It was the one thing he hated about his condition, Harry too he knew; the constant lying. The never ending deflections about how constantly healthy he was, how he could hear so well, olfactory sensitivity, how he could see and do what he could do. The hiding of his true nature now amidst mortal society, amongst normal humans. It hurt him and Harry deeply, even now and it was one of the burdens of their condition that only grew heavier with time, not lighter. 'Bex…' Gwen started 'she…she isn't… one of you is she?' Seb shook his shaggy blonde head and despaired. What could he say? He had to lie once more and it nearly broke his heart doing so. The saving grace of this was in a few hours, she would remember none of it. 'No Gwen,' Seb almost sighed 'Bex most definitely is not one of us, but she is helping us look after you and won't be going with you when you go. She'll say good bye if she can at the station, if we get there in time. You need to be magically off the grid as well as physically gone before things start here, so back to plan A, get your stuff and we'll help Elspeth.' Gwen was still processing what was happening, trying to wrap her head around the fact that the life she had carefully constructed and was organized and to some extent quite routine, was about to be trashed because of something she had no idea about other than being targeted by some mad woman who was about to go off the deep end in some sort of revenge fuelled retaliation. Gwen didn't even know who she was, she was one of Guy's friends by all accounts, his inner circle of VIP connections. Gwen suddenly went cold, was Guy in on this? Did he know? Did he even arrange it? Theories and questions tumbled through her mind like a landslide, what sort of puppet had she been all this time. 'My god, how could I have missed all this?' Seb saw the confusion warring on her expression and guessed her mood. 'Don't beat yourself up about any of this Gwen, it's not your fault. My line of work often reveals a thing known as a long game, you may have heard of similar terms in cold war movies where sleeper agents are embedded and who may never be used but should they be called upon, absolutely anyone could be an agent for another power. We have something similar here only it's not any mortal government operating it, this is way bigger and my guess, much longer played. You're just the latest recipient, caught up in the maelstrom.' Gwen didn't look convinced 'You're not selling it any better you know, though this is nearly the longest I've stayed in any one place, not that I had any immediate plans to up sticks and move on yet. Thanks for that.' Seb looked a little guilty, inwardly pleased she was coming around to what was happening, and it would make the transition easier on her. 'It really is time to go Gwen, go pack for a hiking break, travel light and you can buy anything you can replace once you get where you're going. Think of it as a big adventure.' Gwen got up and thumped Seb hard on the shoulder as she went past to her bedroom to pack. 'You're not funny and don't take my going along with you as happy, I really enjoyed my time here and I'm going to miss it.' Seb didn't bother telling her she wouldn't miss it at all as she wouldn't remember it by the time the bus rolled into Albuquerque.

After the initial objections were swept past, things went a little faster. Within the hour both Gwen and Elspeth were standing at the bus station, surrounded by Bex, Seb and Harry. Harry loaded their rucksacks onto the bus and had words with the driver. Nobody saw Harry's eyes glow golden as he embedded the command to protect his passengers, especially Gwen and Elspeth with his life should it come to it. To not make any unprecedented stops no matter who asked. There were hugs and tears and more hugs but Seb and Bex gradually ushered the girls onto the bus. Both now wearing their New York Herkimer pendants, enchanted by Bex to a capacity that would probably leave every passenger wondering how they arrived at their destination but theirs would wear off after a bit as the charm wasn't specific for them, Gwen's and Elspeths's were. It had taken Bex a full day to work the inclusions into both the gem and the enchantment so that they wouldn't be bereft of their senses or common sense when they arrived. It was a semi direct route and they were due to reach their destination in roughly two days. Bex's charm had the added nudge to encourage the girls to stay on the bus and sleep there. The trio knew they had no way to protect them at their layover, not and stop the demon who was hell bent on retribution any time now, they couldn't afford for one of them to go along, they were too few already. They needn't have worried as Gwen was a Greyhound veteran and knew what to do as she told them between snuffled good byes.

Seb, Harry and Bex watched until the bus was a speck in the distance before Bex broke the silence with a statement that deflated them even further.

'We can't win this you know.' Harry chewed his bottom lip as he considered her word and knew it for the truth, no matter how he spun their options. 'You're right. We need reinforcements.' Harry looked at Seb who shook his head knowing what Harry thought. 'We can't bring the Collective in on this, even Ted can't get that many bodies here that quick and with what's coming, we don't want any more bloodshed than what we're going to have to deal with here. Our own people will be too hampered by keeping the public safe and we don't have time to prepare any battle plan. We need to keep this hard, fast, brutal and messy. I know the same disposal magics as Ted anyway, as do you so clear up won't be the problem.' Bex chimed in with the obvious 'Surviving it will be the problem. You two are built for this, I am not and I've been so far under the radar for so long much of my magic is still dormant, I've used more these last few weeks than I've used in centuries. I can bring some offensive spells to this but I'm more defensive and even that will only last so long, we need more.' Harry asked the obvious 'more of what?' Bex laughed with no humour in what so ever 'More of everything, more of us, more time, more power definitely more luck.' Seb and Harry couldn't disagree but time was ticking and they had to prepare. 'So, plan A, Bex you bag up anything of Gwen's that emanates her, bring it to the park as that'll minimise public collateral damage, keep them off the streets as much as possible. Cast the enhancement upon it and between that and us, it should draw them our way, maybe tap into the obelisk for extra juice?' Bex agreed totally unaware they weren't the only ones looking to utilise the ancient edifice. The sands of time were nearly run out.

Adax had thrown the summons out across the city like a malignant blanket cast across the rooftops and it demanded the attention of every revenant it touched to convene at a point slammed in to their minds by Azazel's will. As Bex, Harry and Seb talked, hundreds of howling revenants screamed in ecstasy and pain as they pushed their tortured bodies – some beyond the trip and they disintegrated before completing it, forcing the demon inside to choose another unwary soul for a host. That night was unlike any the city had seen as a torrent of possessed flowed through the streets and alleyways of the city that never slept and any human caught in its path met a most hideous demise. None were safe, civilians were massacred, as were NYPD officers who tried to make a stand. Their bullets hardly slowing the creatures before they too were overrun and either possessed themselves or ripped asunder. The possessed had but one destination this night, the obelisk in central park, where Adax the demi demon incanted her baleful spell of summoning. It was there and then that Harry and Seb walked into the scene and Adax spun, leaping like a scorched cat at the sudden presence of the two hounds. For Harry and Seb had found it curious there were only a few revenants lurking in the park close to the statue and thought themselves lucky, hoping this was all Azazel was going to muster but when they stepped into the paved clearing and saw Azazel's pet in full incant, they knew matters were nothing like they hoped and whatever was happening had started. The two former SC agents wasted no time on small talk and dramatically transformed into their full hound personas, powerful and impressive, massive and deadly. Each capable of stopping a speeding truck in this form and tearing it to shreds like it were made of paper, but that was just one thing, what they saw now with their golden, lupine, supernaturally enhanced vision was several hundred possessed converging on them from all over the park and moving at speed. Swarming over people and anything living in their path like running locusts. Long, bony, fleshless fingers sharpened and lethal were outstretched as if they could stab and slash and slash at them from a distance. Though they no longer had mortal eyes - for the possessed ripped them away as they inhibited their own deminion sight - Seb and Harry's arcane gaze saw the putrid glow of several hundred baleful magical eye sockets fixedly staring towards them, they were seconds away and both hounds adopted a talon flared fighting stance and howled their battle challenge. It was a sound that carried for many miles and chilled whoever heard it. Suddenly Bex was there, appearing silently beside the two furred behemoths. She tossed a bag of Gwen's belongings down and they began to glow a deep umber, a glow that grew and grew in intensity like a moth catcher drawing the gaze almost hypnotically of the charging revenants. The first to reach the trio died in a blur of talons, blood and bone. Bex looked briefly like she stood within a black and golden hurricane so fast did Harry and Seb move to dispatch the possessed. Adax screamed a bloodcurdling sound no mortal could make, nor should hear and flung the viscous robe that covered her from head to toe to one side. Her form rose then like the fabled Nagas of antiquity, a woman's slick, white, lightly scaled body atop that of a serpent's formed her lower half, rising up to tower over even Seb and Harry. But this was not one of the more benign variety mythology speaks of, this one was corrupt and vile and powerful. Azazel had poured her putrescence into this demonic version and turned it into something else. She was not slow either and Adax sped towards the two hounds nearly catching them off guard and narrowly missed a raking swipe from venom drenched talons that hissed as they sliced past. Harry ducked low and got in a swipe of his own, leaving four deep gouges along her scaly underbelly causing her to scream hideously and slither backwards. Blood flew from the wounds, but as it hit the ground it sounded like a bag of stones had been tossed to the pavers. Her blood droplets had solidified into granite stones between leaving her body and hitting the air outside. 'Look out Seb,' Harry snarled 'she has some of that Gorgon venom in her blood, don't get scratched.' Harry growled and Seb took a step back on the defensive as Adax spun, eyes filled with hatred and a mouth stretched inhumanly wide, displaying an impressive mouthful of fangs. She spat at Seb then and he narrowly dodged clear of the morass that instead spattered over three possessed who were coming up behind him. They howled and thrashed as though potent acid had been tipped on them but quite suddenly they stopped screaming, stiffened and they too turned to stone. 'Useful' Seb noted as he leapt from spot to spot, decapitating and disembowelling with every move, deftly dodging the anti Naga and her fury. Harry was happy she was angry as it kept her from having the presence of mind to cast any more magic. 'Leave her to me!' Bex shouted and both wolves turned to see Bex transform herself. Not since the last planetary shift had occurred had anyone seen the Unc'Anharaphim metamorphose into their alter form, that of the unicorn. Though it bore very little resemblance to the equine version humanity has become fixated upon. Bigger than a Clydesdale she grew, wide of chest and fire blossomed from her hooves. Her flanks and body in general swelled with both magic and strength, like dragons Bex had developed an almost impermeable hide that very little could penetrate and her horn spiralled forth and was as deadly as it was magnificent. Most Unc'Anharaphim were more docile in this form and it reflected that but there were times and they were only remembered in hallowed antiquity by the very ancient when they stood shoulder to shoulder with the Drakarim, fighting wars that even stars had forgotten. The Unc'Anharaphim after those bloody times forswore violence and turned their gifts towards the healing and divinatory arts. Mastering arcane power to rival the oldest in the known cosmos, that of the Hadestrians. After the Kalithine wars and the Covenant when the Unc'Anharaphim were tricked and hunted almost to extinction by renegades of both their own kind, the Drakareth and the newly colonised Nescarii the Unc' Anharaphim went into hiding never to be seen again – until now. Even Adax was momentarily stunned by the sight of the majestic creature rearing up and pawing the air before them. Then Bex charged the Naga and it was fearsome to behold as the head lowered and the deadly horn lanced the serpent woman just below the rib cage and with a head like an armoured truck, spine aligned right down to the back legs Bex smashed into Adax, the horn went clean through rapier style until her head reached the body hit it hard, propelling the serpent body clean off once more and across the open space to crash into the undergrowth and vanish temporarily from sight. This image lasted mere heart beats before the unicorn rose up onto its back legs once more and with the merest of blurs there stood Bex, lightly armoured in articulated scale, helmed and brandishing a long silver sword. 'I'd truly forgotten how invigorating this form can be. I think stars have winked out since I last adopted it, but by triple goddess it is *exhilarating*.' Seb and Harry had seconds to appreciate the Unc' Anharaphim warrior joining them before the swarm of possessed resumed their blood curdling attack. But they were still only three for all their prowess and skill. They moved in perfect fighting precision, constantly circling, never letting the possessed gain any advantage on them but for all they fought well and hard for their lives, this cluster of possessed served only to divert the defenders. Hundreds of others had circumvented them and were pouring out onto Fifth Avenue where cars and buses were crashing and people were dying in their droves as the possessed tore into them. The road for a mile in either direction was soon a charnel house of blood and viscera, guts and gore strewn everywhere as the horde converged upon the gallery where Azazel had directed them. If matters weren't bad enough at that point, a little further back into the park at the largest clearing nearest to the obelisk was where the portals opened. From these 13 portals of circular blue lightning stepped the Kore-Megara, their leader Lysandreth, dressed in flowing scarlet robes and adorned with bone and antler, fur and feather she cut an imposing figure as the staff she held in one hand glowed an incandescent cobalt hued light and she stood as if on guard, deadly magic rolling around her other hand like a serpent of lightning twining around her wrist and through her fingers as her sisters likewise emerged into the park and dismissed their portals. The Kore-Megara were old and powerful and it was from this secretive group did ancient cultures, including the Greeks learn of the legend of Kore and the story of Persephone and Demeter grew. The Kore-Megara were women of power who knew and dwelt in the deep places of the earth drawing power from the Earth's dragon lines to fuel their dark magics. Initially formed before the Covenant when renegade celestials considered it amusing to teach forbidden magic to mortal kind. In those early days, both men and women were taught but the men immediately sought to dominate the women and treated them harshly. At this brutal mistreatment, the Kore-Megara were formed and the most powerful of the women took their revenge upon the men - all the men, though a few escaped they were deemed insignificant and from that day forth the sacred teachings went to the women alone and the Kore-Megara grew in number, power and spread themselves across the known world in search of the conduits of power. They also grew in anger, embittered by their former treatment they took to slaughtering any man who sought their counsel, or came too near or enquired after them until over time they became a feared legend of blade wielding, blood-thirsty sorceresses who brought terror and delivered horror wherever they went. The Kore-Megara were not city dwellers though and took to the caves of the wilds to be closer to the earth and the fonts of their powers, the deep caverns from where we derive the modern word Coven for a gathering of the wise. They were often found by ancient springs and natural wells, deep forests where the dark tales of ancient Germania picked up upon them. The Kore-Megara were older than most civilisations and were still feared by those who knew of them. Most simply believed them myth now and forgot them. None had seen the Kore-Megara for over two thousand years, not a single one but now here stood a full Kavern, thirteen of the most powerful priestesses currently living today and their thirst for blood had not diminished one iota. 'Nuala,' Their priest queen Lysandreth commanded 'summon the Harpies as Azazel requested, let them loose upon these vermin.' Nuala raise a hand and several incomprehensible words later a similar rift to the one they had utilised opened in the air above them and from it flew nightmares. Unnatural fusions of woman and vulture. These were no ordinary women either, for all novitiates attempting to join the Kore-Megara, the trials are hazardous in the extreme and many fail; depending on how they fail determines their fate though the lucky ones simply died. One such fate is that of the Harpy. Minds so irreversibly damaged by the strains of trying to master dark and malevolent magic. Magic designed to kill them and only in their

57

mastering can the neophyte move forward. Failure leads to deformation and insanity at the very least. Failure at the early stages of the trials means the neophyte is destined to likely become a Harpy. Driven to feed constantly and upon the one and only thing that pacifies them – human flesh.

'I don't know who this creature is that has enraged Azazel so, sufficient to demand we attend in person and unleash the carrion but they must be powerful indeed.' Nuala spoke even as she completed the summoning spell and watched the Harpies soar out over the park, screeching and cackling as they rose until they spotted prey, then they dropped like a stone upon the unsuspecting meal. 'What did the demoness tell you mistress?' Lysandreth heard her second even as she scanned the area looking for the obelisk but didn't respond straight away for it was a question that had bothered her too, for Azazel had told her very little, threatened extensively but held many details back. If she didn't know better, Lysandreth believed the demoness was *afraid* of this person. And Lysandreth had – up until now - believed Azazel was afraid of nothing. This roused her curiosity as much as any need to obey. The world had moved on vastly since Lysandreth had last walked upon its surface and if there was a new power abroad then maybe it was time the Kore-Megara became known and feared once more before this new power usurped them. 'Have the sisters bring forth their commanded spells, ready to unleash and blades to hand for the reaping of the chaff should they try to hinder our progress.' Lysandreth spoke her orders knowing they would be obeyed instantly if they weren't already anticipated. The entourage of Lysandreth was comprised of twelve of the eldest and highly trained Kore-Megara within a thousand miles in any direction and she ruled upon this landmass. Within moments arrayed behind Lysandreth were the Kore-Megara, like her, wearing magic upon one hand like a living thing and the other they held their Khopesh, their ancient sickle swords from which the ancient Egyptians drew their inspiration for the weapon. Believed to have evolved from an axe it is little known that that axe was the weapon of the goddess and the ancient Kore-Megara were proficient with the double headed butterfly axe. A weapon created for the female power the same way men later took the concept and created their own swords like Excalibur, in an attempt to exercise dominance once more with their phallic symbols. For several thousand years this has been the way and the female has been overshadowed by this force much to the constant chagrin of the Kore-Megara as well as many other factions but like the planet, much is in the timing. What goes around comes around and the Kore-Megara know this. Feeling their time coming upon them they responded to the overtures of Azazel who sought them out and offered rewards for service too rich to turn down. Lysandreth and the Kavern strode regally towards the obelisk with intent to then descend upon the gallery as directed by Azazel, they were not expecting to be confronted by two enormous Hounds and the one thing that gave even Lysandreth pause. Pause as she couldn't believe her eyes. Her teachings spoke of the Unc'Anharaphim as almost their opposite, healers, warriors and powerful users of the arcane arts. It was some of these arts that the renegades taught in a corrupted version. Their eyes all locked for seconds that felt like an age until Lysandreth pointed suddenly at Bex and unleashed her magic upon her and shouted the order 'Kill them!' Bex was engulfed in iridescent blue fire and vanished from view within the inferno. Seb and Harry reacted with a terrifying speed and launched at the women. Unprepared for their savage martial skills and scorching magical fire. Harry and Seb were protected from major harm by their own innate powers, being born from the origin ring making them almost as powerful as Fenris himself but Harry and Seb were associated to the Seraphim Collective and wore the ancient sigils and charms burnt into their flesh to thwart the worst of spells. Magic poured over them like sewer water but it slid greasily from them like they were non-stick. Their talons rang like a bell-ringers concert as they clashed with the witches Khopesh. The women were more than just proficient and they scored many a hit upon the duo and blood flowed readily. Were it not for their supernatural healing it would have been a very short fight ending badly for the trio. Bex had barely enough time to throw up her own warding as the spell cast Kul-fire washed over her and melted the very brick beneath her feet. It was a rare thing to see a mortal not a Drakul cast this liquid fire so hot that it made being dipped in magma look a cool dip in the sea. Sweat poured from Bex as the inferno raged on, for her shield was only projected inches from her body instead of the several feet that she was aiming for. Bex recognised the Kore-Megara and knew matters had just escalated several degrees by their presence. She hoped Seb and Harry were alright or at the very least coping. With a surge of will power, Bex translocated out of the spot she stood and re-appeared several feet to one side. Throwing her own arcane weaponry out, hoping to catch Lysandreth off guard Bex splayed her fingers upon her hand and golden power poured forth. It was more than just fire, it was like the nuclear core of the sun and Bex channelled it directly at Lysandreth who only avoided instant immolation by swinging her staff into the path of the spell wrought maelstrom. It hit the staff and split to either side of her though not without scorching her shoulder as it roared past. Lysandreth screamed at the unexpected pain and raised her staff to ram it into the molten ground beneath her feet and by doing so, she redirected the energy blast downwards into the ground. 'Good try Seeress, yes I know who you are.' Bex raised an eyebrow at the title. 'Our Kavern dates back before your disappearance and your kind are spoken of as strong in the art but if that was the best you can muster then I'd say our scrolls exaggerate. Bex wasn't being drawn into word games, her need to know was greater. 'Why are you here witch?' Bex asked simply hoping the derogatory reference might provoke her into a slip of the tongue but Lysandreth wasn't who she was for being so easily baited. 'Clearly you have no idea who I am Seeress, I am Lysandreth Sheanna Priest Queen of the Kore-Megara and I answer to no-one, not least of all to an exile who should be extinct yet who hides her craven self among…these human vermin. Not even amongst others of her own kind, what are they to you that you stand between them and our scourge?' As the two women stood off against each other, Seb and Harry's battle had tumbled off another direction and they barely held their own against nine Kore-Megara witches, three would never rise again after feeling the full force of what a Hound of Fenris is capable of when sufficiently pissed. Six tried to encircle Harry and Seb and they were pushed back onto the street of 5h Avenue where chaos reigned as possessed wreaked unholy carnage wherever they went. Any poor human trying to flee the madness who came too close to the Kore-Megara were promptly slaughtered by the savage witches and their brutal and razor sharp Khopesh. Three moved away from the fight, feeling their sisters more than capable of finishing them off and made their way to the gallery where everyone believed Gwen was residing like sacrificial offering.

'Priest queen? That's a lofty title for a harlot who lives in a hole in the ground like a grub.' Bex smiled, all teeth and contempt as she baited the witch to either make a mistake or reveal something of their presence here. 'It's more like Wyrmwitch from what I've heard. Skulking around all petulant at being driven underground by the rise of man and his war like powers. I can only imagine the lies Azazel told you to get you here and under her thumb, I'm sure she neglected to mention how we handed her her ass on a plate a few days back and sent her packing – to you it seems but now isn't your time and were I you, I'd scuttle away before things get really ugly here and you'll regret sticking your head out into the sunlight at all.'

Bex smiled, this time there was no humour or warmth in it and it presaged more than just words to follow. Lysandreth though, couldn't believe the audacity before her. 'You dare to threaten me? Me? It's time you and yours learnt who the Kore-Megara truly are...' at that moment Bex stiffened as an unexpected presence touched her mind in a way she hadn't felt in millennia and it spoke to her. Then one voice became two; Bex didn't recognise them as anyone she knew personally but what they said told her more than she could ever imagine.

'It's been a day of discovery and knowing you live and thrive is something I'll have to deal with but for now, were I you I'd run.' Bex spoke a word and vanished. She re-appeared in the street in between Seb and Harry who had just swatted two more witches over the rainbow bridge and nearly tore into Bex the way she appeared so suddenly.

'That's a fast way to get yourself killed.' Seb growled, never taking his golden eyes off the remaining witches who had taken a step back after the last onslaught.

'We have to go, now.' Was all Bex said as she grabbed a handful of fur from both Seb and Harry. The same word slipped from Bex's lips and all three vanished from sight, leaving nothing on the street but the possessed, the Kore-Megara or what remained of this Kavern and the dead. They re-materialised behind the gallery and Bex looked tired and wilted as reality coalesce around them. Seb caught her as her legs buckled and he moved her to a low wall to sit as he asked what was going on. Bex looked skyward and around her, as though she were searching for something...or someone. Then she saw them.

'There, look there. Use your sight, they're away off right now but it will only take seconds I suspect for them to arrive. Harry hooded his eyes against the sun which they were just under and a little to the left of but he made out to massive figures beating equally massive wings ponderously. It wasn't the frenetic flapping of birds moving at speed but that of what Harry and Seb too could only guess at was that they looked like two dragons.

'Are you shitting me Bex? That isn't some super cool illusion is it? Bex smiled and shook her damp head as she removed her helm. 'Oh no, they're real alright. I'd heard the stories but like most of mortal kind, too much time has elapsed to put much credibility in them still existing. That said, we needed help so I put out a desperate plea in the old tongue, only my kind or the Drakarim would understand it.' Bex looked up once more grinning like a Cheshire cat at how close they were now. There were going to be some very confused possessed very shortly. 'I'd given up hope until just a few moments ago hence here we are, I'd cover your ears if they're as sensitive as mine.' They all did just as the roar of death incarnate rattled every window for twenty city blocks. Those animals still living in the park fled and many of those within the buildings died of fright, as did a few humans. But it wasn't just noise, for that certainly stopped everything in its tracks but the sight of one gargantuan white dragon bearing down on them, accompanied by an equally impressive red dragon was too much for many possessed to comprehend but when both let loose their respective breath weapons. Any time for introspection ceased, along with life – or the puppet like semblance of. Fire of such intensity and tidal wave style in its delivery washed down 5$^{th}$ Avenue, scouring anything and everything in its path. It was simply like dragging the sun along the road. What wasn't burnt to ash melted beyond recognition, the sidewalks became liquid flame and it washed up and over many buildings immolating anything attempting to flee. Lysandreth opened a portal and fell backwards through it just as the living fire ripped through the park area and she escaped with only scorched robes as the portal closed behind her. Her remaining Kavern were not so lucky except for Nuala who did as her mistress had. The harpies fell from the sky like they had been rotisseried mid-air and the possessed crisped to fine ash where they stood. This was far from the end of matters though, for as the big red dragon swooped down the avenue then banked out the other end, the giant white began her own sweep and the ice age she brought with her suspended everything in a frozen, icy tableau as though a tsunami of mythical proportions had thundered down the main - as well as a myriad of side streets - and then froze solid mid destruction. Of the hundreds to bring death and chaos to Gwen's door as well as wholesale slaughter of the innocent, only three escaped. Lysandreth, Azazel and Nuala. Gwen for her part - as the focus and cause of such devastation - was oblivious, sat upon a Greyhound bus, head resting upon Elspeth's shoulder as she told Gwen of New Mexico and what she planned to share with her.

Seb and Harry were beside themselves giddy with what they had just witnessed. Living as long as they had, possessed of such gifts as they possessed, life had become stale. Even with life or death fights like this one, they had been there and done that and eaten the enemy. But this was something neither had ever imagined let alone witnessed. Actual dragons. 'Bex, why did you not ever mention you had friends like these?' Harry was just as excited, like a school boy at his first concert. 'We had heard the stories, done the research and read all that we could, even met a Drakel but this… this is just freakin' out of this world. Are they staying? Can we talk to them? Please?' To hear Harry sounding so plaintive was quite pathetic really and Seb told him so with a nudge and a wink. 'Would be pretty groovy though.' He added both hounds looking at Bex. As they stared at her, they slowly shifted back to their not unimpressive human forms. Still grinning like idiots though but without the big pink lolling tongue of the wolf. 'Let me see if they still hear me...' Bex started but suddenly there was a hideous crashing like roofs being ripped off. They all looked up to see perched upon the building like two magnificent gargoyles were the red and the white dragons. Then the red spoke and it had a Latino accent and both Seb and Harry were awestruck all over again. 'Of course you can talk to us, a friend of Rebecca's is a friend of ours and your heroism here today will not be forgotten.' Heads the size of trucks craned down on necks like trains to stare with the biggest golden oscillating eyes Seb and Harry had ever seen this close. The vertically slit pupil widening and closing with inner mirth as they regarded the two men. Then with a crash of falling roof tiles, the white lifted off and with an agility that seemed improbable it spun mid-air and a silvery, glowing snowfall rained down before them. When it cleared there stood a regal looking blonde woman, hair waving from her head to below her waist, close fitting and lightly scaled dress hugged her form and exposed her bare feet. 'I am the exalted Lady Jenharim Duquesne but you can just call me Jen.' They heard the Southern twang to her voice as she introduced herself. Jen stepped forward then and extended her hand to Harry and Seb like any routine meeting of people. The surrealism wasn't lost either man as they shook politely. Harry didn't dare raise the hand to his lips as he had done with Gwen, he was too in awe. So awed in fact, they barely noticed the red perform the same manoeuvre and in a tornado of fire and multi-hued sparks, there stepped the raven haired, tall and lithe form of the red dragon in her human form. Seb was immediately put in mind of a younger Cher with the huge wildly flowing black hair. Like Jen though, her lightly scaled red dress clung where it touched but unlike Jens, the red was slit right up one side revealing long tanned legs as she walked towards the group though equally bare of foot. Her smokey eyes regarded the group even as she smiled a smile of red lips and pearly white teeth. 'I am the revered Lady Madelena Cortez and you can simply call me Maddy. We don't use those titles much, far too pretentious don't you think?' Seb and Harry nodded like innocent youths as the two women moved amongst them and Jen went over to Bex. 'It is good to finally meet you little sister, it has been too long since we spoke with any of your race, we were so scared the stories of your total annihilation were true, we'd almost given up hope.' 'Then you called.' Maddy added 'How could we not aid you. Though it looks as though we were only just in time.' Bex chuckled, in part with relief and the understatement she delivered 'It was starting to get a bit hairy.' Seb and Harry laughed then lightening the moment as the awe passed. 'That would have been us I suspect.' Seb chortled and Jen turned her attention to the duo. 'Ah yes, the infamous Hounds of Fenris who fight for the light, we have heard of many of your exploits these past years.' They were stunned by that revelation. 'You have?' Harry gasped 'Wow. We're honoured and hope we live up to those tales…' 'Or live them down depending on which versions you've heard.' Seb added ruefully never taking his eyes from Jen. He saw a longer haired southern version of Gwen and Seb found himself as rapt with Jen as he was by Gwen. For in human form, Jen was the same height as Gwen but about a foot shorter than Maddy but as demure and delicate as any snowdrop but it was that haunting and alluring Savannah style southern accent that drew Seb's interest. The initial greetings done, they had matters to discuss and so with a note of hopefulness that it was still standing, Seb suggested they retire to Hannigan's to bring everyone up to date on who was who, who was where and why the shit had the fan so catastrophically as it had. 'Let's do this the quick way.' Bex suggested and they all linked hands then and with a word from Bex, they promptly vanished leaving the late arriving NYPD and New York Fire Department to scratch their heads and wonder just what the hell had happened, not realising how close to the truth they were by that.

# Chapter 2

## Resonance

The long silvery and sleek vehicle pulled into the Greyhound station in Downtown Albuquerque and rolled to a stop with a hiss of air brakes and a final belch of exhaust emissions that gave the station that familiar smell all bus stations have. The greyhound painted iconically upon the side still looking as fresh as ever after his run which was out of the trap on his first outing in 1914, finding his origins in Hibbing, Minnesota. Though the line may have started in '14 the running dog logo didn't make it to the side until '29 and the poor thing has been running ever since. But disembarkation went smoothly for Gwen and Elspeth and in no time at all both girls were outside, giggling and hailing a cab which moments later saw them speeding away into the warming morning. The first couple of weeks went by almost as fast as far as Gwen reconciled time, a non-stop itinerary of hiking and cycling the pathways of New Mexico and Arizona's deserts and mountains followed by hot, breathless and intense nights, both in their combined tent when trekking or back at the queen size bed at Elspeth's adobe home, now thought of as Gwen's home. She felt as at home there as anywhere she had ever been, so natural and chilled. Gwen didn't think she could have felt any happier even if she had been born there.

Gwen sat up and pushed the duvet down and stretched languidly, popping a few joints as she ironed out the kinks of another night interspersed with sleep and passion with Elspeth who stirred herself at Gwen's movement.

'Is that coffee I can smell?' Elspeth drawled sleepily and cast one half open eye – the other remaining closed – up at Gwen who looked down at the tousled haired beauty beside her with rising affection and shook her own blonde locks 'Not unless your nose can time travel, that my girl is wishful thinking on both our parts, I don't even know what time it is yet let alone what day it is and my legs are thinking about staying here for a while longer yet. I can't tell if it was the last few miles on the bike or you pulling them about but I'm holding you responsible either way.' Elspeth just laughed throatily and rolled over, dragging the duvet with her, adding as she did so 'Well now you're up you may as well sort breakfast too, I need a few minutes more here.' Gwen's jaw dropped open at the sheer cheek of the woman and the fact she was now naked and minus the duvet as Elspeth hauled it away and wrapped herself cocoon like in it. 'Unbelievable!' was all Gwen said as she slithered from bed on wobbly legs and padded first into the bathroom setting the shower to warm up as she took the few moments for that to get the coffee on the go. Two hours later and Elspeth emerged looking not much different from earlier except minus her cocoon. She had managed though to drag a long loose tee shirt on as her bare feet slapped on the terracotta tiled floor as she slothed across the kitchen to the counter and perched herself up upon a stool, one hand held out awaiting a coffee cup to be thrust into it. Gwen obliged and smiled at the sight of her friend looking the worse for wear for a change, Gwen knew it was usually her but today she felt quite spritely for some reason despite her vigorous activities the night gone and the day before. 'How do you look so chippy this morning?' Elspeth groaned 'My head is still a day behind I think.' Elspeth sighed and yawned but both girls looked as one at the now empty tequila bottle and they pulled faces of remembrance of where the contents had gone. 'Guess that didn't help' Elspeth groaned. 'No, I don't suppose that one did as that was in fact the second one. We should have called it at the first bottle. Anyway, I'm going down to see Diego for breakfast, I can't be arsed to cook, the fresh air will do me good anyway and it'll give you time to get your shit together. Any preference for anything while I'm there or do I choose for us both like normal?' Gwen smiled disarmingly as she slid into her Sanuks and grabbed her purse. 'I'll have the special,' Elspeth said after mulling it over a few moments 'it usually works after a session, get some fruit while you're at it, I should be good to go by the time you get back.' Gwen skipped over and kissed Elspeth on the forehead before nimbly making the return trip to the back door and slipped out with a wave. Gwen knew – from recent experience - that Elspeth would be hungry by the time she got back so she planned on getting two of Diego's specials for her which was also known as the Southwest Skillet, mesquite marinade breakfast sausage, fire roasted peppers, southwest seasoned red skinned potatoes, Portobello mushroom and red onion, sliced avocado, two eggs over medium and two slices of French toast with cinnamon sugar. Gwen would have the same only difference as she didn't really eat meat these days would be a vege burger, sliced into hers instead, with sweet mesquite drizzle. Checking her watch Gwen noted it was almost lunch time let alone breakfast and Gwen felt a twinge of guilt, just a twinge mind and it lasted a whole three seconds as Gwen was a self-professed day sleeper and not a morning type of gal at the best of times. That had never changed since she was a school girl. In fact she so hated getting up, she had been known to sleep in her uniform just to get that extra nap time before jumping up and running almost straight out the door. Gwen smiled at the memory and slipped her Bluetooth ear buds in she picked some Walela on her phone and pressed on towards Diego's.

Unbeknownst to Gwen, too much tequila wasn't the only reason Elspeth felt so bad but the former detective didn't want to face up to the truth of the matter. She had left work in New York to stay with Gwen after being told her life was as much in peril now as Gwen's but even that memory was fading into the remnants of a bad dream. It couldn't have come at a more opportune time though, free from the pressure of the job for the first time in a long time – although she loved it dearly – it took its toll however much she tried to deny it. The word orbited her like a cruel joke and she couldn't bring herself to say it out loud anymore knowing it no longer had any real substance to it. It was just a spectre, a one trick pony that had lost its power to scare, but sadly it knew enough about dread to last a lifetime. Knowing Gwen was out, Elspeth retrieved the letter she had hidden shortly after arriving back some weeks earlier and re-read it with the same sinking feeling she had the first time she absorbed the words on the page before her. It made no sense. It didn't then and they didn't now. A few days after they arrived off the Greyhound, Gwen had been out fetching groceries and Elspeth had made some excuse about checking in at the local precinct in case they needed her for anything as she still had ongoing investigations in New York. Truth was she had called upon her doctor because she felt the familiar sensations returning as they rode the bus and Elspeth was devastated, just when life looked turning around, meeting Gwen and having feelings unlike anything she had ever felt only to have them overshadowed by another set of feelings, ones she knew all too well and thought were gone forever but her horror was jealous it seemed.

'It's back isn't it?' Elspeth asked the question knowing the answer before the doctor even spoke because she looked at Elspeth with such sympathy that Elspeth broke down there and then and cried like she never had. 'Your white cell count is elevated and increasing.' The doctor spoke to the sobbing woman like she was listening 'You'll need to start treatment right away and we should be able to forestall any further symptoms for now, at least until we can get a better handle on what this is exactly and if it's spread anywhere else.' The doctor talked some more and Elspeth listened but more like a spectator watching herself being spoken too. It was muffled and distant and irrelevant as Elspeth had sworn years ago that should it ever rear its ugly head once more she would take matters into her own hands and not end up like her mother had, bed ridden, in agony and as broken of spirit as anyone could be. Elspeth swore she would never suffer that fate as she was a free spirit, one with the wilds and she wanted to go out that way…but it was too soon, there was Gwen now. She cried all over again.

Diego's wasn't far and Gwen chose to walk, enjoying the rising temperature on her skin and the dry aromas of the burgeoning plants greeting the world. Gwen noted the drier air seemed to make things smell clearer and more pronounced, at least for her as being from an island like Great Britain where the air is mostly moist to a greater or lesser degree she was used to a constant existence of humidity. Wet air in varying guises depending on the time of year but here, in the desert it was so dry she was sure she felt her own sinuses drying up, evaporating before her very eyes. The effect was a clarity she had never known existed, not in all the places she had visited since her travels began. Gwen didn't know it but she felt like a freshly planted shrub and her tap roots were going down, seeking that permanence and nourishment that the feeling of home creates. Gwen was home now and her soul knew it before her conscious mind had caught up to the idea, but she was beginning to feel it. Gwen was about as happy as she could be and she muttered her good fortune to the ether as she walked and listened to her music. 'Damn, you're one lucky chick Gwen my girl. Don't ask how, but somehow you've found your way to this oasis of beauty and wonder, with one heck of a landscape to protect and a really great friend to share it with. Admit it Gwen…' Now as was Gwen's habit of talking to herself, she always reasoned it was the way to get the answer she sought, by brainstorming it out with herself. '…she is probably more than a friend now, you've always loved who you've loved regardless of gender but you've not felt like this before so do not fuck it up.' Gwen laughed at her own advice and knew she would try her best not to regardless. Gwen could smell the food before she arrived and her taste buds lit up into life and the thought of breakfast consumed her thoughts for the next hour.

## TRINITY

Harry hadn't been able to settle at all after Gwen's departure from the Big Apple for the desert. He paced like a caged animal. Seb was somewhat besotted with Jen who kept saying she should leave and head off but always stayed another day; that was a week and a half ago. They had learnt a lot and formed a basic plan but the bigger picture was still elusive. Protect Gwen and by association Elspeth, watch for signs of the Kore-Megara and any influence by Azazel. Revenants were her stock in trade so watch for them first. Seb offered to stay in New York a while longer with Bex and Jen who were getting along famously, Maddy though said she was heading out, she had a premonition and after several readings of the cards and even with a few variations in pattern, the message was still the same which disturbed her more than Jen, sufficient enough in fact to leave and go check it out. It entailed Maddy heading off for the same desert Gwen was sheltered in. The premonition called that shelter into question and Maddy wanted to make sure all was well in the area and by area she meant the entire Four Corners region. They had discussed at length how Azazel had found Gwen and realised that by shielding her they made her stand out, so knowing that, where she was now was brimming with powerful and occasionally conflicting energy, enough to throw any demonic scry off kilter. The SC had a place out there, Harry had been only once, getting along famously with the guardian there, a big Native American who went by Grizzly. Seb had been on another continent at the time. In Sedona there was ample vortex energy to mess with anyone looking too deep there and thanks to the Navajo, Hopi, Apache and Pueblo shaman, there was a constant thrum of power to the land. Gwen was well hidden but Maddy '*felt*' there was something more and she just had to go investigate, Harry offered to come along and suggested a bike trip unless matters got urgent and she really needed to fly for speed, if it was just a feeling, they would only be a few days out. Harry had always secretly harboured the desire to biker up, rev up a comfortable hog and cruise across country, Maddy along for the ride just made that more appealing. Amazingly she agreed and the two set off the moment Harry sorted their ride. 'No bar fights.' Seb instructed as Harry and his bike grumbled up outside Hannigan's and he stepped into the comparative gloom of the diner to pick up Maddy who was waiting for him there. 'You're just sore because you're not coming and wouldn't be a part of such entertainment.' Harry jibed good-naturedly but Seb laughed and spread his hands wide. 'You see what I have to put up with? He's incorrigible, left to his own devices trouble just finds him like a big fuzzy magnet.' Laughter all round and Harry maintained his dead pan look of innocence 'What? What's so funny?' Seb stood and slapped his friend across the shoulders then punched him in the arm like it was a sort of parting ritual they had. 'Seriously Harry, don't go looking for trouble.

You're on recon only and that means just looking. Don't be seen, don't upset the girls and undo the work of the memory charms that should by now have them forgetting this place like a distant dream…' Harry went to interrupt but Seb forestalled him, a serious look coming over his normally smiling, boyish features 'There is danger everywhere Harry without us poking it with a stick and making more of it than is needed.' Harry took a step back to stop Seb poking him as he was doing and held up his hands in supplication 'Okay dad, give it a rest. This isn't my first rodeo but I do understand the gravity of this particular situation which is why I want to make sure things are going as they should be. This seems too important to simply leave to chance.' Bex stood up then and came around the table to give Harry a hug 'We know you know, but all this is unprecedented and we're not there to help if things go sideways. Vital time could be lost you calling me and me trying to open a portal that far away…I've not used these powers as much as I have these past weeks this fully for many, many centuries…' This time Harry placated Bex 'Look, if the shit should hit the fan, I'll not call you anyway, I'll be calling Ted…remember we told you about him? Our boss technically but he can do that portal shit way better and bring reinforcements with him if needed. He is a last resort though and don't forget, Maddy will be there and who is going to piss off a mahoosive red dragon…unless they have a deep and crispy death wish I suppose.' Humour came back and with that, they shook hands, hugged and mounted the Electra glide and rumbled away into the afternoon traffic.

'Think they'll be alright?' Bex asked and Jen – who had kept somewhat silent as the old friends went their separate ways – stood up and raised her glass in a toast, using the gesture to consolidate the fact that a Hound of Fenris and one of the original Red Dragons and Avatar of the Earth herself was along for the ride, little short of a small army was going to bother them and they should rest easy though not so easy as to drop their guard as there were now dangers abroad that would need watching and ideally – eliminating. Humour tried to compete with that ominous statement, failed, gave up and left; then Jen declared she had business to attend to and left also. Seb and Bex spent the rest of the day in a morose sort of silence and drank in an effort to diminish the horror lurking in the shadows just out of reach but that plan failed too.

Azazel wasn't so easily defeated and the rout simply made her even more determined to find both the woman and the reason she was so vital and sought after. Nothing she had learnt so far made enough sense to justify the slaughter that had occurred, the arrival of the dragons – which was a genuine surprise, even she hadn't seen that coming – was overly dramatic for a supposed nobody. The witches were in pieces, many of the upper hierarchy had perished and now Lysandreth was going to have to restock her ranks with lesser powered acolytes. They would be strong for sure, merely to have survived long enough to be an acolyte was testimony to their abilities but would it be enough? Would their lack of experience hinder…not that it did the others much good against the dragons or even the hounds, they were quite prodigious. No, Azazel knew she needed fewer protectors around before trying again. Every scrying spell she could muster came up blank, unlike before where they shielded her, she became a blank spot, clearly they had learnt from that error, they had sent her somewhere saturated with power to mask her…wait. 'Of course. Why didn't I think of that before?' Azazel hissed as she smiled a smile of pure wickedness, a crocodile smile of white teeth and prominent fangs making her appear both beatific and deadly terrifying both at once. 'Don't follow the prey, follow the protectors. Those do-gooder's can't leave well enough alone I'll wager, they'll be checking on their charge no doubt so discover where they are or go and then finish what we started.' Azazel knew she would need Lysandreth for that type of magical net and opened a gateway to the cave she knew the witch queen dwelt within, stepped through and vanished.

The Kore-Megara were not in a pleasant frame of mind. Lysandreth was livid and took her rage out on the acolytes. These…girls were meant to take the places of the elders, they had to for there were no others to step up but they were barely aware of the outside world and deemed novice, there had to be another way, another solution. She had taken the mightiest into battle believing it to be a slaughter and a way to introduce a world who had forgotten them to the sheer calamity they would bring. Once this display was done with Lysandreth planned to take seats of power and bring about a new age of magic and dominion. Things had not gone the way she planned, nobody bargained on dragons. Women she had worked with, lived with, trained with and governed for centuries were simply no more than ash now and if the demoness was right, she had barely days to bring these novitiates up to scratch before they had to be sent out into the world once more. Azazel had just left and in her parting left instruction to seek out the enemy of her enemy; the hounds and the Drak. Azazel didn't think the girl was in the city any longer so a wider net had to be cast and that would take power. They needed a magical sacrifice, not a mere mortal this time – or several as the last scrying had utilised. No, this would require something or someone special.

Lysandreth knew that for the speed required, a trip to the in-between would have to be undertaken and one of the fey needed capturing, ideally one of the Alfar, their blood was like liquid magic. But they were also extremely hard to capture and it would be a useful testing excursion for the Kore-Megara acolytes. If they survived that, then maybe they would do to replace those lost to the New York fiasco. She summoned the acolytes to her and began the ritual to open a bridge to the In-between.

## TRINITY

Gwen returned with breakfast and as predicted, Elspeth cleared the first one and half demolished the second before declaring the desire to go camping again. There was apparently a rock face she had always planned to climb in Mount Zion National Park but had never gotten around to it. Gwen wasn't so sure as they hadn't been back long from the last one and although somehow they had resource to enjoy life as they chose – a fact Gwen kept meaning to look into as it was weird when she thought about it, neither girl worked yet their accounts were always filled but just as mysterious as that was, the longer Gwen thought about it the faster the idea faded and she just carried on like it was perfectly natural, the same with Elspeth. Neither were aware of the active memory charm laid upon both of them to keep them safe and unaware of the peril they were both currently in. But Gwen knew something was up with Elspeth as she had been acting a little out of character these past several days and though she took pains to hide it from Gwen, the wily English girl was a good reader of people but equally discreet and respected her privacy, she would tell her if and when she felt the need. So Gwen agreed to go if it brought a smile to the badly hung over Elspeth who smiled indeed and once replete with breakfast, dragged Gwen back into their sanctum sanctorum and demonstrated just how pleased she was Gwen had agreed. They didn't emerge again until dark.

The trip however needed some planning and that put something of a delay on matters which Gwen clearly saw irked Elspeth. But it was unavoidable, for they needed permission to climb in this certain area and the guy who could sign it off was on vacation so they made do by taking more local trips and buying the essentials they would need. Elspeth had climbing gear but Gwen had never even tried it, so several trips to the indoor climbing centre later and a few hundred dollars' worth of harness and helmet and gear for Gwen later she was as prepared as she was going to get. 'You'll get the best experience on the face itself, these fake walls with contrived hand holds are all well and good but nothing stacks up to the real thing.' Gwen smiled with a hint of trepidation 'Good to know, can't wait yey!' Gwen did a little effortless woo hoo punching her arms in the air 'You know however much you want to do this, if it gets too hairy I'm not clambering up into danger zones, this is your dream my girl, I'm here to see you as safely as I can and be there for moral support when you get your cute ass back on terra firma' Elspeth sighed resignedly, smiled and said she was taking a bath – alone in case Gwen had any ideas as she needed to get her head into the climbing zone she said. The moment the bathroom door was shut Elspeth grabbed her leg and grimaced in pain as it rendered her almost immobile with pain. Grabbing a handful of painkillers from the cabinet as quietly as she could she swallowed them with half a glass of wine and simply stood as the water rose in the tub and the pain abated slightly. Moments later as Elspeth lowered herself into the scalding hot yet soothing water, she felt the pain ebb ever so slightly. Fibrosarcoma. Elspeth merely thought the word and it was enough to set her crying once more. As a child she had developed a pain that grew and grew until it was unbearable and her mother had taken her to the doctors with a sombre expression. Turned out it was something she had herself but had kept to herself as it hadn't developed. Benign they had said, as was the leg tumour in Elspeth. A decade later and her mothers had metastasised and spread rapidly throughout her body. Too late for any treatment she had passed mere weeks after the diagnosis in intolerable pain. Death was a release and Elspeth had immediately gotten herself checked out, but whatever she had as a child had not manifested and she was as fit as a woman her age could expect. Passing the police medicals with flying colours she had put her childhood malady to the back of her mind along with the painful memories of her mother's demise. Not until the leg pain had returned on the Greyhound did Elspeth even give it a second thought, now it was all she could think about. It filled her waking hours and haunted her dreams. Her latest visit to the doctor only confirmed her suspicions and that she needed to make plans and decide her treatment. Elspeth needed this break to clear her mind, focus on the mountain and not her predicament. She would tell Gwen after and they would decide what she was to do next. Once, she wouldn't have cared, a memory of her being a police officer and facing down gun men with no fear surfaced like a dolphin drawing air then it dived deep beyond recall once more. But Elspeth moved on as though she was pulled sideways away from the thought. A trip to Santa Fe came unbidden to the forefront of her mind. Whilst they were waiting for some special order components to arrive, a couple of days there might just be enough to get her mind straight. It had been on the bucket list since they got back but for whatever reason, they hadn't managed the trip yet, there had been so many other things to do. 'But a whistle stop tour through Santa Fe will ease us both into the spirit of the trip' Elspeth reasoned with herself, knowing the Hyde Memorial State Park was place of wonder and beauty, nestled in the Sangre de Cristo mountains would be a good precursor to hiking through Mount Zion.

## CRINITY

The day of the trip came round fast, less than twenty four hours after deciding, Elspeth had booked them a room at a prestigious yet character driven hotel in the heart of Santa Fe, full of rustic lumber furniture, Navajo rugs and Kiva style fireplaces, four poster beds and some of the best local cuisine in the area. The drive wouldn't take long, just a couple of hours and it was another fine desert day. They checked in, parked the Wrangler and had their meagre bags dropped at the room then Gwen and Elspeth were out and about exploring Santa Fe. They aimed for the plaza and were using it as a hub to explore from.

'So what is here then El? Where do we go first?' Gwen asked looking around, then frowning as her eye caught an anomaly 'Didn't there used to be something there?' Gwen pointed to the centre of the plaza where an odd vacant space dominated. 'Ah, there used to be an obelisk there, like the one in New York a bit. Commemorated Santa Fe's war veterans but I think it was removed due to some controversy.' Gwen regarded the space and pondered 'Shame, I like obelisks...I think. Anyway, where first?' Elspeth led Gwen to the Governors Palace and Gwen got talking with a native woman who was selling carved stone animals and silver and turquoise jewellery. Gwen thought she was her own best customer as she was draped in the stuff from a huge squash blossom necklace, enough bracelets it was amazing she could lift her arms, some intriguing Kokopelli earrings and a large sun faced Kachina pin upon her long, vibrant, turquoise and red Pendleton coat which was just off each shoulder and tucked beneath her doubling as a seat blanket. Behind her were dreamcatchers of all sizes, medicine wheels and painted shields. All along the Palace veranda were traders with similar yet diverse wares. From pottery, to fabric to carvings to Kachinas and a dazzling array of jewellery. Elspeth and Gwen spent the morning around the plaza, visiting the famed Loretto Chapel with its magnificent and mysterious spiral staircase, took in the Museum of Fine Arts then retiring briefly for lunch before ranging out further to take in the boutiques, trading stores and arts and crafts stores. A full day saw the girls make it back to their hotel worn out and laden with purchases. 'All in all a good day I think' Gwen summarised as she poured them both large glasses of a local red wine they had picked up earlier at a tasting they'd attended. 'I like it here.' Gwen declared after taking a long pull on her drink and folding her legs beneath her as she slouched onto the sofa beside Elspeth. 'More than Albuquerque?' she asked and Gwen found – much to her own surprise – that she did indeed like it more. There was something beckoning about it, enfolding and secure as well as ancient and steeped in a magical ambience Gwen hadn't really felt before. It was as though it called to her specifically, summoned her on a level she was unfamiliar with. 'I think once you've got you climb out of your system, I'd like to come back here for a longer stay.' Gwen recalled something Elspeth had mentioned 'Did you say we were going up to…what was it, Hyde Memorial park or Hyde Remembrance Park or something tomorrow?' Elspeth nodded as she swallowed then spoke 'That's right. Hyde Memorial, you were right the first time and it's not surprising you like it here, its chock full of artists like you, you would fit right in here I suppose being all arty farty like them.' Gwen dug Elspeth gently in the ribs at the perceived insult. 'I am not all arty farty I'll have you know just because I paint and draw you know. Those kinds of people have a look and I don't have that, I'm not immersed enough to join the uniform wearing brigade. You know what I mean, because you do a thing you have to wear certain things, look a certain way. Do I do that?' Elspeth shook her head knowing Gwen was right, she was always her own creature and that in part is what drew her to Gwen, that individuality. 'But tomorrow, you can't wear those Ugs when we go walking.' Gwen pointed out and at the offending footwear. 'I know you go everywhere in them but they stay here tomorrow, sensible boots only. We don't want you pulling a tendon or a muscle this close to your climb do we?' Gwen was putting on her sensible head, recalling a memory of her mother who once advised much the same when she took the time to pay attention to what Gwen was actually up to. 'Yes little mother.' Elspeth said with a girly note to her voice but as she said it there was a jarring sensation that seemed to sweep over the both of them. Not so much a noise but it resonated in their heads and not so much a physical tremor but both girls became instantly unstable and collapsed back into the sofa for stability. 'What was that?' Elspeth was the first to ask 'I have no idea, are we on a fault line or something?' Gwen responded just as

75

oblivious as Elspeth. But there were two who were not so oblivious and they immediately stopped the bike they were riding and pulled over as a wave of energy swept over them. Nobody for a hundred miles would have even sensed it but these two were way more than normal. Harry and Maddy looked at each other 'What was that?' Harry asked feeling a cold dread settle in his stomach and his instincts shift up a gear in response. Maddy thought for a moment before answering but when she did, her voice was more curious than concerned. 'I think that was a prophecy being enacted. Someone is where they are supposed to be and maybe something has happened or been said to presage and in effect activate the prophecy. Harry wasn't sure what that all meant, he had never dealt with prophecy like this before, it was jarring and even the air felt different for its passing now, he noted that it even smelt different. 'Is it Gwen do you think?' Harry asked focusing on the only anomaly he knew about right now. Maddy nodded slowly 'It could very well be, something about her is attracting some serious enemies, why wouldn't she attract a destiny we don't know anything about too?' Harry agreed but was sceptical 'I reckon we're going to find out a lot more in the near future if you ask me. Things seem to be in motion on a scale we've not seen…well I've not seen at all, ever, even with the Order of Ragnor doing their best to screw the world over they never had this…magnitude to them, know what I mean?' Maddy squeezed the shoulders of Harry gently from behind where she sat upon the big bike and the gesture was both agreement and the desire to be moving again. 'I do Harry' Maddy whispered into his back where she lay her head as Harry pulled back onto the road and gunned the big machine 'I do and that's what disturbs me.'

Elspeth and Gwen spent the following day breakfasting in town, some more shopping where Gwen found a small metaphysical store and added some crystals to her collection. She didn't stay long though because the elderly woman behind the counter, who was so smiley and benevolent when they entered changed her demeanour whilst Gwen shopped. She followed Gwen around the store, almost studying her. Scrutinising her every move as though she was weighing her up, or sizing her up. It eventually creeped Gwen out enough she quickly paid for her items and left before the old woman said or did anything else weird. The afternoon was spent up at Hyde Memorial Park where they took food and stayed long into the evening. It totally took Gwen's mind off the dotty old girl at the store and they spoke more about Elspeth's climb in the coming weeks once all the gear she ordered had arrived. They laughed, made love several times amongst the trees and as the sun set, made their way back to the car for the drive back to Albuquerque. They hit the road back just as Maddy and Harry rolled up into Old Town Plaza. 'Find us a hotel somewhere Harry, just ring me with the address later, there are a few things I need to do first, I'll be back for dinner.' With that Maddy, with all the grace of a hunting feline disembarked from her seat on the bike and strolled off towards an alley way whereupon she modified her density and slowly faded from view and in her now invisible form she metamorphosed into the magnificent red dragon she was and without terrifying the populace for a hundred miles in any direction, she took to the air and beat the sky with massive, sail like, scarlet reptilian wings. Only moments elapsed before she was soaring over the desert arrowing towards Santa Fe. She ghosted over the city until she saw what she was looking for. Gliding down and with the smoothest of reverse transformations, the invisible dragon became and invisible Maddy who solidified her form as she stepped out into the street. Stepped out right in front of a metaphysical store called Earth Angel. Maddy regarded the front for a second, smiled ruefully and stepped inside.

'Just me Cynthia.' Maddy called out and as if on cue, a wizened old lady appeared from behind a curtain that led to the back rooms. The same elderly shop keeper that had creeped Gwen out so. 'Jen not with you?' she asked Maddy, voice surprisingly strong for one of her advanced years. 'Not yet, she is still in New York last I knew but I was...' Cynthia butted right in all excitement and wringing her hands 'She was here, the one we've been waiting for.' Maddy gestured Cynthia to sit on the big sofa they had, fetched her a glass of water and bade her tell her everything. Cynthia spoke unerringly of Gwen, describing her in the finest detail. 'You're sure Cyn? It was definitely this woman?' Maddy showed Cynthia the photos she had on her phone of Gwen taken when in New York. 'Oh yes, it was her alright.' Cynthia confirmed between sips. Maddy slumped back in the sofa in an uncharacteristic display of weariness and despair. 'What's up dear?' Cynthia asked concerned, rarely did she see either Jen or Maddy looking despondent. Cynthia knew these two girls mannerisms because both girls had and still did work at the store with Cynthia and had done so for the last six years.

'It seems Cyn that events have taken a turn. A prophecy is in play or several of them but we didn't see it or them coming nor expect such chaos associated with them. We believe it involves Gwen somehow but we're not sure how yet but she is attracting some dangerous enemies. We aren't sure either if it's all her or something to do with her brother, he is a part of this too also in ways we cannot yet fathom. Either one is affecting the other or the fact the both of them are involved it is doubling up the effect. But I don't know if you felt it, I know you're sensitive but there was a shift earlier, like something big stepped up a gear, don't suppose you sensed it?' Cynthia hadn't and admitted as much but she did notice a larger than usual influx of birds and animals that afternoon, rooftops covered in birds, the urban wildlife quite skittish and seemingly flushed from their daytime hide outs to scamper through town. For many it didn't seem like a lot, but Cynthia took it as a sign. Cynthia was good at spotting omens. 'It must nearly be time then.' Cynthia said with a note of finality 'I'll get preparations underway in the morning. Are you staying tonight?' Maddy shook her raven locks and stood 'No Cyn, I'm expected back in Albuquerque tonight but we'll both be back shortly I expect. Keep your wits sharp and your eyes on Dolores and her cousin.' Cynthia looked bemused 'Why is that? Have they something to do with this?' Maddy wasn't sure and said so; yet although it was just a feeling now, it was a growing feeling and something she and Jen would have to watch.

'Are these all for you?' Gwen asked as the UPS guy dropped a myriad of boxes off on the driveway over the course of several days. Gwen waved once more as he left and she picked what she hoped was the last of them up, huffing by the time she dumped them upon the breakfast bar 'What the bloody hell have you got in here? They weigh a ton and if you think I'm carrying this up a mountain you're having a giggle.' Gwen grumped as she set them down, swapping them for her coffee. Elspeth set about unboxing as fast as Gwen put them down as though it were Christmas and explained everything as she laid it all out. There was a lot of rope and carabiner clips, a helmet, two harnesses, hand ascenders, ATC belay, pulleys, varying sizes of cams, nuts and hexes. Two pairs of new approach shoes and two new pairs of climbing shoes, shorts and shirts. 'Are you going to need all of this?' Gwen asked as the inventory rattled on. 'I am,' Elspeth huffed 'you don't want me falling off do you?' Gwen clearly didn't but was a little dismayed at the stock level required to shimmy up a rock as she annoyingly called it. Not that that she wanted to belittle the fairly pointless – to her at least – pastime, but doing so annoyed Elspeth, so was worth the fun. 'And if I do fall off, I want my corpse to look good at least for when they find me.' Gwen was stunned by Elspeth's off hand manner about falling 'What if I find you? Cheers mate, there you are broken and splattered over the rocks but your shirt matches your shorts at least.' Elspeth knew she had riposted nicely for Gwen's leg pulling but may have taken it a tad too far as the look of mortification on Gwen's face wasn't funny. 'Sorry hun, didn't mean to be so flippant but if you don't put death into perspective we wouldn't do a lot of things. Yes, it's a risk but it's why I have all this, to minimise that risk.' Gwen didn't look convinced and folded her arms across her chest, pouting ever so slightly her disapproval and disbelief.

'Seriously Gwen, I know what I'm doing,' Elspeth explained wearily 'it's just that I haven't done it for a while, moving to New York pissed all over that, there aren't many mountains in Manhattan.' Gwen couldn't disagree with that 'And to prove it to you,' Elspeth continued 'we'll nip up Big Block tomorrow and try this stuff out, you'll see then how cool it is then we're good to go for next week?' Elspeth was clearly keen to get her bucket list climb under way now she had her gear. Gwen agreed and helped her box everything back up ready for the morning and Elspeth's ascension of Big Block.

Oddly enough, descending another mountain right at that moment were three women, but they were not mountain climbers. Nor was the mountain anywhere upon this earth. Nuala the Kore-Megara Prioress and two acolytes were making their way down a steep decline on what was once a path reserved only for mountain goats or maybe at a push, the fleet footed eight legged mountain horses that were known to frequent the slopes in this region. This part of the range was known as the Oakholm Mountain as the hardy and giant oaks flourished in the rocky terrain and moist altitude, their roots weaving through the landscape almost binding the mountain together. These oaks were of such a size that a company could travel many miles comfortably just by using the branches without ever having to touch the ground. This was also a favoured dwelling area of the more solitary Alfar. Those who sought peace, solitude and communion with the land of the In-between. Like many temples and sanctuaries here on Earth, height plays a part. The air changes and the vibration alters with increased altitude and so attracts the scholarly, the seekers of wisdom and enlightenment and those who shun the perceived rat race of their fellows. So it was in the Oakholm, the tallest of the range and so densely swathed in oaks and foliage, one could disappear here and never be found...unless you were Kore-Megara. They sought out power. Their magics were tuned to the arcane and aetheric flows being used for the Oakholm was also known for the practising magi to come to hone their powers, drawing upon the tapped energy of the trees to help consolidate their control. It was one of these fledgling sorcerers that Nuala and her charges had captured. They hunted him down like trained predators and before he could even mutter a defensive spell they had him. He was no match for Nuala anyway had he even tried, as a Prioress her power was only secondary to Lysandreth and her craft had allowed her to live an extraordinarily long life, mastering the subtle enchantments and ancient scrolls that gave her such extraordinary abilities. The Alfar was now gagged and wrapped in enchanted cord that bound him tighter than any chain and allowed him to be moved easily as it held levitation amongst its properties. Their captive was finished with the Skab or Eschar mask. A black mask of dried blood that covers the face, ears, eyes and mouth. It allows the recipient to breath but that is all, total sensory deprivation is rendered otherwise. It has to be made by the caster by pooling almost a pint of the casters blood as well as a few other closely guarded ingredients. Once prepared, the caster can then absorb the Skab back into themselves to fling out defensively if need be with a word rendering your opponent helpless until torn off. A hideous fate awaits should anyone attempt to tear it off too soon. The Skab will take eyes and flesh with it. At least a week must elapse before the thing degrades sufficiently to crack off depending upon the magical strength of the caster. They didn't need a week though to bring their captive back to the Kavern for the enchantment, they would be back within hours. Reaching the edge of the cliff they were heading for the trio stopped and Nuala looked over. It was a drop of several thousand feet for the unwary traveller but Nuala smiled cruelly. 'Do you have your spell prepared?' She asked in such a tone that meant any answer other than yes was not going to end well. They intoned they did as one 'We do Prioress.' In truth she expected no less, these were the two most promising of the neophytes as Nuala grasped the rope binding the Alfar prisoner tightly in her fist she issued her command. 'Then step off.' Nuala did not wait and stepped out into thin air, taking three steps out, pushing the floating Alfar before her then suddenly dropping. Not with the break neck and lethal terminal velocity you would expect, but at a sedate pace like a hawk riding the thermals down, the trio of witches descended like scarlet ghosts past the mountainside. Lysandreth would be pleased with their success and speed of acquisition, little fuss in, capture and out, perfect.

They alighted upon the leafy and mossy ground, moist with an almost perpetual mist where the warm air of the forest below met the cooler air of the mountain escarpment looming above it. Three pairs of booted feet sunk very slightly into the spongy strata as their natural weight took up the burden of motion once more. Soft and supple leather calf high boots that were spell crafted to leave no footprint carried the witches across the In-between. Dragging the bound Alfar between them they made good time to their extraction point. Sometimes when upon entering the In-between, unless you dwell there and are in possession of inherent magic to travel the many realms of the In-between, the point you enter and the point you leave may not be one and the same. The laws of physics were called into question here and space and time as humanity knows it are warped far beyond mortal comprehension, thus making it a dangerous place for the unwary and infrequent visitor, more so if you possess no power to survive its many perils and deadly residents. The Kore-Megara adepts were that rare combination of predator and as such were generally unwelcome in the In-between. The sorceresses were not only magically adept but physically honed for battle. All carried a Khopesh across their backs and were adorned with many blades and throwing stars. Not only were they weapons trained but they were weapons in themselves even unarmed for their hand to hand combat would be a challenge to even the most fearsome of warriors. So Nuala strode through the undergrowth with little fear of what she might encounter, focused upon the bridge and gateway they had to find to return to the Kavern and Lysandreth.

'Mistress, why do we not harvest more of these Alfar for their blood if it is so potent?' the acolyte called Vivienne asked and the other called Judith added her opinion too 'they are not so hard to capture as this one proves, they may study the art but they do not seem powerful.' Nuala didn't look back but spoke all the same, clasping her hands together in the habit she had when teaching her students. The Alfar are more than you know, they are many and widespread and most are vastly more powerful spellcasters than these offerings, and these Alfar are like children by comparison. They come here however, seeking their way onto the path the rest have had centuries to master. We hunt here for that reason alone. Even the Kore-Megara are not foolish enough to hunt more aged and established prey and since you all conducted yourself so poorly at the New York incident, it seems we are not as powerful as we once were or thought we still were. The world has moved on without us and grown in strength and ferocity it seems. Only a fool does not learn from a loss. We do not know everything and pity the dullard who thinks they do. Pride is a great an enemy as any we face. We must learn fast and adapt to these new challenges and grow our strength once more where complacency has left us lacking. This is why some of you will train harder than the rest in order that you may go out into the world as missionaries of a fashion. Learn what can be learnt of mortal kind now and what threat they present to us, recruit even if you can. Learn where best to strike and where their weaknesses lie. We will grow our numbers once more and when the time is right we will emerge once more into the mortal realm and take our rightful place.' To the acolytes Vivienne and Judith, it sounded amazing if a little rehearsed and they imagined Nuala standing before the mirror pool reciting it to herself over and over until she both believed it and perfected its delivery.

The forested lowlands they now traversed led steadily downwards and the valley expanded. Occasionally, walking through the trees the women caught sight of massive creatures, some dwarfing even the legendary dinosaurs of human history, huge reptilian predators and they moved with a stealth that belied their size and the two acolytes wondered just how vast this valley was to conceal such creatures. Through gaps in the leafy canopy, dappled with every hue of green looking upwards they caught sight of the cliff face as the valley rose both right and left. From gaping holes in the rising land they saw great winged beings emerge and soar aloft, rising upon the thermals created by the valley and their keen eyes scoured the forest for prey as they were swept upwards. They were brutal looking things, somewhere between a Pterodactyl and a vulture. Feathery underbelly that leached out onto the wings but graduated into scales then leathery flaps that were the wings proper, bat like but with wicked looking talons upon them. Nuala had told both Vivienne and Judith they sought the river that would run through the bottom of the valley and from that they would locate their bridge. For all bodies of water were catalysts for trans-dimensional travel. They were gateways to many realms if one knew how to use them. Flowing water was best but lakes and reservoirs served well enough if one was desperate enough and powerful enough to create the bridge. Nuala was all that and more. The rest of the day fled before them when they stepped finally upon the shore of the river. Darkness gave it a menace the sun never did. Waters rushed by black and uncaring, the stones upon the shore were various sizes and damp from the river's spray. 'How far to the bridge prioress?' Vivienne asked eyeing the water suspiciously as though it sensed them and their nefarious purpose and would suddenly reach out and overwhelm them in an effort to protect one of its own. It was a story not unheard of in the tales of ancient visits to the In-between. The tales spoke of guardians of the elements and flora and fauna. Powerful elementals who were part of the very fabric of the forest and were even thought to be the life force of some of the majestic trees. Dryads and sylphs of royal power. They would not take kindly to such a kidnapping. 'Here.' Nuala stopped and reached out a hand tentatively. The air shimmered where her fingertips touched and as though a torch had been directed at the spot, it illuminated and showed a bridge of oscillating light arc out over the river though the far side was in darkness and gave no clue as to whether it spanned the torrent or simply stopped halfway. 'Take the offering through, I will remain to seal our escape and ensure nothing follows us back. I have felt eyes upon us these last few hours and I fear we have been discovered by Alfar hunters.' Vivienne and Judith spared enough time to cast uncertain glances between them before Vivienne pushed the lightly floating Alfar ahead of her and stepped onto the bridge. Her every step lit up as she walked out exuding all the confidence she could muster over the roiling depths below her. Judith was quick to follow once she saw nothing happened to her sister. She had not taken more than two steps though when she let out a scream of agony and collapsed. Looking down and causing Vivienne to look back they saw a green fletched arrow punched clean through Judith's calf. The moment of shock passed and several more shafts flew by them before Nuala conjured a shield and the rest bounced harmlessly away. 'Judith get up and move…NOW!' Nuala shouted back at the fallen acolyte as more and more arrows pummelled the shield. As it stood they were no more a threat than a bug on the windshield to the power Nuala wielded but if the hunters had a shaman with them or even a border guardian, for they were just as magically proficient and twice as deadly, they might prove a nuisance. Nuala dug into a pouch at her waist and cast silvery powder ahead of her. A string of muttered words later and stone after stone upon the river bank lifted up until more than half of them hovered six or seven feet off the ground. A sharp wave of her arm and Nuala sent the stones flying from her at such a force they felled every shred of foliage for a hundred paces across as well as deep. As the stones distracted, Nuala stepped upon the bridge and rapidly caught up to the limping Judith. Picking her up like a child, she ran on. Passing the darkness of halfway Nuala was suddenly confronted by Vivienne. 'Pass by mistress, we are home and I shall close this rift.' Vivienne lifted her hands and the river water lifted free and clear of the torrent but as it separated from the cascading rapids below, it began to crack and freeze until over a dozen javelins of ice hung in mid-air and not just tiny shards, these were each the size of a man. Like Nuala, a flinging gesture from Vivienne sent the ice shards tearing across the bridge. Nothing would stand against that barrage as she untied the enchantment that held the dimensional bridge in place. With a flourish it was done and the air closed around the opening until all trace of it was gone. The women stepped out of the rift upon the water and took several steps upon to it before they reached the shore. Had anyone witnessed the spectacle they would have been stunned to see three women step out of nowhere and walk a good forty feet across the surface of the reservoir carrying a floating bundle that resembled a man. Not your everyday sight. 'Where are we?' Judith asked, kneeling finally and breaking the arrow close to her leg and then with gritted teeth, she pulled it through and expertly wrapped the wound with a torn hem of her robe. Standing with a grunt, tentatively making sure it would take the weight and she take the pain, she found it was acceptable for now, a healer would deal with it later. Vivienne looked around and saw a sign in the distance that read Alton Water. Nuala frowned as she scoured her memory for any reference as to why they would have materialized here. A fragment of a memory surfaced about nearby Mistley and Manningtree where legend has it that sisters were mistreated and burnt for their alleged crimes. There was power hereabouts then Nuala reasoned, it was also perhaps somewhere the Kore-Megara needed to revisit and this area looked to suit their purposes. As she wracked her memory for details one in particular surfaced about the area. A place named Holbrook. Named by an ancient family but even unbeknownst to them, the brook in the hollow led to a true hollow. A deep underground system where at some point, an elder Kore-Megara Kavern resided. Utilising the brook and surrounding waterways for their inherent power. Power unused tends to decay and leave a signature to that effect. What Nuala felt resonated with recent use. Clearly there was more to this area and this body of water than was realised. It was however a task for another time, for now Nuala opened the earthly portal to the Kavern and home, such as they had used to escape at New York and she bade the novitiates to step through with their prize. One last glance back and Nuala stepped through herself, closing all sign of their passing behind her.

## TRINITY

'You know Harry, I don't think Gwen is as safe here as we all hoped.' Maddy murmured thoughtfully over a late supper. They had settled into a routine over the days since Elspeth and Gwen took their trip to Santa Fe. Either Harry would wolf up and run up to Santa Fe from Albuquerque over-night, stay the day and head back the following night then Maddy would fly up and do the same. She also kept an eye on Cynthia, the frail looking old woman was convinced her time was up and was preparing for it. Maddy would have said she still had years ahead of her, managing the Earth Angel store and enjoying life but a few casual card readings told a different story and Maddy paid heed to her cards. Then there was Cynthia herself, been in Santa Fe the past forty years, even before Jen and Maddy had settled in the region and she spoke of a shaman, back in her youth who told of a prophecy and destiny. Back then, she just wrote it off as that was what shaman did but by all accounts, enough of what he had told her had taken place she was beyond disbelief now and actively watched for the signs. Apparently she had been awash with signs lately and such escalation had spooked the old gal in ways Maddy had not seen before. It was this recognition of Gwen that had sent chills up the Latin beauty's spine that day she discovered Cynthia and Gwen had met and spoken. She was all for coincidence but not as many as were happening. How Gwen remained as oblivious of everything was a testimony to the finely woven enchantment crafted with deft skill by Bex, the Unc'Anharaphim seer. She made it so Gwen walked through her tumultuous life like a Harold Lloyd movie, blissfully unaware as chaos reigned all around her. It was a rapidly growing feeling that prompted her to share this with Harry. Who simply looked at Maddy, chewed his food and said simply 'I agree.' Then shovelled more food in.

'That's it?' Maddy exclaimed hotly 'You agree? Why didn't you say something?' Harry patiently finished his mouthful as good old English civility prevented him talking with his mouthful. 'Didn't see the point.' He stated bluntly 'What will happen will happen regardless. Seb and I have dealt with witches before, in fact it was what we were doing before we came to New York. Look how that escalated. We are part of the Seraphim Collective, crazy shit is our go to day job. But this has blown up beyond anything we have seen lately and all our intel points at a cataclysm of some sort, a coming together of too many factors creating that perfect storm of a shit show I suspect.' Maddy sat back and reappraised Harry, seeing another side to the man hound before her, an enigma as was Seb but Harry ran deeper, quieter whereas Seb was all out show and tell. 'So? What do we have here?' Maddy probed, hoping his prognosis at least confirmed hers let alone matched it. 'I don't think anywhere is particularly safe for her, I think here we are simply delaying the inevitable. I couldn't tell you how much time she has, we have, we all have before whatever hits hits. All we can do is respond as it comes.' Harry grabbed his beer and finished it in one swill. 'Fancy going out for a run? Or is dragon your only form?' At this Maddy smiled mischievously and shook her mane of midnight hair. 'No, I can assume many forms.' The boast in her voice was evident and Harry smiled 'You do not know much of the Drakarim do you?' she asked. It was one of the few times Maddy had approached the subject of who and what she really was and although it fascinated Harry, he was too polite to ask outright. 'I don't, we don't. Even the SC are somewhat shy on details and we have Drakel working with us. They're pretty tight lipped for the most part though and many of the SC itself doesn't even know about them. Compartmentalization Ted says, it stops too many from freaking out by knowing too much apparently. There aren't even that many who know about us, Seb and I.' Maddy smiled a smile of teeth and torment as she stood and faced Harry with a glint in her eye 'So you want to race me to Santa Fe tonight? I'll play fair and use four legs like you.' Harry's eyes sparkled gold even as crimson sparks leapt from Maddy's 'You're on, loser buys breakfast.' They both ran then outside like excited children, laughing and drawing curious looks from the few late night patrons walking to the next bar. Harry and Maddy ran for the wilderness, oblivious of everything, for they both knew the material world meant very little to them being who they were. Once they hit the shadows Harry went full hound and seconds behind him was Maddy who true to her nature transformed into a massive, deep umber hued timber wolf, all rangy and long legs. Clearly she was no mere timber wolf as she was as big as Harry and with glowing crimson eyes of fire she loped faster than any car and soon caught Harry as he ate up the ground with his powerful haunches driving him forward in a blur. 'C'mon Maddy,' Harry growled 'let's see what you've got.' Harry then internally dropped a gear and all bar vanished, so fast did he accelerate. Maddy smiled her lupine smile with tongue lolling and met the challenge. The sixty four miles was over in a matter of moments as the two supernatural beings skidded to a halt just outside Santa Fe in some wild land just off the Old Pecos Trail. But the night was still young so the duo ranged off the path and out into the wilderness for the remainder of the night, just letting loose and getting to know each other better until the sun began its daily job and lit up the sky with every hue under itself. They returned to the spot on Old Pecos Trail and shifted back to their human forms. 'Well I'd call that a draw young lady but you did very well.' Harry admitted and took and shook Maddy's hand. Maddy was astonished as she clearly felt she had won that and looked agape at Harry who then just sauntered past and with all the audacity he could muster tipped her lower jaw up so her teeth met as he closed her mouth. Smiling then, the two walked the rest of the way into town for that breakfast with Harry getting the occasional elbow in the ribs for something he said, just as Gwen and Elspeth were doing final prep to take their trip to Big Block for the day.

Lysandreth wasted no time slaughtering the Alfar for its blood and was soon elbows deep in the spell of location. Her mind provided images of the wolves and the dragons knowing one or the other wouldn't be far away. Get closer enough to them and they should be able to sense Gwen. Azazel had been making almost daily contact to track progress and with each negative, she grew more and more furiously desperate. The threats flowed now, thick, fast and regularly. Lysandreth was at the end of her tether with the she demon and was keen to be rid of her interference. Lysandreth had plans of her own. Depending on how this seek and locate went, they still involve Gwen and Azazel be damned. The remains of her once prodigious Kavern of Kore-Megara had been decimated, leaving just four of power and a few promising acolytes, Vivienne and Judith the paramount of those. It would be those two Lysandreth would send out to locate their prey once the enchantment was complete. Nuala and herself were too important to lose in another fight should one ensue. Two acolytes they could afford to lose, even if they were the two most promising. If things did go badly however, an escape was planned. The Kavern they currently occupied was deep in the Appalachians and had been undisturbed for over three hundred years. Recent events meant that Azazel knew its location now and there would be no safe haven there if she came with a demon horde in tow. Nuala offered a solution with the discovery of Alton Water in England, it seemed undisturbed and undiscovered. Whilst Vivienne and Judith were about their forthcoming mission, Nuala was tasked in finding the Kavern there and making ready. Lysandreth was taking no chances.

'Is it ready yet Divine Mother?' Judith asked, keen to prove herself and wiping her hands nervously on her indigo blue gown. The red reserved for outside, inside they wore blue as decreed by the High Priestess Lysandreth. 'Soon my child, the right amount of time for steeping the concoction must be observed. Patience, your time is nigh Judith, you and Vivienne. Succeed here and your place amongst the elite will be sealed. Fail and it will not matter.' The hours dragged by as the simmering cauldron bubbled and popped when the blackening, viscous liquid crystalized. Soon enough the desired result was achieved, several black red crystals adorned the bottom of the now empty vessel. Lysandreth scooped these up and strode in to the grand hall and with a word she conjured a world map from magic that hung suspended between them. With little ado, she tossed the crystals out onto the projection and simply said 'seek!' The crystals flew around the map before settling two in New York and two in Santa Fe. Lysandreth pounced like a hungry cat upon the stones, striding through the map to gather the lightly glowing gems. Lysandreth passed them then, one each to Judith and Vivienne pressing each one in to their palm until it almost bled. 'Prepare yourself, you leave within the hour.' The two acolytes ran off in haste as Lysandreth spun to once more to regard the location sourced by the gems. 'So, you thought to hide in the vortex region. Hiding power within power so we wouldn't detect you, clever. But you underestimate the Kore-Megara at your peril.' Lysandreth hissed at the map as though any within it could actually hear her. Twenty minutes later and Judith and Vivienne were garbed once more in the deep scarlet, hooded long coats and robes, Khopesh slung across their backs, blades secreted about them and pouches of spell components hung at their belts. They were as ready as they were going to be. 'We will place you in proximity but you must finish the last. Use the gems to find them, find them and kill them. Leave none but the prey alive and bring her to me.' Lysandreth suddenly raised both hands outwards palms down and upon instinct the two acolytes drooped to their knees so that their bowed heads were beneath Lysandreth's hands.

'Now pray for success, beseech the Kore for fortune as I bless your mission. Deadly ambassadors of the Kore-Megara, bring terror and blood to all who oppose your way.' No sooner had Lysandreth finished speaking than both girls grabbed her hands and kissed the palms as they rose. Saying nothing more, they turned and with a sweeping gesture opened a portal to Santa Fe, stepping through the blue fiery door snapped shut behind them the moment they stepped through. 'So it begins.' Lysandreth murmured to the empty chamber as she began preparations of her own.

'You know they will sense us as much as we them if we get too close.' Judith stated the obvious to Vivienne partly through sense, partly through nervousness about their first solo excursion and it being of such vital import. The stones hummed a steady vibrancy indicating the protectors were close by. By close by, it meant they were likely in the city whereas the Kore-Megara witches were outside it, standing upon a slight hilltop some dozen miles outside the city limits, regarding the bustle that came and went from the desert residents. 'If we just walk in, like this, we may attract attention we do not want yet. They have enforcers. Though they are no match for us, we do not want to give ourselves away. Can you feel the one she wants?' Judith concentrated for she was more sensitive than Vivienne about feeling the flows of power but she sensed very little beyond what they already knew. 'What now?' Judith queried, wondering as much herself. Vivienne considered then decided. 'We go closer then glamour our appearance so we do not attract unwanted eyes. I will mask our presence as best I can so we are not felt then you will cast for a trail. She was here but we need to know where she went. The web will need us to be central.' Judith agreed and they set off walking towards town, as they passed a billboard advertising what Judith took for a potion as two women in long skirts, western boots and waist cut jackets were holding a bottle of something golden hued and apparently called Desert Rose. The two witches didn't know what such a potion might conjure but it seemed pointless summoning a flower and displaying the fact so blatantly. The Kore-Megara witches shimmered as the glamour rolled down over them until they resembled the women above them. Right down to the hair, silver and turquoise jewellery and make up. 'This should suffice.' Vivienne finally answered after appraising their new look. They set off once more and the only indication they didn't belong was the fact they walked along the road where just about every other person was driving a contraption of some description. A couple of miles out, a pick up rolled up alongside them and offered them a ride. A glance between themselves and sore feet as their new look was not designed for pounding tarmac, they accepted. 'Where to ladies?' the driver asked and Vivienne told him the centre of the city. 'Okay, Santa Fe plaza it is, happy to oblige ladies, sit back and relax we're only about eight miles out. But this gotta be better than hoofing it, am I right?' He turned up his music and Bill Miller wafted out of the speakers.

'We should kill him the moment we arrive.' Judith whispered to Vivienne who shook her now auburn locks and explained why. 'We are in disguise Judith, with so many around that would negate the glamour and put us in jeopardy before we find the trail. No, discretion is called for here.' Judith was about to disagree when Vivienne pointed out the bigger reason 'You have to cast a web in the middle of the plaza, we cannot do that in full sight of the denizens of this place. We must wait until nightfall, call upon Hecate and her hounds to reveal the trail and lead the way. I know you crave blood Judith but we will sate that thirst soon enough, for now, patience.' Judith reluctantly agreed and sat back in the twin cab and tried to fathom the music. She failed.

Gwen watched Elspeth pack her kit with a surgeon's precision. Everything in its place, attached and placed in the order she could lay hands to it without looking. Gwen figured it was much the same way as parachutists who pack their own canopies, the best person to trust with your life is yourself...as long as you know what you're doing. Gwen didn't but Elspeth clearly did. Muscle memory must have taken over as she packed and sorted with a mechanical methodology that was fascinating to watch. Eventually though, she ended up just moving things around for the sake of it. 'Enough El, I think it's as good as you're gonna get it, it's why you're doing this practice run isn't it?' Elspeth took a step back and wrapped her arms around herself as she regarded her kit and knew the truth of what Gwen said. 'You're right…as usual and don't be smug…' Elspeth said as Gwen started to smile 'Any last minute changes I can make on the face so it's where I'll need it for the big one.' Elspeth said to herself as much as she did to Gwen, settling things in her mind. 'Alright then, let's get this lot into the Jeep and let's get going while we still have some light left to put up that damn tent you're so fond of.' 'It's my lucky tent.' Elspeth bemoaned and rubbed the tent pack lovingly as though it would coo to be touched so. 'I've used this for nearly all my climbs over the years…' Gwen was not an outdoor camping girl and looked at the dog eared pack and sniffed 'It looks like its seen better days to be sure.' Elspeth scowled and said a silent 'there there' to the tent. 'Pay her no attention, she didn't complain the last time we were in it. 'I was pissed as I recall. I might have well have been in two dozen grocery sacks sewn together for all I knew.' This banter went on as they loaded their gear and didn't stop until they were half way to the camp site. Fortune smiled as there was just enough light left to pitch the tent easily and Gwen cracked a couple of cold ones and set the little fire to blazing as Elspeth finished. They plonked themselves down just as the sun left for the night.

'Going to be an early start tomorrow, so just the one and I'm turning in.' Elspeth stated to Gwen's dismay. Until then she hadn't fully realised just how serious Elspeth was about this climb. Turning down beer and her for a night's sleep felt almost like a snub. Gwen accepted the terms though, and unrolled her sleeping bag. Banking the fire so it would essentially put itself out, Gwen cocooned herself in snugly and rolled over behind Elspeth's already recumbent form. 'Night.' Elspeth grunted a sleepy reply and sleep so overtook them both.

Maddy excused herself and went in search of Cynthia and left Harry to explore the town on his own. He spent some time at the Governors Palace, checking out the merchandise on sale from the artists and craftspeople who held their pitches there. Harry was particularly fascinated by one woman, who had the most hypnotic voice as she told a story to a potential customer about Coyote, the ancient one of legend and some of his antics. Propping himself up against a post, he listened. His hearing was supernaturally enhanced so he heard every word and inflection. It was an incredible tale of lore and once the woman had left with her multiple purchases, Harry - who had gone to fetch a couple of coffees - sat himself down and opposite and offered the woman one of them. 'That's gotta be thirsty work talking yourself hoarse all day, here you go. I've milk and sugar here if needed but I was mesmerized by your story of Coyote and these little guys.' Harry picked up a Fetish carving that he though most resembled a wolf and studied it hard. 'Is this a wolf or a coyote? To my eye they could be similar.' The woman smiled and took it from him and replaced it with another he hadn't seen.

'This is a wolf fetish, carved by my cousin. I don't bring them all out as I'm biased and I think his work is exquisite and I have other carvers work here so I like to balance but something about you makes me feel you need to see this.' Harry smiled and leant back a little to study the carving with a bit more light. She was right, it was magnificent and it pulsed with an energy very few would feel, but he wasn't just anyone. It felt…alive? Dolores then went on to tell Harry the story of Wolf and some of his adventures in the creation of the world and his relationship with the People. All the time she spoke, Harry never let go of the carving. Nor would he. When she finished he asked simply 'How much.' Knowing it didn't matter, the stone was a part of him now and that was that. 'Five hundred dollars.' Dolores said matter-of-factly, almost testing Harry to see how he might react. Truth was, the moment he had sat down every nerve and prescient cell in her body had flared and all she wanted to do was give this man the carving. Somehow it was his before he even sat down, Dolores felt his energy as a palpable thing, much like she did from Joshua, her cousin the carver but this man's was way beyond that. Joshua had power, Dolores was convinced although he always shrugged it off and just carried on whatever he was doing but it was unlike this.

'I'll give you a thousand for it.' Dolores was staggered and was about to argue when Harry stopped her. 'Don't try to dissuade me, I'll gladly give you the five hundred for the carving, to me it is now invaluable and irreplaceable but the other five is for the lesson. I've learnt more today in our time than the last decade about a subject I really should know more about, so thank you…?' Harry angled for her name and Dolores blushed involuntarily and shyly dipped her head as she spoke her name. 'Dolores.' Almost breathlessly and that caught when Harry reached over and grabbed her hand, catching her by surprise and before she knew it, he raised it to his lips and kissed her fingertips lightly. 'Thank-you.' Harry said as he stood. He was about to turn away and go find Maddy when Dolores shouted him back and he turned just in time to catch something small heading straight for his head. It was a small buckskin pouch, just the right size for Harry's new companion. 'This is free from me, made by me. It has a home with you and here is somewhere it can sleep. And here is a bundle of blue corn to be going on with to feed your fetish.' Harry looked baffled by that as surely it was just stone. 'Many think similar, but that stone is a home to the spirit of the wolf and it needs food, spiritual food. Place an ear in the pouch with it, it will absorb the spiritual nourishment from the corn, then you remove it and dispose of it where no other animal will consume it. For it has no nourishment now and will be useless.' Harry understood completely and beamed in gratitude and promptly slipped the Fetish into the pouch and placed it around his neck and the corn into a pocket, inwardly wondering how it would work with his transitions 'something to look forward to.' He murmured and with a wave, Harry was back amongst the pedestrians and his thoughts turned to Maddy and where she was. He didn't have long to wait as she came up behind him in an attempt to surprise him but she forgot about his hypernatural senses and he spun at the last second and mock snarled at her which to her inner pleasure, actually surprised the ancient dragon. 'I must be getting soft in my dotage.' Maddy admitted to no-one but herself. 'What have you learnt?' Maddy asked, changing the subject and getting the conversation back on track. To which Harry smiled and looked thoughtful. 'I've learnt lots I'll have you know.' As he spoke, Harry absently fondled his new acquisition which Maddy noticed and she took one look at the pouch and smiled. 'I see you've been spending time with Dolores.' Harry was shocked this time 'How did you know that?' Maddy took the pouch in her hands and gently fondled the pouch with her fingertips. 'You have one of Dolores's pouches here, I'd know it anywhere…it has a feel to it if you catch my drift and by that feel, you've one of her carvings in there too…nice. Wolf?'

'As it happens, yes and not so oddly really all things considered.' Maddy pursed her lips and shrugged her agreement 'True. Anyway, our eyes and ears have spotted Gwen and Elspeth heading up to Big Block, it's just outside Albuquerque off Highway 337. It'll only take us minutes to get there and we should as Cynthia has a bad feeling.' Harry frowned as he didn't know who this Cynthia was although Maddy seemed to trust her and put stock in what she said. 'I want to say who is Cynthia but just how bad is this feeling she has? Sure it's not arthritis? Or wind?' Maddy's face changed to one of a serious disposition and Harry felt the temperature actually change around him. 'Do not mock me Harrison, I've known Cynthia many years and her feelings are rarely wrong.' Harry backed up and raised his hands in supplication 'Whoa Madeline…I'm just asking, no need to get all feisty, let's get us some privacy then and hightail it outta these here parts. That is what they say here isn't it?' Maddy shook her head in despair as she pointed the way for them to go to make their transition unseen. Maddy was too impatient for running and no sooner had she adopted her draconian form she ghosted into invisibility and launched skyward. 'Charming.' Harry thought as he watched her go. Moments later he was in full Hound persona and to his surprise and pleasure, the medicine pouch was nestled in his fur and had come over with the change. 'True power here.' Harry mused and promised himself when time allowed to explore just what that power meant. Before that however there was the matter of Gwen. Not knowing where Highway 337 was exactly Harry focused instead upon Maddy and the direction she had taken. 'Close enough.' Harry sped off in pursuit.

Madeline landed back from the climbing area and changed back. Walking to the edge she looked over 'Why do humans insist on doing this?' Maddy asked of herself and stepped back. Pressing her hands into the small of her back, she pushed in and arched back languidly and wondered how long she's have to wait for Harry to arrive and for Gwen and Elspeth to make their appearance. She didn't have long to wait for either. Harry was moments behind her and after berating her as gently as he could for leaving him in the lurch with no actual direction. If he hadn't been who he was with paranormal GPS in built, he'd have been stuffed. 'But you weren't were you? I knew you'd be able to follow.' At that moment, the Jeep pulled into the carpark and the two girls disembarked and set about prepping themselves and the camp site, erecting the tent and setting a small fire to blazing to which Gwen went about dinner. Harry and Maddy watched from afar and harry asked what exactly Cynthia had felt. 'She wasn't specific, they never are and with her, she is aware of various outcomes as the future is a malleable thing and every choice changes it ever so slightly so it's constantly in flux.' Harry pondered and looked around at the deepening dusk as the light of the day made way for the star filled night sky and was momentarily absorbed by the illumination of the waxing moon. Like legends would have humanity believe, the moon had no effect upon the likes of Harry. He was a Hound of Fenris, magic, bone and blood were his to control, not an iron based satellite that although it had an effect on many things, it did not control the wolves, supernatural or otherwise. It did however light up the land sufficient to give it an eerie and surreal quality. Almost otherworldly and this – in all his years- had never failed to fascinate Harry. 'So, we're to just wait around for something to happen then?' he asked finally and Maddy had nothing to contribute except a helpless look and a light shrug of acceptance. 'So we wait then,' Harry summarised with a sigh 'At least we know where they are. You sleep if you want,' he offered 'this is my favourite time so I'll keep watch.' Maddy patted Harry on the head affectionately 'I haven't slept like you'd think for aeons Harry. I'm an Avatar of the Earth, I'm sustained by her will and by the power of a world. Jen and I have magics at our disposal that terrify even us, sources of power granted by a living planet, so being the curators of this world we are constantly tuned in if you will. So sleep? Not so much. I'll make a perimeter sweep and see if there isn't anything nasty heading this way that we can't feel yet. If I need you I'll call and trust me Harry…you'll hear it.'

The plaza was virtually empty as Vivienne and Judith entered it sometime after midnight. A few late light revellers were all that remained and they soon dispersed. Helped by a light enchantment of dread, cast by Vivienne to seep into their minds and make them feel like something was looming, or watching or stalking them with foul intent. They sobered slightly and fled the area. It was a variation of a battlefield spell the Kore-Megara utilised to unman the enemy before they engaged, utilised with deadly effect too. 'Get on with it Judith, the stones are insistent and we need to know where to go sooner rather than later.' Judith glowered at her companion and muttered something derogatory but rummaged in a pouch at her hip all the same and withdrew a handful of ingredients. Swiftly creating a circle, Judith drew her Athame, a smaller sickle like blade that also hung at her hip, just as one hung upon Vivienne's and she drew the curved blade across her palm. Blood seeped from the wound and Judith cast it in the four cardinal directions incanting a guttural enchantment, then with a flourish, green lightning manifested around her upraised fist, coiling and writhing about it like a living serpent of power and Judith cast that then into the centre of her spell. It seemed to ignite and what were formerly invisible lines of power and true to the name of the incantation, a web flared out in an ever increasing spiral of a full three hundred and sixty degrees. As it grew it rose. It rose until it was high above the city and then it expanded at such a rate it covered the entire state in seconds. But anyone looking up would not have seen the spectacle unless they were arcane trained to see the flows of magic such as the Kore-Megara were trained in but there were those that did sense the power that flowed above and around them. Birds took flight from their roosts and the nocturnal hunters stopped, confused, disoriented. Several coyotes even wandered into town flowing the direction of a particular power line. Scorpions and tarantulas ran amok, not knowing what was happening.

And several plagues of rats flowed through alleys and streets causing a stir to any who encountered the rodent tsunami. One thread eventually flared brighter than all the others and it gave the acolytes the direction they dearly sought. 'Do you have it?' Vivienne asked impatiently. She asked as the nature of the thread should reveal to the caster the location of that which they hunted. The spell was tied to the stones and for long moments, Judith's eyes were closed as though she watched something in her mind. In fact she did. 'I have it.' Vivienne nodded a curt approval then gave the order. 'So open the portal Judith, let us be done with this hunt once and for all.' Judith agreed and with a flourish and a word, the silvery blue fire of the gateway opened as they had in New York and the two women stepped smartly through. However, even the potent magic of the Kore-Megara couldn't keep up with two powerful creatures moving at speed so the gateway opened for the acolytes essentially in the middle of nowhere at a place Maddy and Harry had been, but were not. Though nowhere wasn't technically true, it was a cluster of trees set back several hundred yards off the Juan Tomas Road, not too far from the Big Block climbing area but in the early hours of the morning where the air hung heavy with Pinyon, Juniper and Mesquite, but wilderness was wilderness and Vivienne was furious. 'You told me you had them!' Judith however didn't back down to the taller Vivienne's lashing tongue. 'I did, but they moved faster than the spell could keep up. It latched onto them here, so they were here seconds ago but presumably have moved on since. She is a dragon after all and I understand they are magically imbued too, so it could be shielding perhaps, moving too fast for another option or simply invisible and staring right at us.' At this last, Vivienne looked around concerned but soon narrowed her eyes once more and stared hard at Judith when no dragon appeared. 'So where are we then?' Vivienne snapped and Judith closed her eyes and held her hand out, sensing the last vestiges of the web spell. 'Close is all I can tell you.' Vivienne pondered their next move as she looked around suspiciously and finally decided their course of action. 'We shall summon the possessors here.' Judith looked horrified and suddenly uncertain of her companion. 'Why do you suggest such a thing? Lysandreth will be furious. It is her arrangement and how do you know the spell anyway?' Judith finally asked warily. Vivienne smiled cruelly and with mischief 'I assisted Lysandreth on a few of the summoning's and Nuala showed me the mechanics of the opening. It is not hard and there are people hereabouts, I sense them at least. They will be unprepared for the possession as most humans are and they will be a useful barrier against the wolf who must also be here about.

95

Stay vigilant whilst I prepare the spell.' The sun was just rising as Vivienne declared herself ready. 'Take my hand, I'll need your strength to support mine as I tear the veil between worlds.' Judith grasped Vivienne's outstretched hand and felt the cold moistness of her anxiety, Vivienne wasn't as confident as she proclaimed and her clammy hand gave her away. 'Don't draw everything Vivienne, I'm holding the ice storm in readiness should the dragon appear. It may be all that saves us if you are busy opening literal wormholes.' For what few realised of the deminions who slipped the rift between the Domain and Earth was that they were almost gaseous and invisible until they found a host but if no host was immediately available, rather than return or perish, they dropped into the ground and by utilizing the energy of the planet, the best they could manifest was a maggoty type of grub. This form could sustain them in the ground until a host happened by. Several months was pretty much the maximum they could maintain this form but rarely had to last that long. Humans infested this realm and there was nearly always some available. Vivienne began to chant, an inhuman sound no mortal throat should be able to utter, but this was the language of The Domain, Nescaria or the place we now call Hell; calling forth the disassociated deminions who waited for such an opportunity as this to once more adopt corporeal form and wreak havoc. Vivienne chanted on and grasped Judith's hand ever tighter until her fingertips turned white then blue and threatened to crush bone. Tiny obsidian spheres appeared in the air by the dozen, growing until they reached the size of a basketball then they fell to the floor and exploded in puff of black smoke, effectively freeing the deminions into our realm. The two acolytes never saw the fruits of their labours but the change in temperature and feeling of dread grew as they grew in number. Soon screams were heard in the distance and some closer as they found hosts. The first of these screams caught the attention of both Harry and Maddy. They had heard it before and knew what it heralded. The many climbers also heard it and their stomachs knotted and ice chilled their blood as they stopped what they were doing. Their initial thought was one they all feared, someone had fallen, but when scream followed scream they knew something fundamental was wrong. From where Elspeth and Gwen camped, they never heard the screams as sound didn't penetrate into the spot they had chosen at the foot of a particularly imposing rock face. It bounced a bit off rocks and harder objects but didn't bend enough to reach everyone. So Elspeth dressed as she would have, geared up and had Gwen check her over making sure she hadn't missed anything and once Gwen declared her as good as she was going to get, Elspeth commenced her practise climb. It was slow at first as Elspeth methodically sought various nuts and cams, ordering them in her mind so she knew better where to reach for what she wanted next time. Gwen watched the progress with a painful expression that spoke of impatience. 'How long are you going to be up there?' Gwen shouted up and Elspeth took a few moments to answer and it was an answer that caused Gwen to groan. 'Most of the day I reckon, I'm rustier than I thought.' Gwen looked up then back the way they had come in. 'Look, as you're not really all that high yet and I'm going to be stuck here for a few more hours, I'm nipping back to town, I shouldn't be more than an hour. I'll top up the coffee and bring back some better supplies than we have here. They were a good idea yesterday but not so appealing now. You have your phone on you?' Elspeth patted it where it was attached to her arm. 'I do, I'll take some pics as I go but I could be halfway up by the time you get back.'

Gwen was torn, it was a nice day but she wanted a few more home comforts than they had and the Starbucks drive through they passed offered those every treats. 'Well, I'll be quick. I'll drive it like I stole it. Sure you're okay?' Elspeth gave the ok gesture and rested back in her ropes eyeing the face, studying it and determining her route. 'I'll be fine, this is child's play even for me; I'm just working out the best bits of kit and testing muscles and fingertips. I probably won't even go all the way to the top. Make mine a large gingerbread latte, I'll reheat it when I come back down.' Gwen jumped up and tossed the keys in the air as she spun, catching them and almost skipping back down the trail to where they left the jeep. 'I won't be long.' Gwen shouted back over her shoulder. By the time Gwen had pulled out onto Highway 337 once more, Harry heard the first scream. He had been running a perimeter the same way Maddy was, doing invisible laps of the surrounding countryside ensuring nothing nasty was lurking. Neither came across the two acolytes who were still several miles away, close enough to have tracked the spell but not pin point for the prey they sought. Hundreds of spheres had been released and the possessed were now starting to amass, still unsure of their surroundings and still in the process of mutilating their hosts so better to function in them. The one thing they all felt was the compulsion upon them, placed there by Vivienne when she summoned them and they made their way towards her unerringly. For their part, Judith and Vivienne began heading towards them as they did so, their crystals grew brighter so they knew they were going the right way and were close. The first possessed deminion hove into view and the moment its eyeless sockets locked on to the two Kore-Megara witches it spoke, its voice was the inhuman hiss, like red hot nails being dragged through broken glass. 'Why are weeee summmmmoned wyytch? Whattt would youuuu have of ussss?' Vivienne stood before the creature and placed her palm upon its forehead the moment it was close enough, transferring images to it of Gwen and Elspeth, as well as Harry, or at least a hound of proportion and of Maddy, in her dragon form. This elicited a brutal laugh from the creature who warned of the wrath of dragons and how taking them on was a fool's errand. It would have nothing to do with that but it would hunt the hound and sport amongst the human populace, those not now possessed and tear flesh where it could. Vivienne accepted this as best she was going to manage in this negotiation. Harry was minutes out by the time the first dozen possessed reached the bottom of the rock face Elspeth was climbing. She hadn't looked back down, concentrating as she was on her equipment, she never saw them ransack the tent and shred their belongings before turning their now inhuman and sightless eyes upwards to where she was suspended some eighty feet up the face. They began to climb. Jamming their now bony fingers into crevices with no consideration for the damage they were doing and they slowly hauled themselves upwards. Harry came skidding to a halt atop the face and managed a quick glance over to where Elspeth was but didn't see Gwen. He had missed her leaving, but before he could descend and clear the possessed from beneath Elspeth, a scream of sheer malevolence drew his attention back to the surrounding countryside where he stood. At least fifty possessed were charging him from all sides, arms out and ducking and weaving in a way to avoid any missile weapon and to keep the eye distracted. They would be on him in seconds so harry did the only thing left to him, he boosted his hound form and took the fight to them, choosing who to attack to buy himself some breathing room and to get away from the edge. With a snarl he leapt at the first half dozen closest to him and with an embrace of fang and claw, shredded them like so much butchered flesh. Back feet raking and talons slashing out, with a fang filled maw vast enough to take heads clean off, which he did. Decapitating, disembowelling and destroying in a haze of fur and blood. The sound though had reached Maddy who likewise transformed, regardless of who saw now as there were probably few left alive to worry about it. Swooping in low, skimming the treetops, Maddy saw the two Kore-Megara acolytes standing brazen in the middle of Highway 337, arms spread wide directing their possessed puppets. One looked up to see Maddy arrowing in towards them and she raised her hands forwards towards Maddy, crossing the wrists and with a word Maddy failed to hear, ice flew towards her, it was the type of ice storm that Jen would conjure. A spiralling cone of decimating cold engulfed Maddy and sent her crashing left across the road and into the trees opposite. A massive frozen reptile that tore a groove across the landscape like a crashing 747. Unbeknownst to Maddy but the direction she had swept in took her over the face Elspeth was climbing and the ice cone flowed on past her once its initial target was engulfed but it decimated the land beyond her, taking out half the possessed who attacked Harry and sending a frozen waterfall of ice shards over the rock face. Right into Elspeth. The wave crashed down over her, knocking her clean off the face and was only saved from falling by the ropes she had secured. She swung limp for a several seconds, stunned by the ferocious cold and razor sharp drenching she had taken, instantly hypothermic and cut in many places by the glass like ice shards but that lasted only seconds more as the cold was so intense that the rope began to freeze and within a heartbeat more snapped. Elspeth plunged eighty foot backwards off the rock face and landed hard upon the rocky ground below. Too hard upon too many rocks at too many angles. Her sightless eyes gazed at nothing as blood flowed from them before they too froze solid along with the rest of her broken body. Harry was keeping up with those left to him and was soon taking the fight to the remaining possessed. Knowing Maddy had taken a hit, he began working his way towards them and the moment he burst out onto the highway he saw the cause of their woes. The two acolytes, surrounded by possessed like a shield screaming obscenities at them, extoling them to keep fighting, find the woman and kill the guardians. But Maddy was far from down. Her inner fire lit up like a nuclear furnace and she exploded into the air once more, shedding the icy shackles that had assailed her as she banked hard, she let loose an incendiary burst that engulfed both the possessed and the acolytes in flame so hot, it dissolved the highway beneath it into a liquid that bubbled and evaporated in such steam and acrid smoke, nothing could have survived. Harry had to shield his eyes as the intense heat wave swept across the land surrounding them, he even felt several patches of fur shrivel before the heat wave. But it was short lived and soon blew clear only to reveal the two Kore-Megara acolytes standing untouched in a blue fiery shield. One gesticulated and the trees for fifty paces all around exploded into a cloud of lethal wooden missiles. They were no match for Maddy's hide and she brushed them aside, incinerated the rest and Harry grabbed a handful of surviving possessed and used them as a shield as they were pin cushioned by the slivers.

'Bloody hell, these witches are a pain in the ass.' Tossing them aside after they proved useful but were falling apart now, Harry bounded forward towards Judith and Vivienne who were regarding him with almost contempt, clearly feeling secure in their shield after thwarting dragon fire the way they had but they hadn't banked on him. Seb and Harry had set themselves up as a kind of supernatural shock troopers. Being insanely fast, pretty much bullet proof and imbued with an innate magic that granted them a kind of immunity to most spells cast upon them – which was why they were hunting witches in New England in the first place - they made dangerous spearheads. Harry was about to find out just how invulnerable he was and how powerful their shield was when he hit it. And hit it he did. Fracturing the enchantment nicely and sending coruscating crimson splits all over the blue fiery shield. A few more hits like that and it would disintegrate. Harry gave his best wolf smile at the two witches who were now staring at him with the horror he expected as his due. Backing up for another run at the shield, he never took his eyes off them in case they had more spells up their sleeves. What they did have instead of spells it turned out was a shit load more of the possessed on command. Harry had backed up a good hundred yards to get a better accelerated impact but that allowed the horde of possessed to swarm into the gap between him and the Kore-Megara. Harry growled a primal battle snarl and tore into them even as they surged all over him. Fortunately Maddy had recovered and was shaking the crash off when she caught sight of Harry's problem. But the shield was weakened, she could see that so Maddy made a choice and shifted back to dragon form and slammed a massive truck sized front foot onto the ground. A crevasse opened up and sped towards the two witches. If their shield was resilient, then maybe not so the ground it stood upon. The road they stood upon parted like opening curtains, which revealed their shield as spherical, interesting Maddy thought but it still dropped like a rock down into the deepening fissure. Deepening and widening as Maddy willed it. The giant red dragon walked over then to the fissure and looked down to see the glowing sphere disappearing into the darkness, with the two witches inside. Maddy took a breath and blew a full lung full of fire down into the deep, liquefying the rock as it poured down and spilling it onto the sphere. Encasing it in the most organic liquid rock she could create. Then she closed the rip. Calling upon her Avatar's powers Maddy drew the earth together and stitched it back almost as if it had never happened. Without the control of the witches, the possessed were temporarily at a loss and Harry took full advantage and shredded them by the dozen. Those that stumbled too close to Maddy met an equally brutal and very final end by the jaws and claws of the massive red dragon. Minutes that felt like hours later and the area was clear of both the Kore-Megara and the possessed. All that was left was the clear up. At the sight of fire in the distance, the human emergency services would be winging their way and as if on cue, Harry picked up the familiar sirens drawing closer. There would be a lot of missing persons reported sadly and that always got the FBI involved when it happened on this level. Calls would need making as this was above his pay grade. It was in the hands of Ted and the Council of 6 now to mollify those who needed it and spells to adjust the memory of so many. This wasn't the sort of war where so many deaths could just be written off as collateral damage. Harry used his speed and strength and gathered as many possessed as he could find and built a pile for Maddy to turn to ash. The sirens drew closer as Harry finished one task then went in search of Elspeth. They found her easily enough and Maddy looked to Harry who couldn't take his eyes off the broken and busted figure of Gwen's friend. So many question. How was she going to take this, how were they going to explain it even? The rock face was a sheet of magical and glacial ice. How had that happened? That was no natural phenomena. But Harry nearly kicked himself as he belatedly realised there was no sign of Gwen. He sniffed and nor could he smell her woody scent. A quick recce proved the vehicle had gone too. They concluded she must have slipped away while they were checking the perimeter, but where had she gone? 'Maddy, get yourself airborne and do a sweep, Gwen isn't here. She was now she isn't. The Jeep is gone so she may very well be in that. She doesn't know what has happened and that Elspeth is dead. We're going to have to change the narrative of the spell to accommodate that.' Maddy shook her reptilian head and spoke to Harry with a voice that shook the leaves. 'We cannot. Bex set that charm and she is not here. We need to make this look natural Harry, like a fall. I'll melt this ice and tear the rock away a bit, a fluke accident is the best we can do. She will have to deal with it like anyone would. Though if she stays hereabouts like the spell insists, Jen and I can introduce ourselves and help her through the tough times to come.' Harry didn't like it but conceded it was the best option. The chivalric in him wanted to protect the innocent from harm and pain but it might serve her better to push through this. Gwen was the subject of some sort of destiny and Elspeth would succumb to something sooner or later being merely mortal. Harry picked up Elspeth delicately and moved her out of the way whilst Maddy blasted the ice away and caused something of a small flood by the sheer volume of ice that adhered to the rock face. Then with a powerful back leg, Maddy ripped a slab clean off and dropped it to the ground below. Harry laid out Elspeth in what he took for the most probable position, then kissed her forehead and wished her well on her onward journey. The sirens were almost upon them now, many sirens as no doubt there would be several police as well as fire service and even paramedics. They wouldn't have much to do though and most of the fire was gone, being of magical origin. There would be a lot of head scratching, milling about and curious explanations. Harry had in mind a seismic explanation might suffice what with the huge fissure remnants across the highway. The witches hadn't re-appeared and Harry assumed that whatever Maddy did to them was permanent. Satisfied they had done all they could do they left matters to play out as they would. Gwen would likely return, find the area covered in emergency services and then discover the casualty. Oddly the only casualty, as the rest had fallen foul of the possessed. Only Bex's charm upon Elspeth and Gwen had prevented the deminion gaining access to her on the rock face. 'I'll go watch for Gwen' Maddy said forlornly 'see if her Jeep is enroute. I'll let you know what I see then you can make your way back to the residence and check on her when she gets home later. I need to reach out to Jen and bring everyone up to speed.' Harry nodded, a sombre demeanour constricting his usual bounce and knowing she took the affirmative from his mind anyway. A brief wind blast and Maddy was airborne and altering her density, she was immediately invisible. The Jeep didn't take a lot of finding, it was the only non-emergency vehicle on the Highway. Maddy watched from above as Gwen was soon stopped, explanations were exchanged and the invariable discoveries shared. A sheet was pulled back to reveal Gwen's deepest fears and she broke down and cried there and then. A police officer escorted her to a cruiser and drove her home, Maddy heard him say someone would bring the vehicle back. Maddy relayed that to Harry who took that upon himself. His own powers of coercion and his fake FBI ID helped too, and moments later he was in the Jeep half a mile behind the cruiser where he could see the silhouette of Gwen sobbing in the back and found himself wishing destiny wasn't so cruel and filled with such pain and death.

## TRINITY

'Judith? Can you hear me?' Vivienne's voice was faint and husky as though she was struggling to breathe but she sighed when Judith answered, albeit with difficulty and filled with pain. 'The shield collapsed at the last but saved our lives at least.' A sharp bark responded that was filled with bitter humour 'Saved us from what?' Judith snapped 'A slow death, buried alive a mile down where nobody knows where we are? How lucky are we?' she drawled sardonically but Judith had a point yet Vivienne was optimistic. 'We are sustained by the shreds of the arcane shield' she replied 'as it broke, I wrapped us in the remnants, we should be able to remain this way for many months maybe years and pray we can locate another sister by sending out your mind's eye or if you can, your astral form. Maybe we'll even locate Lysandreth or Nuala. We do not have the ingredients here for a trans-matter relocation spell nor can we move enough to enact the spell if we did, it will take another to extricate us. Have faith sister, we will prevail you take first watch and attempt to communicate, when you tire, wake me and I will take over.' Judith sighed for her faith was all she had left as she closed her eyes to reach out with her mind through a mile of mountainside.

# Chapter 3

## Imbolc

The next few weeks were a blur. The investigation floundered as no evidence of foul play was found, certainly not by humans anyway. Harry and Maddy had been busy and forestalled the investigation wherever possible until between them and their minor magics, coupled with several high profile calls - many of which originated at the Seraphim Collective offices - but arrived via the FBI local office and, CDC it ground to an eventual stop. Any and all other relevant departments were brought in along the way but were satisfied swiftly with what they found – which was nothing, so they all left again and Gwen was left to grieve in peace. Six weeks after the event, Gwen eventually left the house in Albuquerque where she had sequestered herself and ventured out into the world once more. The Collective had seen to it that the house and effects stayed with Gwen as a will was mysteriously produced to that effect to satisfy any distant relatives and New Mexico law. Of course Elspeth had no such thing but the Collective had been around for a very long time and were experts at tidying up. Elspeth had no close relatives left alive anyway so it was a relatively simple process. Gwen's only adventure out was for the quiet service for Elspeth and after that the door to the house closed and she remained elusive. Gwen being the only real attendee as Elspeth's relatives were either dead or nowhere to be found meant it was over relatively quickly. After those six weeks, her first trip was somehow anticlimactic, as it was only to gather groceries when she inevitably ran out and return to the sanctuary of the house for another month. But time dulled even the worst of pains. Elspeth was more than a friend - that much Gwen admitted - but it didn't stretch as far as soul mate or life partner. They had bonded and the spell enhanced their feelings as it helped keep them close, busy with each other and off the radar of Azazel and the Kore-Megara. Though Harry and Maddy had many a recriminating conversation about what they could have done different as what they did do clearly didn't work. They hung around and watched Gwen in case any more Kore-Megara were sent or worse; but somehow, against all odds everything stayed quiet and peaceful. No sign of any more possessed, no more witches – which was always a good thing according to Harry. They had several zoom calls to Seb, Bex, Ted and the Collective where Summer occasionally answered if Ted was out and about. Gradually then, like a tortoise poking its head out of its shell, Gwen made more and more trips out, soon enough she was getting breakfast in town, running in the mornings and reacquainting herself with all the people who knew her as part of the Gwen and Elspeth double act. Shouldering all the commiserations and well-wishers, Gwen smiled clinically and let it wash over her, normality - as best as can be - began to assert itself upon her once more and her protectors took a deep breath of relief finally. Harry went back to New York and Maddy moved back to Santa Fe where she and Jen held a place. Jen herself arrived shortly thereafter, content matters had settled for now.

Events moved apace and over the ensuing months Gwen got back into her art and had even had a small exhibition at one of the many Santa Fe galleries. This of course warranted her making the trip there on a more frequent basis. Although it wasn't a long trip from Albuquerque, it soon grew tedious with the repetition. So Gwen made the bold move to put Elspeth's…her house on the market and make the transition to Santa Fe a more permanent one. Amazingly the house sold within days and Gwen was left temporarily homeless. Not quite expecting that she hadn't really put any feelers out. She put what little that belonged to her into storage and decamped into one of the boutique hotels near to where the gallery that held her exhibition was located and short walk from the town plaza. It was handy as she could walk everywhere within minutes. In a way, it reminded her of her curating days in New York. But as quick as that memory surfaced, the spell suppressed it once more and Gwen just shook her head and carried on.

One particularly clear and fine afternoon, Gwen had just completed her morning's art time she had allocated herself, caught up on the chores and found herself free quite suddenly. After having spent the morning in her PJ's Gwen though she ought to dress. So Gwen unconsciously slipped on Elspeth's Ugs, her favorite jeans-the ones with no knees and a patch of a large sunflower on her butt, pulling on a light green sweater that refused to sit on one of her shoulders and constantly slipped off down her arm. An embroidered pattern of woven brambles started at the neckline and wove their way across each shoulder and down each arm, sporting small thorns and decorative flowers. Tousling her hair as after one look at it in the mirror, Gwen knew it wasn't going to co-operate so she opted for designer messy. It had worked for her for years and would continue to do so, or so Gwen hoped. Wrapping a light Navajo patterned shawl around her shoulders, Gwen stepped out into the sunshine. After an hour of aimless wandering, Gwen ended up at the plaza and was caught by a familiar melodic voice telling a story that captivated her. Gwen followed the voice and found it belonged to an attractive Native American woman, sat cross legged upon a larger warmer looking blanket like she wore, arrayed before her were treasures aplenty, much the same as what Harry saw but with more added. She was regaling the couple before her with tales of the Kachinas – the fantastic spirits of the ancestors and the time before the Emergence, she held a figurine that was quite bizarre to behold. At first glance, anyone would be forgiven for thinking it an alien, like the famed Roswell variety but after listening for a few moments, Gwen learnt that it was a Mudhead Kachina. It was brown with nodules on its head and big staring eyes. Listening to the woman speak, she wasn't sure if she should be fascinated by the Mudhead or afraid. But before she could make her mind up, the story changed to clowns. The mysterious and contrary black and white striped figures that were before her also. Gwen realized there was so much she didn't know as she listened to the musical voice of the woman. So captivated was she that Gwen didn't even notice the couple complete their transaction and leave. She also didn't notice the woman with the voice like honey, unfold her legs from where she sat, stand, lean back and pop a vertebrae back in and walk over to where Gwen stood.

'Excuse me for noticing, but you haven't moved from that spot for a while now.' Gwen snapped back and realized she had both drifted and was being addressed. Gwen thought she had over stepped with her eavesdropping and started to apologize. 'I'm sorry I didn't mean to…' Dolores stopped her. 'No, no, I'm not worried about you listening. I take that as a compliment but I was wondering…now don't take this wrong but I get the feeling I can trust you and I'm absolutely bursting. Too much mint tea and talking too long squashed up. I was wondering if you wouldn't mind keeping an eye on things here for me while I nip to the rest-room.' Gwen was stunned, it wasn't the sort of thing you asked of a stranger and Gwen said so. 'Well, my name is Dolores and you are…?' Gwen took the cue awkwardly 'I'm err I'm Gwen?' Dolores smiled and grabbed her hand 'There, now we're not strangers but I do have to go, are you okay here?' Gwen said she was swapped places with Dolores who smiled and all bar jogged off. She wasn't gone long and was back before Gwen had to embarrass herself with any customers. 'It's been quiet…thankfully.' Gwen smiled as Dolores came back clearly relieved and looking much more relaxed. 'I had hoped. I'd normally ask Walt beside me but he didn't show today and I'd been lucky up until that couple. You got that showing over at Mike's Gallery haven't you?' Gwen was surprised and nodded, Dolores carried on as though it was a given 'Nice work, you caught that sunrise really well I thought, hard to catch all those colors.' Gwen smiled at the compliment and simply said 'Thanks.' Dolores looked at her and weighed her as she stood there, almost wondering what Gwen would do next and what bearing that action would have. Dolores waited, seating herself back down slowly, watching Gwen most of the time. Just as she got herself comfortable on the big rug Gwen spoke. 'Look, you seem stuck here and I don't know anything near enough about what you have there so why don't I go get us some coffees as the afternoon chill is starting and you can tell me more about what all this is.' Gwen swept a hand over her wares indicating all the Fetish carvings, the Kachinas and the myriad of silver and Turquoise jewellery bits as well as a few artifacts like a Deer dance stick, a talking stick and a few decorative arrows amongst the rest. 'I'd like that. Latte, skinny with an extra shot.' Gwen nodded like that was that and all decided 'Be right back.'

So began Gwen's daily visits to Dolores and after a week, Gwen was covering for Dolores while she went off to a second job. She cleaned houses for the well to do around the city and out as far as Taos. Apparently her cousin was a maintenance guy who looked after the houses that Res – as Dolores said it was what her friends called her – cleaned. They had something of a pattern worked out between them and between all that, Res maintained her pitch at the Governors Palace that she swapped with her cousin Joshua from time to time. He breezed by one afternoon and Res introduced them. Gwen was pleasantly surprised as he was a big fella and looked like he was carved from red stone but when he spoke, his voice was soft and melodious like Res's, a gentle giant. Unless you pissed him off apparently as one or two had found to their detriment. Gwen learnt a lot from Res as days became weeks and it was after the third week that Res discovered Gwen was living in a hotel and Res was furious incarnate when Gwen told her. The subject hadn't really come up and Res was as mad with herself as she was mad at Gwen for not telling her. So it was, two days later and Gwen was moved out of the hotel and into the house Res shared with her Grandmother. Both Res's parents had died when she was young so she had moved in with her Grandmother. Affectionately known by all as Grandmother Yellow-deer. She took to Gwen immediately and treated her like one of her own. This arrangement grew more comfortable by the day and months soon came and went. Gwen still selling her art and painting in the mornings and helping both Joshua and Res in the afternoons usually by covering the pitch as Res – who by borrowing Gwen's Wrangler increased her workload with ease now. Life was looking good. That is usually when the Universe decides to mix it up, and this day was no exception.

Gwen had just sat down and Res was driving off when an elderly woman came right up to the pitch and stopped dead, looking down upon Gwen with a fixed stare. It was a gaze that held monumental expectation but Gwen was oblivious at first, arranging herself so she was comfortable and moving her drink a few times in fear of knocking it over Res's stock and hand woven Navajo rug she displayed upon, by chance she looked up. 'Oh, hello. I didn't see you there.' The woman continued to stare and Gwen matched it for a moment before growing irritated with the woman who so far, had said nothing nor moved in any way. 'Can I help you with something?' Gwen tried, hoping a conversational approach would have more of an effect 'Sadly Res isn't here right now if it's her you're looking for, but she should be back tomorrow.' This had something of an effect though as the elderly woman smiled as though she were privy to a joke nobody else knew and this drew a scowl from Gwen, thinking she was making fun of her somehow. 'Look, I don't know what you want or who you want but it would be really helpful if you either said something or moved along please as because if you're disturbing me, you'll disturb other potential customers I suspect.' Again the smile, but this time she spoke. 'You don't recognize me do you?' It wasn't a question so much as a test of memory. This time, out on the spot, Gwen scrutinized the woman, noting her prodigious teeth. They were of a size that she could have had a part time job breaking them in for donkeys, as an amusing thought it didn't really help. Then it came to her 'You're the lady who runs that little metaphysical store around the corner, yes…I've been in there a few times, Earth…something…wait…Earth Angel, that's it. I don't recall talking to you though, just seen in the background but I was served by a petite blonde girl with the loveliest southern accent.' This time the elderly woman right out laughed as though her secret joke was getting funnier by the second with everything Gwen said. 'Yes, that'll be Jen. You'll get to know her better soon, she is really a true talent and speaks very highly of you.' Gwen was confused, how could she know anything about her, they'd barely spoken. 'How does she…' The old woman stopped her 'That doesn't matter right now, we'll get to that. For now though we need to talk. Can you come over to the shop later?' Gwen was growing both suspicious as well as confused, why would she do such a thing? What was there to talk about? 'Trust me Gwen, all will be made clear when we talk but we don't have much time so would nine be okay with you? I know Res is back from her cleaning job in Taos by then and she'll have given Grandmother Yellow Deer her meal so you'll be available I'm sure.' Gwen was stunned 'How do you...' Again the woman interrupted 'My name is Miss Callaghan but you can call me Cynthia.'

With that declaration, the strange elderly woman spun smartly on her heel and stalked off. Gwen had an immediate image of how Mary Poppins might have looked as she aged less the teeth of course. Gwen resisted the urge to say spit spot as she watched the old gal vanish around a corner. The incident played through her mind all afternoon which was thankfully for her – not so for Res – a quiet one. Gwen told Res all about it the moment she returned, as they packed up and when they slipped into the café for a last coffee before the wine started. 'I know her alright.' Res declared shortly after Gwen's description of her 'she has been here forever it seems. She didn't always have that store as I recall the story. It was something else first when she appeared and bought the building.' Gwen was curious as she didn't really look like she had two buttons to her name by her clothes but Gwen had learnt not to judge books by their covers. Res continued to recount her dredge of memories of Cynthia Callaghan. 'I think she has one the older adobe houses on the fringe of town too. Joshua took her home once one Christmas when the roads were pretty impassable.' Gwen absorbed this and wondered all the more what she could want with her. 'There is only one way to find out Gwen my girl and that's go and see what she wants.' Res said, even as she looked thoughtful for a moment then added 'It had to be a quarter to eight already if I'm any judge.' Gwen checked the clock that there was no way Res could see and to the second it was a quarter too. 'I don't know how you do that' Gwen said stunned 'but it's pretty impressive, you're always right. I couldn't do that if my life depended on it.' Res just smiled and held her wrist up 'No room for a watch with all this here.' There was a small fortune of antique silver and turquoise rattling even as it was wrapped around both her wrists, flashed through with odd bits of strikingly red coral. 'I'll drop you home first,' Gwen decided 'it's only at the store so I can be there and back in no time.' Gwen did just that, saying Yata-hey to Grandma Yellow-deer who once Res mentioned that Gwen was about to meet Cynthia Callaghan took on a whole new look. The wizened Native American stared hard at Gwen as though divining her. 'Pay attention to her Gwendoline,' Grandma Yellow-deer rasped 'the mother speaks through her from time to time as she does me, she is as old as me if not older, I cannot tell for we have not spoken for many years but something shifts and you are a part of it child, tell me all about it when the sun rises tomorrow.' This did nothing to assuage Gwen's growing concerns but she filed them to a recess in her mind promised she would and drove back to the store, parking out back she left the Wrangler and walked to the stoop area at the front and was about to knock when the door swung open before her scaring her back a step. 'Right on time.' Jen answered in her smooth southern accent and she turned and shouted back inside before inviting Gwen in 'You lose Maddy, that's ten bucks you owe me.' Gwen frowned and looked past Jen to see a tall raven haired woman leaning against the counter almost seductively shaking her head sadly and digging a $10 note out of her cleavage. She looked vaguely familiar and as that thought crossed her mind, it occurred to Gwen that Jen looked strangely familiar too. Gwen's night of eerie disturbances had just started. Gwen looked between the two girls as Jen ushered Gwen in finally and closed the door firmly behind her, causing her to spin and stare at it, startled. 'No need to be jumpy here Gwen' Jen cooed 'you are amongst friends in ways you can't even begin to imagine, you're quite safe here as anywhere on earth I'd say.' Gwen thought it a little over dramatic but let it slide. 'Look, I don't want to take up any more time than is necessary but why am I here?' Gwen asked, noting the slight tremor in her voice giving away her trepidation. Jen guided Gwen to a large comfortable sofa that took up almost one wall. It was sumptuous and patterned after the Navajo blankets, like Res's own pitch blanket and the exclusive and collectible Pendleton range.

'Tea? Coffee? Wait, no its time for something a little more fortified I think, Sherry?' Gwen nodded knowing the warmth of the alcohol would steady her nerves and give her hands something to do. 'Sherry will be fine, thanks.' She said 'I'll get it.' Maddy breathed and disappeared out the back to what looked like another sizeable room. Gwen took in the store as she waited, as though seeing the well-stocked treasure trove of shelves for the first time. Barely noticing the stairs leading to the upper floor sales room. The bannister was draped in rugs and artefacts hung off pegs. There was a floor to ceiling glass cabinet filled with Kachinas of every color shape and personification. Gwen recognized some of them from the gallery where she exhibited her own art and knew at least one of them was over $15,000. Gwen began to look at the store with fresh eyes and started to appreciate how extensive it was and beautifully arrayed. Gwen mentioned that and Jen dipped her head coyly 'That's down to

Maddy and I, do you like what we've done?' It was almost as though she asked for permission or approval. 'I love it, you've got a real eye.' Gwen complimented as Maddy came back with a silver tray with four good sized glasses of Sherry and behind Maddy Cynthia Callaghan waddled through. 'You like what the girls have done with the place?' Cynthia asked as she lowered herself into a big comfy looking chair behind the counter where she could see every aspect of the store like the captain of her own ship. 'They gave the place a redo these last couple of days knowing you were coming.' Gwen sat forward at that. 'How could they know I was coming? We only agreed it today.' Cynthia smiled a disturbing smile full of yellowing teeth that would have an ivory poacher getting excited. 'You and I agreed it but the girls and I knew this was coming weeks ago.' Gwen was still a bit lost and said so 'What is coming exactly? I don't mean any disrespect but you're not making any more sense now than you did earlier today. What has anything you do have to do with me? While you're at it, why do I think I know you both from somewhere else?' Jen looked at Maddy and vice versa as both knew they would have to broach this eventually but they had to be careful how they picked the fractured enchantment apart. 'It's because you do...sort of.' Jen started 'We came to New York a few times where you used to live if you remember...' Jen's eyes flashed gold and Gwen was transfixed. 'I did...didn't I? I had a gallery there...I painted and worked at a bar...' Maddy stepped in then and smoothed over the rough edges. 'That's right Gwen, you curated a gallery and did some work at Hannigan's bar. That was where you met Elspeth and the two of you decided to come back here for a while. We came to the bar and the gallery and that was where you know us from.' Gwen heard the word and sighed her name as it registered on her heart like a seismic wave 'Elspeth. Was that real? Because it sure feels real, one minute we were having the time of our lives, the next she is dead, broken at the bottom of a cliff she should never have fallen from, right when I'm not there. It feels like the universe was waiting to take her from me the moment my back was turned.' Maddy reached out a slender fingered hand and grasped Gwen's own hand in hers 'It always feels that way honey, but it does get easier. Think of all the good times you had, remember them like they are photos in your phone. Presumably you have plenty of those too?' The next hour was spent by the three girls all smiling and laughing as they scanned through Gwen's gallery of escapades she and Elspeth recorded during their brief time together. Towards the end of that, Cynthia - who had nodded off in her chair - woke and made herself known.

'I see the girls have kept you entertained, sorry about nodding there. Happens when you're my age and it's always soothing to me to have some good energy here in the store but time is running out, so let's get to the bones of it. Do you like Earth Angel?' Cynthia opened her arms extensively taking the whole vista in. Gwen nodded then realized Cynthia's eyes were closed again though not asleep but lost in time and space somewhere in her mind as she waited for Gwen. 'I do. I've been here a few times but somehow never fully taken in the atmosphere here, it's pretty powerful I have to say. I can't put my finger on it but it's an embrace, warm, soft and assailing every sense with security and protection. A feeling of expansiveness and potential yet as comfortable and intimate as a pair of slippers and not that I've done it for a while now, but a feeling you should get going home.' At that last word, Cynthia opened her eyes and grinned like the Cheshire cat at Gwen, all her prodigious teeth on display. 'Yes, I like that. It was what we were going for and that is ideal because it's about to become yours.' Gwen started 'My what?' she asked and Cynthia shook her head as though she were having a debate with a voice only she could hear.

'Your home, what else could I mean? Sorry this isn't as clear as I saw it but things are getting a little hazy and I'm winging it a bit. I also think I'm going to burst a few bubbles…sorry girls but there is no other way.' Gwen looked at both Jen and Maddy and she saw they weren't entirely happy with what Cynthia was suggesting, as though it was in opposition to what they thought but after a few moments, they acquiesced and nodded Cynthia permission to carry on. 'Good, now let me cut to the chase, I'm dying.' Gwen wasn't shocked after what Grandma yellow-deer said about her being as old if not older but she was slightly taken aback how candid Cynthia was about it. 'Sorry to hear that.' Was all Gwen could muster at that moment but Cynthia harrumphed like it was unimportant and waved a negligent hand. 'I've been doing that for some time now but events have recently hastened matters. You're not like other girls Gwen, you have a something about you that sets you apart. Your aura is off the scale compared to the majority of people outside this building and that tells me something.' Gwen wanted to ask what but didn't want to interrupt either so instead she just folded her arms and leant forward to encourage more of this strangeness. 'When I took this store on, it wasn't as you see it today but it was important to the town. She was a widow of an old frontiersman, a man whose family had come over and settled on this land, originally in California before it was California. What makes that story odd Gwen was that she was allegedly one hundred and thirty seven years old, can you believe that?' Cynthia didn't wait for Gwen to answer and forged on 'I didn't until I dug a little deeper.' Cynthia got up and moved to stand before a faded painting of a woman that was clearly antique 'But I'm missing loads here and with good reason for it would take weeks to tell all of it.' Cynthia sucked upon her teeth, drying out as they had with so much open air exposure 'Suffice to say,' Cynthia continued 'it was true. Her unnaturally long life…and relative health I hasten to add, much like you see me today was a part of a pact. An agreement she made when she took over the store from the woman who held it originally when Santa Fe was a new town back in 1610. So how do you reconcile Gwen that only three women have held this store for way over four hundred years? And I'm one of them. No, don't say anything. I didn't believe it either but it's true. There needs to be someone here in this store and my time is fast approaching when it won't be me but I just can't leave it to anybody; I've been searching for my replacement for a while now and had almost given up hope, certainly when the last load of signs presented themselves. Then as though delivered by the goddess herself…there you were, just standing there. I couldn't believe it.' Gwen recalled the moment too, she was watching Res as Cynthia watched her Gwen was piecing bits together and thought she had the gist of it, for if only three women had held the store to date, they had to be somewhere near a hundred and forty years each. As staggering as that thought was to Gwen she set incredulousness aside and accepted - hypothetically – that Cynthia too was a hundred and late thirty something she had to be sensing her own pending mortality. To top that, she somehow expected Gwen it seems to be number four. Her train of thought was derailed when Cynthia asked quite the materialistic question. 'You have money?' What Gwen didn't know was that Jen and Maddy knew she did due to the sale of Elspeth's house. They had hinted to Cynthia this was so in order to help her make the transition as normal as possible. Gwen realized that dissembling was pointless 'I do.' Cynthia nodded curtly like it was an affirmation 'Good, as soon as the banks open next, I'll get the papers drawn up. No good tomorrow, its Earth Day and we all have things to do.' So far April had been a busy month and Gwen's head was reeling a bit, a heady combination of sherry and bizarre events on top of the uncovered emotion of Elspeth's passing. This was her legacy maybe? But true to her word, a few days later, the festivities all cleared away and a semblance of normality resuming, Cynthia summoned Gwen once more only this time they met at the bank. Gwen had chills run down her back when she turned up at the Bank of America branch on Saint

Michaels Drive. As though by stepping upon it and in it, a head turned somewhere to regard her with loving and protective eyes, slightly wrinkled at the corners with suppressed humor and approval. Three hours later Gwen was, at least in paper for now the proud owner of Earth Angel store, all its stock and goodwill as well as a sizeable adobe home on the edge of town. Cynthia had asked for a few days to arrange her bits and pieces as she called them and set her new plans in motion. After that, it was all Gwen's.

Shifts in the Universe don't always come with earth shattering revelations, sometimes they go totally unmarked. The moment Gwen put the pen down, Tomas was crashing a helicopter deep in the Siberian wilderness and after surviving that, he was hot footing it as best he could with a hungry pack of wolves nipping at his heels. Events were in motion and nobody really yet knew what they heralded. Though they soon would. Cynthia's eventual parting words were simple, that Maddy and Jen would explain everything and take care of her. Cynthia waved and clambered into a beat up Chevy Impala and the last Gwen saw of her was a hand waving out of the window as the car disappeared from view.

'Well, guess I'm in your hands now, what do I do?' Gwen asked plaintively looking between the two girls who looked between themselves and Gwen was sure something passed between them she wasn't privy to but she said nothing, choosing to wait for them.

'Well why don't you go fetch whatever you have at Dolores's house and meet us at your new home so we can get you settled then we'll meet up at the store in the morning and make a start making it yours and go through all we have in store, sound like a plan?' It did and Gwen allowed herself to be led and that's how they functioned for the next two years as Gwen grew in knowledge and confidence as proprietor and focal point for the holistic and metaphysical store that as Gwen learnt, attracted more of the city than she realized. Seekers one and all. Either through desire to know more, or seeking solace, or an anchor point in a sometimes wildly spinning universe. Gwen continued to help Res and Joshua and the girls were invaluable at running the store. It was an arrangement that suited everyone but as is life, even the best of things must come to an end. Thing is with ends that until they happen, nobody knows what form they'll take, how fast they'll come or when.

Gwen stepped out of the Santa Fe mini-market and immediately wished she hadn't left her coat at home. The icy cold air gusting through the holes in her knitwear led her to think that she couldn't have gone far wrong with a thicker sweater either. Gwen shivered as another gust of what she called *lazy wind*, put goose bumps on her goose bumps. She called it that, as she had explained to Res once, *It's called lazy wind because it doesn't bother to go around, it just goes right through.* It also made her aware that she had foregone her warmer underwear as well today. *That'll teach me, lacy doesn't really work in cold weather - though I suppose if I got my sorry ass out of bed a bit earlier I might be able to remember these things instead of simply where my coffee is. It's a shame to have to get out of bed at all.* Gwen sighed as she silently berated herself for her recent slothfulness. Having jumped up at the fourth alarm she had simply grabbed whatever came easily to hand, Gwen had poured her coffee in to her travelling mug and literally run out of the house.

It was however, this days freezing temperature that actually kept her moving. Gwen was aware of odd memories that had been slipping in and out of her mind a lot recently and she found them an unwanted distraction; disturbing her sleep, causing her to forget things when they took precedence. A fact she was growing increasingly annoyed about. Gwen attributed them to the high altitude and the bizarrely cold weather but her gut said otherwise. Focusing on the task at hand whilst shivering involuntarily…again. Gwen picked up her pace across the lot and made a bee line for her little car. It had been warm enough in her store, but when she got dressed this morning, she had been so distracted by these odd memories and dreams, she had also somehow forgotten she was visiting Dolores today, how she managed that was another mystery, because she had been visiting regularly for years now. Gwen attributed her mental fragility to having not long returned home from a visit to the UK she would rather not have had. Her mysterious brother was absent though it was hinted he was KIA but that disturbed her less than the fact that her mum and dad were dead. She hadn't really been close. Barely before she left and not at all after. But the fact they were suddenly dead, never affording her the opportunity for any sort of reconciliation ate her up. The month she was in Newcastle sorting the affairs were some of the worst and darkest days of her still short life. She met with a friend of her dads at the service, a pleasant elderly man who said he had served with her dad and been a friend of his for many years. Apparently he was a general too, though he insisted she call him Ted. She met with Ted several times over the course of her visit, he said it was to honor her father and make sure she was safe and taken care of. He supplied her with a driver who was to take her anywhere she wanted to go. Of course, Gwen had no idea he was a highly decorated and highly dangerous asset of the

Collective, up there with Tomas for out of the box action if required. Truth be told, Schofield had volunteered and was happy for the respite from dealing with incursions of possessed, let the other teams deal with them for a while. The Revenants - as the Collective termed them - were increasing for some bizarre reason and had even engaged with the general public to a horrific end in particularly nasty incident. The Collective had spun it as riots and a terrorist plot using a deadly nerve agent. The media reported it as they were told. They knew however they couldn't keep that pretense up much longer if they kept attacking and growing in numbers and frequency as they were.

Gwen was oblivious to the true nature of the Collective, instead it was under the aegis of Horus Securitas PMC and close protection Ltd and Gwen asked no questions about them being distracted by the details of the funeral. With no Tomas and no heirs, the estate was hers. She couldn't face dealing with the larger aspects such as property and Ted said he would have it all sorted for her by their legal team 'they're pretty good at what they do Gwen, don't you worry. Here's my card...again,' As Gwen rummaged for the last one he had given her '...if you've lost the other one I gave you.' Also the invisible ink sigil embedded in the card allowed Summer to keep tabs on its whereabouts easier. 'You call me if you need anything...anything you hear me?' She did and it was strangely reassuring, so she just took the liquid assets and returned home. It replenished her accounts after the acquisition of Earth Angel and that was all she cared about for now. It made life comfortable and allowed for a replenishment of stock as the business was doing a good trade. Gwen was solvent right now and at a certain level of peace and that would just have to do for now. She hadn't been back more than a few weeks but her sleep was nothing but disrupted and she had been out of sorts since her return. Forgetful, distracted like she hadn't wholly returned. She hadn't remembered her Santa Fe routine until it was almost too late and pulling up at the store where she swore and beat the steering wheel of the Wrangler out of sheer annoyance and frustration; now she was paying the price for the trip and the morass of inadvertent memories it roused having disturbed her delicate routine. *I don't know what's going on in my head these days but it's starting to take the piss now, though this'll teach me to not pay more attention to stuff in the past than what I'm doing in the present - Focus Gwen girl, for pity's sake you've got too much to do today! Thank heavens for the girls, I'd be stuffed if they weren't there. Days like this I wonder if I'm cut out for this shop keeping lark. I've never been a morning person, but just lately it's got out of hand, reminder to chat to 'Res about it, I'm sure she's got the answer and I bet I won't like it'* Gwen chuckled to herself at the prospect of Dolores' reaction. For she was always full of sage advice and enjoyed handing it out.

As Gwen slalomed across the parking lot, deftly avoiding the slush and desperately trying not to get her Ugs wet, for she loved her Ugs, having had them for some years now, the last thing she wanted to do was get them ruined in the filthy water. Though they weren't her Ugs, they were Elspeth's though she had been wearing them for some time now. Gwen's heart skipped a beat as she hadn't thought so sentimentally about her friend for a while now, not really since Cynthia sold her the store and did a vanishing trick but something was definitely adrift. So she carefully navigated the puddles as she watched the other customers coming and going. Struggling in the very premature Santa Fe winter. The thing about being several thousand feet above sea level too was that the air was thinner, making it feel considerably colder too, add some wind and it turned brutal in heart-beat. Some days the air hurt to breathe and its thinness generated so much static electricity that it played merry hell with many of the women who swanned about, all trying to look like catalogue models. Having spent hours getting their hair just so, the moment they stepped outside it sprang out in all directions. Like stepping on to a Van Der Graff generator. Much to their annoyance and Gwen's constant amusement. They amused her for other reasons too, for as much as someone could be a product of their environment, they were that. The South Western influence was prevalent in just about everything in Santa Fe. Brimming with Pueblo and Navajo imagery as well as the Spanish and Mexican. From the adobe buildings, chilies and even down to the luminaries, essentially paper bags with little candles in which adorned many homes and lit up pathways - which people were now putting out in readiness for Thanksgiving and eventually, Christmas. There were simply so many minute things that together, created the ambience that set this city apart from all its other charms and it was that what attracted Gwen to it originally. It did though, seem to try and stereotype its inhabitants. Gwen, not being one for conformity, noticed this almost straight away and had purposely shied away from the subconscious uniform that many of the women who lived and worked within the artist's community had adopted. That of the cowboy boot, long colorful skirts and western style cut bolero jackets. Gwen conceded it did looked nice, a bit frontier, a bit Spanish all mixed with a goodly bit of Native American and rolled then into traditional American female sensibility; but it wasn't her. She had been called a hippy chick, little miss flower power and all other variations

117

upon a theme as she grew and travelled, not that she cared - she was in fact, quite proud of her individuality. But it appeared many who moved here from all over the world, seemed to succumb to the unwritten dress code, some sooner, others later, but most, eventually. Gwen had learnt early in life that however free and easy something appeared, there was always an undercurrent of conformity, of regulations and rules. There was always someone seemingly in charge, ensuring things got done their way. It was subtle, but the world was full of these manipulative individuals, trying to shape people and events to meet their minds ideal. Gwen figured she was either paranoid or especially observant for she refused to become embroiled in these invisible entrapments. When it began to look like life was being interfered with again, she would up sticks and leave. She could see it happening here, but there was an attraction to the land that seemed to hold her stronger than her own instincts. *Another odd thing for the list.*

Having made it both inside to check on the girls and explain her dumb blonde moment, she made it back unscathed to her car, Gwen had pulled back out on to the road and was roaring off as fast as she dared considering the treacherous conditions, back to her own adobe styled house she'd left not long before. She still called it a house, a remaining idiosyncrasy left over from her British heritage. In truth, it more resembled a glorified mud hut with timbers poking out. Even though it was state of the art inside and historically in keeping with the indigenous peoples and environmentally conducive, it never failed to give her that Neolithic feeling when she went home at the end of the day. She had affectionately named it the cave. It amused her friends, Dolores and her two shop assistants Jennifer and Madeline. *Maybe it's just for them I stay here. Them and the mountains, the desert and the feeling that the land wants me here. I must be getting softer in the head.* Gwen chuckled to herself. The sweet sound of her laughter echoed in the confines of her Jeep Wrangler - whose loosely fitted soft top was letting in cold air as fast as her warm air-con was trying to do the opposite. As much as she moaned about the arty farty women hereabouts, they couldn't affect her enough to make her forget just how beautiful the New Mexico desert and surrounding Superstition and Sangre de Christo mountains were. Not forgetting her number one favorite retreat, Hyde Memorial Park, she loved her time away up in the trees. Not so far away she couldn't get there on a whim but once there, she could be a million miles from anything. She would tolerate their sideways glances and whispered mutterings a bit longer for that, though she knew she had been saying that since moving to Santa Fe. *Suppose I'll say it a bit longer then, and do what I always*

118

*have and leave it up to the Goddess to determine where she wants me next. So home it is, Jen and Maddy can survive without me for a bit longer, I am the boss after all. I'll make it up to them and bring them those sickly chocolate mocha lattes they like so much and some lemon pound cake. Damned if I know how they pile it in without piling it on; still, good luck to them, if you've got it, use it I say.* The days niggles so far, settled down in her mind, Gwen settled in for the remainder of the drive home to pick up her coat and bits, singing along somewhat out of tune to Buffy Saint Marie and Robbie Robertson. Content for the time being, humming as she made the round trip. Even still singing tunelessly to herself as she arrived back in town with the promised supplies. Laden with steaming beverages, Gwen skidded expertly on to the road that headed for the town square.

Dolores Begay, or 'Res to those who knew her well, her friend pretty much since the day she had arrived in Santa Fe. Dolores, her mother – who had vanished when Res was young - and her Grand-mother were all of the Long Turtle Clan and had lived in Santa Fe all their lives. Dolores worked part-time with her cousin who held a pitch on the porch of the Governor's Palace where Gwen had met her that first distant day. It was a place where Native Americans had been trading almost since it was built. Which was some time ago as Gwen had learnt, for the building had been recognized as one of, if not the oldest public building in the US. The Pueblo and the Navajo had been around as long as anyone currently living there could remember, and in the desert for centuries. Even bequeathing their pitch to their children to continue. It was a tenuous living, but it was all there was for some. Dolores and her cousin were two of the fortunate ones, both held down several jobs to make ends meet. When Res covered for Joshua Stonerook, her cousin, he went off and did house maintenance and mountain tracking with a small guide business he ran too, when they swapped back, she did housekeeping for some of the wealthier families, some as far away as Albuquerque and Taos and Joshua relaxed at the pitch or at home and carved.

Ever since Gwen's arrival in town, she had been helping Dolores out. It started out as a debt repaid, for it was Dolores and her family who put Gwen up for what ended up being several months, initially it was only to be a week or two while she found a place of her own, but the trio enjoyed the arrangement and it just seemed to go on and on. It would have probably continued were it not for what happened with Cynthia when her own place found her. But now they were good friends, it was just fun for each of them. It gave Gwen a break from the tedium of shop work – not that it was that tedious, but Gwen liked being outside too - and it helped Dolores out of course. Occasionally Res would have to run her Grandmother into Albuquerque for hospital appointments with increasing frequency, which was more than a little alarming. During summer it was a thoroughly enjoyable time out for Gwen, she met all manner of fascinating people. Her favorite time there was during the Earth Day celebrations each year. The world, his wife and their dog, literally, came out for that and the atmosphere was phenomenal. However, it was days like this one, when it was colder than a cold thing, with the hot soup and tea she had brought which was a godsend, that it wasn't quite so much fun being outside. *Freezing your butt off and losing all sensation in your appendages as that icy wind whistles around your nether regions, lovely. The things I do for friendship.* But Gwen's conscience pricked her then, for Res' Grand-mother, wasn't taking the cold well, that was the reason for today's excursion and Gwen's cover; a lovely old lady who everybody called Grandma Yellow-deer, her actual name was Eleanor, but according to Dolores, no-one had ever been heard using it, and she was considered by many to be a true wise woman. Her forte was weather, but she was no mean healer either, and a few months back she had predicted a winter unlike any the people had ever seen. *I hope this weather is as bad as it's gonna get.* Thought Gwen, not being a fan of the cold as she parked the jeep in the square. *But I can't shake the feeling that it's not and that something much worse is coming.* But Gwen kept her morose thoughts to herself.

Grandma Yellow-deer hadn't looked well when she saw her last and it was cause enough for concern. She was believed to be around the ninety six years old mark and having outlived her own daughter, looked as though she had earnt every year of life and was in fact closer to a hundred and six. Her history was etched within every line of her weathered and parchment thin skin. But even though her body had become frail quite rapidly of late, her eyes still looked as though they would bore holes through mountains and could read your every thought. Which occasionally she did. *Now that was unnerving. Lovely old gal. Lovely but bloody scary sometimes.* Gwen would muse as she sat with her.

Dolores was busy with a customer when Gwen arrived, so she mouthed a silent hello and held up the Styrofoam cups which steamed slightly in the cold air. Dolores acknowledged with a flash of her big brown eyes and an almost imperceptible nod. Gwen backed up and parked herself down on a nearby bench to wait. Watching and listening to Dolores go through her sales pitch, feeling her mind drift again. She

120

had heard her go through this often enough in that haunting and musical voice of hers. Gwen just loved the accent and knew she could listen to her friend tell stories for hours upon end. And had. It cast Gwen's mind back to when she was a little girl herself and she had listened, rapt, as her mother had told her stories. Not of animal spirits, Gitche Manitou the Great Spirit, White Buffalo Calf Woman and a host of other equally fantastic tales, but they were powerful nonetheless. And they now were part of all she had left of her parents. Memories. She had been eventually notified – wondering how they had even found her - that they had died mysteriously in some macabre explosion, something that should never have been able to happen according to the coroner. The odds of such a localized blast doing so much damage was highly improbable at best, but even though no further explanation was forthcoming, it didn't alter the outcome. They were dead.

Gwen didn't remember it and Ted had reminded her inadvertently of the story when he asked what she was doing now. She told him about the store and Ted had mentioned the connection having been at several parties with her parents it seemed; but her mother had told her the story too. It had come from an old record that her father had first asked his future wife to dance to. Both Tomas and Gwen had been conceived out of wedlock. Her parents always told them that they had been difficult days back then, her parents met when they could, when her father's duties would permit. That and other concerns had driven her mother to guiltily turn her life over to the Church toward the latter part of her life. It was in part the thought of how her mother had gone a bit strange, that made Gwen turn her thoughts to the other strange woman in her life. The former owner of her shop and home. *Now she was a right peculiar one. This place must attract them like some huge geophysical magnet. Maybe that's also why spiritual places always seem to be up mountains or at height? Attracting those who don't fit in with what society deems 'normal', pah, who wants to be normal anyway. Certainly not me.*

Gwen's stroll through memory lane was interrupted by the customer leaving. Dolores sighed deeply and rocked back onto her heels, one hand rubbing a stiff neck as she balled the other into a fist and blew hot air into it.

'Yata-hey Gwen.' Dolores greeted her friend gratefully as she took charge of her latte, sipping and moaning in pleasure with equal intensity. 'That was a hard one.'

'Yata-hey 'Res, sorry I didn't get here earlier, long story involving my stupidity, and, I think I just broke the land speed record getting back in to town, lucky I didn't get a ticket. I called ahead to make sure Ernest had the soup and bread ready and warm' Gwen inclined her head in the direction of the woman's receding back as she fished out the aforementioned lunch and handed Dolores hers. 'She buy much?'

'Yeah, eventually.' through mouthfuls of chunky vegetable soup and warm cornbread 'Though she wanted to know the ins and outs of everything, it's amazing I've got any voice left. This helps.' Dolores held up her soup to emphasize. 'She was here an hour before you arrived and I've been talking non-stop. Still, she bought just over five hundred dollars' worth so it was all good. Don't worry too much now if you have a quiet afternoon, today is paid for.'

'I've told you before Res,' Gwen nudged her friend to make her point 'you'd be brilliant at giving talks properly, look how many times you have to do it, why not get paid for doing that alone? You should give the college a call? Maybe even the Cultural Centre over in Old Town, don't they want speakers?' Dolores looked wistful a moment as though the notion appealed, but she shook her head slowly, the raven black braid at her nape swishing gently back and forth. The abalone and turquoise chips she had tied into the braid clicking as they swung. Gwen looked at Dolores, she was one of those who had followed the fashion trend of the region, but being part Hopi and part Navajo, and with those dark mysterious eyes and skin as red as the desert itself, she carried it off with a natural grace the others couldn't hope to emulate. The abundance of silver and turquoise at her wrists, the fetish carvings she wore and especially the huge squash blossom necklace just enhanced the image. Standing, Dolores pulled on her ankle length beaded sheepskin coat. That alone would have fetched several thousand dollars if it had been in a store, but she hadn't bought it, she had made it herself, taking just over two years. First curing and stitching the hides, then meticulously beading the back, shoulders and lapels.

'The coffee was lovely, the soup as good as ever and even the corn bread was still warm; Ernest bakes the best cornbread outside Grandma's kitchen. Another truism. Grandma Yellow-deer made the best cornbread in the southwest, at least that's what everyone told her. Gwen wasn't inclined to disagree, it was gorgeous. Moist and as yellow as the sun, with juicy pieces of corn interspersed throughout. Many a cold night had passed with that and her famed dark, spicy, chili bean soup. She had no doubt the old girl would take the recipe to the grave with her as well just to spite Ernest, who had been badgering her for way over a decade now to give it to him, under the guise that it would be a shame to lose such a valuable national treasure, but Dolores and Gwen just thought he was just desperately jealous.

'You know how I could sit and yarn with you for hours,' Res said with the concern in her eyes making that statement a closing one. 'Great Spirit knows we haven't done plenty of *that*, but I must go fetch Grandma. Her hospital appointment is at two, which leaves me about an hour and a half by my reckoning.' Dolores never wore a watch, there wasn't room on her wrists for one thing, but it never failed to amaze Gwen how she kept almost perfect time. It was as though she had an internal time clock that kept her on schedule.

'Spot on Res, that's a knack I really could use. Half the time I don't even know what day it is, let alone what time. If it weren't for you, Jen and Maddy keeping me on the straight and narrow I'm not sure even the Great Spirit and the Goddess combined would have a clue when and where I am. But it's all been getting worse of late. I've been so distracted by sudden surges of buried memories' Gwen raised her eyebrows and struggled with a wan smile 'though apparently not buried enough. What do you reckon Res? Am I finally losing it?' Dolores frowned, an expression marring her normally flawless and serene expression. The look she gave Gwen was one of concern and Gwen was instantly worried. She'd seen that look on her friends face before, and it hadn't boded well then either.

'Grandma too,' Res whispered as if not wanting the spirits of mischief to hear 'she has been recalling her family since the Kachinas came in December; I was worried then, but not as much as I am now - now that you are re-living your past as too.' Dolores looked at her feet and scuffed her boots absently against the wood of the porch. Several rebellious gusts of icy air danced and spun around the two women briefly; eliciting shivers and curses from Gwen. But for Dolores, her shivers weren't just for the cold. They were the shivers of prescience. The sensation felt by many prior to something momentous taking place. Unfortunately, like so many of these things, it seemed stronger with malevolent activity than with the benign. Res looked hard at Gwen then, right in the eyes as though searching.

'What really concerns me though is that Grandma is rarely wrong' Res said as she looked deeper 'and she has been saying that the Kachinas are actually coming back; Wolf, Ogre and many more. I do not know what this means, but she has been muttering this in her sleep for several weeks now. I had originally thought it was due to the forthcoming Powamu ceremony in February as Grandma was planning to attend. Maybe the

Crow Mother's appearance would calm her and these dreams would pass. Now, as I say, I do not know. What do you think Gwen?' Res seemed genuinely concerned and Gwen knew a little about the Kachinas, she had seen several dances and carried many of the cottonwood carvings in her store. In fact she had a lot in her store from the local craftsmen and women of the Zuni, Hopi, Acoma and other Pueblo tribes as well as Navajo. The one thing she did know, was that there were some two hundred and fifty plus of these supernatural beings in the Pueblo pantheon. Not all of them were nice. The Ogre Kachinas especially, or as they were known, The *Nataskas*. These were used to terrify the children at the dances if they were disobedient; but some of the older stories she had heard from the elders implied that that they were much more fearsome and destructive in real life. It would be a sign of very bad things indeed should the *Nataskas* return in their own form. And that was an understatement similar to the Grand Canyon being a little crack in the ground.

'I don't know 'Res, it's a bit far-fetched really, in this day and age I mean. It's probably just a coincidence that Grandma and I are having flashbacks. These old memories have to surface at some time I suppose, I just went to a funeral of my parents that's all they're doing with me. Grandma? Well, she is old 'Res, after all.' Gwen grimaced, hoping her expression would lighten her friend's now thoughtful mood, but it didn't seem to, Res appeared graver than before so Gwen tried to change the subject. 'It's quarter too now, so you've got an hour and a quarter to play with, get off with you, I'm fine really, just letting my imagination get the better of me; you go get Grandma to her appointment and I'll see you about five at the store. Jen and Maddy have got a few appointments of their own booked in for tonight, and I said I'd be there for teas and coffees.' Gwen reached out and clasped her friend by the shoulders and gently turning her in the direction of Gwen's jeep, which Dolores borrowed, the Native woman was propelled with affection towards it. Res allowed herself to be ushered off and it finally brought her smile back.

'Yes mother,' Dolores fawned, knowing that Gwen hated that, but knowing also that she did have a tendency to mother everything she encountered. Maintaining it was genetic, her own mother used to do the same with everyone she met. *It's a Walker thing.* She would simply say. With a final wave though, Dolores completed her short walk and climbed in to the Jeep. Firing it up and turning the stereo on, Gwen could hear Douglas Spotted Eagle even as the car pulled out of the square. The haunting flute music carrying on the morning breeze.

124

Gwen pulled up the little cushioned stool she had encouraged Res to use more though it was as much for Gwen as was Res to give her butt respite. Gwen settled down for a quiet day with her book. With her flask of soup beside her she sat and let her mind roam once more. It wasn't a conscious choice, but it seemed easier than fighting her minds current penchant to dredge up the plethora of random images that she thought were filed away but had been assailing her. The first series of images that coalesced into a coherent mental picture was that of her first day at the store. Greeted as she was by her two newly adopted assistants. Both smiling broadly as she parked her Jeep and strolled over to the door. Jennifer Deveraux, blonde hair falling like a golden waterfall to her waist, her fringe sweeping gently to the left, exposed her big blue eyes, vibrant and glistening. They had the effect of making the New Mexico sky appear cloudy. Shapely and petite, she stood only an inch or two taller than Gwen. Dressed in faded denims and pink angora sweater. The neckline plunged alluringly and exposed her flawless skin, Gwen thought a tad too much. But she seemed to carry it off without looking cheap. A large silver set moonstone hung at her throat and it seemed to pulse with a life of its own. Beckoning the eye to it the same way the sea calls to the soul, tempting the unsuspecting to plunge into its mysterious depths. With an exertion of her will power Gwen had turned to the other woman who stood at the doorway to greet her.

Madeline Cortez, she was everything Jennifer wasn't. Tall and well-built with a cascading mane of the darkest auburn hair ever. In one light it seemed as black as night, in another it flared the deepest red. Almost as though it were a smoldering fire and merely waited for the signal to burst in to flame again. Where Jennifer was pale, Maddy - as she preferred to be called - was dark. Her mocha skin reflected her Latin American heritage. Gwen never did know exactly where she originated, they never spoke of their homes, but it could have been anywhere where dark sultry women hailed from. The Dominican Republic, Cuba, anywhere in South America such as Brazil or Argentina, even as far as Spain itself. When pressed, all she would say was 'Oh, I'm from all over' and that was about that. Jennifer wasn't much different about her true origin. She was cagey about her exact birthplace but her Southern accent limited the option a bit more but even that was vague as 'the South' covered a lot of ground. Beyond that, Gwen knew very little except that they were always around. They were at the store every day before her usually, with fresh coffee brewing and warm croissants ready. They had a small apartment only one block over apparently. Gwen had visited it once and was stunned. For two apparent single girls, who appeared so casually flawless, it was virtually empty. No TV or ornaments, only two beds, a lounge and a serviceable kitchen which was more a just for looking at room. The bathroom was basic as well and conspicuous by its apparent lack of the usual girly enhancing products. They just shrugged and their explanation was just as sparse. 'We don't need a lot. And as for looks? Well, I guess we're just lucky that way. Maybe it's in the genes.' They were certainly an enigma, far unlike any other females she had ever known, but she had quickly grown to love them like sisters all the same. And talented, Gwen had never seen the likes. Maddy was probably the most gifted Tarot reader she had ever encountered and people would flock from all over the region to see her. Some even flew in from neighboring states. That kept them solvent and they insisted that Gwen only pay them a cursory salary for the sake of the I.R.S. Jennifer insisted the same for she had a thing going with her psychometry. She received a stipend from the local and state police for her services. Her ability to locate missing things and even people had earnt her a reputation too as well as a tidy bank balance. Not that they needed money really. They rarely bought anything. On the other hand, they seemed to draw people to the store like moths to a flame and thankfully, they found plenty of things in store to spend their money on. Gwen often joked that she would adopt the girls as sisters properly one day and the last time she had said that they both stopped what they were doing, looked at each other seriously, then at Gwen and said together 'We'll hold you to that Gwendoline Walker.' That had been a little over two weeks before. Gwen had been a bit creeped out by that for a few seconds, but then the moment passed and all was as it had been.

The sound of Douglas Spotted Eagles flute wormed its way into her daydream and it took a few seconds of hearing it for her to fully realize what it meant. The Jeep should have been long gone by now, why could she still hear it? Gwen was fully snapped back to the present by that revelation, her mind instantly taking in her immediate environment. Seeking danger, seconds passed and she was satisfied that she was in no imminent peril, expanding her awareness then, mentally seeking the source of the music, Gwen jumped up, her stomach sinking with that familiar feeling that something was wrong, however much she hoped to the contrary, she just knew it to be true. Quickly throwing the Navajo blanket over the wares on display she called to the man next to her.

'Keep an eye on this will you Miguel?' The man who always sat next to her when she did her turn for Dolores nodded all was in hand, as it was whenever she asked.

'Thanks, I'll be back in a minute…I hope' He smiled a toothless lopsided sort of grin and in broken English said 'Pro noblem Gwen, you know that's Latin for everything's fine' he chuckled to himself, for he always said the same thing, and Gwen smiled back wanly as she jumped off the porch and began to run in the direction that she last saw the Jeep go. But she hadn't gotten more than a dozen paces before the screams started. Skidding to such an abrupt halt at the unearthly sounds, Gwen very nearly went head over heels on a particularly icy patch. But she still had to know what was happening, walking now instead of running; leaning forward in order to see before her body reached the corner, what she saw made her gasp in shock and disbelief.

There were people running down the street towards her and past her like the end of days was upon them. They were running in what could only be described as sheer panic and terror. Then Gwen could see why, looking beyond their fleeing forms. Eyes drawn upwards, Gwen watched amazed as the sky darkened ominously. Not only by the sky darkening with the look of an impending storm but by flocks of birds. Large and small filling the sky alongside swarms of insects. *Insects? How could that be, it's bloody winter, there shouldn't be an insect for months yet. What the hell is going on?* She saw her Jeep a hundred yards in front of her, Dolores apparently still sat within it, but making no move to get out and run. Gwen began to make her way towards her. Pushing past screaming and running people much like a salmon battling upstream. Then she saw why they were running. *How could this be?* Was she seeing things? Though she soon ruled that idea out. *Obviously not judging by the way everyone's running.* But it can't be, it just can't. They're not even real. But several giant Kachinas were looming in the distance and heading this way at a frightening pace. Their shadow driving all before them to flee in terror. It was like an attack of the giants. As though Gwen and all around her were ant sized and humans were coming towards them. But these weren't humans, they were Ogres. The Ogre Kachinas of legend and they were truly fearsome, not the wood carved, feather and paint versions that lived in her cabinet but very much larger than life, horned, fanged tusked and ferocious creatures right out of nightmare. Gwen felt the world tilt.

'They are very real Gwen, just as real as you or us.' A southern voice was suddenly by her ear reassuring her and explaining 'That is why the animals do their bidding against their own will and nature for they are magical and supernatural beings with power Gwen. We must help them, it is time. A time we hoped would never come, though all the signs told a different story it was a tale we hoped could be averted. Seems we were wrong Gwen. Events have transpired to expose you to the enemy and their scouts have found you.' At the sound of the lilting southern accent, she had spun to see both Jen and Maddy standing behind her. Just standing there as though they had been there all along.

'How did you get here? How? Wha.. Scouts? Found me why?' Maddy put a finger to her lips, gesturing for Gwen to stop talking seeing as she was making a hash of it. A hundred questions were hurtling around in Gwen's head but none of them would form up and come out of her mouth in anything that resembled coherence. 'But I..'

'Not now Gwen, one thing at a time. First let's help these peoples. Two, four and six legged.' Gwen blinked her eyes a few times and took several quick breaths to steady her racing consciousness before speaking again.

'They're Kachinas! Bloody huge and very real looking Kachinas! How is this possible Jen, what the bloody hell is going on?' Jen spared a quick glance to Maddy

'Long story Gwen, one we promise to go through with you if we survive this.'

'*What do you mean if we survive this?*' Gwen's voice rose as she felt her grasp on reality begin to slip slightly and her head felt all light and swimmy as though she were about to faint. The towering figures of the war painted and horrific Ogre Kachinas could be seen from a great distance, denoting just how big they really were to be visible from town. But amazingly they were not the immediate threat. That was coming from the animals that were now pouring into town. Wolves together with deer, badgers, foxes, coyotes. Not to mention the scuttling forms of scorpions and the very flesh creeping spiders that leapt and ran up and over all in their path, biting and stinging indiscriminately. All manner of vermin were swarming into the streets and buildings too, screams could be heard and occasionally someone would come crashing out of a shop window, desperate to escape, covered in undulating fur. Or worse. Screaming in agony for a few brief seconds until the rats, mice or spiders poured into their throat and silenced them. Seconds later the flesh stripped or bloated corpse would be left sprawled in the street. Skin either shredded or garishly swollen and dissolving internally from so much venom, and the furry swarms scurried off looking for their next victim. The roars and howls, barks and screeches were getting louder as the stampede of ravaging animals poured into the built up areas. Gwen saw people caught in the onslaught, impaled on wicked looking antlers, several were decapitated as wild eyed and frothing black and brown bears stood and swatted at those trying to escape, others went down beneath the slavering and fang filled maws of the wolves. They were experts at hunting and bringing down prey much bigger than themselves, humans stood no chance as they turned their backs on the animals to run. Walking amongst them however, were lesser sized Kachinas, almost human in size but really big humans, eight to nine feet tall maybe and in part resembling the dancers who portrayed them. Except these were real, solid, something akin to flesh and bone but looking harder and horrifically more malevolent. What flesh she could see was a putrid green like that of a decomposing corpse, for all that though, they were no less lethal. They carried brutal looking weapons and were not slow in using them. Within moments the ground was slick with the blood of those too slow to flee or too stunned to accept what was happening until it was too late. The deadly torrent of animals and those that drove them on were less than forty yards from Dolores now and she still hadn't tried to get away. The haunting flute music from her stereo was still playing and it cast a surreal atmosphere on the tableaux unfolding before them. Gwen turned to her friends in desperation. Looking at their calm yet concerned expressions. They seemed to be waiting for her to say or do something.

'What can I do?' Gwen virtually shouted at them in her rising panic.

'Gwen, do you accept our help with your own free will? Are you prepared to do whatever it takes to prevent this? Will you make the ultimate sacrifice?'

'What? Sacrifice? What are you saying? Sacrifice what? Myself? But..' Again, Jen and Maddy silenced her. They moved to stand either side of her and placed one hand each upon her shoulders. They stood, three women against the tidal wave of brutal, animal and supernatural Kachina ferocity that was thundering towards them.

'Gwen, you must choose now!' they all bar shouted 'You must decide if you are willing to give up everything to save these creatures, and you must decide now, or Dolores and all these people will die. Horrible wasteful deaths. You can stop this, we will help you, but you must choose, *Now!*' Gwen felt their fingers grip her like steel bear traps as she was forced to face the torrent of teeth, claws and blood. She watched horrified as the first wave of animals broke like the ocean upon the shore over Dolores. Sitting rigid in the Jeep, it afforded her some initial protection and bought her a few seconds reprieve. It was buffeted by powerful bears, their teeth grating and salivating hungrily upon the windshield and side windows as they sought to get at the warm flesh and blood within. More wolves had bounded over the roof, their claws scratching at the vinyl roof, but as they pounded on to within feet of Gwen, she saw flocks of crows descend and begin to rip at the roof. Cawing rapaciously. They would be through in seconds. Gwen was out of time. She had to choose now or it would be too late.

'Okay!' She shouted desperately 'I'll do it, whatever you want just make them stop!' Gwen screamed out her acceptance and with the last syllable hanging in the air, time seemed to slow. The air thickened to the consistency of tar. Gwen could see the eyes of the creatures, rolling up in their heads white and livid. Enraged beyond comprehension at their inability to move.

'We have little time Gwen, I have brought us a few seconds, let us go fetch Dolores for her time hasn't yet come.' Gwen had no idea what Maddy was on about, but her sense of the practical asserted itself, whilst the animals weren't moving and she was, that was good enough. She would worry about how later. The three girls ran between snapping wolves and slavering bears. Stepping over and around the smaller but no less ferocious animals. It was the queerest sensation for Gwen could see the eyes of the animals following her, their jaws working in the weirdest slow motions. They reached the jeep and pulled the passenger door open. With that sudden movement, Dolores seemed to come to her senses. Her eyes went wildly spinning at the sight before her and she promptly passed out. Slumping forward just as Gwen reached in and grabbed her.

'Help me, she's too heavy, I can't budge her' Jen moved Gwen out of the way and took hold of Dolores. Now if the Kachinas and the animals wasn't strange enough for Gwen, the sight of little delicate Jennifer, manhandling Dolores and carrying her away down the street to safety as though she were no more than a child, sent the last vestiges of her sanity running screaming for a dark safe corner in the secure recesses of her mind.

'It's your turn now Gwen, you must break the enchantment cast upon the creatures by the Kachinas. They are still not strong here in this world, however you are, you're a fundamental part of this world, more than you know and as such your will should be the greater. For the moment at least as the Kachinas are not quite solid here it is within you Gwen to repel them, you must dig deep to release it, do it now Gwen, we can't hold them much longer' *How are they holding them at all?* Gwen was desperate to know as she could see that much was true. Several of the wolves and a couple of the larger bears had begun to forge their way forwards, walking haltingly as they struggled against the thick air. Air that shimmered about them like rippling transparent treacle. Gwen looked between her two friends, looking for any sort of a clue.

'But what do I do?' Taking a faltering step towards the animals, she kept one eye on them and one back upon Jen and Maddy searching for any indication of how she was to do this thing.

'You'll think of something Gwen, you have to, it's your destiny.' *Destiny? Now what are they on about?* Gwen looked once more at the wolves and again at her companions, then took a deep steadying breath and strode up what she took to be the lead wolf. Was it not for the fact it was still moving slowly and inexorably forwards, it would have passed for a stuffed one. *Okay, here goes nothing.* Gwen reached out a hand a placed it upon the wolf's head as though she were petting it. She simply said the first thing that came to her.

'*Stop!* Stop now I command it in the name of the Goddess!' On cue, there was a blinding flash of light and a silent concussive explosion that blasted Gwen off her feet and sent her sprawling backwards. Landing awkwardly upon her rump, it took her a few seconds to regain her balance, her equilibrium and for the lights to stop spinning before her eyes. She sat up in perfect time to come nose to wet nose with the huge shaggy wolf she had touched. Its vivid yellow eyes mere inches from her own and she could feel its lupine mind burrowing into hers, questing, searching for something. She could smell its breath as it panted and the wild and rich odor of its wet fur. Gwen's mind began to swim with images of mountains, trees and waterfalls. Of rivers and then of wolf cubs, dirt and caves. Other wolves drifted into her field of vision then, all sitting now in that inimical wolf fashion. Regarding her with curiosity and a frightening intelligence. The smells of pine and fresh mountain air assailed her nostrils. Gwen blinked and the image intensified when her eyes were closed. It was as though she were up on the mountain herself. Opening them again, she saw that the wolf had sat, like the ones in her vision. Back legs skewed out to one side, the big furry tail slowly beating the ground beside it. Head cocked to one side it regarded the small female two legged before it. Gwen spared a quick glance beyond it, looking for the Kachinas, but there was no sign of them. Whatever she had done it had been sufficient to send them packing. Part of Gwen's mind tried to rationalize that maybe they had never been there in the first place. Just her over productive mind giving her hallucinations. Though a smaller, but no less insistent part spoke to her about the complete opposite. It had gained some credibility as she looked into the eyes of the wolf before her. For more images flooded into her head. These ones however, were not so pleasant. She saw the Ogres and Kachinas smashing through the forests, herding all creatures before them. In voices that defied description they ordered the wildlife to do their bidding - it felt like a blanket had been thrown over their will, suppressing it. Succumbing to the urges of the malevolent Kachinas any that fought the unnatural compulsion were destroyed. It brought tears unbidden to Gwen's eyes as she saw how many died at the claws of those Dark spirits. Something in Gwen's soul died with them as she experienced their agony. But just as she thought that she could take no more and blackness had begun to edge in around her consciousness with oblivion looming just out of reach; the wolf blinked and the mental assault came to an abrupt end. Gwen fell forward exhausted and she would have hit the ice covered tarmac of the road hard, were it not for the big shaggy wolf moving forward to catch her. Gwen scrunched into the shoulder of the animal. Instinctively throwing her arms around its massive neck to support herself, she buried her face in to its ruff and cried.

What she couldn't see at that moment was that all the animals involved in the provoked attack had ceased their rampage. Birds of every description lifted up and alighted upon all the roof tops and watched intently. Herds of deer and coyotes all stood together. Bound by a force that removed any dissention amongst them. They waited. A great breathe was held and all eyes were on the odd couple in the middle of the street. The two legged female and the four legged pack leader. She had spoken a word and the fog that shrouded their minds had lifted. This was a conversation worth hearing.

Gwen eventually sat up, her eyes were red with prolonged crying. She had never experienced such an outpouring of emotion, not even when her parents had died. This was primal, dragged from deep within her, the part that humans tended to bury as they lost their connection to the natural world around them and become indifferent to the plight of what they considered lesser creatures. Sitting back up and drawing several ragged breathes to steady her nerves, Gwen realized that she had not relinquished her hold upon the wolf, nor had it pulled away from her embrace. With a feeling of compassion that nearly had her crying all over again, the wolf licked Gwen's face, running its previously lolling tongue up the tracks of her tears, twice upon each cheek, then it leant back slightly and regarded her once more. Gwen spoke to it then, softly as one would to a beloved pet.

'You shouldn't be here you know!' Gwen saw intelligence and recognition in its eyes, but what she didn't expect, was a reply. 'I know this two legged, but we were not ourselves.' The wolf said 'We came against our will and our will is strong. This is not a good thing.' It paused for a heartbeat then it added 'How is it you speak wolf?' Gwen almost laughed out loud, instead she replied 'I was just wondering the same thing actually, I have no idea what just happened. I was thinking how you speak human. Who were those things herding you and how it is I stopped this and how I can understand you and you me. Tell me I'm not dreaming!' The wolf looked at her askance and said in a dry yet bemused tone. 'You are not dreaming.' It said matter of factly 'I am the speaker for the ground dwellers here...' He looked skyward and barked a couple of yelps to the roof tops, whereupon a large black crow swept down and alighted upon Gwen's inadvertently outstretched arm. She hadn't raised it for that purpose, but to protect her face as it caught her off guard with its shadowy dive. It cawed a few times and by the last caw, Gwen understood what it had said too.

'I see,' Gwen said in amazement 'the people of the sky were affected just the same by these creatures. Of course you were, you wouldn't have done what you did otherwise would you?' Gwen looked into the obsidian eye as it responded 'No, two legged land bound, we would not have. It was a good thing what you did, though you should have done it sooner, before many of my brethren fell!' Gwen felt a stab of guilt however irrational for she couldn't have anticipated this catastrophe. It seemed that the crows felt otherwise. Their belligerence seemed somehow fitting for them in a crow sort of way. Gwen had always imagined them as the bouncers of the bird world. If birds had clubs then they worked the door. 'It has gone now though, it's all over, you can return to your wilds' Gwen tried to reassure but the wolf and the crow both corrected her on that point. 'One at a time please, this is hard enough already without having to separate one voice from the other.' The wolf spoke next.

'It is – they are - still out there two legged, the unnatural ones. These are the dark sprits of our ancestors legends, returned to exact vengeance. We cannot fight them, they are too powerful for us. You must do this thing, you stopped them once, but they will return stronger now you have repelled them, they are not gone.' Gwen was about to protest but the wolf forestalled her 'I know your soul two legged, I have seen it. You are the hand maiden of the Mother. A strength abides within you and there is no deceit. We trust you. You are a sister to the land bound.'

'And to the sky born.' the crow added. Then with a move so fast, Gwen had no time to avoid it, the razor sharp and hooked beak of the crow flashed out and with a cruel twist, tore a chunk from Gwen's arm.

She squealed and nearly dropped the massive corvid, but its impenetrable black eye held her firm. It then pecked its own leg, then the outstretched paw of the wolf. Blood welled from all the wounds as would be expected, what Gwen didn't expect was the crow hopping along to let its own blood flow into the wound upon her arm, then it hopped back as the wolf placed its shaggy paw upon the wound, letting its own blood mingle. Once that was done the crow cawed out an exultation and the entire rooftop burst into life and sound. It was terrifying and exhilarating both at the same time, the cacophony was immediately joined by the wolves, coyotes and all other land dwellers.

'It is done little sister, you are a part of our circle now. You will be spoken of in our legends to come. Walk in harmony two legged it is time we were away, this place is too strange and alien for many of us and I feel the fears returning.' Gwen was about to agree when the magic was exploded by the deafening wails of several police sirens.

Before the animals could turn and flee, a dozen police cars came screeching in to the square and skidded to a side on halt. *This is just like the movies.* Gwen thought with an eerie detachment. She watched as the sheriffs men leapt from their vehicle with all the expected drama and gung ho trigger happy behavior expected of boys with guns. Gwen could see an impressive array of weapons trained upon them all, mainly focused in the center, more accurately upon her and the wolf, for there were simply too many targets otherwise. Nothing moved, a thousand eyes were riveted upon the new arrivals. Gwen sensed a few snarls and some general disapproval. Perhaps they had seen these two legged out with their weekend guns. A wave of anger at these so called hunters flared within her and it was picked up by Jen and Maddy, who had stood silent up until now.

'Don't do anything silly Gwen, not now.' Maddy almost whispered 'These men are as innocent in their way as the wild folk. Ignorance is no excuse to punish them, I can feel it building inside you. You have released something dangerous Gwen, and now you need to control it. Now isn't the time to let it free. Be calm and let us guide you.' Gwen stood releasing her hold upon the wolf reluctantly, and allowing the crow to glide a few feet away to bounce upon the top a parked car. The wolf just stared at the men, a combination of contempt and pity showing in his golden eyes. The sheriff, bullhorn in hand, shouted his demands to the women.

'Move aside or we will be forced to open fire. Those are dangerous beasts, killers and need to be destroyed before they kill any other humans. They might even be rabid.'

Gwen couldn't contain it any longer and she openly laughed then, at their ludicrous reasoning and their equally ridiculous premise to get their guns off.

'I don't think so sheriff,' Gwen spoke normally but her voice carried in an unnaturally loud way ensuring she was heard by the lawmen. Jen just winked, implying it was her doing 'I suggest that you and your men be the ones to pack up and go away, everything is in hand here thank-you very much. It doesn't need several overgrown boy scouts with guns to solve this. I grant you, we can't undo what's been done, but shooting won't undo it either. It's a long story and maybe one day you'll hear it, but for now please, just go away.' It seemed polite enough to Gwen's ear, but apparently it had somehow gotten misinterpreted somewhere between her and the sheriff and he seemed to hear something completely different, for he grew immediately enraged. Snatching up his bull horn, he bellowed out his indignation.

'You were warned! *Open Fire!*' The noise was deafening as all the weapons that were levelled at them spat their lethal missiles. Copper, brass and lead roared towards them, death inherent in every shot. But it seemed to Gwen that the air thickened again, like before and the bullets were travelling in slow motion, she spared a quick glance to Jen who winked and raised her outstretched palm.

'You too Gwen, we can help you channel your energy!' Gwen did likewise.

The police couldn't believe their eyes when they saw the three women raise their hands and instantly, the bullets and lead shot from the pump shotguns exploded into a cloud of multi colored butterflies and wafted off towards the wild lands beyond the town.

'*Fire again, Fire at will!*' The sheriff was on the verge of apoplexy. Again, the girls raised their hand and uttered a simple 'No'. And again the sky was filled with rainbow hued insects. Hundreds of shots later and a lot of butterflies, the police stopped shooting. Whilst they stood and looked to each other for some sort of explanation, the wolf simply nodded his shaggy head towards Gwen, turned and loped off. Gwen heard two voices in her mind, those of the wolf and the crow.

'I am Kavan of the wolves, call me if you need help!' the crow added its own name. 'I am Shan of the sky born, you may call me also for aid. If I hear it I will come.'

Gwen didn't know what to make of it, so she merely thanked them with her mind and hoped that they understood. A brief acknowledgement told her they did.

The police watched in utter confusion as the sky born took wing and arrowed off towards the mountains and forests beyond. Within minutes the streets were deserted once again, as though the animals had never been there. The only sign that anything untoward had taken place, was the destruction of property and the unfortunate dead bodies left behind. The Sheriff and his deputies were standing stock still, wide eyed and slack jawed. Each looking to the other for some sort of rational explanation. No-one spoke at first, there weren't that many words that came close to describing what had just happened. The Sheriff himself, a veteran of some twenty years on the force was at a loss as to what he was going to put in his report. In fact he was unsure how he was ever going to come to terms with the whole episode. It was at that moment, one of his deputies gave them all a way out.

'We missed! That's it isn't it?' Another picked up on the thread

'Yeah' his southern drawl was slow and unsteady at first, but as he got his head around it, the idea grew fatter and more believable than what had just happened.

'I had the sun in my eyes,' one said 'so I must have fired high.' Another 'me too, I must have put faulty rounds in the shotgun. Maybe they were wet, you know, all smoke and noise.' Much nodding went around the police then as they all got their stories straight, because it just had to be. It couldn't have been the mystical spectacular that had just unfolded, those things just didn't happen outside the movies. Jen called out to the Sheriff.

'Perhaps you boys should all be on your way now, the fun is over and I'm sure there are a lot of scared people out there in need of some reassurance. Ya'll surely the people to do that. We'll take care of matters here if you want to send for an ambulance or two to take care of these poor people' Jen's gentle southern voice was almost hypnotic to the stunned policemen. When they hesitated, Jen slowly repeated it, only this time it was delivered with a different cadence - this time, it was less of a suggestion and more of a command. Issued by someone who was used to her commands being obeyed with little opposition. Again they hesitated, heads reluctantly turned to the Sheriff for his approval, but it was clear in their eyes that they really wanted to go, and sooner rather than later would be good. The Sheriff took off his hat and rubbed his sweaty head before making his decision. With all the speed of a sloth running a marathon, the Sheriff made a choice, and luckily for him, it was the right one. The compulsion was evident in his voice as he answered.

'Okay ma'am, if you're sure?' Jen placed her hands on her hips and struck a pose as if to say 'Of course I'm sure, now go!' The Sheriff replaced his hat and adjusted the chin cord, then with as much authority as he could muster, he ordered his deputies to pull out. And rendezvous back at the station for further orders. The three women stood and waited until the last taillights from the retreating cars had disappeared before Gwen collapsed in an ungainly heap upon the road. She sat as though her bones had been removed, more resembling a rag doll than a living, breathing woman.

'This is no time to rest Gwen, here, let us help you' Gwen looked up from her prone position to see both Jen and Maddy reaching down to her, offering their hands to her to pull her up. Limply placing hers in theirs, she was lifted clean off her feet by the two girls, nearly pulling her shoulders from their sockets.

'What the...' This second display of strength reminded Gwen that there was more to these two than she had ever known. Having watched them effortlessly carry Dolores to safety, how had they appeared at her side from nowhere? They were simply there, where there had been only empty space seconds before, she was sure of it. There was no way on earth they could have gotten from the store to her side that like that. The flurry of questions that had been stilled during the encounter with the police began to reassert themselves, and she looked between the two women who she no longer knew, mentally deciding which question had the most importance to ask first.

'Why aren't we dead and where did all those butterflies come from...' Maddy just smiled annoyingly. '...and don't you be smiling at me like that, I don't even have a word for what I'm feeling right now, but it's not very pleasant. I don't take kindly to being lied to and ...' Maddy waved a casual hand and Gwen's mouth continued to move but no sound issued. Jen and Maddy stood and watched their friend as she spoke, or at least went through the motions, casting slightly amused looks between them, waiting. It took several seconds before Gwen realized that they were taking no notice of her rant whatsoever.

'Gwen, save your breath.' Jen advised 'We understand your obvious annoyance at being probably the only one who doesn't know what's happening. An explanation is also overdue, but certain things had to occur before one could be forthcoming. Today qualifies for that. But here amidst the general populace isn't the place for it. They've had enough shocks for one day, they need to let the dust settle before the crap really hit's the fan. You on the other hand, need to calm down and put aside your pre-conceived notions of how the world works and what your place is within it.' Gwen tried to ask what the hell she was on about, but it was much like a silent movie without the sub-titles. Only this time, Gwen realized there was no sound. Her eyes flew open in fear and she grasped her throat in panic as though the gesture would do any good. Maddy smiled again, but quickly stopped as she sensed Gwen's growing discomfort. The horror of being unable to make any sort of vocalization was playing across Gwen's features. With a repeat gesture, her ability to communicate was restored, but now, Gwen remained silent, but glowered at the two strangers before her. Too enraged to speak coherently anyway, she needed to calm first before she gave these two a piece of her mind, what there was left of it.

'We have given you back your power of speech, for now,' Jen warned, waggling a finger at Gwen like a disapproving school ma'am 'but it is conditional you stop fuming and pay attention. Matters have moved on, and there are certain items that need to be addressed, and soon. Things will go easier and faster if you hold that vipers tongue of yours and utilize that latent intelligence you possess.' Gwen knew she was being rebuked and insulted in equal measure. She also knew that she was seeing a whole new side to her friends that she hadn't even imagined existed. They emanated power and authority now in such vast quantities that world leaders would have been intimidated by them. Gwen however, had always had a problem with authority. It seemed to bring the worst out in her, but even she capitulated to these two women. So all she did was simply agree.

'Okay' with her concession, Gwen began to notice other details around her. It was as though her consent raised a veil which seemed to have fallen over her. For a few seconds she couldn't reconcile what she was seeing. Then it hit her. This was winter. The square had been dusted with snow, slush and icicles hung from the trees. At least they did a few minutes? Hours? Ago. Now, the grass around her was clear, lush and verdant. The trees were free of ice and were in fact blossoming. Spring had descended upon Santa Fe during the middle of January. She watched in rapt fascination as flowers sprang up through the grass where only hours ago, there was snow. As she watched, she removed her jacket and scarf, subconsciously aware that the temperature too, had increased in line with what she was witnessing. With a spongy, not quite associated to her surroundings feeling, Gwen asked a question in a voice that seemed small and afraid, overawed by all that was going on.

'I know it's repetitive, but what's happening? I mean what's *really* happening. This…' Gwen pointed at everything in general '…This isn't right, how can this be?' Gwen knew her questions fell short of what her mind craved by a country mile, but it was all she could manage. But the spongy feeling increased, along with it came a feeling of spinning. Moments later Gwen's disorientation had escalated to a point where her mind refused to take any more and promptly switched off. Gwen crumpled in an almost slow motion action and the lights kindly went out.

She woke to the soft, heady smells of blossom and new grass. Fragrant flowers sent wafts of their delicate scents to mingle with the others. Before she opened her eyes, Gwen was briefly transported to the meadows near her home in England, where she used to run to when she couldn't bear school during the summer months. Laying out amongst the wildflowers and butterflies, Gwen imagined that she was merging with the very ground, becoming one with the natural order. So still would she lay, that on more than one occasion grass snakes and adders would slither over her intent upon their own agendas, field mice had clambered up onto her, investigating her clothing, even taking threads that had been loose. Rabbits, one fox, a weasel and even the odd mole had happened upon her during her excursions. At the time she hadn't thought it strange, only wonderful and totally natural. Now, her mind was reconfiguring the memory, implying that there was more to it than she had ever believed possible. Her present predicament came rushing back to her then and she sat bolt upright so fast, it made her dizzy all over again.

'Easy Gwen, take it slow, here, drink this.' A bottle of water was placed in her hands which reflexively grasped the cool bottle. She took a long pull then hiccupped twice before drinking some more. Eventually sated, Gwen looked at the two women who had passed themselves off as friends. She flashed through the many nights that they had shared doing the girly slumber party thing. Sleepovers with a chick flick for the DVD, a bottle of wine, or two and lengthy discussions concerning many of the male populace as well as some more cerebral issues, though they usually degenerated as the night wore on. Instantly those memories were dashed by the events of the day. Her trust was shredded and lay in torn fragments at her feet. Feeling more herself, she turned to her former companions and requested a rational explanation for their behavior. It was it seemed, turning into a day of disappointments.

'I see you are feeling a bit better after your little nap, something akin to your old self. An interesting phrase, but more about that later, for now, are you up to a little chat?' Jen asked not really expecting a negative answer 'There are a few things you need to know' Gwen adopted an exaggerated look of surprise. 'No shit!' Gwen snapped 'I expect there are several things *I need to know*. Starting with just who you too really are. You *aren't* just two convenient shop assistants are you?' Gwen knew that the moment the question left her lips that she didn't really want to hear the answer, but unfortunately there was no avoiding it.

'No, we're not.' A leaden blanket of disappointment dropped over Gwen.

'Thought not' Gwen sighed at the knowledge 'You've been taking me for a mug these past years, having a good laugh at my expense no doubt, pretending to be my friends but when my back is turned you're up to heaven only knows what. Can you imagine how such a feeling of betrayal hurts?' The emotion began to creep through the anger Gwen was feeling and her eyes welled up, causing the world to take on a distorted and ethereal like quality as she looked out through salty tears.

'Firstly and most importantly, you must believe us Gwen when we tell you that we are still your friends. We love you, we have never stopped, nor will we. However, you must realize that everybody has their secrets. It doesn't alter the fact of who we are, it's just our particular secret is a tad larger than most peoples. Though like so many things, an individual can only know what they are capable of and likely to excel at when they actually try and do it. Until then they could live under the belief that they are normal and unexceptional. You Gwen are neither. Your ignorance of what you are and our secrets have much in common - as you are soon to find out.' Gwen listened, fighting an urge to interrupt with more, she realized then inane questions about matters she didn't understand. Instead she let Jen continue her explanation, seeing where it went. 'Have you ever wondered about your affinity with wildlife? Your mother never had one, nor your father. Why you are a vegetarian, your parents weren't. Why in all the world did you really settle here in New Mexico? Why do you find such a kinship with the Native Americans? These and so many other questions can be answered comparatively easily. We could sit here for days and go over each one. Over all the events and choices that have steered and guided your life up to this moment. You are Gwen, the sum of your experiences.' Gwen chewed her lip as she listened, preventing herself asking questions or blurting something angrily 'For the most part, you don't need us to tell you any of this, in your heart of hearts you already know the answer. But how many times have we sat up late and debated the power of coincidence and fate.' Gwen thought about answering that but didn't 'Whether there is really such a circumstance as

140

being in the right place at the right time? You are always where you need to be when you need to be there. Humanity has a phrase that says that there are more things under heaven than be understood, or something like that, but essentially it's true.' Jen stopped and took a drink from her own bottle of water, while she did, Maddy picked up the thread and continued.

'There are people with incredible gifts, their evolutionary journey has accelerated them ahead of many others and these souls perform certain tasks. Imagine them if you will as prefects, monitors for the sake of humanity. Though not all are consciously aware of the role, those that are, often find themselves the focus of ridicule and persecution.'

'I understand all that,' Gwen eventually said 'but without seeming selfish, what has it got to do with me?' Maddy patted Gwen's knee affectionately but Gwen twitched like she had been bitten and the sadness was clear in Maddy's eyes.

'These monitors for want of any other title,' she continued 'need something to monitor wouldn't you say? No don't answer, let me. They monitor those individuals who are destined to do great things. In every generation there are these individuals. Though they don't know who they are, nor are they likely to unless they're called upon. None have really been called in an age. It would take something of epic proportions and having catastrophic consequences to consider making such a call. It seems that we have surpassed such time. Matters are beyond calling. Warriors have been dispatched to locate and actually fetch the remaining destined ones.' Gwen felt another question that she didn't want to hear the answer to rise in her throat and it was out before she could stop it.

'Destined to do what exactly?' Maddy looked to Jen and vice versa. An unreadable look passed between the two that had Gwen wishing all the more she hadn't asked that.

'There's no easy answer to that, suffice to say for the moment - whatever it takes.'

'Whatever it takes to do what? You know how I hate it when people start rambling on in riddles. Why can't some people just damn well say what it is they've got to say without running it around in circles until it means nothing and they've effectively said nothing, it's bad enough that politicians do it.' Gwen felt her rage rising 'Most of them wouldn't know how to speak the truth now if their lives depended on it, they've dissembled for so long it has become as natural as breathing. It's like that saying how do you know a politician is lying? Their lips are moving. I expect it from them, *not* from you, now will you just say what you mean, I'm struggling enough with this already; c'mon, be fair!' Again the look passed back and forth. It was like watching a tennis match as Gwen followed the gaze back and forth. Then it hit her.

'You're talking to one another aren't you? Telepathically?' Gwen blurted excitedly. Her own predicament temporarily forgotten over the revelation at what her so called friends could do. Maddy simply nodded and Jen closed her own eyes and looked down. Weighing in her own mind just how she was going to make what she had to say credible enough for Gwen to swallow without her freaking out again. Jen looked up, adjusted her clothing and ran her hands through her hair, flicking it back so it sat right where it did before she interfered with it. But the ritual complete, she began to speak. Maddy reached out and Gwen let her take her hands in hers, as outraged as she was, the comfort it gave outweighed her annoyance.

'I'm cutting a very long story extremely short here so bear with this,' Jen spoke softly 'the blanks will be filled in later I promise. For now, suffice to say you have been chosen, destined if you will to be the vessel. We might have known this long ago but you were hidden. You and your brother have had one too many close calls with Death and that has fractured the spell that hid you both, it seems it has crumbled now and left you vulnerable and exposed.' Jen saw Gwen's frown at that so she embellished. 'Since the Earth was young and long before humanity, we have served the planet as her Avatars. Maddy and I represent the elements of this world. Myself for air and water, Maddy for fire and earth. We acted directly where she could not. We are the scalpel where she would be too devastating. We have always known a third might be required, but we never anticipated it actually happening, so we are almost as surprised as you.' Gwen made a face that said in no uncertain terms were they as surprised as her, but she remained silent and gestured for Jen to continue her tale. 'No one knew who the vessel would be, not even the Earth, it simply manifested itself in each generation of humanity. Guardians were chosen and they continued through each successive bloodline. Again, they may not have known their role unless they were called to act. Not every generation called. Hundreds of years have passed since any had to act, and then, not for the doom that faces us now...' Gwen couldn't help but leap in at that last bit.

'Doom? What bloody doom? You never mentioned a doom, oh no, I'd remember a word like doom, it has a certain impacting quality about it.' Maddy squeezed Gwen's hands to interrupt her flow before it could pick up any momentum.

'Guardians were chosen as I said, to protect the vessel, whatever force led you here was fortuitous indeed; you remember the lady who sold you the store? Of course you do. Well it might surprise you to know that she was a guardian, but she was killed, brutally, shortly after leaving here, as were many other guardians. Let your imagination do its worst, matters are that dire. It seems that there are few guardians left.' Gwen's jaw dropped at that revelation, thinking she had just gone off to enjoy what life she had left, a cruise maybe? But dead? Murdered? That was so horrible Gwen couldn't quite grasp it.

'Those individuals who weren't called still tended to gravitate towards greatness, two of your ancestors, to whom you owe an addition to your bloodline, are none other than Boudicca and the woman who was eventually portrayed as Guinevere in the romances. But they weren't called. They were not to become the third in the Trinity. It seems you are.' Gwen pulled away from a Maddy before she could stop her this time, shooting her a look of *'back off a minute'* Whilst she was unconscious, they had moved her to the center of the square under the comparative shade of one of the trees, Gwen leant back against one now and looked long and hard at the two women. A tinge of barely contained hysteria was evident in her strained voice.

'You're telling me you've been around since the dawn of time and you now want me to join you? Do you know how that sounds? Really?' Jen shrugged her shoulders sympathetically. Gwen knew that they had some idea of the enormity of what they were telling her, what they didn't know was how she would handle such news. Gwen thought she was handling it fairly well all things considered. There was still the option that *they* were off their trolley and not her. That much of what just happened was due to some mass hallucination brought about by a sudden outpouring of natural radiation or gas.

'We have a pretty good idea of how it sounds, yes. Though the dawn of time is a bit melodramatic, it hasn't quite been that long' Maddy piped up at that and flourished her hands as though it were a ludicrous idea.

'Though there are some days' she conceded 'when it feels a lot longer, but I shouldn't complain, it hasn't been all bad, a lot of it *has* I grant you, but not all of it.' Maddy looked at the expression of uncertainty on Gwen's face warring with outright disbelief. 'You need something a bit more definitive don't you? We have so little time to convince you, maybe desperate times require desperate actions, what say you Jen?' Jen nodded

'I'm inclined to agree, but here isn't the place, we could use somewhere secluded, these poor people here have had enough shocks for one day and I can hear the paramedics trucks arriving, we need to let them recover before they get any more, which is likely the way things seem to be shaping up though the severity is in your hands Gwen.'

'Mine? Don't you go laying the blame for this on me, I had nothing to do with it!'

'Granted, though I suspect it was you they were after and subject to your acceptance of certain truths, you may prevent any further bloodshed. Personally though I think it might be a bit too late to avoid that, but we must try all the same.' Maddy and Jen stood, both offered a hand to Gwen to assist her in rising, but she looked at the hands as if they were a pair of poisonous snakes.

'Thanks but I can manage, I may appear calm and rational but I assure you I'm not. I still don't trust you two, not after what you've done and what you apparently seem to be capable of. I'm not entirely over the bullets to butterflies thing yet. I've never felt so betrayed in my life, I thought you were my *friends?*' Gwen's plaintive accusation struck home with the girls and they finally gave in to their own conscience. Tears bubbled forth like mountain springs and their mask of authority slipped a fraction, the pain glimpsed beneath caused Gwen to catch her breath as a lance of empathy struck her. Gwen knew then, that with everything that had happened this day, it wasn't the intention of these girls to hurt her. It seemed to hurt them as much, having to put her through this. They were as tormented by having to give the explanation to her - as she was in dealing with the implications of said explanation. She had always sought phenomena to substantiate many of the *new age* beliefs she perpetuated in her store, witnessing it first hand was another thing altogether and she had over reacted. Knowing that now, didn't make it any easier; her own guilt at having given her friends such a hard time wracked her even as she watched her friends break down and cry before her. Ancient beings they may be, but she had lived with them for years now, as close as any family could be. That was what they were, family. Standing, Gwen went to them and upon reaching them, she spread her arms wide and encircled the two softly blubbing girls.

'I'm so sorry, I've been a right shit' making the admission triggered Gwen's own tears as the emotion of the moment overtook her, her voice cracking and failing she tried to tell them how sorry she was for giving them such a cold shoulder, the girls in the same weepy voices tried to say they understood, but to soon it all fell apart and the conversation dissolved into the three of them, arms encircling each other all crying their eyes out together, heads pressed into each other's shoulders.

They wept like this for several long minutes, each finding their own catharsis from the release. When they were in a fit state to find their voices again without breaking down, which they did after three attempts, they pulled their faces back from each other but didn't break the embrace. The trio stood and gazed at each other's red puffy faces and it was Jen who managed to speak first.

'We are sorry too, but we understand, it hasn't been easy for anyone, it's a lot to take in, but please, know this one thing, first and foremost; We are your friends and have always had your best interests at heart. We had fervently hoped that this would never have to happen, but it has. It's always the same - the less you understand, the more you fear - the more you understand, the less you fear. Once you understand what it is that is expected of you, you'll accept it with little to no fear. We wouldn't do anything to intentionally hurt you. You are as a sister to us in more ways than you could possibly realize, though you will. Maybe we could go to that place you like so much, up the other side of Hyde Memorial Park? Near that rock the shape of a mushroom?' Gwen was startled, she had never taken the girls there. It had been *her* refuge.

'How did you know about that? I've never taken anybody there, not even Elspeth. Have you been spying on me?' Gwen felt her indignation begin rise again, but kept it in check. She was glad she had when Maddy explained how they always kept an eye on her, for her own protection. It was why they were with her and as matters progressed elsewhere, or rather went downhill, her safety became more of an issue. Today's events were testimony to that. They begged her forgiveness and that set Gwen off again on her emotional rollercoaster. Tearfully, she forgave them and agreed to go to Toadstool Rock as she called it. They would take the Jeep once they had seen Res safely home, she lived on the way to the Park and in all likely hood, there would need to be some explaining to Grandma Yellow-deer. When Gwen mentioned this little fact to the girls even they blanched. Ancient beings they might be, embodiments of the elements, but Grandma Yellow-deer was another power altogether, her reputation was equally formidable, and both Jen and Maddy grimaced at the thought of trying to explain to the canny old Hopi wise woman just why her day had been so disrupted and why she had missed her appointment. Inwardly, all three secretly wished for the Kachinas to come back, for that seemed a much safer option than facing her. Placing the still unconscious form of Res back into the Jeep, they all headed off out of town, just as the first ambulance turned up to tend to the dead and try to make some sort of sense from the macabre scene they pulled up into.

# Chapter 4

## Propagation

Gwen was beginning to wonder just why they had to hike *so* far from civilization for their demonstration, after all, the spot they proposed was her favorite and she had picked it with the express purpose of being as far as possible from any other humans. It wasn't that she was particularly xenophobic, but there were just some days that she never wanted to see another human again for as long as she drew breath. Those days, she would pack up all she could carry - sometimes even her tent and sleeping bag, and trek up here for some Gwen time and to calm herself back to an acceptable level. She could scream if she so chose and no one would hear her, which occasionally she did. It was very cathartic, nearly as good as punching something. She simply had to expel whatever had built up inside her. Once, she had punched a mossy looking tree in pure frustration - only to find it wasn't quite as mossy as it looked. She had cracked a bone in her hand that day; Jen and Maddy had no sympathy for her when she eventually came back and held up her hand forlornly.

'That's what you get for hitting trees; it serves you right if you ask me, I hope it hurts.' It did, for a good ten days after. Gwen didn't hit trees again after that. She kept a punch bag hanging in her garage, which she took her frustrations out on now. Serving a dual purpose, it calmed her and kept her fit at the same time. Which was just as well, Gwen realized, after a traumatic day like she had just had, nearly having her ears chewed off by a very irate Grandma-Yellow deer; the girls had backed out of there as quick as possible once it was evident that Dolores was now simply sleeping, and unharmed. They had driven to the Parks car park and abandoned the Jeep there and started walking. Gwen knew how far it was, and it was apparent that the girls did too - having spied on her each time she came out here, though they said it wasn't spying; rather it was more a case of protecting. They insisted that they kept a respectful distance, but were in range should trouble occur.

'What trouble? There's nothing out here but me, the trees and maybe a few animals. Give me the animals any day. At least you know where you stand with a bear, whether it wants to eat you or not, it's just people you can't trust' the girls just shrugged, for there was little argument from them as far as that went although they knew she was having a pop at them.

The day was still cold and Gwen was glad she had picked up her coat, but her Ugs were fast deteriorating, they weren't designed for hiking in the woods and she muttered frequently about it. All the girls did was to assure her it would be okay, if things worked out as they hoped, footwear would be the least of her worries. Gwen wasn't sure if that was all that reassuring. The more she ran it through her head, the less confident she felt about their impromptu excursion. Gwen also knew from the one time she had encountered a ranger up near her retreat that gunshots were unlikely to be heard either.

The trees had a certain mystical quality to them this time of year, for even though many of them were evergreen, they seemed to know it was winter. The frosty sparkles on the leaves of the ferns and the red mulch from the cedars which gave the ground a moody contrast to the deep greens managed to give off a magical woodland feel. Ancient gnarly roots twisted and twined around the occasional rocky outcropping. Some were even deep enough to shelter in should the walker be caught in one of the sudden storms that could spring up without warning at certain times of the year. Gwen distracted herself with the familiar sights of the forest as they drew closer to Toadstool rock. Gwen couldn't imagine what had happed to this stony outcropping to leave it in this formation, but it was a distinct umbrella shape, almost as though water had worn it away, but she couldn't imagine enough water this far up to do such a thing, and, not wear away the foliage. It was too big for someone to have carried up here. It was just one of Nature's mysteries she supposed. Looking across to Maddy and Jen, she figured that they were another of Natures mysteries, for they seemed totally unaffected by the weather. Granted, they never really over did the warm clothes - they always seemed to be warm to the touch, but this day, they were hiking through a winter forest, bare foot and only wearing thin and not very long summer dresses. The spring effect of the plaza hadn't followed them out of town. Yet for all its insanity, they seemed more in place here like that, than they did back amongst civilization. This seemed more their element, the wild and untamed. Which, she figured kind of summed them up quite well. 'You two do know that it's going to be dark soon, and we'll never get back to town in time. The temperature is already dropping and you're not really dressed for this are you?' Maddy skipped ahead and twirled around a tree laughing as she did so. *That's it, they've flipped and I'm out here with a couple of nutters.* Maddy leant back against the trunk of a mossy cedar and placed one bare foot up on the bark. She ran both hands through her flaming mane and held it up, exposing her swan like neck. Gwen thought she looked more like some sort of tree spirit then, the sort that tempted mortal men out in to the woods never to be seen again. Seeing her there, many would think that there were worse ways to go.

'Gwen, dearest, have you not worked it out yet?' Maddy chortled as she spun and danced away like Jen had.

'Worked what out?' Gwen asked frustration tainting her words 'That either you or me is off their trolley? That much I've considered; the fact that you're not normal is increasingly apparent as well Let me guess, we're not going back tonight are we?' Maddy shook her head and smiled benignly.

'And don't smile like that either, it's not charming anymore, in fact it's quite unsettling now. I only mention this because we didn't bring any supplies for a camping trip. You know essentials like food? Water? Shelter? Any of the above ring any bells in that pretty head of yours?' Jen laughed then and joined Maddy a few steps ahead.

'Gwen, will you stop worrying, we've already said that no harm will befall you, surely that's enough to simply enjoy the forest and the company of your friends. Relax, don't worry about us, I assure you, this weather won't bother us one little bit, it's not even really cold yet, look…' Jen held out her slender arms '…can you see any goose bumps?'

'Well…no actually,' Gwen looked hard too 'but that's beside the point, it's just not natural.'

'Ah, that's where you are wrong Gwen, it is in fact more natural than you can possibly imagine. When you were born, were you born with clothes?' Jen asked innocently which somehow managed to get Gwen's back up further. 'No, but I wasn't born with fur either,' she snapped 'things that live in the cold are usually covered in the stuff, I'm not, nor are you.' Jen put her hands on her hips and tilted her head at Gwen, a gesture Gwen had seen on many an occasion; it meant she was getting a lecture.

'Gwen, how do you move your limbs?' Jen asked in her best school ma'am voice. Gwen stopped walking and considered the question, wondering where she was going with this one.

'I suppose…they just move because my mind says so?' Gwen's open expression implied that was that, did they want anymore? It seemed they did.

'More Gwen, there's more to it than that.' Jen snapped her fingers in rapid succession 'Think how fast your mind works, manipulating muscles

148

through electrical impulses, exciting the molecules and guiding them to obey your every command, however complicated at phenomenal speeds. I'm sure the medical people have a much more detailed version of how those simple operations occur, but the crux of it is in your mind. So is temperature; it is the control of your molecules, your mind keeps them warm therefore you are warm, however cold it is. Many of the older cultures still have a degree of mastery of this. It is *very* natural, for it is *your* mind, *your* body, *your* control so how unnatural can that be?' Gwen didn't know how to answer – unfortunately it made total sense.

'Expanding from that control of your own molecules - through frequency manipulation - comes the ability we call telekinesis.' Jen continued, joining dots for Gwen now 'It is simply tuning the radio of your mind to the frequency of whatever it is you are trying to move, as though you were tuning in to a radio station. When the two sync, you get music. With telekinesis, when your mind comes into sync with the object, it becomes an extension of you, granting you the ability to move it the same way and with the same instantaneous speed that you move any limb on your body.'

'So, that's why the weather doesn't bother you?' Gwen tested, though suspecting that there was considerably more to it than that. She wasn't going to be disappointed.

'More or less,' Jen replied cryptically just to annoy Gwen more 'now why don't we press on, the sooner we get to the clearing, the sooner we can explain properly. All your questions will be answered then, if that's alright with you?' Gwen knew she was outnumbered in this and they were just humoring her, trying to ease the enormity of what was happening. She knew she wasn't the boss anymore out here…they were. She was now the novice, the neophyte. *Sacrifice?*

'Sooo are we planning to be out here long then?' Gwen drawled in a last attempt to try and figure an agenda, but they were still having none of it, smiling infuriatingly.

'We'll be out here as long as it takes, but like I said,' Jen reinforced 'we'll look after you.' Gwen smiled thinly at that and knew that they knew what she thought about it.

The rest of the journey was uneventful though apart from Gwen's occasional question, and she was running out of sane sounding ones, but the girls weren't answering any of them anymore, sane or otherwise. They just strolled through the darkening forest like it was a stroll on a sunny day, one or both sometimes would walk beside her and hold her hand in a familiar and strangely comforting way, other times, they would leap away and dance about the trees and bushes like a pair of mischievous school girls who had slipped away from the teacher. But eventually, like all journeys, this one ended as they stepped through the tree line into the familiar surroundings. About half an hour before arriving, Jen had slipped away and Maddy didn't let on why. But to Gwen's amazement, when she broke cover, the first thing she saw was Jen, sitting before Toadstool rock, blanket spread out on the oddly snow free grass, a series of small fires blazing in a ring about the rock. On the blanket, Gwen saw bottles of water, and piles of fruit, bread that was still steaming - her mind couldn't process that little gem - and a selection of cheeses were also apparent.

'Thought you might be hungry - told you we would look after you. Once fed, and cozily warm, we'll get down to why we're here, seem reasonable?' Gwen just nodded dumbly as Maddy led her to the flickering fairy ring. Gwen soon found that she had to divest herself of several layers of her own, for it was, as Jen said, cozily warm within. Taking her Ugs off and depositing them to one side to hopefully dry, she placed her coat, sweater and one of the tee shirts she wore on top. Sitting bare foot in her faded jeans and kami top, she tucked in to the surprising repast.

'This tastes like Ernest's bread?' Gwen exclaimed, mouth full as she munched on warm, buttery corn bread with a soft cheese spread upon it, Jen smiled excitedly and nodded, her own mouth full of warm buttery bread.

'How on earth did you manage to do that?' Gwen asked when she could 'It's still warm for Pete's sake.'

When Jen had finished chewing, she answered just as enigmatically as before.

'You do ask a lot of questions Gwen, which is odd when you already have an inkling of the answers. How did we get to you so fast when the animals appeared? No don't try to answer that, we'll show you shortly, how's that?' Gwen still wasn't so sure, for during the impromptu meal, she had been having serious second thoughts about all of this. It was fast becoming too weird for comfort. She had sought phenomena all her life, but now she was faced with it, she found she was scared. That was the word she had been avoiding all the way up here, scared. Gwen had read enough pagan lore to let her imagination run free a bit, here she was in the woods, alone, with two mysterious women who were growing increasingly scarier by the minute. They were like strangers to her, for they no longer behaved like the girls she knew. Doppelgangers of the girls she had known or alien pod people who had taken them over. Her mind ran amok. A whole new side to them was manifesting and it hinted at danger and an irreversibility that would affect her life forever more. She didn't know if she was up for that sort of change. She enjoyed the routines she had, they had stabilized her and for the first time in who knew how long, Gwen thought she was putting down roots. What she didn't know, was just how truthful a statement that was going to turn out to be.

Jen and Maddy watched Gwen carefully, silently communicating between themselves about her suitability, but in the end they concluded that she was the one, the true conduit as Seb, Harry and the Collective had suspected and she had accepted the role back at the square quite enthusiastically – all things considered. After all, the power did flow through her, were she *not* the chosen one, nothing would have happened and things might be going a bit different about now. Yet, for all her acquiescence so far, Gwen still had that scared bunny look. What was termed in animals, the fight or flight reflex. Gwen's looked very much like flight. But matters had gone too far to turn back now; she needed to see this through, to understand what she had accepted.

Fed and watered, Jen cleared the remains of their meal away, though where it went, Gwen had no idea, but go it did. And by this time too, it was also full dark, the thin sliver of the moon barely lit anything - so the only light came from the circling fires and it cast macabre shadows to leaping and flicking in and out of her now limited visibility. Maddy stood first and walked a ways out in to the clearing, far enough that Gwen lost virtual sight of her beyond the firelight, barely able to discern her shapely silhouette. Then Jen stood, stretched and told Gwen to sit still and watch. But Gwen had determined that as soon as Jen joined Maddy in the dark she was going to be off, already discreetly slipping her Ugs on, she knew she could pick up her coat and be gone in a heartbeat. The moment Jen stepped from the circle of firelight, Gwen was up and running. Or at least tried to. Firstly, she hit the sticky air that she had seen before in the square, holding the animals fast. Then the word hit her.

'*Stay!*' The force of the word absorbed her like a wet mattress moving at thirty miles an hour. Gwen was lifted off her feet and hurled back through the air in a pseudo slow motion manner, as the dense air cushioned the impact. It was the oddest - as well as a painful feeling - slammed between two invisible forces. The air driven from her lungs by the impact making the world swim disconcertingly; and as she landed with an undignified thump, back on the grass before the Toadstool, the air returned to normal and she rolled several feet, before coming to a tangled, sprawled stop.

'Now sit up please Gwen and sit still, like we asked you to do. Don't try that again, for your own safety more than the inconvenience of fetching you in the dark. We didn't take any pleasure from having to do that, but you were asked nicely. This behavior is beneath you, we asked you to trust us, you need to understand certain things Gwen and it's not just our opinion. It seems you have been chosen by a power greater than us certainly greater than you. It's simply better for you to know what is happening to you in advance, don't you think?' Gwen nodded slowly, a horrified look still etched upon her features at the preventative steps taken to stop her running. This was real, her slightly battered body and very battered mind finally accepted that this was much bigger than her and that if beings of obvious power wanted her to be involved then perhaps she should see it through. For now. Especially as it turned out that running was a wasted exercise.

'Okay, you got me! I won't run again, here see?' Gwen said as she pulled off her Ugs once more and threw them out of reach along with her coat, 'How's that?' Gwen could see the glow of the girl's eyes from where she sat, even if she couldn't see their bodies. It was as though two massive feral cats were watching her from the darkness. They didn't answer. *Ha! How much more strange could it get?* Gwen thought to herself. *Crikey, what am I thinking? They just did magic on me, bloody hell. Magic! It's real. Oh hell, if that's real, what else is real? What else is out there? What really happened back in town?* Gwen, her mind racing was about to find out as she turned her attention back to the girls again. She could still see their eyes glowing, but she was sure they weren't that big before, or that far apart. And getting bigger by the looks of things. *Oh no! What now?* Gwen backed right up against the solidity of the Toadstool, in the vain hope that the rocky, dolmen like overhang would shelter her from whatever was taking place before her in the darkness. The more she looked, Gwen realized it couldn't be the girls, for it now appeared as though two cars were parked out there with their head lights on, but hang on, why were they going upwards? And since when did cars have golden headlights with vertical slits in them? The lights began to weave from side to side before her, still ascending and growing further apart until one pair were off to the far left, the other, the far right.

Gwen wasn't sure what happened next, but a sphere of light began to grow around her. Magnesium white, it grew brighter and brighter. It took a few seconds for Gwen to ascertain that it was the Toadstool itself. Gwen leapt forward again with a horrified squeal as though burnt, yet she wasn't harmed. Gwen alternating her gaze between the two pairs of hovering lights and the now incandescent toadstool. But it was on the alternating glance to the floating lights that the illumination did its trick and she saw what the girls truly were. She slumped like every bone in her body had just been removed and she simply stared slack mouthed and wide eyed for several seconds before promptly passing out. Again.

As she lay unconscious, her mind swam with fantastic images. Of creatures she had only ever dreamed of, they were all around her, smothering her and this feeling of suffocation brought her back to reality with a start. As her eyes focused again, all she could see was a wall of metallic, iridescent red scales the size of shields, flashing before her eyes oscillating through every hue of red imaginable. They surrounded her but did not constrict her so Gwen was able to turn about furtively and look around her. She wished then she had stayed unconscious. For looming over her, were two enormous reptilian heads, way bigger even than a large semi-truck, the massive golden swirling headlight eyes were fixed on her diminutive form.

Gwen couldn't work out where she was in relation to their heads at first, then as the initial shock wore…not off, but down a bit; she found that she was cozened in the coils of a glistening red scaled tail.

'It seems she's awake again Jen.' The sound was booming in her ears externally at first, but then it was Maddy's voice, gentle in her mind. Gwen lay there too stunned to do much else other than stare - not that there was an awful she could do anyway considering where she found herself - but look up in awe at the two great draconian faces looking down at her. The other face was as white and as pearlescent as fresh snow and as it moved, Gwen saw that she flashed through more colors than the most precious opal. Her dimly remembered physics told her that white held every other color within it, so it made a kind of sense. But they were *Dragons!*

It was difficult to tell what they were thinking as they gazed upon her recumbent form, were they smiling? Or were they like crocodiles, a mouth full of enormous teeth just look like they are smiling, usually just before they eat you.

'We're not going to eat you Gwen, don't be silly,' this time, the voice was only in her head and it was definitely Jens. 'What do you think now? Not something you see every day is it?' That did it for Gwen; she just burst out in bouts of hysterical laughter. *Not something you see every day? That's a good one, I've been living with two dragons that look like Victoria's Secrets models and now they decide to share? Damn! How many more were there out there?* It seemed the girls had maintained their mental link with Gwen and answered her thought for her.

'We are it,' Jen answered 'the only two Drakarim you'll be pleased to know and before you ask, there are only a few individuals who know about us in our mortal form, including you now.'

'But why are you sharing this with me?' Gwen asked almost plaintively 'Fantastic as it is, there are so many hows and whys going through my head I can't even begin to start to ask them.' Gwen wasn't sure she could maintain her sanity and conversational skills together much longer, her mind was sorely tested with what stood before her.

'We know,' Maddy answered this time 'but most of them will be answered as time progresses, patience is something you are going to have to develop you know. That is always assuming we survive the coming storm, humanity has weathered many before but this is unlike them. This is serious. That's why everything it seems was sent to find you; and you Gwen, our beloved sister, are to set a precedent. The likes of which has not been known since this Multiverse was born.' Gwen was not at all reassured by that statement.

'What?' was about all Gwen could manage at first, then she added 'would you mind kindly putting me down now, I don't think I'm going to faint again, at least not yet.'

'That's good, but why is this all so hard for you take in? I mean, you run a new age store, one that's called Earth Angel, you're friends with Native Americans who have shared some of their most private rituals and ceremonies with you and you are familiar with many more; you've even spoken to a wolf and a crow just recently. Are you not a blood sister to them now?' Gwen looked at the fresh wound on her arm and recalled the surreal conversation that brought it about. There were in fact, a lot of dead people back in town to testify to her encounter.

'But it's all just so… *fantastic*,' Gwen bemoaned 'how can any of this be real? It's like I'm reading one of those books I stock, full of elves, fairies and bloody elementals. I used to think they were on something, or were having flashbacks or something. Maybe there's some truth to it all now?' A bass rumble emanated from the throat of the Dragon that was Maddy that sounded more like a rockslide than mirth.

'No, not a lot of what you call truth really. Maybe some lost genetic memory or pure wishful thinking based on much older legends.' Maddy explained 'Like your King Arthur story, by the time it was romanticized to fit the age, it barely resembled what really happened. Legends have a way of doing that. Take us for example, a lovelier pair of innocent girls you couldn't wish to find…' Gwen snorted derisively and added a 'yeah right', which earnt her a little tail squeeze before she was deposited back on the grass.

'Hey! Easy with the little human,' Gwen snapped 'I've been battered enough for one night thanks.' More rockslide and Maddy continued with her account.

'…anyway, as I saying before I was insulted, we have been portrayed and identified in just about every culture across the entire planet. Every civilization has stories of dragons, many red and white. For the most part it was us, but we didn't do a hundredth of what was attributed to us, but it made a good story. Though on saying that, our brethren have been known to visit this world, and some of those may have overstepped the mark. But not since pre Babylonian times as I recall, centuries after the Great Kalithine War saw them all off. That was about the last time I remember feeling their presence.' Gwen sat down and put her head in her hands and scrunched her fingers through her hair, dreading the next question that she knew she had to ask, it was almost expected, but equally she didn't want to hear the answer. In light of her life over the last twelve hours or so, it was going to be something radical. And just cap things, she was getting a headache. The sort that pushed hot pokers into the backs of your eyes from the inside out and made the rest of your head feel as though it was in one of those medieval torture devices that screwed no end of metal rods in to your head. Gwen looked up through her lids, without barely moving her head and nearly jumped again as the face of Jen, the white dragon was looming down to sniff her, then her long snake like and blue, forked tongue lashed out around her, tasting her and the air about her.

'It's started hasn't it?' Jen whispered and Gwen looked up this time, though it was a struggle.

'What's started?' she asked despondently. The pain taking a swift and miserable hold on her.

'The headaches.' Jen stated matter of factly 'I'm guessing it's not the first of these headaches you've had, am I right?' Gwen nodded weakly and bizarrely the pain was escalating much faster than it usually did and her medicine cabinet was some miles away. She groaned and rolled on to her side. Pulling her knees up into a fetal position, groaning some more as the agony sent waves of sickly heat cascading across her body.

'We were hoping to resolve this matter with you before it became an issue, seems matters are even more advanced than we thought. There is a permanent cure for these headaches Gwen, it is called acceptance.' But

Gwen only groaned more, turning her face into the grass as the telepathic voice of Maddy resonated through her already tender skull.

'Not so loud please,' Gwen whispered 'accept what anyway, what have you two done to me?' Gwen managed to get out her questions before another wave incapacitated her again. 'Shit! Where did this come from, one minute I'm fine, the next my skull is being squeezed like a lemon for a margarita.'

'These are conflict headaches. When your destiny conflicts with what you are actually doing, the greater the conflict, the greater the pain. It seems you are still fighting your destiny Gwen, and as yours is pivotal to the cataclysm at hand, your pain will probably kill you.' Gwen screamed then as her suffering flared again. She began tearing at her clothes as wave after wave of inner heat surged through her. It wasn't like she was wearing much anyway, but the kami top and the jeans went, leaving her just in her skimpies, then even they had to go. If she could have unzipped her skin and languished in her bones she would have done. Through one squinted eye, Gwen was wondering if she could crawl to the snow.

'*Make it stop!*' Gwen sobbed as she was writhing uncontrollably, her nails digging into her skull so much so, one broke and blood was evident through her blonde hair.

'The only thing we can suggest Gwen, is to fully accept your destiny now, wholeheartedly and of your true freewill, deceit will be recognized and the pain will increase. Unfortunately, explanations will have to come after rather than before as we would have liked.' But Gwen had heard enough.

'*For god's sake, will you stop talking and tell whoever I need to tell that I accept.*'

The pain stopped immediately.

Or at least it stopped getting worse which Gwen took as good enough. Gwen lay on her back, perfectly still, chest rising and falling as her heartbeat slowed once more, with one knee raised and her hands still entangled in her hair. She lay like this for a good twenty minutes as the pain gradually abated and she slowly regained her bearings. The only outward sign she lived at all, was the now steady breathing, the rise and fall of her chest. Her naked chest. Which Gwen slowly came to remember, as lucidity returned to her with the gradual abatement of the pain so too did the recollection of how she came to be in that state.

'Did I just do what I think I did?' Gwen asked when she felt her voice return.

'I don't know' Jen responded in her usual slightly amused voice, it wafted across the night air and caressed Gwen's ears as though she lay next to her. 'What is it you think you've done?' Gwen opened her eyes slowly, it was still dark and she could just make out the outlines of trees, silhouetted against the moody night sky. Gwen hadn't noticed, but the Toadstool had gone out as well, it had dimmed to its original rocky look. Conspicuous by their absence as well, were the two dragons. But as her eyes became accustomed to the gloom, walking lithely across the clearing towards her, she saw that Jen and Maddy were their comparatively normal selves…except they too, were naked.

'I think I've just committed myself to something I'm probably going to live to regret.' Maddy responded with the one comment Gwen didn't want to hear.

'We hope you do live to regret it as well, in fact, it would be nice if we all get to live to regret your choice. For that to happen, we need to finish your education.'

'What do you mean finish? I didn't know I'd started, I thought I only just accepted this?' Maddy and Jen slipped down beside Gwen, Maddy began stroking Gwen's hair and Jen slid an arm around her shoulders, pulling her closer until their skin touched.

'In part. You accepted our help back in the square and it opened you up to the Earth. You survived the contact as the power flowed through you, but the biggest change is yet to come, and your heart had to accept that wholly. It is only unfortunate that we couldn't break it to you gently, before destiny took it from us. It was touch and go there for a moment, even we couldn't tell if you were agreeing to ease the pain or were genuinely accepting your role in the upcoming battle. It's a good job the Earth knew the difference.' Gwen perked up somewhat at the mention of the word 'battle'.

'What battle?' Gwen looked at each girl in turn, waiting to see which one provided the explanation. 'You never mentioned anything about a bloody battle?' There were now even more questions clamoring for answers, but she couldn't get them out; she couldn't even get her mouth and mind working in conjunction with each other sufficiently for a coherent sentence to come out. But her face told the girls as much as they needed.

'No, we didn't. Though what do you think the presence of the Kachina spirits we fought earlier heralded? It is because of a battle so great, that you have been raised to fulfill your destiny, a prophecy so old it was almost forgotten.' Gwen shook her head as though to clear a fog over her mind, it seemed to be getting progressively harder to both think and speak clearly. Gwen recognized the feeling as being similar to the time she had tried a friends Diazepam for a giggle, it had the same sensation, for her at least, of knocking back a bottle of tequila, or two. She ended up as good as useless for the best part of sixteen hours because of it. Gwen could feel the same creeping lethargy insinuating itself in her head and limbs as it often did after the usual headache wave passed, this one was something else altogether.

'Destiny?' Gwen asked struggling 'isn't that another word for the fact that your life is no longer your own and all choice has been removed? I get the distinct impression that I've been railroaded into accepting this and choosing whatever it is I've chosen. Now, I have the weirdest feeling that I've been drugged. I haven't though, have I?' The vehemence was palpable, even in Gwen's strained voice - she didn't like being manipulated, it brought out the confrontational side of her, much like it did with her brother. All her brief life, Gwen had always sought to remain a free spirit, answerable only to her own will and not subject to the will of others. This was beginning to feel very much like somebody else's increasingly bad idea.

'It is destiny Gwen, it always has been we suspect. And before you fly of the handle, let me finish.' Maddy still stroked her hair and was still laying seductively naked next to her, but her tone had changed once again to that of the school ma'am, correcting a misguided child. *Which I annoyingly have to concede I suppose I am, but that doesn't make it any easier to swallow.*

'As we have said before, this is all about you and has been for some time now. And you are right to one extent that any choice is limited; however, there is a but. It's like all things in life, you may be steered in a direction you did not opt for, either through work or relationships, financial limitations or any other number of reasons, but the fact of the matter remains is that within those parameters there is still choice.' Again Gwen tried to disagree and Maddy silenced her.

'Let me try another analogy, you drift along life's river, you must deal with staying afloat and what interacts with you from the riverbank. Yet through all this, you are still susceptible to the current of the river, it propels you, when you reach a fork and the current takes you left or right, it is not of your choosing, you merely deal with the consequences and adapt to the change. You do not rail at the river for its choice in which direction you ended up taking. Maybe, had you gone the other way, it would have ended in a particularly nasty waterfall culminating in your premature death. Such is life. For however important your choices are, it is equally important how you deal with the choices made for you. In this instance, the Earth has chosen for you. Do you believe that she would have done so lightly? Or without compensation?' This watery explanation had somewhat doused her simmering anger. For as though she wanted to lash out, to blame someone, something, anything for her predicament, what Maddy said made sense. She had always maintained that fate guided her and she just went along with it, sending her where she needed to go, providing her with what she needed, by adhering to this philosophy, she believed that was how she ended up in Santa Fe in the first place. The enormity of what that implied struck her. The Earth had already steered her life through all its twists and turns, educating her in the knowledge she needed to be the girl she was today, where she was today, facing the choice she had made today. Gwen gave up, and flopped flat back onto the grass. It was making her head ache again. Even through all the lightness and spongy feeling, Gwen smiled to herself all the same. Looking up at the two beautiful girls who in turn, looked back down upon her.

'I give in,' Gwen sighed 'you're right, the Earths right; I've seen the signs for years and paid them little to no heed. It has been brewing for a while hasn't it?' Jen nodded sadly and lay down alongside Gwen, head propped up on one hand, her elbow resting in the grass alongside Gwen's head. Jen started to trace spirals on Gwen's belly with a long, well-manicured fingernail. Gwen's pale skin reacted by raising the blood to the surface showing where Jen traced. It was also slightly ticklish, but in a nice, slightly rude way. Gwen closed her eyes and let herself enjoy the sensation. Maddy began doing the same the other side of her and in addition, she began to sing quietly, yet hauntingly. Gwen couldn't identify any words, they were more sounds than real words, but the melody was hypnotic. Then Jen added her own voice and Gwen was transported. Stretching languidly like a spoilt cat, Gwen lost all sense of time as the girls expanded their tracing to encompass her legs, up over her breasts and down her arms. Over and over they went. Gwen wasn't sure when it happened, but at some point during proceedings, one of the girls had leant over and kissed her. It just seemed the natural thing to do. Gwen, so thoroughly caught up in the rapturous feeling, responded in kind. She barely felt the hand that slipped between her thighs, only the sudden increase in pleasure which elicited several little gasps from her. Her breathing was becoming labored as the girls continued their teasing exploration of her body. The kisses became more frequent and more fervent. As matters escalated, the trio soon became a writhing mass of female flesh, entwined and thoroughly lost in each other's bodies. Moans and gasps became more and more frequent as they took each other to new heights of pleasure using their bodies, hands, fingers and tongues. It was a bonding session that Gwen wasn't going to forget in a very long time.

Hours or maybe days passed this way, and it was just before a dawn, as the sun began to creep over the horizon, that matters reached a crescendo and Gwen's world became a swirling mass of lights as her body could take no more and peaked in a mental and physical way. Wave after wave then crashed over her; she gasped and cried out in an ecstasy she had never before experienced, and believed then was unlikely to again. It was like being drawn deep into the Earth and then exploding like a new born star, every fiber of her being was torn asunder and renewed, over and over again. Stripped to her core and turned inside out, then reassembled only to have it happen again. It was a joy she never wanted to end. But end it did. Draining her so entirely, she was truly like an empty vessel and Gwen slept then. Slept while the Earth filled that emptiness with something new.

It was the smell of food cooking that eventually brought Gwen back to the world she had left behind. Slowly, she opened her eyes, just a hint, to determine if it was day or night. The dazzling sun told her it was day. *At least I haven't slept too long.* Then it all came back to her *Oh my God! What did I do last night?* As memory returned, Gwen became more and more aware of her surroundings, of the fact she was still naked and that she was not alone. 'It looks as though someone is stirring Jen.' Maddy's voice reassured her that she was still in the company of friends; they hadn't left her alone in the woods after *that.*

'It's food.' Jen chortled 'I swear that woman instinctively knows when there's food to be had.' Gwen opened her eyes fully then, followed by a bone cracking and muscle popping stretch, one that any cat would be proud of. Accepting she was still naked, Gwen smiled sheepishly and looked around for her clothes but couldn't see them anywhere.

'Err girls? Where are my clothes?' though as she asked, she noticed that neither Jen nor Maddy had dressed either. Subconsciously, she admired their lithe, well-toned bodies, the seductive curve of the backs that swept down to shapely buttocks which topped long, muscular legs. These were bodies which she had gotten to know *very* well only a few hours before. She blushed again as she was assailed by images and memories of events involving those body parts. Gwen was open minded about such matters though, having experimented when she was in college

160

and more recently with Elspeth. She was content she knew where her sexual preference lay, but there was something more than sex about the previous night, it was more binding and ritualistic, seemingly more of a natural bonding than simply crude sex for sex sake. She had never thought of the girls that way before, well, she corrected not with any serious intent at least. It was undeniable that they were gorgeous, worthy of admiration, but they were her friends and her employees and that was that. Though apparently that *wasn't* just that anymore.

They however were going about the mundane business of cooking and tidying up the little campsite as naked as they were the night before. Seemingly oblivious to the incongruity of it. Somehow, in the dark it didn't seem so strange; in the light of day though, it felt a bit weird. Not unpleasant, she amended to herself, there was a definite catharsis to being naked in the woods in broad daylight; probably why there were so many naturalists, but it was still just a bit weird for her was all. She looked between the two for an answer to all that had occurred, any sort of answer would probably help at this delicate stage, but all they did was smile at her and offer her a bowl of fruit and some scrambled egg on a wooden platter. Gwen took this without question - even though they hadn't spoken much since she had awoken, her stomach suddenly reminded her of how hungry she was. She always got the munchies after... she blushed at the sudden resurged memory of the previous night's activities. Diverting herself from those lewdly embarrassing thoughts she started to pick over her food hoping the girls would offer some sort of clue to the morning's events.

'Okay, so you don't want me getting dressed yet, I get that, though you gotta understand, I'm not entirely comfortable with this daylight nudity thing - all it'll take is some meandering hiker to come stumbling through here and he'll think all his Christmas's have come at once. I have a reputation here and I'm *trying* to build a business.' Still no reply was forthcoming, so Gwen carried on. 'I won't be happy to find myself in the papers or online with some scandalous headline like *'local business women romps in woodland lesbian escapade'* or some such nonsense.' It occurred to Gwen then that she needed to be at the store, she had lost all track of the day and it had clean slipped her mind. 'What time is it?' she panicked, nearly dropping her food. 'Have I slept long? I've got to get to the store!' Gwen shoveled steaming egg in to her mouth as she waited for the answer. Eyes frantically scanning for her elusive clothes. She nearly sprayed her egg across the clearing when they finally spoke. 'It's about two in the afternoon; you've been asleep for three days!'

161

# ACT 2

## Chapter 5

### Triskelle

'*What?*' was about all Gwen could manage as her ability to talk coherently had seemingly left her bereft. In fact, all rational thought had abandoned her petite body, packed its cases and gone on a long vacation rather than face what Gwen was experiencing right at that moment. She couldn't work out what to do with her hands or seem able to co-ordinate them with her mouth. A light breeze blew, raising goose bumps on her presently unfeeling skin. Gwen couldn't decide whether to explode or carry on eating and wait for the punch line; so she simply stood and stared at them. Frozen. Plastic fork halfway to her mouth, empty now as the egg had fallen to the grass - it was hard enough to keep scrambled egg on a fork when it had her full attention. Long seconds passed before the power of speech returned to her though, and then it came gradually, haltingly; though emotions vied for attention within her, it still only managed to come out in a flat monotone. Gwen couldn't put her finger on what emotion best suited her for what she was going through and Jen and Maddy seemed to be taking some perverse pleasure in her stunned predicament. She gave up with the food; her hunger had vanished like so much morning mist with the revelation anyway.

'Girls!' Gwen finally managed 'Tell me you're kidding; tell me I haven't been crashed out here in the bloody woods, naked, for three days.' Jen nodded as though it were the most obvious thing in the world to have done. Standing opposite Gwen, only a few feet away.

'Yep. You haven't been crashed out here in the woods naked for three days.' Jen answered and Gwen relaxed ever so slightly as she sought refuge in that clarification 'Really?' she asked and Jen shook her mane of blonde hair and said with way too much humor 'No, not at all but you asked us to tell you, so we did. The reality is you've been out cold for three days like we said, though I'd forgotten how much you mutter in your sleep.' They giggled between themselves and Gwen scowled in return, not liking being made fun of at all. 'Very insightful,' Jen smiled as she spoke though 'remind me to sit you down one day and go through some of the odd tit bits with you and then…' Jen smirked lasciviously, '…you can confirm just how true they are. Some bits even made Maddy blush. And who is Jason again?' Gwen was horrified and it obviously showed on her face, though this just seemed to amuse the girls all the more. For they started giggling amongst themselves. Gwen found a bit of fire and she threw her platter to the ground. Though the effect was lost as she stamped her naked foot, looking quite ridiculous. It seemed the girls had a warped sense of humor, making fun of her this way, but Gwen's anger quickly turned tearful, she had gone along with these two with more than enough faith and after all said and done, they still tried to provoke her. It was just too much to take and she dropped to the ground, burying her face in her hands, she started to cry. How had things gone from comparatively normal to this disaster so suddenly? They must have drugged her, though she couldn't recall taking any, but what would she know? She'd only taken what she called serious drugs the once as well as some skanky looking mushrooms. All they managed to do was make her sick, so she wasn't what you could call an expert on symptoms and signs. Now here she was, naked, deep in the woods, far away from all she knew, her business in jeopardy and no obvious way out. The dragon thing was probably her hallucinating, part of their drug induced plan to break her. They had succeeded Gwen accepted, she had no more to give. The fire that blazed within her, what gave Gwen her feisty character, finally and sadly, went out.

'I give up.' Gwen sobbed 'just don't kill me, please. You've had your fun now let me go *please.*' Gwen implored and had dropped to her haunches and was slowly rocking on her heels. Elbows tucked in and her forehead resting on her knees. She didn't see Jen and Maddy slip up either side of her and drop to their knees, flanking her. Gwen squealed in surprise when the two girls put their arms about her, she tried to struggle away from them, irrational fear had replaced the usual pragmatic Gwen, but the girls held her firm.

'Gwen! Please, relax.' Maddy had a note of concern in her own voice at Gwen's outburst. Squirming in their grip, Gwen was desperate now to get away from them but she couldn't move. They held her down no matter how she bunched her legs to spring away. With a quick push, they drove Gwen back. Off her heels and dropping her onto her bottom, where she landed with a squeal of surprise and moderate pain as she had landed on her plastic fork and it wound up sticking into the meat of her buttock.

This seemed to break her train of thought from flight to fight. Her spark rekindled vengefully with the sudden pain.

'Ow! Shit, Christ that hurts.' Gwen turned to remove the broken plastic utensil from her bruised flesh. Seeing that she had calmed momentarily, the two girls let go. Though they were poised to restrain her further if she made a bolt for it.

'Calm down Gwen, you silly thing, we're not going to hurt you, kill you or anything else grizzly to you for that matter. There are some things we need to explain to you to be fair, and we had hoped that your mind had adjusted well enough after your rest, maybe you needed more sleep.'

'*More sleep*? You *are* taking the piss now?' Gwen shot back furiously 'Three bloody days! How much more sleep do you think I need? I'm not poxy hibernating.' Gwen resigned herself to not being able to get up so she sat back, wincing as her stabbed posterior squashed up on the ground, but definitely calmer now. It was then she noticed the spirals.

'*You've bloody well tattooed me in my sleep?*' They were all across her abdomen and down her legs; Gwen saw a myriad of tiny pale blue spirals. She began to examine the rest of her body. They were all over her, feint but definitely there. Her rage began to build again and she started to rise, shrugging Jens hand off her shoulder, but as she turned to do the same to Maddy she saw the baleful look in the tall red heads eyes - unless she was hallucinating again - which she doubted considering how she was feeling, Gwen came face to face with a pair of blazing reptilian eyes. Black vertical pupils set in a liquid gold surround, they pinned like her like a bug in a specimen tray as they bore into her mind. She stared transfixed at the tiny flames licking out from the corners of her eyes.

'*Sit down Gwen!*' Even her voice had changed. Deeper and more sibilant. It resonated with power that Gwen felt vibrate through her very bones. Gwen sat. Her own eyes wide and fearful; red rimmed from her recent tearful outburst. She looked to Jen quickly, checking to see if the other girl had changed - she hadn't. In fact, Jen was smiling as benignly as ever, and if Gwen wasn't mistaken, a look of pity played across her serene features.

'I'm sitting okay?' Gwen almost whined 'I'm sorry. Look I'm sitting. What do you want from me?' Gwen's nervous, edgy voice served to somewhat pacify the fiery woman before her. Maddy stood and walked off a few paces before turning back to Gwen. The fire in her eyes had gone out and had returned to normal, but she wasn't smiling. And Gwen had the distinct realization then that it didn't bode well for any forthcoming good news.

164

'Your prolonged sleep was a necessary testing Gwen, to ascertain your genetic compatibility with the Earth and to prepare the way for the next phase of your journey. Without her assistance, your molecular make-up wouldn't be able to sustain the transition. In short, the Earth has altered your Deoxyribonucleic Acid and increased your chromosomal content. It seems in doing so; it has disrupted your mental and emotional capabilities. We had hoped that you would adapt better, certainly faster, for your next step will in all likelihood be even more traumatic than this one.' Gwen was horrified, and this started her crying again. She couldn't believe what she was hearing.

'You've been messing with my DNA?' she sobbed, her mind was registering all the information slower than usual it seemed. Her ears seemed to be full of cotton wool and her own words sounded spongy to her. Glancing over Maddy's shoulder, the trees had started to sway in a most disconcerting manner, round and around. No it wasn't the trees, it was her, swaying this way and that, and then with a gentle pop, Gwen passed out. Though not for long.

Gwen came too moments later - gradually, like a swimmer caught deep below the surface, she could see the light playing on the surface but try as she might, she found it hard to reach. Her mind swam furiously, desperate to break the surface before the emotional turmoil she swam in, drowned her. Distant voices seeped through to her consciousness. Recognizing them as her companions, Gwen concentrated on trying to hear what they were saying, but try as she might; it was just so much gibberish. Though two words did manage to slip through, and with them, Gwen broke the surface.

'She's awake.' Against her will, for she felt as weak as a new born kitten, Gwen was lifted up into a sitting position again and something cool was pressed to her lips, refreshing liquid trickled down her dry throat and relieved her now dry, cracked lips. Coming fully back to her senses, Gwen gasped. Whatever it was they were giving her was absolutely fantastic and she drank greedily, grasping it in both hands to get more.

'Easy, little sister, easy. Not too much at once, you'll give yourself a head rush.'

Gwen was reluctant to heed the warning until one of the girls - Jen - pulled the goblet away from her moist and searching mouth. Finally opening her eyes fully, Gwen saw that nothing had changed around her, yet everything seemed brighter and more colorful than before. She ran her tongue around her lips, making sure none of the drops escaped her.

'Wow! What was that?' Gwen's eyes fixed on the goblet that Jen held as though she could will it back to her mouth. But Jen simply shook her head and the magical liquid, goblet and all, simply vanished.

'That my dear was a little known beverage, mostly consisting of nectar but with a few other little things thrown in for good measure, totally natural though don't worry, we haven't drugged you if that's what you're thinking, you were weren't you? Hopefully that brew will bring some clarity to you.' Only a few seconds had passed but she did feel better. Gwen smiled, an embarrassed sort of twist to her usually ditzy grin, she found herself much more relaxed than her earlier awakening.

'How much do you remember about our conversation before your little three day nap and mini meltdown?' Jen asked. Gwen scrunched her hands through her hair again as though it would help her memory, mentally wandering through her minds filing system, which wasn't much better at best than tossing things into the various already cluttered corners of her head.

'Not much really, something about acceptance, destiny and pow...' as she spoke, the words prompted a surge of buried memories, recently swept into a darkened corner by Gwen's subconscious as it seemed a bit too much to tackle at the time, part of her had hoped she wouldn't have to tackle them again at all. So much for that.

She was bombarded with images of slavering wolves, giant Kachinas and smashed corpses, lying strewn across the street. Then the memory of two enormous Dragons slammed into the forefront of her mind. Gwen looked back and forth then, rapidly between the two girls. They retained their silence, though it was clear they could virtually *see* the memories flooding back to her, based upon her own mix of shock and horror playing merry hell with her features.

'We need to be serious now Gwen, as you apparently remember what has happened to you to date, you will also appreciate that matters are going a little against the expected norm.' Gwen laughed despite herself *against the norm? What planet were they off?*

'You could say that,' was all Gwen actually said though 'and all this has something to do with me I take it?'

'Yes!' Maddy said quite emphatically 'To do with you and partly because of you. You've seen firsthand what has started to happen. It is not only happening here, but all over the world. It's only going to get worse. Before too long, matters will be irredeemable. Now, we've laid the groundwork with you, but the final choice has to be yours. You accepted your destiny three days ago; you recall the pain in your head

166

subsiding?' Gwen nodded' but that acceptance only brings us to this moment.' Gwen sensed with a deepening anxiety that there was more to come, though she had seemingly passed a point she hadn't been aware of - because she felt relaxed and steady now - eager in fact for more information, even knowing it was probably more doom and gloom. Her previously turbulent psyche was gradually finding a purchase in reality again. Though that reality had irrevocably changed, Gwen found she didn't really mind. She hadn't been overly fond of the previous one anyway other than its relative stability. Her earlier trepidation was being steadily replaced with enthusiasm, a keenness to know more and what her place in all this was. She was however soon discovering the true meaning of ignorance being bliss.

'Go on!' Gwen encouraged 'I've had about all the shocks I'm going to have, I think that it's either the nectar or, I'm actually ready to hear this. Either way I've got to know what I am, what you think I am and what is expected of me.'

'Very well' Maddy exclaimed, casting a quick glance to Jen, making sure she concurred. Jen nodded that she should continue. Maddy took a deep breath and started.

'You recognize the fact that Jen and I are Dragons, we are of a race known as the Drakarim. We were the oldest of the four races.' Gwen couldn't stop herself butting in.

'Four races? Who are they then?' With the patience of a teacher instructing a child, Maddy deviated to accommodate her curiosity.

'Us, the Drakarim, our twin race who branched away at the beginning of our rise - the Unc'anharaphim, the Ch'drnOmThophilim and yourselves. One you know as Dragons, the other as Unicorns and the latter as Angels. But try not to concern yourself too much with them for now for its not as simple as it sounds, suffice to say, there have been times when certain individuals have been elevated to positions above that which they were born to. A few of your kind have evolved to join the ranks of the Ch'drnOmThophilim but that is another tale for another time. As well as far too many of your kind being taken by the Nescarii and subverted to their foul ways.' Gwen butted in again.

'Nescarii? Doesn't that make five? You just said there were four including us. Are trying to confuse me? 'Cos I don't think you'll have to try too hard.'

'Yes and no, the Nescarii are what the inhabitants of the Domain have termed themselves to differentiate themselves from their brethren, the Ch'drnOmThophilim. You would know them as demons.' Gwen mouthed a silent 'Ah' not wishing to pursue that avenue just yet. Rolling her finger to Maddy, she gestured she should carry on.

'You…' Maddy started again, exasperation just starting to creep in to her teachers level tones. Gwen was good at getting her to bite every now and then. Maintaining that she took matters a little too seriously. This was definitely one of those times, but the residual effect of the nectar was still tingling through her system, making Gwen a little mischievous. The closest to this feeling was once, when she was a girl, having to take a trip the dentist. Somewhere she hated, she had to have a wisdom tooth taken out and they had sedated her partially before the operation. During one particular case of verbal diarrhea, she had nearly bitten off the dentist's finger. But, as she recalled, there was no pain and that was the important bit.

'…have the opportunity to rise above your species now. That is the choice you must make. We are the Avatars of this world, and we are currently just two, yet now matters have escalated to such desperate proportions, it is now unlike any other time in the history of the known Multiverse, whereupon the Earth, weakened as she has become under the onslaught, has been caught off her guard so much so that she is unable to rally herself to fight back, others must do so on her behalf. It is for that reason alone that two is no longer enough and we now need to be three. For the first time *ever*, anywhere, another is called. You Gwen must choose to become the third Avatar.' Gwen was grinning inanely before Maddy even finished speaking. 'Fine.' Maddy recognized the look on Gwen's face and turned to Jen, placing her hands on her hips in that age old posture of female irritation.

'You've given her too much, look at her! She's in no fit state to make such an important decision. We really don't have time for this you know, we…' Gwen jumped up.

'Shut up for crying out loud,' she snapped 'you're giving my arse a headache.' Gwen frowned at her own analogy, not having a clue what *that* meant, but she continued regardless.

'Giddy I may be, but I'm still quite capable of making my own choices. I don't know if it's the nectar or somewhere in between, but I've never felt more free. Unencumbered by the practical and logical starchiness I must have inherited from my folks. Anyway, things were getting boring back there if I'm really honest, don't get me wrong, it's not that I didn't like every one or the store, I loved all of them, you, it, but - I'm not the best at settling down, frankly I don't know how I managed to stay in one place for as long as I did, have, am, oh you know what I mean.' Maddy looked for a second like she was going to say something, her mouth opened then she thought better of it and closed it again, looking momentarily unsure. Gwen took the pause as her cue to carry on.

'I mean, it's not every day you get to talk to wolves and stop bullets in mid-air is it? No it's not' Gwen answered her rhetorical question for them before either could speak and so she forged on. 'I know it's not every day as well, that the likes of me' Gwen struck a pose 'one cute English storekeeper - gets to do something like this, something profound. If what you say is right, then I'm needed. It's actually nice to be genuinely needed for a change. Not simply needed just because I supply people with objects or the odd coffee, but *really* needed. I like that.' Gwen shook her head then, in a happy, dizzy, fly buzzing around her head sort of way. One that had the strange effect of endearing people to her when she did it. It wasn't the reaction they had expected and probably for the first time in longer than even they could remember, the two earthly avatars were speechless. Gwen hopped from one foot to the other gently clapping her hands alternately in front of her and behind her, smiling and looking from one to the other. She cut such a comedic figure, capering about like she was and naked to boot, that it broke the precarious tension and sent the two Avatars into fits of giggles.

'Now you seem to have lightened up a bit,' Gwen continued smiling herself and thinking that she had never felt so uninhibited, she really ought to get the recipe for that nectar, she could make a fortune. And every one would be a lot happier for it. Gwen mused inwardly as she considered the argument. *Always assuming it was a legal concoction; some prissy anally retentive git in the government would still try and ban it though. I swear those miserable bastards want everyone to be just as miserable and hacked off as them. They certainly do enough to piss every one off already - what's another one to add to the list? Tossers, I swear it's a conspiracy.*

'Maybe you can tell me then exactly what being an Avatar entails?' Gwen chirped before they launched into another lecture. This time it was Jens turn to look stern; Gwen thought they must take it in turns, sort of good cop bad cop. Though her happy thoughts soon vanished, just like a balloon popping when Jen spoke.

'Firstly, you have to die!' All of Gwen's previous vindication came flooding back along with her renewed fight or flight adrenaline rush. Gwen eyed up her route as she spoke.

'Hah! I knew you were up to no good, and I'll be damned if I didn't let you drug me *again*, I must be some sort of pillock.' She started to back slowly away from the girls, her eyes darting left and right, trying to figure out where she was going to run to. Though streaking through the woods didn't exactly fill her with enthusiasm or brimming confidence, but at least she might stay alive a bit longer.

'Relax Gwen, you really must get a handle on this fight or flight reflex you seem to have. It's not death in the physical sense; we're not going to beat you over the head with a blunt object if that's your worry. It's like the death card in tarot, its change or transformation. The 'cute English storekeeper' will be no more, as such, you'll no longer be the proprietor of Earth Angel either; you'll hand it over to another's keeping. Much in the same way as it was handed over to you. Dolores will make a fine shopkeeper don't you think?' Gwen stilled her urge to flee, but narrowed her gaze to scrutinize the girls suspiciously. 'You mean you're *not* going to kill me then? But you are going to give all my stuff away, my hard earned and worked for stuff?' Both Jen and Maddy shook their heads simultaneously, rolling their eyes skyward as if to say 'silly girl'. Gwen saw the look and responded hotly, repeating her words in poor mimic of Jens accent.

'*Firstly you have to die*! What the bloody hell was I supposed to think? It doesn't really leave a lot to interpret does it? It's not like 'firstly you have to die' means *would you like sugar with that?* No! It means you bloody well have to die! Of course I'm going to run away. Do I look stupid?' Gwen was standing ankle deep in grass, naked in the middle of the woods, jabbing her forefinger at two equally undressed girls who stood smiling at her. Jen spread her hands wide in a gesture of resigned innocence.

'Well, yes, actually.' Gwen froze. Without moving, she gave herself the once over. She had to agree with them. Her expression said more than words. Slowly lowering her arm and folding her wrists over each other behind her back, Gwen kicked one foot through the grass, grimly noting even her feet and ankles had the feint blue spiral trace-work upon them.

'Fair comment,' Gwen conceded 'okay, I admit it did look a little bit like dummy spitting. I'm sure it's all this standing about with my bits swinging in the wind that does it. That's my excuse and I'm sticking to it.' Maddy walked over placed a comradely arm around her shoulders, slowly she turned her and led her back to the fire pit, which by now had burnt down to a few smoldering embers. Maddy winked at it and it roared back into life, blazing merrily away on what appeared to be nothing but rocks and stones which made Gwen's eyes widen once more.

'There is a phrase Gwen' Maddy cajoled 'one that you have heard before. It says that to give up everything - potentially then, you have everything. So it will be with you. Look at us, are we unhappy? Do we ever seem to lack anything? No, for all the Earth is ours - so too will it be yours. You will become more than mortal Gwen and you will be able to do many extraordinary things. Now sit down again and take a breather, you've had a little too much excitement in too short a time. Here - have a drink' Maddy passed Gwen some water and waited patiently while she obeyed. Jen had joined them and sat on the grass next to Gwen, folding her supple legs underneath her. She started to twiddle with Gwen's hair, in a way she often had when they sat in the store, she would braid little bits while Gwen sat and did paperwork. It was a feeling of familiarity and Gwen started to relax again. The girls saw the tension slowly ebb from her taut, wired frame. Rigid shoulders dropping as her bunched muscles unwound.

'Better?' Jen asked softly, for she sat only a few inches from her friend, legs touching as she stroked and fondled Gwen's head and hair. Not in a sexual way this time, but in that indescribable way that brings a sense of comfort and security. Gwen nodded sheepishly, all too aware of her recent behavior. It all seemed so irrational in hindsight and her head swam with memories of her yo-yoing emotions. It was all so surreal; like something she had read about in one of her paperbacks. It was the sort of chain of events that only ever happened to someone else, not her. Though not any more it seemed. She was about to embark on the adventure of a lifetime if any of what they said was true. Oh it all sounded fantastic, and Gwen was appreciative to at least still be alive, though even that was about to change apparently. *I hope it doesn't hurt. I wonder if there's any more of that nectar up for grabs, I'm sure with enough of that in me I won't feel anything*. With bravado she didn't really feel, Gwen steeled herself to do whatever it was that they required her to do, telling herself repeatedly that it was for a good cause.

'Okay, I feel better now, what do we do next?' It was at that point though, that Gwen realized that something was missing. In fact, the more she thought about, she realized that it had been missing for some time. The sounds of the forest. The creaking of the trees and the sound of the birds. Squirrels barking as they capered amongst the high branches and no end of other sounds that made up the constant cacophony of the woodland. She sat in silence now and that - more than anything she had seen or heard since she had arrived at toadstool rock - bothered her.

'Why is it so quiet?' Gwen found she was whispering, as though to speak any louder would disturb the eerie silence.

'Why are you whispering?' Jen whispered back conspiratorially. Leaning to better share the secret. Before Gwen could answer though, Maddy dropped to her knees beside them both and leant in towards them. And in a hushed tone, she had Gwen look around.

'Gwen, look at the forest edge, slowly and quietly and you'll see why.' Slowly, ever so slowly she began to study the tree line. Focusing intently on what she didn't know. But as she concentrated, images began to appear; hundreds of pairs of eyes looked back. She was being watched in return. The branches were jam packed with all manner of birds, sitting silently - even reverently - together, riveted upon the clearing and the three two leggeds within. Gwen gasped as she saw bears and mountain lions, badgers, coyotes and wolves. Squirrels and deer, and what she took for grassy clumps were in fact knotted bundles of snakes all entangled yet calm, watching with their intense reptilian gaze. It was fascinating and terrifying all at once. If Gwen had any doubts about the two girls even up to that point, seeing the animals there, together, dispelled them like a gale force through mist. Creatures that should be attacking and eating each other sat side by side like the best of friends. As her eyes adjusted, she could see further and further into the woods beyond and there were still more of them. There had to be hundreds and hundreds. Whole herds of deer, millions of birds. A disorientating sensation swept over Gwen, causing her to close her eyes and grab her head with a grimace of unexpected pain. Both girls were instantly attentive, cradling her and speaking soothingly.

'Let it go Gwen, let it go. You're not ready for that yet, you're only half way there, let it go.' the pain diminished slightly along with the dizzy swimming sensation that had come over her unexpectedly. In a weak but still awed voice Gwen sought the answers to a myriad of questions that had sprung unbidden to her slightly overwhelmed mind.

'There are so many whats and hows I don't know where to start. I'm guessing though that we are the why?' Maddy nodded. 'Your mind is reaching out to them already, but it's not quite up to that task. Trying to see through a hundred thousand pairs of eyes will give anyone a pain in the head. In fact, these animals are here to greet the new Avatar, you Gwen. They all came to be the first to see the birth of the one who will nurture them and protect them. Succor them in their time of need and defend them from all who would do them harm. They will become a part of you and you of them. Because you have part way undergone your connection to the Earth your mind was susceptible to the draw of the animals. Their need and desire pulled at your unconscious, fragmenting it into a hundred thousand minds. Your eyes saw from all of theirs at once. Fear not though, for after your rebirth, you'll find that a much more pleasurable sensation.' Gwen was relieved by Maddy's explanation and a little frightened. Assuring herself that a little fear was a healthy thing and that everything would become apparent soon enough. Jen whispered in her ear, keeping her voice low so as to not rattle her delicate sensibilities any further.

'We need you to lay down now Gwen, flat on your back as though you were doing snow angels. Arms wide and legs spread.' Gwen blushed uncontrollably.

'Behave yourself you minx, we're not doing that again' the humor in Jens voice relaxed her a little, but she was still nervous. Her stomach tied itself into several knots.

'No matter what happens now Gwen, you need to relax. I know it sounds lame and we've probably repeated that fact so many times already, but it's true. The more relaxed you are now, the easier it will be. Especially for you. Close your eyes, the next time you open them, you'll see the world as an entirely new place and it'll break your heart. Focus on our song and breathe deeply.' With that, Jen started to sing. Not real words but sounds that appeared like words. It was almost another language and the sounds made the skin on Gwen's arms and legs prickle like a small electric current had been passed through her. She realized then that it *was* another language. The language of Magic. It was a language she had yearned for all her life, hearing it was as though a missing piece of her soul had finally been found. Seconds after Jen had started to sing; Maddy picked up the melody and repeated it in counterpoint. The effect was phenomenal. Amplifying the sensations coursing through her and bringing tears unbidden to her closed eyes.

She never saw the seven intricately cut stones push their way out of the ground around the trio, ringing them with spiral carved stone and crystalline menhirs. Chunks of precious and semi-precious gems protruded from their granite structures and caught, reshaped and subsequently scattered whatever illumination hit them. Tiny sparks of light flitted between the crystal and spirals on the rocks and the subtle sub-dermal spirals indelibly imprinted into Gwen's body. As each sparkling mote flashed upon her skin, the pale turquoise spirals began to glow from within. In only a few seconds of this pyrotechnic display Gwen was almost invisible, cocooned within a halo of soft blue light, emanating from her glowing spiral markings. It would have fascinated her had she been able to see it, for she had long been an exponent of the significance and importance of spirals in the governance of the Earth and all around it. The ancients obviously knew this, for why else would they utilize so many spirals on so many relics and historic archaeological finds. Stone circles, art, jewellery and even within caves; Gwen recalled Newgrange in Ireland. Somewhere she had always wanted go but hadn't quite made it yet.

The chanting sing-song melody of the girls continued. Wrapping Gwen in a musical sheath to the total exclusion of the outside world. All she now knew was warmth pulsing from her core and the tingle of the magic - as she liked to think of it - dancing across her flesh. Time began to mean little to her as the harmony carried her along. She could have been laying there for hours or days again for all she knew, so entranced by the internal and external stimulation. *External?* This was new. Gwen thought that they weren't doing the touchy feely stuff again? But the more she concentrated on the touch the less it felt like hands or fingers. It felt more like some snake was coiling about her leg. Legs? And getting higher? She knew she shouldn't open her eyes, they had said so. Maybe it would break the rhythm of whatever they were doing. But Damn! They were getting higher. Any second now they would reach her...Gwen gasped as whatever was coiling itself up her thighs pushed itself gently into her. That was it, she was going to open her eyes and see just what the hell was going on. A wave of indescribable pleasure ripped through her, temporarily cutting off rational thought. *This was wrong.* Gwen started to panic and when she tried to open her eyes she found she couldn't even do that. Her mind said she wanted to but her body refused to obey. As self-preservation began reassert itself, Gwen tried to bring her arms and legs in to protect her vulnerable body. They were firmly pinned down as though she had been crucified upon the ground. Staked out, star shaped just like in some old western movie or serial killer slasher horror. Gwen tried to scream then, vocalize the horror she imagined was being perpetrated against her, but the moment she parted her lips to yell - another tendril like thing pushed its way into her mouth and began to force itself down her throat, just as those below her waist pushed up higher into her again. More coiled over her chest, constricting her breathing, every time she breathed in the coils move further down her throat. She couldn't move, fight, scream or prevent the invasion. Her mind was howling at her that she was about to die. To effectively drown on dry land as her body was invaded by who knew what. Lights began to flash before her closed eyes as the last remaining vestiges of life giving oxygen left her traumatized and now stress wracked body. Had she been able to see herself laying there in the woodland clearing, she would have seen thousands of tendrils, resembling prehensile tree roots, thrusting out of the earth around her and binding her to the ground like an organic, over excited Gulliver, over and over until she was virtually invisible beneath them. Then, as the life Gwen knew began to swiftly diminish, seconds before she lapsed into sweet oblivion, the tendrils began to sink back into the earth, taking Gwen with them. Heartbeats later, she had totally vanished, leaving no trace that she had ever been there at all. Gwen, the tendrils and even the disturbed grass had all vanished, the area was as unruffled as it was before they arrived. Jen and Maddy stopped singing and sat in a contemplative silence for a good hour after, just looking at the spot their friend had occupied moments beforehand. Slowly and quietly, the decorative and energized stones too sank back into the loamy soil from which they had originally arisen until they vanished completely as well. Quietly and deliberately, Maddy and Jen tidied the makeshift campsite. Eventually, when they were satisfied that all traces of their presence had been removed - they manifested their hiking clothes back on, Jen tidied her hair as a matter of habit, not through any real need, but it made her feel better.

'Might as well head back home' Maddy suggested in hushed tones, 'she won't be back for a while. I imagine Dolores could do with a hand adjusting to the new life she knows nothing about yet. I suspect it's all going to come as something of a shock.' Jen agreed, nodding sympathetically.

'I also suspect my red headed friend...' Jen responded levelly 'that there are some very edgy people back in town, trying to piece together just what has happened to their lives and their ordered existence. I reckon we should have a go at diffusing any potential situations. People have a way of going off the handle when something untoward happens to them. They might even get it into their heads to do something stupid.' Maddy flashed Jen a concerned look which said 'Really? Do you think they would?'

'They're humans Maddy, it's in their nature to overreact and retaliate with excessive violence. They don't understand what's happening to them and that lack of understanding makes them unpredictably predictable if you take my meaning.' Jen spoke as though she had said this many times before and knew she had.

'I do' Maddy agreed as she too had many times in the past 'and I think you might be right again, though I don't know that we'll accomplish much, once people get a bee in their bonnets they're historically hard to discourage, I just hope they haven't done anything stupid already.'

'Well, let's do what we can, I like this little town, it would be a shame if it all went horribly wrong and we had to move somewhere else. Did you keep her car keys?' Maddy patted a pocket and the familiar jangle answered 'I don't think they need to see two dragons swooping in on them just yet, it might be better to arrive normally, anyway, I happen to quite like that CD Gwen has playing in there at the moment.' Maddy laughed richly and huskily even as she shook her head forlornly.

'You're incorrigible! Momentous events are taking place all around us, the world is probably ending and all you want to do is listen to Robbie Robertson.' Jen shrugged as if to say 'And?' Maddy gave up, tossed her mane of darkly smoldering red hair off over one shoulder as she rummaged in her pocket and produced the set of keys. She tossed them to Jen who caught them deftly.

'You drive!' Maddy called back over her shoulder as she wandered off towards the car park where the jeep sat. Minutes later it was kicking up gravel as it slewed out of the parking area.

They were right in their assumption though for the moment the girls pulled up at the town square again covered in yellow warning tape like a gigantic tape spinning spider had been on a rampage too. They were immediately confronted however by several irate police officers demanding an explanation from them both about their most recent whereabouts and what their involvement was with the massacre days earlier. Maddy and Jen sighed resignedly and cast weary glances at each other before they set about what they had to do. It took most of their combined powers of diplomacy and coercion to convince them all that what they had experienced was something far beyond their capability to handle and that emergency measures should be instigated to protect those individuals still living and working in the immediate vicinity. They explained that they were off duty doctors had been away doing similar for the outlying areas and Gwen was still out there doing what she could. With a mental nudge, the policemen bought the tenuous explanations though they seemed at a loss as to what to do next then, for this really was something they weren't geared up for. It didn't conform to any of the procedures they had in place. The girls didn't like to 'nudge' them too much as it sometimes had an adverse effect and knocked other more useful stuff out, but these poor officers did need a prod in the right direction and had to be galvanized into the correct course of action. Mainly getting everyone together and getting the hell out of dodge. There was no telling how long it would be before whatever had attacked days ago decided to attack again. With themselves and Gwen temporarily out of circulation, they would all be vulnerable and completely defenseless. Frankly, the girls were stunned they hadn't already wiped out the town in their absence. The ferocity of the first attack had been expected, but Gwen was more of a priority than the town. It was part hope and part acceptance that the town may or may not be there when they got back. They had both sighed in evident relief when they saw the centuries old town still stood.

They helped with the clean-up operation for a full day before finding Dolores. Who upon being briefed as gently as the girls could, took it rather well considering the circumstances surrounding it and vowed to continue the work started by Gwen during her few years as custodian. Though Dolores later confessed that it now made some sense of Grandma Yellow-Deer's most recent dreams. The girls didn't pursue it then for they had great respect for the elderly wise woman and her foretelling. Instead they ran through the books with Dolores making sure she was happy with all the wholesalers, the bills - for both the store and the house. Hoping a basis in normality would help ground her and make her ready for what was inevitably coming. The Native American woman had been stunned for several hours when she had been given the news of what she was to inherit. In fact, she still felt - some twenty four hours later - that it was all a dream, Maddy assured her it wasn't and it would take some getting used to but not to worry too much. There were more immediate and infinitely more important things to be concerned about. There were few assurances and little solace to be had, but what they had - they gave to Dolores and her Grand-mother. A most pragmatic pair, both acknowledging the dangers and the hand of Great Spirit at work. They would be vigilant and do all they could. Satisfied that they had achieved as much as feasible in the short time they had to prepare the townsfolk and the new owner of Earth Angel, the morning of the third day Maddy and Jen left Santa Fe and Dolores to fend for themselves once more and headed back up to the woods to see what, if anything had occurred at Toadstool rock.

Maddy and Jen didn't know what to look at first. What should have been a familiar drive to the oft visited car park and woods soon became a journey into the unknown. Had they not known better - they would have sworn that they had slipped back in time to a more primordial era. Hyde Memorial Park as it was known previously, no longer existed it seemed. Something much more vast and brooding had taken its place over the course of forty eight to seventy two hours. Huge trees had burst forth, bromeliads the size of cars hung from their trunks and upper branches. Ferns that could have hid elephants covered the ground, vanishing into the darkness of the immense forest. Jen and Maddy were Avatars of the Earth and as such, they feared very little but even they felt a touch of trepidation as they drove in, for as Maddy pointed out, the forest was closing ranks behind them as they got further in. There was it seemed, no turning back.

'Interesting don't you think?' Jen commented as casually as she could as the jeep bounced over a bulging root that pushed up across the road. Maddy had to agree though her eyes were scanning everywhere at once it seemed. In truth, they didn't know what to expect as a consequence of their actions. All that was transpiring was, as they had told Gwen, was so unprecedented. Winding their way up many of the trees and spanning the gaps in between, were wickedly barbed ropes of bramble and dog rose. Stems as thick as mooring rope and covered with spines the size of daggers, some even larger. As archaically beautiful as the forest now looked, closer inspection revealed it to be infinitely more deadly. Stopping in the small clearing now that used be a sizeable car park area, Jen and Maddy abandoned the jeep and commenced now on foot. They saw the lethal undergrowth writhing and twisting dangerously before them, almost daring them to enter. They looked at each other, silently communicating their concerns. But they needn't have worried, for the moment they drew close enough, the writhing tendrils parted like a bead curtain revealing a mossy pathway beyond, Jen even wondered if there was a yellow brick road there somewhere, so surreal did it look beyond the thorn wall. The moment they both put foot to the path, the briars snapped shut behind them like a monstrous organic and sentient bear trap. For all the intimidating display of menace and danger the forest put on when they had first arrived, the path itself was now a journey of amazement and beauty. Plants long since extinct flourished. Massive flowers with the most vibrant and intoxicating aromas. Huge fruits of every shape and color hung from branches big enough for two people to walk along side by side. The girls adjusted their clothing to suit their new environment. Short halter dresses and bare feet were the order of the day for them as they strolled casually along the meandering pathway. They were ensorcelled by this '*new*' ancient forest. The wildlife had certainly taken to it. They could be seen in their droves darting and running through the undergrowth. Occasionally one would stop and stare at the visitors, recognizing them on a deep level for who they really were, the curious animals bowed slightly in acknowledgement and moved on. Secure in the knowledge of their now total safety. The sounds of birds wove a musical accompaniment as they walked. There was little doubt that this forest was alive, not just with wildlife, *but in itself alive*. It was a freshly born and very living entity and the girls respected that. A fitting residence for the next earthly Avatar they thought together. A huge stag, complete with an impressive rack of antlers stopped mid-flight across the path and stared at the girls. Proud and majestic it appraised the visitors. Yet for its own royalty, owner of a bloodline any king would be proud of, it lowered its great head and bowed in silent reverence and respect to the two Avatars. Jen and Maddy bowed their heads back in acknowledgment. With a last glance from its intense liquid brown eyes, it leapt away and vanished once again into the forest, a wraith that flowed like mist amongst the trees. Agile for one of his size and musculature. And bizarrely Jen noted, its entire hide was covered in subtle blue spirals. 'Who does that remind you of?' Maddy quipped watching the beast vanish. Jen's eyes sparkled her answer.

The sound of burbling and trickling water caught their attention next. A silvery splashing brook had materialized alongside the pathway and was growing in size the further and deeper they ventured. As they stopped to investigate it, they saw flashes of silver and gold darting below the surface as schools of fish explored their own newly acquired environment. Toads could be seen wandering around the mossy embankment along with frogs and newts. Maddy was enchanted; she didn't know where to look next without seeing some new wonder. Clouds of butterflies and dragonflies filled the air above them, as multihued as any rainbow, thrumming their wings like little rotors. Whatever was happening to Gwen was definitely having a direct effect on the surroundings. The closer they got to the area where they had left her - for they no longer had any idea where they were in relation to the forest they knew. They simply walked now at the mercy of the meandering path. Resigned to the fact that they would eventually be deposited where they needed to be - the girls recognized many of the features that they had spoken of with Gwen during some of the quieter moments in store. What she had described as her ideal woodland was now apparently manifesting around them in all its lush and spectacular glory.

Progressing onwards with their journey, they saw the babbling brook grow to stream size then up into small river proportions. Not necessarily deep, but wide enough to move over the landscape. Every now and again it would deviate from the path and vanish into the trees. Some of which were so vast, that their root system spanned the watercourse like a bridge and the river flowed beneath it. Bees swarmed around the upper branches, hives formed and clouds of workers were busy gathering the copious amounts of nectar from the myriad of flowers. Jen commented on the fact that it must make the most wonderful honey. She had a bit of a weakness for honey, it satisfied a sweet tooth she vehemently denied she had.

Yet for all their exploration of what the forest revealed to them, what they didn't see was what the forest still hid from them. Just how much and how vast it had grown. It had spread out and encompassed the original Hyde Memorial Park like it was a pot plant in the midst of a forest. Losing track of all time in the semi-permanent twilight of the forest, the girls eventually found themselves in a small clearing; though clearing wasn't exactly the right word for it was filled with huge clumps of spongy moss, enormous geodes had been pushed up and cracked open, revealing the sparkling crystal formations within. They knew they were at their destination, for before them was the biggest tree either of them had ever seen in all their long lives, it dwarfed even some of the huge Redwoods for girth and it surpassed the brazil nut tree for height. It loomed over toadstool rock making it look like a real fungus, the rock however had split, it had cracked in half and the origin of the river sprung forth from within it spreading out different directions, creating at first a good sized pool which the river then ran off from. In the middle of this pool- though to call it a pool was a disservice, for it was more like a small lake, and upon it was a raised island of grass. It was the same area of grass that they had left Gwen laying on before she disappeared beneath it and upon which now grew this fantastic and majestic tree. It grew upon the island in the midst of the pool like a reverential island shrine. Chalky lines of pale blue spirals could be seen interlacing through the long grass and even under the crystal clear water like some ancient powered-up hill drawing. Knowing instinctively that they had arrived at the right place, Jen and Maddy sat themselves down on the soft mossy outcroppings that rose to meet them and prepared themselves for a bit of a wait.

'I like this grove Jen.' Maddy commented, her eyes roving around the secluded woodland sanctuary, as they sat listening to the abundant birdsong and general animal chatter. 'Why don't we have anywhere like this?' Jen laughed and gave Maddy an affectionate shove.

'Because up until now, where could we have gone where humans wouldn't come venturing and trying to get into? Nowhere would have been sacred. And if we had guarded it the way Gwen has this forest, they would have been all the more determined to gain access under the guise of 'exploring, studying'. No, they weren't going to be ready for such places as this. They had no way though to have warned Gwen not to be ostentatious like this for it was too late for that now, with all that is happening, their world is about to - if not already has - change irrevocably. The Adversary has inadvertently brought about an evolutionary metamorphosis for humanity. 'No matter who wins now, nothing will ever be the same again.' Jen whispered and Maddy could do nothing but agree with Jens stating what she herself had already told herself.

'So that means we can have somewhere now?' Maddy stated suddenly looking eagerly at Jen.

'If you like Maddy, but you and I both know that there is so much for us to do that we would never find the time to enjoy the benefit of having it.' Maddy shrugged, not entirely letting go of the idea even in the face of Jen's pragmatism.

'I don't know, you know how that desert looks in summer, I'm sure there is a secluded canyon I could call home. Even you could find a little retreat out there. Or, you know how I've had a soft spot for Death Valley. It's not too far away and you don't get many humans wandering around out there, even before this.' Jen shook her head resignedly. Looking at her friend with affection, yet at the same time with the weary look of one who has spent so many long centuries in the same persons company, so much so, a familiarity with how they thought was as ingrained in them as much as their own thoughts.

'How many times have I heard you say this now? Why don't we wait and see if we even have a world to call home first, because if the Adversary finds whatever it is he's looking for and we don't stop him, then none of it will matter will it?' Deflated but realistic, Maddy had to concur. With a deep sigh of her own, for she had always been the more romantically inclined of the pair of them, she accepted what her sister told her and knew it for the stark truth, but it didn't hurt to have dreams, she thought to herself sadly.

'Fair comment Jen, but enough talk. We should start the song now, I can feel the Earth calling, and she's almost ready.' Jen giggled at the comment.

'You make her sound like an oven ready meal.' And just for a moment, they both succumbed to the humor of the image. Hearing an imaginary *ping* and the ground spitting out a well basted and slightly steaming Gwen. But it was hard to try and *not* imagine where the sage and onion had gone.

It was late in the afternoon when the two Draconian Avatars of Earth, Fire, Air and Water began their song of power. Their voices raising the vibration of the grove to an electro statically charged environment. The creatures of the wood added their own counter harmony to the girl's voices. It became a song the likes of which had never been heard before, nor was ever likely to be heard again. Its power reached out in ever increasing sound waves. Pulsing form the forest like the ripples from a pebble dropped into a pool. Only this time, no physical embankment was going to prohibit their passage. Every single living thing on the planet became aware on a level that caused a moment's pause in what they were doing, enough to acknowledge that something fundamental had changed, but not as to what.

The song continued in to the early evening and it was just as the moon had waxed to its zenith that the sound of wood cracking and splitting began to be heard. Maddy started several little fires going, placing them where the geodes were growing, letting their crystals magnify the light around the grove. It created a spectacularly magical effect. The sound of creaking and splitting wood continued for about an hour. They stopped singing as the sound abated. Then, with a thunderous retort, the huge tree cracked open. A vertical rent a foot from the ground and finishing some seven foot above. The bark had peeled back to either side giving the rent a distinct vulval look. A mist began to slip out of the opening and creep along the ground. Swirling around the little fires and dabbling along the water's edge. It lent the whole scene an air of magic and mystical anticipation. Many of the animals, like before, had come to see what was transpiring; their own instincts told them that it was a transcendent moment, never to be repeated. This experience would be passed down through their genes to their own young forever more after this night. Another little evolutionary change for the immediate wildlife.

Jen and Maddy rose, and with the ethereal delicacy of their nature, stepped over to the dark, moist entrance of the trees core, stepping on massive stepping stones that rose from the water to meet them as they walked to the island. There they waited patiently, knowing it was only seconds away. Time was measured now in heart-beats. The primal rhythm pulsed within them all, the blood coursing through their bodies keeping time to the natural flows that throbbed within the magical forest. It was almost a countdown to the moment that Gwen would make her reappearance within the living world. Ba-boom, ba-boom, ba-boom; the cumulative hearts beat, then, upon the thirteenth beat, a glistening, slightly emerald hued foot extended out from the darkness. Immediately followed by the calf, the thigh, and then the woman herself. A vision of natural perfection. Her eyes bright and liquid, her hair lustrous, her breasts pert and defined, flawless skin, though being tinged slightly green, with underlying pale blue spirals wasn't considered a flaw. Gwen stepped out fully into the night and drank in the atmosphere as though it were her first breath ever. She closed her eyes and spread out her arms as if to embrace everything. A shaft of moonlight materialized around her, bathing her in its silvery glow and sparkling motes of light refracted the moons glow. Her skin flashed and sparkled like the scales of a magnificent fish or cuttlefish. Cascading through every color over her body like mother of pearl flashing in the sun.

Then the moment passed, and she relaxed. The shaft of moonlight filtered in to the rest and what could pass for normality in this fantastic place returned. For a moment, Gwen looked at everything as though she had no idea of where she was, or how she had come to be there. Even to looking directly at Jen and Maddy like she had never seen them before. Tilting her head to the side, bird like. First left, then right. Gwen blinked, and with the one movement of her now double lids, memory came crashing back in. Filling the void her transition had created within her. Everything that had happened to her from the moment her life started to go sideways, her time in New York and beyond, right back to childhood; it all came flooding through her, bringing right up the moment she now stood within at the speed of light almost. Emotions tore through her like internal explosions as every aspect was amplified, love, hate, betrayal… and loss. Elspeth's face lingered before her mind's eye before hurtling on.

'Come here Gwen, come sit for a moment.' Jen broke the spell as she called to Gwen 'I imagine this is all very disquieting and you may need a moment to reorganize your thoughts, sort of get your bearings.' Gwen allowed Jen and Maddy to lead her by the arm to one of the spongy mossy seats and she sat, with no real idea of what she was doing. The girls could see her assimilating her thoughts by the way her eyes flashed, but her body just reacted like an automaton.

'How are you feeling?' Jen ventured, hoping that some gentle conversation would help her friend return to herself. Gwen looked up slowly as though there was a subtle time delay in her hearing what she did and her ability to respond.

'I er...I.' Gwen shook her head lightly and coughed. Maddy instantly reached over with a manifested stone goblet of cool water from the little lake. Gwen registered the movement slowly, but took the goblet and drank. Slowly at first, then with a growing need. She finished six goblets in all before she tried to speak again.

'I think, that all things considered, I'm actually quite fine.' Gwen eventually said and even her voice had taken on a slightly more enriched and melodious tone. Gwen noticed this and her hands flew to her throat, thinking that something might be wrong, but there was nothing there to cause or indicate any need for concern. She tried speaking again, as much to hear her voice and get used to it, as it was to actually hear the answers. But as she spoke, she took in her surroundings and then the questions flowed much more freely.

A good hour later, Gwen had run out of her most immediate and pressing questions and was beginning to relax a little. In fact she was fast becoming quite enamored with 'her' grove and all it contained.

'It's all so fantastic really...' Gwen murmured as she thought more about her experience '...little bits of what happened in there keep flashing up and clarifying themselves. I get a rush of details and it's like I'm there again, amazing' she exclaimed like a school girl 'just so bloody amazing.' Jen and Maddy had noticed though, that one thing was conspicuous by its absence. That of what she had now hopefully become and they were concerned deeply about that more than anything because it would mean the transition was complete and successful.

'Gwen? Did you see anything else during your sojourn? Anything... Draconian?'

Gwen looked thoughtful for a moment then nodded slowly as images came to her.

'Yes I did now you mention it. I saw another like you two, the same liquid golden eyes; only this one was more of an emerald green in color. There were roots and ivy's milling about her claws and entwining up her forelegs, I remember that it was...' The final memory slotted into place and Gwen's face froze in awe and amazement.

'That was me?' she squeaked eventually. Maddy and Jen nodded, smiling encouragingly as they did so. 'I'm a…green…I'm a green…'

'Say it Gwen, its okay' Gwen looked between them again and gave it another go.

'I'm a green Dragon?' The girls beamed then, each jumped up and hugged Gwen like the true sister she had now become.

Gwen sat back then, seemingly more relaxed even though she had never been more overwhelmed due to the revelation and sipped her water thoughtfully. Her mind briefly took a turn inwards then, for as much as it was incredible, the implications of what she now was and how she now looked crept up on her. Looking at her wiggling green toes she mused on trivial things, like wearing sandals again, shopping and those general day to day things that entailed her mingling with the public.

*It's all a bit eco, and if I was in California I might get away with it. But being green and covered in pale blue spirals might pose a tad difficult anywhere else. It's going to play havoc with my social life.* Gwen laughed out loud then, surprising her companions and eliciting a look of concern. *What social life? Bloody hell, I don't think I've had one of those since much before or since Elspeth.* Gwen quickly pushed that memory away as in her current state, the pain was almost unbearable; she quickly changed the subject.

'So, is this going to fade at all?' Gwen's abrupt question startled the two girls who were still hovering anxiously. Concerned that even though she had come back physically, her mind may have not made it all the way back. 'Or am I going to be green for the rest of my life?' Gwen asked glibly, looking between one girl and the other.

'Sorry?' Jen responded, quickly regaining her thoughts from assuming the worst.

'I mean,' Gwen continued as though she had never been answered 'you're not white and Maddy's not red, so why the bloody hell am I green? It doesn't seem entirely fair.' Gwen pouted. Yet before either could respond to her query, Gwen clapped her hands together and jumped up grinning. The girls looked worried again.

'I've got it! I'm not ripe yet! That's it isn't it? I'm like a little green tomato, maybe I should curl up in a draw for a week or two? Will I go red or yellow?'

'Are you quite finished?' It was Maddy this time, almost stamping her foot. Exerting her authority. Both Gwen and Jen turned to look at the annoyed looking red head. Gwen had the good grace to look contrite at the rebuke, bowing her head slightly, though she kept her eyes on Maddy, giving her a coy, shy look.

'Sorry miss, won't do it again miss,' Keeping her knees together, Gwen scrubbed one foot back and forth like she was putting a cigarette out. Holding her hands behind her back completed the image. Maddy threw up her hands in consternation and stomped off several feet, muttering. Jen smiled and knew that Gwen was just winding up the easily baited Maddy.

'I take it you are actually okay Gwen? Not traumatized by it all to the point of...?' Gwen looked up then; straight in to Jens eyes so there could be no misunderstanding.

'Insanity? No, I'm fine, really. Shocked, surprised, a bit giddy I suppose. It is, after all, a lot for a girl to take in. But if you are referring to my marbles, well, they are all there. However many there were before this anyhow. So - joking apart now, am I going to stay green?'

'Not if you don't want to.' Jen assured her in her most reassuring tone. 'But that said, there are some things you need to master before any chameleon games. And quickly.'

'Go for it, after the last few days or weeks or however long I've been gone again, I'll have a go at anything.' Maddy rejoined them and took her seat again, glowering at Gwen. She hated being wound up and set off like some clockwork toy. Gwen always said she took things a little too seriously and Gwen made it a point to demonstrate that at every opportunity. Almost without fail, Maddy bit.

'You saw us in our Draconian forms, so how do you think we get all that in here?' Jen patted herself on the chest and waited to see what Gwen came up with.

'Pass, next question.' Gwen shrugged and at their silence added 'I have no idea, dehydration?' She ventured. Maddy groaned, looking askance at Gwen, who shrugged as though butter wouldn't melt in her mouth.

'What? How the hell should I know,' Gwen blurted as they stared at her, expecting a better answer 'I'm not a physicist or a biologist. It doesn't seem possible to get all that into that' Gwen mimicked something big being squashed into something considerably smaller, by flinging her arms out then bringing them back into hold something tiny in her hands, pointing them in the girls direction. 'I imagine you are going to tell me though otherwise it would be conversation going nowhere wouldn't it. Please!' Gwen implored 'Don't be treating me like a mental case, I'm fine now, but I'm still as impatient as I was and even though I've just gone through some incredible shit, which ...'She forestalled their imminent interruption, '...I know - it will all become apparent in due course. But for now, I'm finding I have a need for some simple facts, not science lessons. And don't be asking me questions about what you want to tell me, I hate riddles and they make me crabby, correction, crabbier than I'm already feeling. So please, again I ask just tell me what I need to know to get a handle on all this. Don't beat around the bush, no pun intended.' It was the most coherent speech that Gwen had come out with for a while and it took the girls back. They had been dealing with denial, fear, paranoia and no end of other human emotions all vying for attention within Gwen. This had the semblance of rationality and they both felt a weight lift. Maybe there was hope after all.

'Very well. The abridged version it is. But do stop us if there are any questions, much of what we tell you has to be mastered by you, not just known about.' Gwen nodded and waved impatiently for them to continue. Jen stood, adopting unconsciously the role of the teacher; she began to speak as though she were instructing a class. Gwen assumed it was another of her incarnations and sat back to listen. As she did so, without any conscious thought, she reached up and an obliging branch dipped down, depositing a big juicy apple in her outstretched hand. Jen stopped and watched, stunned. Her mouth paused halfway through shaping a word. Gwen took a bite of her apple and with a little spray of juice; she mimed a 'What?' Jen mimed back holding the apple with a question of her own. Suddenly Gwen realized what had happened and she blanched. Looking in horror at the apple as though it had crawled into her hand of its own volition.

'I don't know how I did that, honestly.' Gwen blurted quite shocked herself now 'I wasn't thinking about it except that I really fancied one right then. Wow. Neat trick. Want one?'

'Gwen, you are now capable of many such neat tricks, obviously your subconscious has adapted to your new role, it just maintains to adapt your conscious mind to accepting what and who you now are. You are Gwen, the Avatar of Nature. The living embodiment of flora and fauna. The natural world responds to your will as easily as you lifting an arm to scratch your ear. Your thoughts are their actions. The same principle applies to your body now. It is as malleable as your thoughts.' Gwen scrunched up her face as though she was concentrating on understanding what Jen just said.

'You are saying, right? That I can change my body by thinking about it?' Jen was nodding. 'Basically, yes.' She answered 'Its simple name would be molecular manipulation and density compression or expansion.' Gwen looked agog and shook her vibrant and lustrous blonde locks in a mock confusion.

'If that's the simple term, you can keep the technical one to yourself. What's that in idiot terms? Green dragons for dummies? I'm not up on the science part that much, I know the basics, to an extent but complex stuff I never really got along with.' Jen smiled, she knew Gwen's dislikes.

'You're a shape shifter.' Maddy blurted impatiently wafting an irritated hand as she did 'You can be anything that this planet naturally contains. You have the capability to rearrange your molecules to conform to whatever your mind requires. It is an exterior process though; you are still yourself within whatever form you adopt. Likewise, as you demonstrated a few minutes ago, you can also manipulate the flora to your minds will.' Gwen looked thoughtful as several memories spun up within her. Disjointed images from her incubation, she knew that they weren't hers but she couldn't decipher what they were trying to impart to her. They were hazy, messy as though she were seeing someone else's thoughts through a crystal ball. But amongst it all, Gwen felt certain impressions. It felt as though she was now the repository of an accumulated wealth of information. Provided by any number of souls over the course of the Earths lifespan. *Maybe I'll add my little bit to whoever comes next. That won't be much then.*

'I don't know,' Gwen mumbled 'you'll have to bear with me but I think that I'm kind of remembering stuff that I didn't have before…' she grimaced slightly at the memory 'I'm seeing a woman, tall, lithe almost willowy, long white robes I think, crap!' Gwen looked mortified 'Sorry, I sound like one of those people who invents mystical looking spirit guides or the likes, but I'm not I assure you. I remember her thoughts if that makes any sense, let me see.' she paused while she organized what she wanted to say so it made sense to her as much those who would hear it.

'I think she is saying that I can 'borrow' molecules from all around me? Does that make sense?' Maddy beamed and came rushing over, and gave Gwen an impromptu hug.

'Thanks Maddy, but what does it mean?' Maddy sat back and pondered for a second how she would explain it all. There were no easy options, so she bit the bullet and went for it.

'Well, in a nutshell…' Maddy was interrupted by a groan from Gwen.

'Very droll.' Gwen moaned at the unintended pun 'Nutshell? Get it?' Maddy rolled her own eyes skyward, smiled wanly that she did and tried to carry on.

'Absolutely everything is comprised of highly charged molecules, all resonating at their own individual frequencies and speeds. They are in all objects, water, rocks and even the air. You now, as with all the higher races to an extent, have the ability to add and subtract the number of molecules you need at any given time. If you opt to take your Draconian form, which you now possess by the way.' Gwen's facial expression told Maddy all she needed to know about that little revelation. 'I take it you've seen that in one of your new memories too?' Gwen nodded dumbly. She *had* seen several disturbing images of flight and of seeing a pair of massive emerald hued reptilian wings that seemed to be where her arms should have been though Gwen knew she had four limbs and wings, it was very disconcerting. Although it had been most disconcerting it was yet an oddly exhilarating experience too.

'Good, now to continue' Jen interrupted her thoughts 'all your little spherical molecules are held together by a force. A current, a charge. Call it electricity but is fundamentally more vital than that. It is the force that holds your molecules together and binds them, constructing the physical form and all that goes with one. Blood, bone, tissue, sinew, veins, and that list is endless. Everything relies on this life-force. Once the alternator or generator that is you...' Maddy poked Gwen in the chest, eliciting a disgruntled *ow* '...stops supplying the energy, or put another way, death.' The word had some finality to it 'The electro-magnetic field that holds the molecules together ceases and the binding capability stops; they just drift away from each other in every random way imaginable. Decomposition is the result. No power, no life. You've seen no end of those TV doctors give the patient a jolt when they have a cardiac arrest, well, it's much the same thing. It's like giving a car a boost, infusing power. You can now manipulate that force. The looser your molecules the less dense you become, eventually you would become gaseous if you loosened them too much. Alternatively, you can compress those you have and become heavier than lead and harder than diamond. You would become as immovable as a mountain should you require it to be so.' Gwen was assimilating this news as fast as she could; the implications were astounding. The more she thought about it though, the more questions sprang into her head.

'This all sounds like so much science fiction. Why haven't our scientists figured this out yet, it all sounds so simple. Like me tuning the radio of my mind into the frequency of whatever it is I want to connect with. Hey,' Gwen squeaked excitedly 'Like that branch with the apple on. I didn't even really think about that. It just...sorta happened if you follow me, shit, I'm blabbering now, calm down Gwen' she muttered to herself.

'You're right Gwen' Jen picked up the thread of the conversation then 'It is a logical science; the trouble of course is *knowing how* to tune in to something. That's another matter altogether. You can do this because you are now genetically superior to your fellow humans, you are now Drakarim.' The process was almost visible on Gwen's face, her flawless brow furrowed briefly as she put the pieces together; and they were coming together, with frightening clarity.

'So what does that mean? Genetically superior?' I'll keep my hair when I'm old? Or what? What exactly have I become?' Gwen couldn't help but wonder how many more times she was going to ask that.

'Drakarim Gwen, are the eldest of the four higher races as we explained to you before, they have moved even closer to the fiery hub of this spiraling solar system. Closer even than the race you currently know as Angels, this means they have evolved even further physically as well as spiritually. Whereas before, as a mortal, you had only a double helical DNA strand and a mere forty six chromosomes...'

'Mere?' Gwen snapped 'You make it sound like we're a bunch of amoebas. Ah, look at the little single cell organism.' She whined in a peeved sort of way, letting the girls know she didn't like being condescended to, nor should they do it to others. Especially her.

'...well, you have a few more now,' Jen continued smoothly 'Four hundred and twenty two more to be precise, and if you can imagine your double helical DNA strand as one of thirty two others, giving sixty four strands in total. That's what you have now. Mortals to you now *are* as close as that amoeba to you and that's not being condescending, it's a fact. One you'll have to get used to I'm afraid.' Gwen was stunned. She didn't feel any different. She had become something from a fantasy story. She was a genetically altered fucking Dragon! Not even human anymore. Gwen was numb, her emotions had seized up on her. What was she supposed to feel about this? *I know I volunteered to do this - but what have I done to myself? I'm not even Gwen anymore, I can't be; I'm not human.* Gwen's mind was reeling at this new bit of information. But there was no going back now; she had to get a handle on it, and fast. Somehow that prompted her to look down and realized for the first time since

190

emerging from the tree, she was still naked. *Starting with my bloody clothes, enough is enough.*

'If that was your potted version, I think I'll hold back from the detailed one for a while, what I do want however, is my damn clothes. By your reckoning, I've been out here and naked for ten days or so, that's quite enough don't you think?'

'So what do you want to wear?' Maddy returned, putting the ball back Gwen's court.' Gwen frowned as she considered the question.

'What have you got?' Gwen batted back, used to this tennis type conversation.

'Actually, Gwen, it's more like what have *you* got, have you not been listening?'

'What?' Gwen shot back, getting annoyed again at the ambiguous and riddle like statements of her so called friends. They wanted her to do something but couldn't manage a straight answer when pressed.

'Look. I'm a bit frazzled at the moment, can you just take some pity on little old me and just tell me what you're trying to say.' She dropped her shoulders and gestured to them imploringly to give up what they knew.

'Do you remember what I said five minutes ago about molecular manipulation? If so Gwen my little fruit bat, close your eyes and manipulate some molecules. Choose something you are familiar with, try your favorite sweater and jeans. Imagine you are wearing them, visualize yourself in them. She did. A light tingling rippled over her body and caused her to open her eyes and see what had happened.

'Oh my God! That's incredible!' Gwen didn't know which bit of herself to look at first. Her favorite sweater was indeed there, and it felt so real. Her jeans were fitting her as though they were made especially for her, which in a way, they were. She clapped both hands on her buttocks and admired the way her jeans hugged her rear.

'Does my butt look big in these?' The girls clapped their own approval at Gwen's initial success. Jen held up a hand and water from the pool leapt up to gather around her outstretched fingers. She rolled the water around in the air pulling it this way and that, and then she flattened it, compressing their molecules into disc shapes. This had the effect of creating a floating, ever so slightly rippled, watery mirror.

'Take a look.' Jen offered, Gwen wasted no time twirling and spinning before the mirror, checking her reconditioned figure. She got up close to have a better look at her face and skin. Other than the slight green hue and pale blue spirals, it looked fresh and toned; even the tiny crow's feet that she had noticed forming had gone. *I didn't look this good at eighteen. Gwen you lucky girl, this is one perk you can certainly live with.* It was as though Jen had picked up on her thoughts, moving to stand beside her. They both looked at their reflections. Each looked no older than their mid-twenties, but by Jen's reckoning, she and Maddy were several thousand years old, if not older. And they looked like that.

'Can I do anything about this green shade? I suspect I'll look a bit sea sick in certain lights.' Jen told her to try the same thing as she did with her clothes. And she managed it with equal effect. She squealed and hopped with excitement, just like a ten year old at Christmas having been given every present they had asked for and then some. Gwen was scrutinizing herself like she had never seen her reflection before.

'I'm sorry to seem overwhelmed by this, well I am but it's incredible, and you're telling me that I'm going to look like this for a very long time?'

'I don't like to say forever, considering the crisis we are currently in the midst of, but essentially, yes. You are reborn Gwen, quite literally. You have become the epitome and living embodiment of Nature. The sap that flows through your body now will perpetually rejuvenate you, you are as perfect as you can be and will stay that way for as long as the Earth endures - which won't be much longer unless we don't get down to business. After all, there was a reason this was done to you, and it wasn't so you could gaze at yourself all day after a holistic makeover.' Gwen felt the gentle rebuke by a warming of her cheeks.

'You're right, I'm sorry, I've been incredibly selfish about all of this. Chucking my toys *way* out of the pram. It's been all about me hasn't it.' The rhetorical question wasn't lost on the girls, they nodded sadly. 'All I've thought about is what I've lost, not what the rest of humanity stands to lose. So...' Gwen stood straighter, more determined than any other time she could recall, 'I've accepted my fate, my destiny or whatever it is I have now, so I guess it's about time you told me what it is that is expected of me.' Without thinking, Gwen made to sit down. Used to having her sofas in the store. As she moved, several roots rose up from the soil and tied themselves into a chair shape. A slightly surprised Gwen sat in her makeshift furniture. Giving it a quick once over she tried to create the same for the girls. Two more chairs wove themselves into existence and the girls sat.

'Very good Gwen, it is as well you are a quick study. Let's hope you adapt as well away from your grove.' For the next hour Gwen badgered them about *'her grove'* and where her new power would be the strongest.

And they in turn broke the news to her about the nature of her quest. This stemmed the tide of her questions like a tap being abruptly turned off. All the elation that had started to stir her in ways she had never dreamt of - well actually *had* dreamt of but never expected them to come anywhere near true - evaporated like so much smoke. Her very natural high came crashing down around her ears. She mentally weighed up the implications of what they told her, her mind turning over like a book having its pages flipped. But not on any one of them could she see the answer she so desperately sought. Within several heartbeats, she had run out of options. Gwen began to pace the grove. Her once more bare feet sluffing through the wet grass at the edge of the pool. With a nervous habit she had never let go, Gwen began to chew on her little finger. The enormity of what they had just asked of her began to assert itself and her earlier panic started to rise in her breast again, threatening to stop her breathing altogether.

'I have absolutely no idea where to start!' Gwen finally blurted out to the girls who had waited patiently for their friend, but this wasn't the news they wanted to hear.

'You have to know something Gwen,' Jen protested 'you were the chosen one for the Earth, does nothing stir in your memory now? What with all you've gained, has it not unlocked the answer?' Both Jen and Maddy, for the first time Gwen could recall, looked concerned, genuinely concerned. Gwen was stunned, angry and terrified all at once and not for the first time she realized. *The ups and downs of this are more likely to kill me than anything at this bloody rate. Get a grip Gwen old girl, breathe, that's first.* She took several long deep calming breathes. Regulating her erratic heartbeat and relaxing suddenly bunched muscles. Slumping down on a mossy pad, Gwen tried to tackle it from another direction.

'How is it that you don't know its whereabouts?' Gwen asked the girls 'Or for that matter, how is it the Earth herself doesn't know? Surely of any of us, it would be her.' Gwen looked desperately between the two but they only shook their heads sadly to the negative.

'Crap!' Gwen spat suddenly angry 'Well I just don't know. How do you hide something like that?' Gwen had started to fidget again, putting her left foot on top of her right, monkey fashion, toes gripping the other foot. That was the least obvious sign of Gwen's agitation; the more blatant indication was the undulating and writhing foliage that was giving the forest a malevolent demeanor. Reflecting its mistress's anxiety.

'Gwen, you must understand, it was hidden long before the Earth grew to the sentience she now possesses.' Maddy had stood and had picked up the pacing started by Gwen. 'She hid it to protect herself from just this type of predicament,' Maddy tried to explain 'let's face it, if it was that easy to find, we probably wouldn't be having this discussion now, nor would the Adversary be in the position he - through pure ill fortune - finds himself in.' There was no denying the logic to hiding the damn thing, but some clue would be useful, Gwen thought, her irritation just making the forest rustle all the more.

'It's amazing really isn't it, when you get right down to it. You railroaded me in to this big transformation...' they started to protest but Gwen held up a silencing hand and they held back their expected argument 'I've sacrificed my humanity, my life and everything I was to assist in this great calamity, only to find that the one thing you had me do it for, puts us absolutely no further forward than we were before we did it. Why didn't you just ask me before? I could have told you then I had no idea.' The venom was taken out of the comment by the beatific smile Gwen wore. She knew that she had reached a point where rollercoaster had reached the end of the ride. Beset by irony and conflict on all sides, she knew the only way forward was going to be a physical search. Whatever clues or ideas she might have, would have to be tackled by her direct presence. And that meant a serious amount of travelling in a decreasingly short time. It really was *how long a piece of string was*. The Adversary could complete whatever it was he was up to at any moment. Then what? The End? Just like that?

Sitting for what seemed like hours, though in truth it was only a few moments. Gwen tried to formulate a plan. She had to put on a brave front, for there really was no going back now, a thought that made her stomach flip. She was good at ignoring what she didn't like and press on with what she did. Stubborn and mule headed had been a couple of the names she'd had applied to her. There wasn't much to like here, the end of the world and all that, but it was, for the moment at least, outweighed by things that she did like. Certainly for the time being the benefits she had gained would help her deal with what she didn't have, which was an answer.

Her mother always said that first things were first. She wasn't going to go searching anywhere unless she got a handle on what she could do. Adversary or no, she needed at least rudimentary capabilities if she was to get by out in the big bad world. That meant trying the shape shifting thing that the girls had mentioned. After all, if things were as bad as they made out, there probably weren't any planes flying. Not commercial ones anyway. So birds might not be a bad place to start. Resolved. For now, Gwen stood and approached Maddy with a determination she didn't fully feel, but was adamant that she would be seen as having. Stopping before the girls, legs braced and arms folded.

'Right then, we're not going to do much sitting on our collective arses and blowing smoke up mine to make me feel better. There are some things you need to show me if we're to go gadding about on this wild goose chase.' Another crash.

'We?' Jen and Maddy looked surprised for a second before their grim visage took over again. 'Sorry Gwen, but there are other matters that we have to attend to; this quest will be yours alone. We won't be coming with you.' If the rugs beneath Gwen were as numerous as cat's lives, then she was on her last legs. Just when she thought that she was over the big shocks. *Wrong again, maybe I ought to just expect the worst of everything every time, that way I won't be disappointed. This is* not *going the way I had planned.*

'Marvelous. Kick me a bit more why don't you. How long did you two have to get used to what you are? A bit longer than me I bet. This is getting ridiculous, back forth and back again. Its bloody well like passing your driving test on a Monday and on Tuesday, being told you have to chauffeur the Royal Family around, in an unfamiliar car on foreign roads, I mean, how do you handle something like that? - I'll tell you how' Gwen continued 'Not very bloody well that's how.' Her mood didn't improve when they just smiled at her. *That's all they bloody well seem to do, smile at me like I'm some kind of pet that's learning to perform its tricks. I'm not some performing seal or the like.* And Gwen told them so.

'Well I'm not a pet, do you hear me? I'm not. Stop grinning like that - it's driving me round the pissin' bend. What?' she growled 'What do you find so amusing *now?*'

'What else? You - you ditzy object. What are you blathering on about pets, we know you're not one of them; they do as they're told. But *that's* not in your make-up is it?' Gwen shook her head in tacit agreement, though she felt slightly manipulated at that point and her suspicious nature took over again.

'What are you getting at then, what are you saying now? I'm having a moment here, and I can't figure out why don't you take me seriously anymore?'

'We do Gwen, believe me we do' Maddy and Jen flanked Gwen and herded her to the center of the clearing 'that's why we think you'll make a formidable Dragon. You need to know your secondary form; it's who you are now.' It hadn't even occurred to Gwen that she would have to assume this other shape. Her mind had accepted the fact but only on a tenuous, sort of surreal kind of way. The abrupt change of subject put her off her pace. They were good at reading her moods and steering her back on course. Gwen nodded her agreement and let Maddy continue her *lesson*. 'So why don't I go first, then you try to copy me, okay?' But for Gwen's nervous annoyance, she couldn't help but be thrilled at the prospect of *'going dragon'*. Her stomach started to turn somersaults and she found herself grinning like a simpleton. This was the first time since her *cocooning* - as she had come to think of it - that she had seen the dragon forms of her companions. Other than being incredibly exciting, it would still the final nagging doubt in the back of her mind. The one that said she was hallucinating after too many wild mushrooms.

In less time than it took to think her thoughts, Maddy had swiftly executed her change. Gwen was impressed at the speed she had done it. *God! I'll never do it that quick. I'll probably end up looking like a big iguana or something.* Inwardly amused and terrified at the same time, Gwen walked out into the clearing. Looking around her to see if she had enough room. Mentally, and without any direct intent, she imagined the trees moving back out of the way, and to her total amazement, that's just what they did. Amidst rustling and crackling of branches and leaves, about sixty feet of tree line backed up creating a much wider clearing. A voice in her head spoke clearly to her as though the speaker were at her ear. It spoke words of encouragement and was accompanied by a very strong sensation of love. Warmth and affection that mere words had no conception of. It swathed Gwen in an aura of well-being and made her breast swell with a love and pride of equal intensity.

'Your mastery of your new abilities is so instinctive Gwen, well done, bear that in mind in future, for it will aid you more than rational thought. Let your intuition guide you. Perhaps that knows where you will need to concentrate your search.' It was Jens gentle southern tones that spoke to her. It put her in mind of the difference in her old radio, of how the sound was monotone and flat, whereas the voice in her mind came through in nine point one surround sound. It was almost four dimensional.

'For now though' she continued, her tone firming ever so slightly. 'I want you to concentrate on Maddy, close your eyes and visualize her in your mind, picture every scale, every muscle, horn and fang. Create an image in your mind; of course, you'll want to pick your shade. Green I expect, but the details are yours Mon Cherie, but once you have it fixed firmly in your mind...' Jens voice was fluid, as watery and musical as the rivers she presided over, it was almost hypnotic but it held Gwen's full attention and she focused on every nuance and magical syllable as it echoed within her skull.

'Okay, I've got the image there, I can see it. It's looking right at me with those glorious golden swirling eyes you have, and its long reptilian tongue is flicking out at me, tasting the air.' Gwen felt Jens mind touch again, soft yet powerful, it was as though her mind could snuff her out with barely a cross thought so potent was its presence.

'…and once you have the image there - move your consciousness into it. Imagine you are behind those golden eyes and looking out. Take a deep breath and fill your lungs with the sweet woodland air, taste the multitude of scents that abound. Be the Dragon Gwen; Be it.' Gwen opened her eyes and after a sudden rush of vertigo passed her by, she realized that she was, or at least her head was some considerable distance off the ground.

'*Oh - my - God!*' Gwen thought back out to the girls, or at least so she hoped 'this is just bloody fantastic.' She swung her own massive head around to check herself out. She flapped her wings experimentally and much to her joy and surprise, they flapped. Her tremendous forelegs were like her arms and she inspected the sword length talons on her car sized feet. It took her another good hour of this scrutiny to fully acquaint herself with her new form. But once she had given herself a thorough inspection Gwen felt pleasantly comfortable as the huge fern green, blue spiral patterned Earth Dragon.

'So this is what I am now? At my cellular level, I'm genetically a Drakarim?'

'You most certainly are Gwen Môn petit, a most impressive one at that, well done.' Jen swiftly adopted her own ice white Dragon form and there - for the first time in the history of the solar system, and of this sequence of planets, the trinity of Avatars were together, standing as one in the first sacred grove of the Avatar of Nature.

The atmosphere was palpable, charged with raw primal power. The air became thick with the magic emanating from the three. They were living conduits to the Earth herself and the power she wielded; even in her weakened state it was cosmically spectacular. The devastating force of the oceans, the winds and of the volcanoes and mountains. She could feel it all thrumming through her bones. She was connected to these forces in a tangible and very real way. Intuitively feeling her own power. That of every living thing that swam, crawled, walked and flew. Everything that grew from the living soil. Every single blade of grass to every fragrant blossoming flower on the vine in the highest tree of the most distant jungle. She felt connected to her core. She expanded to the size of the planet in an instant only to shrink to the size of a grain of sand in the next. She experienced the microcosm and the macrocosm in as many heartbeats as it took to say it.

Gwen lost track of time as the images flowed through her and around her. Binding her to all she saw. From the most diminutive and minute to the most expansive, she touched it all. Gwen knew then more than she had ever known anything in her brief life, that nothing was insignificant, that everything was an intrinsic part of the weave. The warp and weft of the delicately balanced collection of life on Earth. And if she thought that was sufficient to blow her mind, she hadn't counted on the Earth herself making her presence known. There was a concussive shockwave like she had stood on a nuclear warhead and it had gone off beneath her. The wave resonated up her legs and with a blinding flash in her mind, she felt and saw *all* the dragon lines that permeated the Earth, the lines of force and life giving power that mortals termed 'ley', taken from the old English term, but were nothing less than the veins of the mother. Gwen wanted to express her joy, astonishment, elation and wonder in words, but she couldn't find any that could do what she was experiencing justice. What came from her was nothing short of a cry of exultation, torn from her gigantic lungs and ripped from her throat that sent every bird skyward and stopped creatures dead in their tracks for hundreds of miles around. The town's folk in nearby Santa Fe, Albuquerque and even distant Brazil stopped, curious as to the ululation that raised the flesh on the arms of those that heard it and felt it. It was the first cry of the Earth Avatar and its sound would resonate out for all time, as the shockwave from her cry rippled out over the planet's surface, connecting with every living thing out there, bonding and binding with all on a cellular level - touching everything on the Earth before cascading off and out into the cosmos.

Far away upon the Jezreel plain, a massive contingent of Chdrn'OmThophilim gathered. Angels to mortal kind, phased out of density so the desert looked empty but there they stood, readying themselves for battle. Raphael and Uriel stopped what they were doing as the shockwave rippled through their camp and they all looked to each other for an explanation but nothing presented itself except a feeling of well-being and a sense of promise.

Jen and Maddy, in their draconian forms, stood back a step from Gwen in a sign of both respect for her ascendance and out of awe for the untapped wellspring of unadulterated power Gwen seemingly possessed and bowed their heads in acknowledgement. It demonstrated yet another factor that was unprecedented for they truly had no idea of her limits or potential. Nor at that moment did Gwen. Swept along as she was by the outpouring of emotion and energy from the Earth. It built within her like a pressure cooker and Gwen knew of no way to expel it before she exploded. The only thing she could think of was to bunch her muscular hind legs, extend her huge leathery wings, veiny membranes catching the minutest of breezes, she flexed her talons and with an explosive thrust, she shot herself skyward. So fast she created several sonic booms as she tore through the sky. Upwards and upwards she screamed - only stopping when the sky turned from a vibrant blue to the hazy black of space itself.

Coming to her senses somewhat, Gwen was exhilarated at her new found abilities and the connection forged with the planet and all upon it. With that connection however, came a new feeling. A profound sense of purpose and possessiveness. This was *her* world. The Adversary, if he did but know it, had made a powerful new enemy this day and Gwen vowed to herself as she soared high just above the atmosphere of her world, that she would do all she could to thwart the machinations of this demonic pretender.

*Return to us Gwen!* The twin voices of Jen and Maddy reverberated through her skull, with - she noted, a hint of concern coloring their call. Reluctantly and relishing the power of flight, Gwen arrowed downwards towards her grove and the clearing way beneath her. Of course, it never occurred to her that she would send no end of military installations into a tail spin as they tracked her sudden arrival and subsequent disappearance. As though they didn't have enough problems already. Poor old New Mexico had yet another Roswell in the making. She was a UFO alright - the *ultimate flying object*. Gwen thought wryly.

Returning to her grove and making a better landing than she thought she would considering the fact she had never done it before. It wasn't something she had considered when the moment inspired her impromptu flight but instinct and innate intuition made her look like an expert. Once on the ground though, Jen and Maddy spent the rest of the afternoon with her practicing some of the more peculiar shapes she might employ. Birds, fish, insects and even plants. Mostly in the hope that her intuition might provide some insight into the nature of her quest and where that which she must seek might be found. But nothing presented itself. The sun eventually set on the most strange, yet amazing day of Gwen's life. She only hoped she lived long enough to appreciate the sweet memory. A memory she would treasure in the dark days to come.

The trinity relaxed by the pool in the clearing, Gwen was quite adept by now at adjusting her clothing and she had been having a mighty fine time donning various ensembles to find one she felt '*Avatarish*' in, but she couldn't decide on any one thing. So, settling for her own clothes for the time being, she munched on an apple - kindly provided by the forest along with a number of other woodland delicacies - and asked the question that had had been haunting her.

'Tell me again, just so I can get it fixed in my mind what it is I've got to find. I've tried to think about throughout this afternoon but I keep coming up blank.' Maddy swiped the dribbles from a particularly juicy nectarine, from her lips before speaking. The little humanistic trait made Gwen chuckle. Such human mannerisms from two creatures so otherworldly and powerful that they seemed so out of place now.

'It is simply Gwen, nothing other than the First Tree. The original tree that seeded all that we now have. The tree that appears throughout human culture. The tree of life, tree of knowledge, Yggdrasil the world tree, so on and so on are based upon this one. The one and only tree that can kill or cure the Earth depending on who finds it first. We pray that it be you Gwen.'

*So do I.* Bombarding the girls with questions about the whys and the hows after an hour bore no more fruit either about its previous locations and why the Earth herself didn't know its whereabouts. Gwen mulled over what and where she might have to go to locate such a thing. The enormity of the task and what they expected of her was almost overwhelming and the prospect of scouring thousands of square miles of jungle for one tree didn't fill her with joy either. *There has to be a way, or a place, something we've missed. Something that has slipped from the records. Knowing my bloody luck it'll be in somewhere obscure like Atlantis or Avalon or some such and look how much luck humanity have had in finding them.* Gwen snorted in disgust. *Instinct they say, well, they obviously don't know my track record with that particular ability, or lack thereof, though I suppose I ought to have more faith in it now, all things considered.*

At some point during the conversation, Jen excused herself. Citing an important errand that needed attending to. Jen crossed over to Gwen and hugged her; long and with an intensity that brought a lump to Gwen's throat and a knot of panic to her stomach. It was the type of hug that friends did when they thought they would never see each other again. Where was she going? Or equally importantly, where did she think Gwen was going? When they broke apart, Gwen held on to her newly acquired sister tightly and looked her straight in her cobalt blue eyes, searching for some meaning to this display of parting.

'You are coming back, right?' Gwen asked, her voice catching as she spoke, tripping over the emotions that she barely held in check. But Jen smiled, almost reassuringly and hugged her again.

'I hope so, though if I do, you may not be here when that happens Gwen. Don't forget that you too have an important mission to undertake now and I doubt you'll be able to complete it without leaving this grove. But I've done all I can to prepare you, so too has Maddy, and you mustn't be afraid if we have to part. This is war Gwen, with cataclysmic consequences and we must do all we can. I have to find Raphael now and bring him up to date on you and your role now in the fabric of the cosmos. Your arrival will hearten the warriors and fill them with renewed hope in the times ahead. You do understand don't you Gwen? Please tell me you do.' Putting it that way, Gwen did, she realized slowly she was having an irrational reaction to the separation. It was just the thought of setting off alone with all new abilities and no-one to guide her while she learnt just what she was capable of. They had learnt from birth over aeons, she had only days. Maddy joined the pair and an emotional group hug ensued. There were tears; but eventually even they abated and they stood back from each other. 'If there are two of us together, any two we have enough power to communicate anywhere any this world Gwen, as we just called to you. So occasionally I expect we'll be able to catch up wherever we are' Gwen nodded, reassured by that hope. Acceptance had been reached then and Jen, backed up and took her silvery white dragon form, and with a last meaningful and love filled look from the great swirling golden eyes Jen spoke privately to Maddy 'I'm going to have to employ some serious magic as Raphael is some nine hours ahead and they'll have questions as to Gwen's shockwave. I'm going to have to warp time a little to arrive there shortly after they experience it, I'll do it high so not to draw too much attention.' Jen knew what she was doing was risky and rarely done. 'Use the magnetic field between the moon and the Earth, that'll help you warp the time differential without draining yourself.' Maddy advised, being the more arcane savvy of the two of them and Jen nodded, reassured as she bunched herself up and launched herself skyward so fast, to the eye, one minute she was there, the next she was gone. Just the rustle of leaves and swaying of branches as she tore past them, marked her passing.

Gwen had a thought then as the image of Jen was lost even to her now extraordinary Drakarim sight, or perhaps it was more of an urge, maybe it wasn't even her thought but the subtle intimation of the earth herself -

but the result was the same. *I need to meditate.* Gwen concluded somewhere *and see what this alleged intuition they rate so highly comes up with. This grove is spot on for that. Maybe my subconscious knows more than its letting on, otherwise I've no bloody idea where to start. And I'll need to get my nose into some books too before I embark on this wild tree chase.* Gwen knew a trip to her store would be a first port of call. *The girls pray that I'm the one who finds it,* Gwen repeated their earlier hope to herself but *at this point, no one's praying bloody harder than me.*

# Chapter 6

## Quaesta

After Jen's departure, leaving Gwen tearful and Maddy contemplative together in the grove, Gwen started thinking seriously about what lay before her At first she thought about how her quest was going to start before the realization hit her - with a sinking feeling like a lead weight in her belly - that she had more than started already. The mind blowing transformation and the revelations of the past few days had been integral to her journey; to simply cap it all - all she needed to do was to actually go somewhere for the quest to be fully on. For all her pacing and nervous fidgeting around the grove, chewing her lip and fiddling with her hair, it wasn't the same as making those first steps out in the world. There would be a massive distinction between her little steps here and the first monumental, physical steps upon her journey. A part of her mind rationalized that it was a very normal and human psychological barrier. The anticipation of a thing was nearly always far worse than the thing itself, though probably not in this case Gwen mused. Her imagination conjured no end of disastrous scenarios, each more horrific than the one preceding it. Of course, reality was now a whole new ball game.

The basis of her quandary was that man, the voracious explorer that he was, had been just about everywhere in the comparatively short time he had been on the earth. There were few places left that had not been colonized or interfered with in some way by him - so how had this tree remained hidden for so long? Quite literally, where on earth could it be? Maddy seemed to sit patiently as Gwen muttered and mumbled to herself, organizing her thoughts into something that she hoped resembled some sort of coherent and cohesive plan. She didn't think she was doing very well. The serene Avatar of the Earths Mountains and minerals, fire and flame, sat upon the ground lost in her own thoughts, her long tanned legs curled beneath her demurely, and the blades of lush green grass brushing gently against her flawless skin. Maddy leant upon one hand, head tilted slightly so her lustrous locks of flaming auburn hair cascaded over one shoulder, with her free hand she swished it through the grass as though she were draping it in a lightly flowing, if rather green river. She had issues of her own to sift through and welcomed the tranquility of the grove to do so, though for all Maddy and Gwen were both lost in their respective musings, they both knew that they didn't have the luxury of a lot of time to muse with.

When Gwen got nervous or thoughtful about an impending situation, she got hungry. That illogical sensation that said food would solve everything. Ah, but what sort of food? That was the question. Her first thought was a large tub of her favorite chocolate chip ice cream, but she didn't think she could rustle up any Ben and Jerry's out here. Plan B came without thinking. Snaking from the woods came a thick branch, laden with lush, juicy looking grapes of varying hues, swinging ponderously as it dangled its bunched fruit just where it would be comfortable for her to reach it. Gwen picked one bunch for herself and one for Maddy. Once she had what she needed, the branch receded and vanished back into the woodland once more. Rising easily and strolling over to her friend, she proffered the fruit which Maddy, looking up and smiling, took graciously. Of course, it hadn't occurred to Gwen that neither of the women actually required to take sustenance this way anymore, she supposed that some old habits died harder than others.

'Thank-you Gwen, this looks lovely,' Maddy popped one casually into her mouth and her eyes widened instantly in pleasant surprise. She had another then another, chewing and swallowing before speaking again. Gwen had done much the same. She couldn't believe what she had in her hand was simply a grape. So sweet were they and the juice was a nectar that would have revived the dead, she was sure of it.

'Gwen, this has to be the best fruit I have ever had, and I've had plenty I can tell you. This is a testament to your worthiness as the third Avatar Gwen, well done and let's not imagine what the wine these would make would be like.' The thought made them both smile.

'Thanks, I think, but I didn't do it consciously again,' Gwen was a little miffed with herself for that oversight 'I just thought of fruit because I couldn't manage ice cream and this vine of grapes appeared, how's that for weird?'

'It's not weird Gwen, this is your grove and unlike anywhere on the entire planet, it is more attuned to your will than you can possibly imagine. It knows what you require as your mind first thinks of the requirement. It is attuned to your every fiber as much as your arms and legs are, they respond to your will just the same way.' Gwen looked both happy and incredibly sad at the same time, causing Maddy to frown with sudden concern. She asked if she was alright and Gwen nodded she was, yet she still looked forlorn.

'There are moments Maddy' Gwen embellished at seeing the expression on Maddy's face 'much like this Maddy, when I think it's all just too much and I'm going to wake any moment and find it all a fantastic dream; I've been having that feeling since I left New York as close as I can remember at the moment. It leaves me feeling like a newborn child, or a foal who is learning to walk for the first time, all wobbly and overawed by absolutely everything. I've no idea of the extent of just what I am now capable of and that frightens me just as much – if not more - as the prospect of failure and all that entails frightens the bejeebers out of me.' Maddy just sat silent and listened, trying to understand how she felt, but it had been so long since she had been born to her own role as Avatar, though she was already Drakarim, that she now believed that she had always been this way and never had to experience what Gwen was now feeling, it was an alien concept to her.

'I mean...' Gwen wavered as she carried on '...think about it. I'm a Dragon and so are you, now don't get me wrong, that's so fantastic I can't even imagine words suitable to describe the feeling. But, and there is a *but*, who else can I tell? Where could I go now as a dragon? There aren't any conventions for enormous supernatural reptiles are there?' It was rhetoric and Maddy just let her get it off her chest. Gwen wasn't finished either.

'For all I am capable of that could help humanity' Gwen bemoaned ever so slightly 'I have to keep it a secret. Who could I tell who'd even believe me anyhow? I could show them but mark my words, within hours or less I'd be hunted by the very people I'm trying to protect; desperate to either catch me, kill me or cut me up to see what just makes me tick.' Now Maddy knew this for a truth. A young but heavily afflicted Drakareth had crash landed in its iron based geode back in July '47, just outside Roswell New Mexico. The occupant was sadly but luckily dead upon arrival and were it not for the swift intervention of the Seraphim Collective, matters may have turned out differently. Instead, they left the government focused on a new idea; that of space aliens instead. A harmless diversion...or so they thought. Gwen's voice popped the bubble she had slipped into 'It's what they do for some peculiar reason, nice eh?' Maddy said no not really, for she knew the truth of it. All she had to do was remember that Roswell incident. The outcome was less than discreet and several members of the human race had to be *tampered* with for want of a better description to muddy their memory of events, not something they liked to do. A total wipe would have caused irreparable damage and that was unacceptable, but the partial wipe had caused as much disruption as if they had simply removed everyone concerned. The absence of several hundred people would be easier to gloss over than the muddle they were left with. The resulting confusion had only fired the human's naturally suspicious nature all the more, making them even more unstable. So on this matter, Maddy sympathized with Gwen.

'Looks like you know what I'm saying,' Gwen observed noting Maddy's thoughtful expression 'it's all amazing but bloody pointless for day to day stuff. In fact, I probably feel even lonelier than I did before in an abstract sort of way, being so different from humanity now. Because I'm not am I? I'm a...what was it again? Drakarim? I just look like a human. Damn, now I know how that Clark Kent feels. I used to think he whined too much about being alien, but now I see where he's coming from. There's a lot to be said about that trouble shared thing.' It made Maddy thoughtful, for the realized that she had never been without the company of Jen, even though they had been worlds apart on occasion, she was always there. Gwen was new to this and still felt the solitude she had known before as a mortal. There was no easy answer, it was something she would either learn to live with or not. Maddy hoped it would be the former, for her sake.

Gwen ate her fruit then, letting silence now reinforce her words. She bathed in the lake that now surrounded her tree island, the water was surprisingly warm. Gwen ran through several clothes changes before some hours later, finally reaching her decision.

'I think it's time I... that is' she corrected quickly 'we, take a little trip back to town.' Gwen had, for all her changes, finally settled on her good old favorites. Tight fitting faded jeans, the ones with the torn knees, tucked into her fawn colored Ugs, topped off with her soft angora, fern green sweater, the one with the low neck and flowers embroidered on to it. To complete her look, she added a necklace of moss agate with a silver ivy leaf design chain. She rarely went anywhere without one of her myriad of necklaces and pendants gracing her throat. Why should being a dragon be any exception she thought wryly. Her change, though didn't come without sensations. She got the feeling that she was visiting someone else's life now. That surreal feeling people got when they visited the sets of TV shows they followed. The transition from years of watching, to actually touching the reality of it was too much for some people. That separation from fantasy to reality and back to fantasy again blew their minds. Gwen was about to visit a world she would never know in the same way again. For she had been on first name terms with many of the residents of Santa Fe, now, she felt like a stranger.

It was Maddy who pointed out a relevant point to the new Nature Avatar.

'Are we going to walk all the way back, on two legs I mean? I take it you remember the walk up here and how long that took, even after driving to the car park.'

How could she forget, it was the night her world had changed irrevocably.

'I hadn't really thought about it to be honest, what did you have in mind?'

Maddy laughed her rich and throaty laugh, the one that had the boys drooling after her back in town. With a toss of her fiery hair, Maddy stood, held both arms out before her and fell forward, as though she were about to do push-ups. Except by the time she landed on what used to be her hands, she had flowed into the sleek and russet coated form of a long legged timber wolf. Ears pricked and tail wagging playfully, the deep, golden brown eyes regarded Gwen with an inherent intelligence. But it was Maddy's voice issuing from its fang filled mouth that made her start.

'This might be a more suitable form for running through the forest don't you think?' She flowed again into the form of a muscular and fine limbed deer. 'Or this perhaps? You choose, but the exercise will do us some good I think. A good run will work wonders for your muscles, and after all, your muffin top does need some work.' Gwen's mouth fell open in horror and indignation at the accusation. She pulled her sweater up and investigated, paranoia that Maddy had seen something she hadn't filling her.

There was, as she thought, no such thing. She was a petite size eight with an ideal figure for her stature, if anything, a pound or two wouldn't have been noticed on her lean frame.

'You cheeky cow!' The Avatar of Nature chided. But Gwen smiled to lessen the insult and show she could take it. But Maddy was right about one thing. A good run would help her. She knew how energized she felt after one of her infrequent gym visits. Things had a way of clarifying themselves that only hours before had seemed impossible to fathom.

'You're on, but go back to the wolf look, I like that; here, let me have a go.' Gwen concentrated, and she too shimmered and flowed, dropping to all fours. Her own honey blonde coat shone with a vitality that was reflected in her emerald eyes. Her pink tongue lolling from the side of her panting mouth. Maddy gave her a once over, scenting her a couple of

207

times then howling an approval. Gwen spun a couple of times and howled back excitedly. Getting the hang of her form. But Maddy had seen enough and was keen to go the desire to run was growing stronger.

'That's enough preening, Gwen, now are you up for a little race? Last one to town is a lizard!' With that, Maddy bunched her powerful hind quarters and bounded off. Gwen didn't even have the time to say that she already *was* a big lizard. As Maddy's tail vanished into the undergrowth. A second's hesitation and Gwen leapt away, bounding off, hot in pursuit of her friend. Catching the odd glimpse of the rusty wolf dodging and loping with a relaxed grace. Gwen had to concentrate to just keep up, but as the miles sailed by, it became easier and she even began to catch up.

Which was fortunate, for they drew close to the wall of thorns and deadly protective brambles. Gwen could see the lethal tendrils snaking and writhing amongst themselves as she neared. Not even a mosquito was going to get past that barrier without running afoul of her guardians. *Now that's my idea of a burglar alarm.* But she needn't have worried, for as the two loping and speeding wolves came within range of the lashing barbs, the barrier simply parted before them as though someone had drawn back a curtain. They bounded through and loped on. Not before hearing the bear-trap closing of the barrier behind them. It sounded as though it were made of steel rather than wood. But putting it almost immediately from her mind, Gwen once again lost herself in the exhilaration of the run. Tongue lolling, ears back and legs stretching out, Gwen and Maddy raced on. Soon arriving at and passing through the empty car park and onwards towards town. It took a little while, but Gwen began to notice the subtle shift in the weather and the temperature. Since leaving the balmy and temperate climate of her grove, the winter that should have blanketed everywhere began to reassert itself. It didn't affect her, but she was aware of it. The crisp clean smells of the snow covered woodland soon faded to the more disquieting aromas of the town. Her heightened wolf senses picked up as they drew closer that all was not as it should be. There was a foul stench in the air. The smell of death and corruption. Putrescence and decomposition were all around them as they reached the town limits. They stopped together, all thoughts of their race forgotten in an instant. Resuming their own forms, Gwen and Maddy stood in the middle of the street and looked about them. Silence deafened them. The absence of the usual noises, of the hustle and bustle of daily activity. Cars, music, people, trucks and so many other day to day becoming evening and night sounds. Their absence was totally alien for the time of day it was.

'Is it just me Maddy or this definitely not right?' Gwen asked sniffing the air curiously 'That smell, its rank even for my human nose. Like something, or a lot of somethings have died and just been left out in the sun to rot.' Maddy was looking all around her, one hand shading her eyes against the light, the other resting upon her hip.

'No, you're not wrong Gwen, but I can't see anything from down here. Look, let's take wing and slip up to the church tower by the square, see if we can't get a better view from up there.' Seconds later, two dark bodied crows flapped slowly upwards, catching the weak thermals still inherent in the cooling day and rising smoothly. Granting them a much better over view of the streets below and what was - or as it turned out, wasn't - going on. The streets were barren. Totally bereft of life. They glided high enough to avoid detection, but still able to see clearly. But the only thing that saw clearly, was the number of fires that must be raging, for there were several plumes of black smoke roiling up from no end of buildings. Where were the damn fire department? Why wasn't anyone doing anything?

They settled upon the tower and watched for a few minutes. But there was nothing to see or hear. It was as though all the people had been evacuated and nothing was left but an empty shell, the ghost of civilization. Gwen turned to Maddy and said one word.

'Dolores.' The meaning was not lost on Maddy as they both took wing and flapped off, heading as the crow truly flew, directly towards Earth Angel. The one place that Dolores might be if she and her Grand-mother hadn't fled town already like everyone else seems to have done. The sensation that she was flying towards her shop came and went as she realized that she owned nothing anymore. Not even her own life, it was the tool of the earth now, for her to do with as she saw fit. That aside, it still grated a little. It was always harder to fully let go of something the more it meant to you. Earth Angel meant an awful lot to Gwen, it had been her salvation, giving her purpose and an identity for the first time, and she would never forget that. Alighting gently upon Old Man Travis's roof, which was the store opposite hers. A general hardware store that had been there almost as long as the town itself, it was rumored that so had Old man Travis himself, he looked like a walnut in dungarees' and nobody knew his true age. He just always seemed to have been there.

Though the moment they settled upon the ridge of the roof and gazed down upon Earth Angel, they got at least one answer. Not everyone had left town. It seemed that about a hundred of them were milling around some twenty feet from the shop front. What looked odd - or odder still, considering the circumstances - was that they were all intent upon the shop, but every time someone reached out to get closer, a flash of blue sparks would flare up and the person would recoil their hand as though it had been burnt. Watching this happen every few moments as differing people tried to get closer, sent shivers of icy dread up Gwen's spine. This wasn't right. Focusing her sharp corvids gaze upon the scenario, Gwen noticed that there was a shimmering kind of heat haze emanating from the ground, directly before the clamoring horde. It was that what prevented the people from getting any closer, *but why? And equally how?* What was wrong with these people that they should be withheld from getting any nearer? Gwen got her answer before Maddy could point it out, for they both saw the same thing at the same time as several of the populace turned suddenly to stare straight at them. Then they screamed, an unearthly howl of rage and agony. Gwen couldn't have been more horrified. If she had hands, she would have clasped them over her mouth to prevent herself screaming and vomiting in equal proportions. Every single one had ripped their eyes from their heads, Gwen could see the ragged tears where nails had scoured the sockets, dragging the last vestiges of the squashy orbits clear. Their faces were drawn and sunken as though the life was being gradually sucked from them and as their flesh pulled tighter, so it tore at the weakest points and gaping wounds were rife. The smell of faeces and corruption was almost overwhelming as the breeze turned and sent wafts of their decay directly over Maddy and Gwen. They took off instantly, that or be overcome by the suddenness of the powerful stench. They banked around to the rear of the building and into the wind, letting the cooler, fresher air clear their heads.

Gwen spoke to Maddy, using their mind to mind method, for talking as a crow, flapping in the air and over the screams that had started below where the horde had seen them, was to just too hard.

'What's happened Maddy? What is wrong with them?' Alighting on a flat roof of a two storey building, before Maddy answered she resumed her own form and walked to the edge, leaning on the parapet, she leant over and looked down and around. Sure enough, her fears were realized as fifty of the filthy abominations that had once been the townsfolk, came scrambling into view, still pointing and screaming. Their hideously disfigured faces looking upwards towards the roof. Some began pounding on the doors and windows in an effort to get in and get to them, others were making futile leaps for the metal fire escape ladder that hung suspended several feet out of reach. Gwen went to see to make sure none made it and asked again.

'What are they Maddy? Talk to me! There's people down there who used to be friends of mine and yours, how could this have happened?' Maddy leant back, but still keeping an eye on them as well as one on the roof door as she spoke.

'Gwen, there is no easy answer to this. I've seen this before, but not on this scale for millennia. They are the possessed. Demons and minions of the Domain who are not yet strong enough to take corporeal form on this world, they cannot affect their own density. They take hosts of mortal kind. A type of insulation. A skin suit if you will. Their essence is still too powerful for the body to contain so it breaks down and rots. They generally tear the eyes out for mortal vision limits them, they see more without them if that makes any sense to you. Ramping up the pituitary gland they utilize the third eye capability that mortals have but rarely use. It enables them to see the auras of individuals. That's how they spotted us the way they did. We tend to glow a bit brighter than most.'

'So they're dead then?' Gwen asked, her mind filling with visions of what humanity had always considered possessed. All head spinning, pea soup spitting and growling. Not this, these were far too capable. Running and howling, and in packs too. That had to be bad.

'No, not dead yet at least, though they soon will be, the body can't last long before it fails completely and the minion has to cast about for another before it is pulled back to the Domain.' Maddy was cut short of her explanation by a pounding on the roof door.

'They're here! We would be a great prize for them, that's why they are so motivated in chasing us and getting to us. Any ideas?' Gwen had one as it turned out.

'I know it's risky, but I'm thinking that that fizzing barrier is only going to work on them, so let's drop down to the store and see what is causing it, cos I know it wasn't something I did.' The door slammed open with a tearing and ripping of hinges and several possessed flooded out. 'Now might be a good time too.' Maddy just nodded and ran for the ledge, jumping up smoothly and diving out into oblivion. Gwen was hot on her heels as Maddy transformed in mid-air to the crow form and flapped away. Gwen, a few seconds only behind her did the same just as the possessed leapt at her. Or at the spot she had occupied only a heartbeat earlier. With slightly less grace, Gwen dived over the edge, falling a few feet at first before affecting her change. Then the crow she became swooped over the surprised heads of the possessed below and she flapped away, catching up with the slowly circling Maddy. The possessed on the roof had been so close that their momentum had carried a few of them

211

over the edge to crash into their comrades in the alley below. The sickening crunch of bones snapping from the impacts still managed to reach Gwen as she flew higher and caused her to mentally wince.

Risking Gwen's idea, Maddy spiraled down to perch on the bench that sat upon the sidewalk in front of her store. The haze didn't affect them at all, as she hoped, but their arrival sent the possessed the other side of it into a frenzy. They threw themselves against the barrier with renewed vigor. As though their perseverance alone would be sufficient. The two crows – as Gwen joined Maddy – staring in amazement at the horde with their corvid's glossy black eyes for a few moments before hopping off the bench and returning to their human forms. Still watching the possessed, Gwen couldn't take her eyes off them. For now, all they were achieving was the speedier destruction of the mortal host they occupied as each burning flash seared more and more flesh from the bodies. Maddy looked askance to Gwen and saw she was crying. In a choked voice, Gwen turned to Maddy and asked.

'Isn't there something that can be done, this is awful?' Maddy shook her head resignedly. For the outcome was already determined.

'Unlike zombies Gwen, these people are still alive. Their bodies have been hi-jacked, their own souls suppressed. The moment a minion takes over, the body is as good as dead anyway. There is no such thing as exorcism for these, it's a placebo that your kind came up with to make themselves feel better, that somehow there was hope. There is only one way that a minion leaves its host. When that host eventually dies. Whilst they are in them, they are hard to kill, but not impossible. The host feels all the pain while the minion is insulated from it. To stop it, you have to kill the host. The minion escapes and all you've done is to kill an innocent. Truly diabolical. It is a sign of how advanced the Adversary is for so many possessed to be taken. If this is happening the world over, we are in more trouble than we first realized. All they need to do is infiltrate the silos where your weapons of mass destruction are held and release them. It's a miracle they haven't yet, there has to be a reason he hasn't but I can't imagine what it is.' The smell of burning flesh began to assail Gwen's nostrils now as possessed after possessed threw themselves against the magical fiery barrier. She saw their charred remains fall to the ground simply to be replaced by new ones stepping on and over them to carry on where they left off. Frustration caused many to scream and howl until their throats tore from the exertion. Those that weren't screaming began to taunt and threaten. Their hideous voices bastardized the human's vocal chords and the result was a thousand times worse than fingernails down a chalk board. They suggested all manner of foul practices and obscenities. Now Gwen was fairly unshockable, but they were getting very graphic and very creative, to the point even Gwen had to put her fingers in her ears to quell the torrent of abuse.

'Why do they have to get all nasty like that?' Gwen asked snippily 'it isn't going to do them any good is it, don't they think we have our own share of sexual deviants to spout this vitriol?'

'Where do you think your deviants get their ideas from?' Maddy spoke calmly but what she implied was horrendous. 'There are two types of possession. What you see here is known as greater possession, where the host is subsumed completely, lesser possession is more like whispers in your ear, voices in your mind. Voices that will sound just like you. Making you think it was your idea all along. Dreams that fill your thoughts with depravity and sickness until you accept them as reality. Humanity has never been any good at identifying these tortured souls. In one time they were banished, another they were executed, another burnt at wooden poles, stoned and any other number of equally hideous torments. These simply added to their own inner torments and helped not at all. Now of course, you have all manner of long winded names for them. Categorizing them as different mental illnesses - when in fact many of them truly *are* hearing voices - and pumping them full of drugs to try to *cure* them. They can't be cured. Once they are in, that's it. They are very parasitic. Then, like a time bomb, they wait to go off.' Maddy stopped talking, her voice just fading away as she looked at the minions, killing themselves to get at them. She too had tears cascading down her cheeks as she stared, helplessly at the people she was sworn to protect and knowing there was nothing she could do for them. Death was just a matter of time and that would be their only release.

Standing there for the few minutes they had, drew some other attention to them. The door to the store burst open and a very relieved looking Dolores came crashing out. All bar flying into the arms of first Gwen, then Maddy. But her relief and joy soon turned to despair as she looked beyond them to see the forms of the terrifyingly determined possessed still trying to get in.

'Why do they not leave Gwen?' Dolores asked plaintively 'It has been three days now, I do not know if I can take much more of their inhuman cries.' True enough, panic was evident in her voice. 'Thankfully they haven't been able to get in, but nor can we leave. It is only by the grace of Great Spirit that Grand-mother was with me when whatever this is started. I understand what you told me Maddy but this...' Dolores gestured to the mob outside. 'I was not expecting.' Maddy turned her away from the possessed's efforts and guided both Dolores and Gwen back inside the store. Closing the door on their hateful and filthy cries.

'It is as though the spirits of the Dark Kachinas, such as the ogre and the more other vicious aspects have taken the souls of those poor people and now they seek to exact their revenge.' Dolores speculated 'The good spirits and the powers of the earth and harmony seem to be absent. A great darkness is coming and it suppresses the light.' Dolores spoke softly of her theory as she made tea. It wasn't that they needed tea, but it kept her hands busy and stopped them from shaking too much. They moved to the rear of the store and closed the inner storefront door. This was much more effective in silencing them. They were able to think a little clearer - it also allowed Gwen and Maddy to see Grand-mother Yellow Deer, who was reclining on the sofa that Gwen kept in the back room. More hugs and pats on the back as the old woman was just as pleased to see the girls all well, as the girls all were to see Dolores's grand-mother, though she looked decidedly less well than the last time Gwen had seen her. It made Gwen worry all the more for her fading health and although Gwen rarely spoke of her fears to Dolores, knowing it would upset her all the more as she was already beyond concerned, Gwen remained silent once more as Dolores was barely hanging on now as it was, Gwen could see it in her eyes and the tight set of her usually smiling mouth and how she wrung her hands over and over.

Over tea, Dolores explained, with the odd word and nod from Grand-mother Yellow Deer, that the townsfolk had started showing up a few days earlier, and at first, they just looked like they always did. Though they all had a sort of blank look to them, vacant and distant. It wasn't until the night of the first day they appeared that their faces started to change and the first sign came that there was some sort of barrier around the store. Those that stood within the perimeter were vaporized where they stood, those on the edge were blown back with the now familiar blue flames.

'Thank-you for giving us this shield, I do not know what we would have done without it.' Maddy looked confused, looking between Dolores and Grand-mother Yellow Deer. Gwen, was equally lost, looking between all of them.

'I'm sorry Dolores.' Maddy started. 'But we're not responsible for this, we thought you were.' Dolores shook her head and denied all knowledge of it. They were still looking for answers between them when the smoky spiral began to rise from the shop floor just behind them

214

beyond the now closed door. However, Grand-mother Yellow Deer came instantly alert and grabbed her turtle shell rattle that lay across her rug covered lap. Her rheumy eyes fixed on the door beyond the girls and she began to incant softly in her native tongue, gently shaking the rattle. This caught Gwen, Maddy's and Dolores' attention. They stopped their conversation and spun to see what was bothering Grand-mother. They didn't have long to wait as the specter ghosted through the door to hang in midair before the women. At first it was just a diaphanous cloud of gently swirling smoke, but as it coalesced, it took on another form. A form that both Maddy and Gwen immediately recognized, yet neither could believe they were seeing.

'Mrs. Callaghan?' Gwen both stated and asked at the same time, she and Maddy looked at each other quickly, making sure that they were both seeing the same thing.

'Is that you Cynthia?' Maddy asked tentatively, senses alert for some trick by the enemy. It was not unheard of sending a wraith to commit some foul deed under the guise of a familiar face. It was a peculiar image of the old lady hanging in the air before them. She was like a charcoal or pencil drawing, all outline and no color, everything was a dull grey, grey eyes, lips, skin and clothes. Yet for all her grey amorphousness, she fixed her grey eyes on the girls and actually smiled at them. Then in a voice that sounded distant and all around them at the same time she spoke, it was a voice Gwen wasn't likely to forget in a hurry, it was the voice of the woman who had given her the life she had.

'Yes dear, it's me. And I must say it's good to see you both looking well, actually, if I'm honest, it's good to see anything at all, it's been a while, but even I could do without seeing them... things outside, they look pretty nasty to me.' Gwen laughed in spite of herself, drawing an odd glance from both Maddy and Dolores.

'No really, you guys, its fine. But isn't that just the understatement of the decade? Nasty they certainly are and I for one have to say that I'm bloody glad they're out there.' Realizing how bad that sounded Gwen added 'as opposed to in here I mean.'

'Yes dearie, me too. I sure am pleased that I protected this place when I did. It wasn't easy mind but the result was worthwhile don't you think?' Gwen was stunned.

'This is your doing? That shield out there? Thank you again then Mrs. C. You're just full of surprises aren't you?' Gwen could have hugged her. The spectral old woman chuckled and wafted back and forth as the breeze from the air con unit caught it. As her misty form broke up a little and reformed again it made Gwen wonder about the important question that hadn't been asked yet.

'So are you dead then Mrs. C. or something else or what?' Unsure of the etiquette of talking to a spirit. 'Sorry to ask like that, just that I haven't spoken with many ghosts before and up until this moment, and to be fair, I didn't even think they existed.' Maddy plonked herself down on the arm of the sofa, next to Dolores who had sat next to her Grand-mother. Shock and relief making Dolores's legs a tad unstable. The wraith of Miss Cynthia Callaghan simply smiled benignly and shook her head, sending little wisps of greyness floating off to dissipate in the air.

'No dear, not technically yet at least. I can't remember exactly what I told you when we met, I know we didn't have long. Events were in motion and I had to move fast, but I was, I am and I expect to continue to be a practitioner of the craft. As my ancestors were before me. And I suspect were many of yours, but I mustn't digress. A short while after I moved here, now, when was that?' Cynthia tailed off and looked thoughtful, at least thoughtful for a smoky grey cloud with human features. 'It must have been shortly after the war, we had just dropped that dreadful thing on Japan. Boy, if those goons knew anything of karma back then, still I suppose economic karma will have a similar effect. Anyway, I found that there were several naturally occurring areas of vortex energy. Both here and as far over as Arizona. Coincidentally or not, but there is one directly beneath this store. It's why I chose its location. It boosted my craft a hundred fold once I learnt how to tap into it. Its good stuff.' She smiled toothily. 'There's method to my madness Eh?'

'I'll say Cynthia,' Maddy responded 'but how is it you never told me or Jen about it? Didn't you trust us?' Maddy sounded a little hurt at that implication, for she and Jen had spent a lot of time here with the old woman apparently. Staying on when Gwen took over.

'It's not that dear,' Cynthia explained 'but the fewer people who knew what I was doing the safer and more secure it would be. I've focused and concentrated the vortex energy beneath us by utilizing various relics and ancient artefacts. Buried and secreted all around the store. It took several years searching to gather them all together, and even longer to get them where I needed to without rousing suspicion. After all, I couldn't just go out and dig up the street, I had to wait until there were road works close enough for me to slip out and plant my bits. So forgive me if it's not quite circular, but beggars can't be choosers. Of course, it's the effect that counts and that's all just theory until it actually has to work. Glad about that. In fact, it's that what summoned me.' Gwen looked a touch confused then and scratched her head as though trying to work it all out.

'So, if you're not dead, what are you then and where are you for that matter? How is it you're here at all? Sorry to sound a bit thick, it's been a trying couple of weeks.'

'Not at all dearie, my body is lying in a hospital somewhere close to the center of Mexico city, apparently, I'm not expected to last the night c'est la vie. Or not I suppose, but something has to give. It's the balance you see dear, body or spirit. For one to be strong, the other has to give way. I prefer my spirit to endure, so there's the rub. Now I hope the next part of my plan works with equal effect, that'll be just wonderful.'

'What's that then, if you don't mind my asking? It might be nice to be one step ahead instead of one behind for a change.' Cynthia wafted a little closer, still smiling.

'Not at all dearie, I'm quite pleased about it really. Most of the artefacts I buried to boost my powers were connected to me by blood. So I was able to bind my life force to them, that's how I knew it had been activated. My body collapsed as my spirit was drawn out and pulled here. I'm guessing it was when the first of those creatures showed up. Now however, I'll be able to boost the shield with my own essence and fuse with it, effectively becoming it. Though I guess my journey onwards will have to wait a while until I'm no longer bound to the shield, however long that might be.' A sudden ripple swept through Cynthia and she sucked in a misty breathe. Her form solidified slightly afterwards and she looked more substantial.

'Oh dear.' Cynthia sighed with a finality that said exactly what had just happened. She moved in close to Gwen and hugged her with a tangible presence that hadn't been there before, Gwen reacted and hugged her back, whispering a thank-you in her ear as she pressed in close. When she stood back, there were tears in both their eyes. Cynthia smiled and quickly moved over to stand before Maddy, who jumped up from her seat.

'Tell Jen I'm sorry I missed her, but it seems the body has finally passed and it's time for me to join the vortex. Never having done this before, I don't know if I'll be able to come back again, but I'll try if I can. Bless you child, stay safe and look after them all for me!' Cynthia hugged Maddy then and stepped back, looking at her hands as they began to lose color, becoming transparent then fading from view altogether. The entire process took mere seconds before Cynthia Callaghan, craft worker extraordinaire, once more vanished completely. Joining the mystical shield she had created around the Earth Angel store. Through all the conversation and ghostly goings on, Dolores and Grand-mother Yellow Deer sat in silence, watching and listening. Dolores was a modern day Native American and she accepted more than her Grand-mother who was muttering slightly about it being a bad idea having ghosts hanging around like that. Gwen smiled at the pair, glad they were here and realizing that they would perfect to carry on the work there.

The presence of Cynthia and the power of the vortex helped Gwen overcome some of her trepidation about the milling horde outside.

'We really ought to do something about them Maddy. It's not fair to leave them like that.' Only days ago, they had been comparatively happy and unconcerned souls. Going about their business and caring for their families. Then the Adversary, for he is behind all their woes, came along and destroyed their lives, their hopes and futures. It has to stop she mused and she was going to do all she could to make sure it did just that.

'I take it you're referring to the possessed out front,' Maddy thumbed their general direction 'what did you have in mind?'

'Something swift and as pain free as possible. I think they've suffered enough as it is don't you.' Maddy agreed. Humanity didn't deserve this, well, she amended to herself, not all of them anyway. Not that these creatures were human anymore. They were just meat. Fleshy overcoats for a sinister enemy that had as much concern for the suffering of humanity as much of humanity had about stepping on a bug. Their lives were as good as over and Gwen was right, it was time to put them out of their misery.

Knowing what she had to do didn't make it any easier for Gwen, she couldn't stop the tears streaming down her cheeks as she emerged from the store and walked as calmly as she could to within a few feet of the barrier. The horde whipped itself into a frenzy at her presence and threw themselves all the more at the barrier. Maddy came and stood next to her, placing one hand upon her shoulder for support. Gwen laid her own over it and closed her eyes. Wishing she could close her ears to the sounds too, but she gritted her teeth and concentrated, putting their hideous ranting as far from her mind as possible.

Visualizing and summoning to her, all the roots from all the trees in the area. And there were plenty. She massed them beneath the horde, knowing that there were more than enough beneath them to carry out their grisly task. Maddy spoke in her mind, *Do it.*

With tears still brimming in her eyes, Gwen released her deadly subterranean forest.

The possessed had no time to react. The devastation was so abrupt that it was as though the massive pin cushion of razor edged and barbed spears had always been there. Each possessed was impaled on at least three barbs. Death was almost instantaneous for the now wretched townsfolk. The screams of the minions went on for a bit longer as they thrashed and sought other hosts. Those that by some miracle had escaped the first wave invariably fell to the second and third. None must get away; and none did. Maddy closed her own eyes and focused briefly. The street further back split apart with a thunderous crack. The tarmac and bedrock pulling apart ponderously, revealing a deep, deep chasm.

'I think we should reacquaint these souls with their mother don't you? Let them learn the true meaning of earth to earth and ashes to ashes.' Gwen nodded enthusiastically. Focusing some more, Gwen managed to manipulate the barbs to deposit their flailing and parasitic refuse into the chasm where many fell screaming and cursing. Flames licking out of the chasm as the bodies fell. Consuming their corpses and freeing their souls. Or so Gwen hoped. When the last had been sent plummeting to the depths, Maddy and Gwen restored the area as best they could. Closing the chasm as though it had never been and Gwen retracted the roots, allowing them to return to what they were supposed to do. Maddy fixed the road to cover the carnage left behind. It made little difference, but it wouldn't remind and disturb Dolores and her Grand-mother too much should they come out the front again.

'We won't be able to be that respectful for all the possessed we encounter,' Maddy warned Gwen 'time and events simply won't allow it, but for now, it was the least we could do for them.' Gwen nodded automatically. She heard the words but they simply washed over her in a buzz of fuzzy sounds. The roaring in her own ears drowned out most of it.

'I can't believe I just killed that many people. I...Maddy did I just really do that?'

Maddy came and took Gwen by the shoulders 'It's alright Gwen, they were already dead, and you did them a favor' turning her gently, Maddy guided her back into the store, past the awestruck Dolores who had watched it all. Seen it with her own two eyes and was still struggling to comprehend what her two friends had just done. Through the store to the back room where Grand-mother was still sitting, eyes closed and chanting quietly to herself and intermittently shaking the turtle rattle in time with her chant. She didn't even notice as Gwen was softly placed beside her. A flash of lucidity lit up in Gwen's eyes and she looked at Maddy, Grand-mother then at Dolores who had followed the pair through to the back room. Gwen smiled in a lopsided sort of way.

'I'm really sorry about this, but I've never killed that many people before and I don't know if I can…Is it hot in here or is it just m…' Gwen eyes rolled up in her head and she fainted dead away. Sliding bonelessly from the sofa and collapsing in a Gwen shaped puddle on the floor. Maddy simply took one of the Navajo blankets that adorned the sofa and laid it over Gwen's prone form.

'Let her sleep, for a bit. It was a bit traumatic for her I suppose. Though unfortunately, I expect she'll get used to it. We on the other hand…' Maddy spoke directly to Dolores now, '…have some serious work to do.' Dolores looked bemused. What sort of work could *she* possibly have to do? Dolores figured that she was the least empowered one there. Even a ghost had more power than she did. Grand-mother was in one of her chants, communing with who knew what. She could be like that for days, and had been on more than one occasion.

'So what are *we* going to do exactly?' Dolores asked, trepidation evident in her voice as she wasn't entirely sure she wanted to know the answer. Sensing the Native American woman's nervousness, Maddy put her out of her misery with a smile.

'It's nothing you have to worry about Res. Gwen has a task ahead of her that requires some research. What we need to do is scour all the books here in hope of locating something that gives us a clue to the possible whereabouts of the First Tree. That was part of what drew us here initially, it's what Gwen wanted to do first before setting off. Like a supernatural route planner for want of a better description. You start down here and keep an eye on our girl and I'll start upstairs with her personal collection. Let's hope we find something useful here or else we'll have to head to the house. I know she's got some more books there.'

Though after a couple of hours searching, they hadn't turned up much more than Gwen had already surmised. Her route of possibilities was almost a straight line, for none of them stood out above any other. Across the Atlantic, coast in at Ireland, there were a few sacred sites there that may offer further clues, across to mainland Britain and the obvious places like Stonehenge, Avebury and Tintagel in Cornwall, Rosslyn up in Edinburgh, the Orkneys as well as a few others. Then it was off to France, Carnac, Rennes le Chateau, through Spain and Italy and out across Central Europe. Eventually arriving on the shores of Syria, for there were a few options in the Middle East. After all, it was a country beleaguered by myth and legends. It wasn't called the Holy Land for nothing. Beyond that timeframe all bets were probably going to be off. Gwen didn't have an infinite amount of time to go gallivanting across the globe. She had to be precise and focused. If she started in on the Dark Continent or the Russian landmass, she could be gone forever. Jen and Maddy would willingly help her eventually, but in this, only Gwen would be able to recognize what it was she sought. That was why she was chosen. The more Maddy looked at the enormity of the task before Gwen, the more her own heart sank. It was doomed from the outset.

Gwen came shuffling upstairs soon enough, looking for her friend. Scrubbing her hand through her slept on hair. And annoyingly, for any woman who would have seen it, it just sorted itself out into lustrous perfection with a gentle shake of her head.

'What have I missed?' Gwen asked a little groggily as the last vestiges of her shock induce sleep left her. Maddy chuckled at her question.

'You sound just like somebody else I know. Never mind Gwen, come and sit down and we'll go through it with you. How about some tea? I'll do it. Res will bring you up to speed.' The Pueblo woman nodded vigorously as Maddy disappeared off to the little kitchenette, her usual easy smile back in place after the horrors of earlier. She patted a cushion next to her and Gwen plumped herself on to it, looking down to what the girls had amassed. A prodigious amount of papers and open books with all manner of book marks. They had scavenged the store for everything remotely useful. *Why not, sales would be a bit down for a while anyway.* Gwen reasoned to herself, *why not put it to some use, that's what it's for anyway.*

'So what have we got here then?' Gwen ruffled through a few fragments before Dolores slapped her fingers away playfully. A mock annoyed expression on her face.

'Leave it alone, you'll mix up the order!' Gwen looked at her with surprise.

'*That's* in order?' She looked at Dolores sideways and added a 'Yeah right!'

'We don't have anything definitive Gwen, I'm sorry, but we have a sort of direction. Though I don't know how you're going to cover all these places in the time we apparently have.' Gwen elbowed Dolores softly in the side and winked at her.

'Ah Res, I've got one or two tricks up my sleeve now, like you wouldn't believe.'

'After what I've seen today, I bet I would.' Dolores paused briefly before asking.

'Do you…I mean, do you *feel* any different? Cos you don't *look* all that different other than looking as well and as fit as I've ever seen you. I don't know what you're on but I wouldn't mind a basin full myself. Your skin, hair eyes - well just about every damn thing you cow. Seems you got something of a tradeoff out of this deal.'

'It's just as well, the bloody stress of what they want me to do would have me looking like Grand-mother otherwise.' Dolores nodded and tried not to laugh at the image of Gwen looking as ancient as her Grand-mother. Who as it turned out had finally stopped her chanting and had fallen into deep sleep. Still propped up in the chair where she had been the last three days.

'I think Gwen, that for my people, you may well be the personification of the White Buffalo Calf Woman, according to Jen and Maddy, you embody much of what legend says of her, that and what your arrival heralds.' Gwen didn't look so sure.

'Don't mind my cynicism Res. But it's been my experience that people rarely accept something that doesn't conform to their preconceived notion of what they expect to see. I appreciate your people are closer to the land and the spirits of nature than many other cultures, especially us in the West, but humanity isn't known for its rationality when it comes to things sacred. The diversity of cultures and each having their own notion of who and how they will be returning and when, doesn't allow for much deviation. I'm not sure I'm what they had in mind.'

'Maybe this conflict will make that allowance, when what they expect to happen doesn't. They will know the disappointment that my people felt, when many of the things they expected to happen didn't. It is accepted that the calf was born to us. What follows would be at the discretion of the spirits. For that is how they work. It is not for us to question Gitche Manitou, but to do what we must within the great web that Grand-mother Spider weaves. I'm a little more pragmatic than our elders. I'm not saying they are wrong to hold to tradition, but to see perhaps, how tradition works in this time. Allowances must be made.' Gwen had heard much of this before from Res. For all her traditional upbringing, she had a modernistic and contemporary slant on the future of the people. She would adapt them to this world as best she could, convinced there was a happy middle ground between the two. Time had been their enemy as much as the white eyes.

'We have, like so many other peoples of the fourth world, where we exist presently, become stagnated in our ritual and belief. It has grown solid and immovable through habit. Time without change has created a complacency that has proven to be our undoing. You and your kind must make all new believers from the people and from the rest of the world. Show them what they have forgotten in their rigid ways.' Gwen had the distinct impression that she had just had a pep talk from Dolores, the sort given to soldiers before battle, or fighters before they get into the ring. Dolores believed in her. That was the bottom line and it touched another raw nerve in Gwen. Causing her to break down in tears again. Clasping her friend in a tight embrace as she did so. Feeling a love for the woman whose friendship had supported and guided her more than she knew.

'Ah Yeh Gwen! If I thought you were going to react so, I would have kept quiet. But you are closer to the gods now than us mere mortals, our future is in your hands, you know what I mean don't you?' Gwen snuffled and sighed in a mock exasperation. Before holding Dolores out at arm's reach and looking deeply into her dark eyes.

'Of course I do you swine. But I'm a bit delicate right now, and all that sentimental gush, got right to me that's all. But I thank you for your belief Res. I really do, it means a lot. You're the best friend a girl could have, excluding her rabbit of course.' This broke the tension and had them both hugging again and laughing.

Maddy came back in with a tray of steaming tea and hot buttered crumpets. As she placed the tray down she looked between the two women, trying to ascertain what had just passed between them, settling on the fact that whatever it was, it had been good for Gwen. There was a glint to her eyes that she hadn't seen in a while.

'Look what I found, they were lurking at the back of the Aladdin's cave of a refrigerator of yours Gwen. You really ought to get to the back of it from time to time. I took the little blue bits off, and they seemed fine, but there are things in there that are about to evolve. I'm sure I saw legs on a vegetable. Oh and before I forget, the printer is out of paper.' Gwen slapped her forehead. Recall flooding back. It was one of the things she was going to do after meeting Dolores on that fateful day when her life as she knew it went so far off the rails that a whole new form of transport had to be invented.

'Arse. I meant to get some before you know what all kicked off. Can't you find any more anywhere else?' Maddy said she couldn't and it was a pain because there were a few things on what remained of the net that might have been useful, but she would just have to do without it.

'I think I've got more than enough stuff here anyway. I'm not going to be able to take half of this with me, there's just too much.' Dolores pulled out a sheet of paper.

'That's why we knocked this up.' Dolores passed it to Gwen. 'It's a very rough track taking you eventually towards the Middle East. We were thinking that if you haven't found it by then and if we are all still alive, maybe you can return here. I'll keep looking, though I've no idea how I'd get a message to you, guess we'll cross that bridge should we get that far, yeah?'

Gwen was reading the extensive list avidly. Mentally working out where many of the places mentioned actually were. Geography hadn't been one of her strong points.

'Bloody hell, this is going to take an age as it is. Have you seen how many search areas there are on here?' They just widened their eyes at her. 'Of course you have, duh! You put them here, but I don't know. These are just sacred sites that anyone can visit now, I don't know how a bloody great tree could hide there for so long without someone discovering it.' But it was Maddy who pointed out that these sites may be for her, access points to these missing realms that humanity has sought and lost. Atlantis, Lemuria, Avalon, the In-Between. After all, wasn't Avalon known as the Isle of Apples? That was a tree. It was a long shot. But that was all they had, long shots. Gwen was full of doubts and questions. What would it look like? How would she recognize it, How would she access these sites? What would a door look like? She could sit here for a month just running through the questions this quest brought up. But that wouldn't help her. She knew them for what they were. Reasons to postpone actually leaving. A part of her knew that she would have to make some harsh choices in the field and on the spot. There was little preparation for a journey such as hers. Knowing that however, didn't make any of it any easier. They sat back and contemplated the array of books and paperwork and research before them as they polished off the tea and crumpets. Hoping that some revelation or answer would leap out and present itself. An hour later, it still hadn't. And time was ticking like some infernal bomb. She had to make a definitive choice. A plan of action needed a beginning.

'I'll be leaving first thing in the morning then. No point putting it off any more.'

Her two companions simply looked at her. Both equally aware of the weight about to be shouldered by their friend and honoring the courage it had to take to make such a monumental decision. Starting a thing was always the most difficult. It was akin to pushing and enormous rock. That initial effort took the most strength, but once it was rolling, maintaining momentum was much easier. How many developments in humanity's brief lifetime had failed, because of a lack of initial strength? Maybe if

224

they had asked for help and those asked had actually provided it, rather than considering only their own self-absorbed lives, things might have been a little different today.

'Look you guys, I've slept enough today - albeit on an involuntary basis - I feel as refreshed as I'm going to with this hanging over me, so why don't you get some sleep yourselves. I'm going to sit outside for a bit and get some air. Let some of that good old Santa Fe air clear my head a bit. 'The moment Gwen mentioned sleep, Dolores' eyes drooped a little lower. The pressure of the day's events catching up with her suddenly.

'Good idea, now that you mention it, I feel like I've been dropped down a mountain side. Grand-mother seems okay, what harm can a few hours do?' Dolores stretched, stood and yawned. Stretched some more and went to find somewhere comfortable to curl up. Maddy waited until Dolores was out of earshot before speaking.

'I'll break the news to her when she wakes up, but I'll say good-bye now. You don't get away with it that easy you know.' Gwen was stunned. For she had only just thought about slipping away under the cover of darkness, foregoing the emotional good-byes she thoroughly detested, and embarking on her first steps while her friends slept.

'How did you guess that?' Gwen had to ask. 'Did you read my mind?' Maddy shook her mane of fiery locks and smiled ruefully.

'Not really, it's just what I would have done were I you and that thing you have for good-byes.' *Sussed.* Gwen grinned at the girl who had been her assistant, mentor, lover and now sister. This girl could read her far too well and that wasn't good. Gwen liked her air of mystery and figured that she had become far too predictable. That would have to change too. It smacked of what Dolores had said about time and repetition. It made bad practice and worse habits into permanent fixtures. Gwen embraced Maddy with an intensity that surprised them both. Breaking apart, both girls had tears streaming down their flawless cheeks. Leaving red rimmed eyes and moist salty tracks in their wake.

'I'm not going to give you any big speech about the student graduating, or the fledgling about to take her first flight or any such nonsense, I know how that would grate on you. So all I'm going to say, is good luck sister. May your journey be fruitful, literally. And stay safe. Don't do anything you're not sure of and most importantly and I can't stress this enough.' Gwen rolled her eyes which said get on with it woman. 'If you get into trouble you don't think you can get yourself out of it, call us. We will come if we can.

'Are you quite finished? I wanted to avoid all this as - you - well - know!' Gwen emphasized the last words with a pointy finger, prodding Maddy in the shoulder.

'Thanks anyway, and yes I'll call.' Gwen rolled her eyes 'But if I don't drag my sorry arse out of that door sooner rather than later, it's only going to be that much harder. So yes, I really was going to sit and take in some air, maybe a few memories while I'm at it - but yes, you were right too. I was just going to slip off. While it's quiet and I can try out a few shapes as I head across country.' Maddy nodded she understood. There were no more words that could add or change anything for her or between them. So instead, they hugged again. This time when Gwen stood back, she really stood back. Taking a couple of backward steps. Maddy nodded once more, almost imperceptibly and she hooded her eyes. It was more of a deferential bow. That done, she turned and headed back in to where Dolores went. She just heard Gwen's last words as she closed the door.

'Look after them Maddy, look after all of them.' Then Gwen herself stepped outside into the chilly night air. Not that the cold affected her now, but she could see it sparkling on the glass and laying on a multitude of other surfaces. Winter was increasing its stranglehold on the town again, and it looked like it was going to be a harsh one. She looked up but there were no stars to see. Just the dark roiling clouds that threatened the mother of all snowstorms. Gwen hoped and prayed that her friends out in the Pueblos and upon the Mesas were going to be safe enough and provisioned enough, for she got the feeling that when this hit, life here was going to get pretty rough. Maddy will help them. Gwen tried to convince herself but she knew deep down that there was only so much one Drakarim, however motivated, could accomplish. Especially when she had duties of her own to attend to. *Damn! Why are there so many things to think of, and why is everything spread so thinly. If it isn't one bloody thing it's another. And I've got an extended lifetime of this now. I bloody well hope that valium still works on me - I'm gonna want shit loads of it before this is finished I expect.* But a much deeper part of her mind replied. *No you won't.*

Gwen sat outside for about another two hours, reliving moments and pondering the variables of her future, both immediate and long term. But two hours later she still had nothing definitive and concrete to give her any peace. In fact her head was swimming with scenarios and possibilities, merged with vivid images spawned from her over active imagination. They didn't help at all considering what she had done earlier that day.

'Sod it. If I sit here much longer I'm going back in.' Gwen stood and stretched her muscles, feeling them pop and expand. 'Well, here goes nothing.' Gwen closed her eyes and re-imagined the crow form from earlier. It was only an hour before dawn, so she wouldn't stand out. The spiraling and shimmering emerald vortex spun up around Gwen.

When it dissipated, what remained was a blue black, glossy crow, sitting perched on the back of the bench. With three good throaty caws, Gwen flew up from the bench and circled several times as she gained height. She glanced down, looking at the earth below her. But not just with corvids eyes, but with the eyes of the Avatar of Nature. She saw the flashing dragon lines that ran throughout the planet, burning bright and flaring every now and again as they criss-crossed the globe. They gave her an innate sense of direction, one she had never had before. She was notorious and could probably get lost on a straight road if left to her own devices. With a few powerful beats of her wings, she was off.

Gwen flew steadily for a while until she had passed what she knew to be the city limits. Knowing also that habitation was thinner out here and she was less likely to cause a stir, Gwen shimmered once more and the sky was momentarily full of gigantic forest green Dragon. Gwen bunched her powerful muscles and with a mighty down thrust, she tore across the sky. Not only breaking the sound barrier with a thunderous boom, but smashing it into thousands of tiny pieces that fell unseen and unheard upon the desert sands.

Though to say entirely unseen would be somewhat presumptuous. Unseen by human eyes she may have been, but the two deep set and muddy yellow eyes that watched the transition of the crow to monstrous reptile were not human. At least not any more. They hadn't been human for a hundred and fifty years. Not since his newly appointed lord, freed from his imprisonment had ventured forth to this world at the sufferance of he who released him, to recruit as many warriors as he could in the turning of the moon. His mining camp had been decimated. None escaped, those who did not survive the turn were doomed to become food for those that did. It was why he was here now. His rise through the ranks of Fenris' hounds had earnt him the opportunity to return to this world and scout. To be a scout warranted slightly more intelligence than a mere hound. They were the infantry to his sergeant major. Brutal and relentless hunters. They killed on command and that was what they did best. It was the likes of himself who told them where to kill. He stood to get a better view of the rapidly receding creature. He was a good nine feet to the shoulder and built powerfully on the upper body, designed there for strength with the ability to tear a human or an animal clean in two with its bear hands. It narrowed at the waist and ended with long, rangy legs, meaty thighs for distance running and speed. There was nothing on earth that could match it in a one on one contest. Its wiry grey fur covered its body in its entirety. Topping off on its pricked ears, down over its muzzle and completing the journey on its huge padded and taloned feet. Feet that could disembowel with a stroke. Currently it was one of a thousand Hounds – werewolves to the mortal kind it hunted - that were spread out across the land, seeking and searching for vital news for their lord and for fresh meat for his growing army. It had not been told of such incredible beasts as what just flew over its head. It would have to report this back to his lord as it would have the rise of possessed and how it was curious how they gathered at that store. Now not so curious. But something deep in its animal brain, the bit that governed survival, told it that this wasn't going to be greeted as good news. Perhaps it should find another to pass this news on. Fenris considered these lands undefended and ripe. He wouldn't take kindly to being told - however round-about - that he was wrong about that. But someone would tell him and he would decide what they were to do next. Whatever and whoever it was, the beast growled in pleasure to itself, humanity was about to slip once more several notches down the food chain.

# Chapter 7

## Serendipity

Gwen mastered the art of shapeshifting mid-flight as she left Santa Fe. So over excited by the concept, she was like a kid who had just gotten their first bike and not only were the stabilizers off, she was discovering all new roads to traverse. So it was with shapes. Gwen dug deep in her imagination and her newly expanded - though still hazy - memories and she took form after form after form. Gwen initially - and inadvertently to some extent - flew a southerly course a she practiced shifting. Part of her mind contemplated Mexico anyway with Palenque and the numerous and magnificent ruins of that ancient land. Gwen recalled the legend of Quetzalcoatl or Kukulkan, the feathered serpent and with all the trees that jungle offered, it seemed a good place to find her feet and maybe the first tree. Though in her heart Gwen somehow sensed she wasn't going to find it on the land mass she was currently on, that would be too easy and she figured surely the girls would have sensed long ago without her help. Help it seemed they needed urgently too. It was with an unconscious thought but incredible speed that Gwen swept south and banked up once more to follow the coast north until she ranged back up over the Everglades and once more in more or less conspicuous forms, hugged the coastline of the Eastern Seaboard for as much of her journey north as she could. Soon enough soaring up past New York, she caught a glimpse of the fabled Lady Liberty as she held her flaming brand as high as she could. *Liberty! Now that's an interesting concept.* Gwen mused. *Was there such a thing anymore?* With credit referencing, DNA profiling and database compilation, heightened passport control and immigration crackdowns and more cameras than a stick could be waved at just who was at liberty to do or go anywhere anymore? Gwen recalled all the questions the man from the bank had asked her when she bought the shop and house, it was all bar her blood type and inside leg measurement. To go buy, or even shop anonymously was an almost impossibility now, *not without big brother watching and monitoring your every single bloody move,* Gwen thought sourly. *There were domestic cameras just about everywhere these days; then there was the NSA, CIA and who knew who else with their spy satellites watching everyone and everything from space.* Gwen's sour humor vanished as she wondered what they saw now, some poor soul having a fit as the blip on his screen thundered from one side to the other, appearing then disappearing as she assumed something small for a bit. She was in no doubt that she was creating some significant stir on someone's radar, she was after all, when she adopted her new draconian form larger than any domestic craft and infinitely expanded upon any fighter aircraft as well as being considerably faster too if she put her mind to it, but oddly, she hadn't seen many aircraft of any description for some time, not since she left Santa Fe and New Mexico generally. There she spotted a few military craft as there were bases close by but otherwise, the skies were oddly bereft of any other flying craft.

Based on what Jen and Maddy had told her and what she had seen herself, she suspected the military had their hands full. Though the skies should have been busier with both military and commercial aircraft, as it wasn't every day a superpower was invaded, certainly not by what was attempting it this time and this made any attempt by the Russians, Chinese or Koreans or whoever else who wanted to have a go seem trivial by comparison. Gwen suspected too, that there was an awful lot of *denial* going on. *No doubt the God botherers would be flocking to their respective churches and probably dying gruesome deaths, trapped inside while demons tore them to shreds. Possessed and deminions secure in the knowledge that the house was unprotected by any such deity, just like the poor souls within.* Their alleged house of God proved no more of a sanctuary for the religious than did the bunkers and homes of the non-religious. There was no discrimination in what these demons were attempting. They wanted *all* humans dead it seemed. A meat suit was a meat suit and all skeletons look alike with the flesh torn off them. But should humans have been surprised by this sudden downturn of events? They had been systematically wiping out species after species since they got up off four legs, why shouldn't another more aggressive species come along and want to wipe humanity out like the parasitic vermin it resembled?

The home forces it seemed were faring no better than those *extinct by our hand species* did. Human armies protecting the populace – or trying to -had to be spread pretty thin as well, though Gwen could only speak for her adoptive homes soldiers, what with so many in the Middle East still and Homeland Security still being a comparatively fledgling force when compared to what it faced. A force as ancient as the Earth herself; Beings that taught humanity about war and death, and how to kill in a multitude of nasty ways. Even for all their cruelty, violence and devastation, humanity was still the pupil to their mastery of all things abhorrent, brutal and malevolent. Though Gwen hoped futilely that the Adversary's invasion hadn't become so widespread and destructive in such a short space of time as to create such global chaos as she witnessed in Santa Fe, chaos and death as he no doubt intended; because Gwen was still laboring under the impression that she stood a chance, that she had been summoned in time - *before* matters degenerate beyond salvation - but if she was honest, judging by the state of the world as she remembered it, she couldn't see how it couldn't not be. *We let him in.* Her moment of sour humor passed. Vanishing like snow in the desert as she considered the consequences for the hundredth time of a demonic rampage. Not just on a tiny and ridiculous scale like those seen on TV, but on a scale unprecedented at any time in history. The Romans failed, The Persians failed, Alexander failed as did Napoleon and even Hitler didn't accomplish what the Adversary was undertaking. That was merely nation against nation, and this didn't even come close to that. It was greater still than the eradication of a single species – a fact humanity knew all about, having tried it several times and luckily failed; some were however still trying it – but this was something else, it was an entire world against world. Races immeasurably older than humanity apparently now faced extinction too at the hands of the Adversary, a creature that was clearly insane. What sane being sought to accomplish what he was and have so little care for the chaos and death left in his wake? Gwen was having trouble wrapping her mind around that scale. Though what scared Gwen more than that threat even, was the fact that humans still fought amongst themselves like crazed children even when faced with a common enemy of this magnitude. Not space aliens from outer space but real demons from a realm much closer to home. Gwen flew on as her mind spun, troubled and uneasy, lost in her own thoughts as she saw the imagined horrors in her mind's eye over and over, again and again with no happy ending in sight.

Leaving US and almost Canadian airspace with sonic boom - one of many she had accidentally done as she initially powered across the vast open expanses of middle America unaware of her speed before turning south then back north again up the coast. She didn't know exactly what she was seeing or where she was, as there were no signs that high up and geography wasn't one of her strong points, but it wasn't long before she saw less and less land and definitely no giant tree. That gave her all the clue she needed then, more so as she watched the passage of the occasional floating ice flow. Sensing then the current of the Earth's magnetic field, she banked slightly and was soon skimming out past what she took for Greenland. It was from up there she saw her first wild whale sign. Excitedly, this prompted her to take a change of travel plan, angling down and southwards to follow them. Gwen loved whales; she had always had a soft spot for them. She had no idea what it was that attracted her to them. It was as irrational as many other human emotions. They touched a place within her that blossomed like a spring flower when she listened to their song or saw them on TV, but this was just the icing to her cake. The ability to actually watch them in the flesh. Suddenly realizing she could swim with them too Gwen felt a touch foolish for not understanding that nuance earlier. The thought hit her like she had flown into a wall. In one swift move, she folded her massive fern green draconian wings back and dived. Braking at the last minute so she didn't hit the concrete hard water's surface, she shifted form, slipping shape into that of the Orca. The huge killer whale slid gracefully through the roiling ocean surface and her whole perspective took a radical turn then.

Gwen swum in circles for several long minutes as she acclimatized herself as a mammal in the vast sea and got her head and senses around this new and – to Gwen -alien environment. Satisfied eventually with her new mode of travel, Gwen shifted once more, adopting the larger and more ponderous form of the Humpback whale which had drawn her attention in the first place. She figured the bigger species of Cetacean was going to be more suitable for powering across the ocean depths anyway. Re-aligning her senses she drove her great tail and swept her flukes down, propelling her hulking form away at a speed that surprised even herself. She marveled and felt joys unknown in this new form and sported amongst the ice and waves like a new born experiencing the joy of life for the first time. It was then she heard her first whale song in the ocean. She wasn't anywhere prepared for the intensely spiritual, profound and subtle change that dropped over her mind like a fine web at hearing it, hearing it *as* a whale not just as a human with human limitations. Her thoughts began to slow then and elongate. What before would have been a transient idea now took on a deeper and more deliberate thoughtform. She began to sense currents and undercurrents to even the simplest of concepts. Realizing like a child learns something new that there was little that was truly simple, and that *everything* had a purpose, implications and repercussions. Their meanings just weren't always obvious. And how so many of them were devastatingly far reaching.

Gwen began to reflect then more and more upon her own life in this intense and thought provoking whale manner. Initially, it made her uncomfortable as she went over her many inadequacies. Too many, but they paled into insignificance as she expanded her awareness to include the rest of her two legged species. The results stunned her. She had never delved this deep before and it made her wonder just how superficial her life, all life had been up till that moment. Just scratching at the surface of their existence, oblivious to what lay beneath like a stone that skimmed the surface of a lake unaware of the vastness below. Her humanity took another pummeling - what little remained anyway and her former self was re-forged almost like a fine and ancient Japanese blade. Heated and hammered then folded and the process repeated over and over as every nuance was exposed to her, tempering her perspective from not just a whales point of view but every ocean dwelling soul. Perspective from their place in the cosmos and how they understood it. Sounds travelled through the water from thousands of miles away as a council of Cetaceans convened and were overjoyed at Gwen's presence, awe, reverence and even relief colored their multi layered thoughts and they came together as one mind then and taught Gwen what they could to best help the new Avatar of Nature.

Time then became a casualty of her transition. She began to measure it by different imperatives as her perception took twist after twist. Gwen began to imagine humanity as mayflies - it was as though her mind's eye had put her view of mortal life on fast forward - so brief and short lived, yet they hurried through their tiny insignificant existence missing so much; they were fleeting in comparison to the ponderous and gentle pace of the whale. And It didn't help either, that in the back of Gwen's mind she recalled the prospect of outliving everything and everyone she currently knew if what the girls had said was true, and she had little cause to doubt them. She was Drakarim now, and though she was yet to fully understand what that truly implied - Gwen shivered involuntarily at the thought of finding out too - she knew that unless something unpleasant happened to her, she was up for - potentially at least - a long and significantly extended life. Such that even the whales would be short lived, along with trees and mountains but she couldn't quite get her head around that prospect yet.

Beyond the philosophical ramifications she meandered through, there was one abiding sensation that pervaded her soul above and beyond the rest of her introspections – that of a deep and abiding peace. Far below the waves and turmoil of the surface world, she felt peace like a gravitational effect, couple with a kind of serenity unmatched above. Total escapism to the point she could have been traversing space and encountering the creatures that called it home and that humanity would likely never see, let alone understand. It was so unlike anything she had ever experienced or imagined. The whales feared nothing down here, they were nobility here for there was nothing to fear below. This was their world and all the secrets it held were theirs to share alone, were they inclined to do so - which they were not yet apparently as they relayed such to Gwen – but it was only when they had to surface did they have cause for real concern; And it was the same cause that had much of Mother Nature's children living in mortal dread. Humanity.

Gwen caught up physically with several of the leviathans as they ghosted majestically through the dark waters, smaller fish flashing by like shooting stars and she began to converse, slowly at first with these sixty five ton plus gentle giants as she was initially an actual stranger to them, they were naturally wary, but somehow, before even Gwen could fully introduce herself - unfamiliar with whale etiquette - they recognized her, not for who, but what she was. Reverently, they began to communicate then with her, politely, softly and with a gentleness that made her heart wrench until it broke. They spoke not with words, but with a pure sound and emotion. The sound and vibrational equivalent to hieroglyphics. Images flashed through her mind as she discovered their telepathic language up close and personal and she was soon reduced to tears by the plight and total incomprehension of humanities genocidal attacks on their kind and that of the oceanic creatures who they felt a responsibility for. Failing them and failing too to understand the humans single minded compulsion to kill so much and so many, with them least of all. They had endeavored over man's brief history to communicate with the two legged land bound, but for the most part, they were met with only fear and ignorance. There was a brief moment of communicative success with a primitive race who later became known to humanity as the Inuit, but even for all their respect and reverence of the great whales, it didn't stop them killing them. Though many willingly gave up their lives to aid these two leggeds in the hope that they would eventually come to learn what the whales tried to instill in them, but unfortunately, it never happened.

For all their tales of death and torment, Gwen never once felt hate or vengeance from them, only sadness. That and pity, though not the condescending type humanity proffered. It was a deep, soul destroying sorrow at failing to bridge the gulf that separated their world from that of the land walkers. There were things that lay in the great depths and ocean beds that man would never know and what the whales had endeavored to share. It was more than just a tragic loss, it was a loss which they saw as such a waste of knowledge. For the knowledge they had was phenomenal, world changing and lost on the petty and tiny minded humans they hoped to teach. If it couldn't be achieved with a harpoon or a sharp blade, they didn't want to know. For a long time, Gwen knew only shame.

They took Gwen to some of the deep places and shared many of the wonders with her that man knew nothing of and Gwen wept all the more. Her salty tears mingling with the salt of the sea. Where the seawater containing her tears washed over rocks and touched the sea bed, new plants and life bloomed and sprouted. Yet for all the new life that blossomed as she swept past, Gwen came to understand, tragically, that the whale's song, for the most part, wasn't just them communing; it was their living eulogy. They sang their own death song as they died slowly, one by one, not so much from humanities depravities, but equally of a broken heart at their failure to reach an understanding.

The question that kept repeating and echoing through her mind was '*Why?*' With all man's ingenuity and feats of engineering, scientific discovery and supposed intellect, what on earth could he want from a whales corpse that he couldn't fabricate or reproduce otherwise? Surely we had gotten past the pathetic idea that it was okay to keep making the same mistakes and committing the same acts of heinous cruelty just because our predecessors did. That didn't make it okay at all. Habitual death. It made no sense to her whatsoever, no matter who it affected. Images of Oriental whalers filled her mind and she grew angry all over again as the combined imagery from both her own mind and that of the whales filled her head with blood and terror. That would stop. If they survived this catastrophe, Gwen swore she would see to it personally that the barbaric practice would cease once and for all or else her rage wasn't going to be a healthy thing to be around. She swam on as the whales talked. There was one area they covered that intrigued Gwen almost enough to break off her quest to explore as it was just too incredible to be true. She said so much and the whales took Gwen to where she could see the truth of it. Antarctica had been the last great mystery for mankind for many decades now as what was below it was a growing mystery. The whales knew and they took Gwen deep below the surface, into a darkness untouched by the sunlight but with a thought light blossomed there as a massive profusion of bio luminescence illuminated the viscous waters where no man had ever been. Deeper and deeper they dived and with a suddenness that almost stopped her heart, there it was. Looming out of the stygian aquatic gloom like a light at the end of a tunnel that had gone on for days. It grew brighter and brighter and for a second, Gwen couldn't compute what she was seeing based on how deep she knew they had to be. An opening so massive a small country could be pushed through it, the actual country. It was a tunnel of such magnitude and crystal filled where every shred of light was reflected a thousand times magnification until it was brighter than daylight. Something was different then and Gwen couldn't figure it at first, she felt different and with something that resembled mirth the whales told her. Breathe. Was what they said and that was it. Gwen took a deep breath of the illuminated water and she was flooded with oxygen. The water was so rich that her body could breathe the water the way lungs breathed air on land. That explained how these majestic creatures dived so deep with no fear or need to surface.

'What is here?' Gwen asked 'Where does this go?' One image bearing sound came back to Gwen and her mind translated that image into words, Mar-Terasherah, The Deep Under-realm. Gwen was stunned and wanted nothing more than to go further to see where this fantastic portal went, but the whales who were escorting her, swum before her and barred her way. 'Why?' Gwen was confused, why show her yet prevent her taking a proper look. 'It is not for you yet Avatar, in due time.' Was her cryptic answer. Gwen was confused and took another tack. 'Surely the Lady Jen, Avatar of water and Air is privy to this realm, so why am I not?' There was amusement in the tone of the response and that threw Gwen all the more for the Earth was keeping secrets from her own Avatars it seemed.

'Jen doesn't know?' Gwen couldn't believe it that in all the aeons she had resided upon the Earth and done her bidding, this realm wasn't known to her. Jen knew the whales kept secrets but had never pressed them for them, so why now?' Gwen asked as she absorbed the enormity of the situation. 'Erithia is not the realm it once was Lady' Gwen's whale escort relayed to her 'monumental events are reshaping our home and as ancient custodians of her greatest and oldest secrets, your presence has been foretold by our eldest and wisest; with your coming all knowledge is to be shared for who are we to decide what must be done. We believe that responsibility is now yours and that of the Lady Jenharim of the sea and Lady Madeline of the flame, your trinity unleashes a power beyond us and we bow to your sovereignty here Lady Gwendoline. But the time for repose here is not yet, soon a time will come to unravel the secrets of Mar-Terasherah but now is not the time.' Gwen was speechless, a feat for her as she usually had something to say about most things. The whales filled her pause though and a glimmer of hope ignited within her breast.

236

'Should we survive this cataclysm Lady, you may return here along with the ladies Jenharim and Madeline for that too is foretold that all three of you must attend as one at a time yet undecided.' Gwen frowned inwardly, she hated cryptic answers. 'You must be upon your quest lady Gwendoline, The realm Mar-Terasherah will await your return.' A deep part of Gwen's psyche knew this, she couldn't really afford distractions, least of all not of this magnitude but she was fast learning there were no such things as coincidence. She's definitely be back. Allowing herself to be turned, they began their journey back to the surface.

## CRINICY

Gwen got a sense of the whale's numbers from their shared consciousness and was both furious and saddened that there were only a few hundred thousand left on the entire planet. Once humans had driven them to extinction, what would they do next? And more importantly what would happen to the world? It had no idea how dependent upon the whale's stewardship they were. How many more species would suffer the same unnecessary fate? What would replace the whale for whatever it was they wanted from them? If they would have to find a substitute at that time, why not find it now and evolve ever so slightly, leaving these beautiful and gentle creatures in peace. Sadly and shamefully, Gwen knew the answer to that all too well.

Gwen just swum then with the majestic whales for a time then, once they had finished speaking, for there was only so much to say about what they couldn't change and before they all grew too morose. Were such a thing possible, for Gwen didn't think she had ever been so sad for both a species and to leave a place. It seemed odd to hear from a whale that life was too short to be miserable all the time, not in a world of such utter beauty and tranquility as the one they swam in. Her new found companions began to sing again as they soared through the waters only this was a song of joy and power and her spirits lifted slightly. It was easy to see how some artists had envisioned these huge beings gracefully propelling themselves through the timeless void of space as the fish and other denizens of the deep waters sparkled and flashed their lights and colors like a myriad of living stars around them. Though the world beneath the waves was far more alien to man than space was, it made sense that humanity should not comprehend them. Too busy flinging lumps of metal upwards into space trying to understand worlds that held no connection to them and hurling their refuse into the oceans, rather than exploring downwards trying to understand the very world they were an intrinsic part of. Humans were mostly water in their composition after all, yet it was the least understood aspect of their world. Good only for plundering and dumping. Though she knew she was being unfair to those few who did try, but they were just that, too few - and probably too late. Gwen closed her eyes and drifted serenely, carried along by the powerful ocean current.

Many years ago, long before her time at Earth Angel, Gwen had been a member of a small new age group who had tried to teach her meditation, Gwen had since pondered the subsequent irony. They were constantly going on about *going inside*, plumbing her inner depths and discovering her own mystery yada yada. Back then, for all her increasingly desperate need to find *something,* she doubted that they ever really knew what the hell they were talking about, but it sounded good, especially to those who knew less than nothing and were finding it for the first time. Gwen had plumbed and plumbed, but the only thing she ever explored in any detail, was the inside of her eyelids. That was of course, when she managed to stay awake long enough, she quit soon after when she nodded right off and snored so loud she opened her eyes suddenly to see every single member staring at her. She didn't go back after that. Searching for meaning in her meaningless life didn't stop her partying whenever she got the chance though. Gwen used to say that it wasn't the partying that did you in, it was the recuperation. It never helped her meditation because they used to insist on sitting in a gloomy, semi-darkness with just a few candles to stop people treading on each other and some smelly incense wafting in a corner to add its cloudy atmospheric sixpence worth. Hour after hour as her buttocks went from one degree of numbness to another. Her carefully crossed legs lost all sensation and she dreaded the pins and needles she would get if she ever moved them again. But mostly it was like having an epidural. She gradually lost all feeling from the waist down as she sat cross legged. She would try to forget the discomfort to come and focus on her eyelids. Her strategically placed elbows would be located just so upon her soon desensitized knees. Her hands would come together to form the pyramid, thumb and forefinger touching as the remainder wove themselves together giving her the illusion that she was an experienced meditator. Usually it was only when one of her well placed elbows slipped off her knee as sleep robbed her of control, that she would be dropped unceremoniously back into reality. The undignified jerk that brought her back would cause her to move more than she had that last hour and sensation would flow back into her bloodless limbs.

Closely followed by pain as blood and feeling flowed back in. Eight sessions of this were all she could deal with. She rarely tried it again after her snoring session, except when she was alone in her own bed or on her sofa with a little too much wine coursing through her system. She usually started well but invariably ended up curled up in a weird shape either on her sofa, on the floor. She would then stumble up to bed, sometimes shedding her clothes first and sometimes not. This was her most abiding memory of her meditative experience to date. She didn't include her encounters with Grand-ma Yellow Deer and Dolores as they were more like mystical experiences than mere meditation. But here, deep in the dark and vast ocean, she felt the pull of the currents, the pulse and hum of the electromagnetic waves that resonated through the water. Much in the same way a bee sees something completely different when it looks at a flower, so too did the creatures of the oceans. They felt and followed the natural ebb and flow of the Earth's rhythms. As each frequency was conducted through the water, so too did its color field change. To the fish and ocean dwelling mammals, what was darkness to humans was a multihued color laden extravaganza. Their world was illuminated by a suffusion of every shade, hue and color imaginable and then some we hadn't. For there were frequencies that were beyond a humans perception and they had their own color. Gwen discovered as she moved with the whales, just how limited human vision was, how much they missed. For they seemed to categorize the entire universe as they saw it and perceived it, because that was all they could see. *Limited.* Humans couldn't even see the world the way over half of the animal life they co-existed with saw it. She was more connected now to the natural flows of the world than she ever had been before, synergistically connected to something so big and vast she felt so tiny and insignificant. As though she existed on a world that was no bigger than a grain of sand and it was adrift within a desert the size of the Sahara. Gwen wished she could bottle this feeling and share it with all of humanity, things would be different then, she'd put money on it. At the very least, go back and share it with her little meditation group. They'd really know what the meaning of those empty sentences that they spouted were all about afterwards.

As she floated outside time and lost within her newly discovered world, other creatures came and went; introducing themselves to her as news of who and what she was spread far and wide. Much in the same way as the whales had, they transmitted their thoughts and feelings via images and emotion. It made Gwen well up on more than one occasion as these humble beings *spoke* to her and told her of their families and lives. Each in their own way and individual styles. It made sense now to her why the Earth was seventy percent water. At least seventy percent of the world's intelligent life was down here. Yet the one thing she was particularly pleased about, was that in her presence, nothing attacked anything else. Both prey and predator came and went with none wanting to insult her by eating each other in her vicinity, even the massive and greatly misunderstood sharks. Gwen wasn't so naïve as to think that they wouldn't revert back to their natural ways once they were at a sufficient distance from her, such was the nature of Nature after all. As cruel and harsh as it was serene and beautiful. Harmony. Balance. The one principle spoken of by many cultures, yet rarely practiced.

Gwen mused over intelligence then and wondered about its measure. Granted, humanity had built machines and tools to further their progress, but on a like for like basis, humanity couldn't hold a candle to the creatures of the natural world. What would humanity do when in the long term, there were more unnatural objects left over, than there was *over* to spill out into? Deserts were increasing, land was falling back into the oceans at an alarming rate, water levels were rising, only partly due to global warming, the remainder from the heat of the ever increasing size of the molten core which was due to hatch from the pregnant Earth sometime in the near future. Jen and Maddy had briefed her on the natural order of progression and how the planets fed the furnace that was the Sun, keeping it alive until the last planet was eventually sucked into it. Apparently, the Earth was due to shift and replace Venus, with our moon moving closer to the Sun to replace Mercury and the ejected, white hot and bubbling core would cool and replace our moon, becoming the new moon for a new Earth, the former Mars. So on and so forth. Its creatures progressing and moving on as they evolved, or not, as the case may be. In her heart of hearts, Gwen knew that the vast majority of humanity wouldn't be moving on. They had lost all sense of what it means to be human, of what being connected to the earth entails, its responsibilities not only to the other creatures that shared this world, but to each other. They had become intent on destroying each other and everything else with as much brutality as possible as well as doing everything conceivable – to the planets detriment – to leave it and venture into space. There would be repercussions for that. What the Adversary was doing could be considered such a repercussion. But Gwen had been told that there was far worse out there than the Adversary. It wasn't him in himself who was so terrible, just what he was doing, misguided as it is. Oh no, there were species out there who had been exiled beyond the Covenant and prohibited from ever stepping foot on any other living world ever again. Now they *were* to be feared, should one of those decide revenge was the order of the day, then humanity would be in really big trouble and they would scream to have the Adversary back. So what did humans do? Send out probes and tons of space garbage to draw attention to themselves. Curiosity was all well and good, but humanity weren't mentally prepared to find anything. The moment they got any alleged visitors, all they wanted to do was shoot them down in the name of national bloody security. Surely the answer is obvious. If you don't want visitors, don't send out invites. If humanity had any inkling of what was out there, they would run for the shelter of the deepest cave, seal it up and pray nothing found them ever again. Gwen only imagined the fear if they ever knew of the Kalithine Empire that preceded them and those beings exiled into the void had not only landed upon this planet but settled it and ruled it for millennia until only a few thousand years ago. They might be gone but how many more lurked in the wings waiting for their day? Gwen shuddered.

Gwen was Drakarim. Her newly adoptive species was one of those from *out there somewhere*; Jen and Maddy had implied as much, though they had kept their exact location to themselves. For her own good they said, until matters here were dealt with, there was no point in over burdening her with specifics. *All in good time* they had said. Damn, how they irritated her when they did that. But powering through the ocean, Gwen found herself arguing with herself, though she amended that to debating. She considered the other side, that not all humans were stupid and self-destructive. Some were seekers. Souls who hoped for a brighter future for their kind and those of the animals who shared our world. Considering us more in the role of curators. They sought enlightenment and guidance, fueled by a genuine need to be and achieve something better with their lives.

Poor saps. They stood out like flaming beacons to the predators of human kind.

There were those who wrapped themselves up in the guise of teachers and gurus. Spouting banalities and incomprehensible rubbish that when broken down, meant absolutely nothing. Talking in riddles to disguise their own lack of substance and wisdom. But if it sounded remotely credible - with the best lies having the most truth in them - it usually did, they drew the seekers to them like moths to their parasitic, vampiric and eventually, doomed flame. These teachers raid and plunder the ancient cultures and fuse it together, often nailing square pegs into round holes to try and find something new and exclusive to them. An ancient and forgotten wisdom that only they can impart. *Bollocks can they* Gwen fumed to herself. Her mental debate was having its usual effect on her, she was getting annoyed again. For there was no real way to police these frauds and tricksters and she knew they knew who they were, how could they not. Sitting in their mansions and vast country houses, paid for by the gullible, and inventing some new ruse to bolster their egos and bank accounts. For all their so called intellectualism and technological prowess, humans still hadn't managed to find or lose the *stupid* gene. Only mere hundreds of years ago, if a person said that they had heard voices from beyond, they were either revered as some sort of prophet or they were stoned as a madman. Nowadays, there were no end of individuals who allegedly spoke to the dead, or some high powered, high ranking spirit guide who had nothing better to do with their afterlife. Yet the majority of humans accepted this all in their stride. Of course, the rest just categorized them with humanities newest set of tools. Illnesses. They were delusional, schizophrenic with some sort of multiple personality disorder or some other sort of *ology*. Just as well they didn't have these illnesses back in biblical days otherwise the world might be an entirely different place. For as much as Gwen could remember - she was never big on religion. *Bloody waste of time* she used to say, earning a clip around the ear from her mother. She still thought that if she was honest. Look what sort of trouble it had gotten the world into she would argue - there had been people all over the place hearing voices, talking to burning hedges, shafts of sunlight and numerous other tales of disembodied voices. *Their padded cells would await them if it was nowadays.*

Take Joan of Arc Gwen would say, *now there's a fine example of female empowerment* thought Gwen, getting into her mental stride. Why did she never come up with gems like this when she argued with Jen and Maddy? Now if some young girl today was to start claiming she heard what she did, no army in the world would drop everything and follow her to war. She would wind up in a lovely cushioned room with all the medication she would ever want, and a lot more she didn't. Certainly the Church would see to that if nobody else did. Absolutely no-one was allowed to be in communication with the divine except them of course. Apparently the divine in question had no say on that matter. Its self-appointed invariably male toadies were the only ones who could dictate who could or who couldn't, which means to say no one could but them, that way their will was and still is unchallenged. Gwen thought that attitude was up there with the epitome of arrogance. Such arrogance from an institution that claimed such humility, even allowing some females into the clergy. Then, Gwen added to her rant, there was this so called division between the religious and the scientists. *How does that work then?* For if they abhorred science as much as they claimed, why was it that when one of their flock - Gwen had always thought that apt, for most of them followed blindly like sheep - had a spiritual experience, why did they insist on then subjecting it to every scientific experiment and test they could come up with to disprove a thing, when they believed in the biggest disprovable thing of all time. They wanted the poor soul to reproduce their experience just because they said so. Another arrogance. It was as though they could call the lightning to strike again in exactly the same place or the wind to blow on command and by that very reasoning, both wind and lightning couldn't be real as they couldn't be replicated on command.

How humans had such an elevated opinion of themselves had been a never-ending source of disappointment and concern for Gwen and she now knew that it was the same disappointment for the leviathans of the deep. But unlike them, having to surface for air every once and a while, Gwen didn't have to. Reluctantly leaving the whales then for some solitary time, though the moment they were gone, Gwen fought the urge to slip back and into Mar-Terasherah just to see what it was all about. It was a tough mental wrestle but her new found sense of responsibility won out and Gwen reluctantly consigned such rebellious thoughts to a far distant corner of her mind. Gwen then plumbed the bottomless trenches instead, investigating chasms that split the ocean beds and even once, she came upon a magnificent, tentacled beast of mythological proportions, making even Gwen in her whale form appear small. It regarded her as she drifted close to it. She didn't know if it was fear or excitement that coursed through her but either way, she was in awe of the giant squid that watched her. It had to be in excess of two hundred and fifty feet tip to tentacle. And it had to have been ancient, even by their standards. Though it was just as well that humans couldn't get this deep, for if they came across a terrifying creature such as this - though Gwen sensed nothing hostile from it, just a sense of gentle curiosity at seeing something different in its world. It felt no fear, for what had it to fear from Gwen as Avatar – only humans were to be feared, for all they would probably want to do was kill it, cut it up and or eat it.

These thoughts and more resounded in Gwen's mind as hours became days and she traversed the vast Atlantic. She totally lost all sense of time as she swam. So rarely had she been alone with herself long enough to ponder the many things that irritated her, and not in such depth as she had been. But now that found herself in such a place and her mind opened for them to have a voice and it seemed that with that voice, they had a lot to say. More time passed.

Something in her mind triggered a memory as Gwen swam and introspected. It was a memory of time spent in Santa Fe, enjoying a summers day with Dolores. Who for once, wasn't working but spending the day in the store with her. Her store, Earth Angel. The one that lovely old lady had bequeathed her. As well as her two lovely shop assistants. Jen and Maddy. Boom. *Jen and Maddy! Drakarim! The quest!* It all came crashing back in on her like her mind had imploded. The enormity of what she faced and the implications of her failure. Suddenly Gwen found it hard to breathe. She shifted through several forms, but it didn't help. She wasn't claustrophobic, she just needed to get to the surface. Fast. Gwen reverted to whale form and with powerful strokes of her massive tail and by sweeping her equally massive flukes downwards, she rocketed upwards like some Trident missile being shot out of one of the many non-existent nuclear submarines that she *hadn't* passed during her journey.

Gwen broke the surface with little regard until after, of what might have been up there. She managed to get her entire body, flukes and tail so far clear of the water that had there been any of those whale watchers nearby, other than wetting themselves at seeing her erupt the way she had, they might have thought she was going to sprout wings and be the first in a new species of flying whale. They might not have been far wrong, had they been watching, for before her gigantic body could slam back down into the undulating waves, Gwen morphed into a sea bird and alighted upon the surface of the heaving sea. Had there been anyone in the vicinity watching a whale turn into a bird, well that would have been one fish tale that would need to have a lot of rum to have been believed. *I really ought to be more careful though where I change, too many questions and I'm in no position yet to have to try and explain myself.* Fortunately for Gwen, though, there were no dinghy driving anoraks up there. She was safe, for now.

Gwen had discovered that during her mental meanderings, she had drifted much further off course than she had ever intended. She had wanted to merely cross the Atlantic, instead, she had been drawn in by the Gulf Stream and the oceanic wonders the whales had shared with her as well as her own solo discoveries. If she was honest with herself, she could spend years down beneath the waves, just exploring. But she also knew that too much now depended on her to succeed in her quest to dally any longer than she already had. Gwen bobbed on the murky and choppy sea, riding wave after wave up and down until she found herself facing yet another coastline. It seemed an age since she saw one last, and that last one would have been Greenland, a rough looking inhospitable terrain what she saw of it from the air, bereft of any life that she could see. The one she was looking at now didn't look any more inviting. She hoped it was the one she had been aiming for originally, though she wasn't sure which bit she was looking at. Not that it mattered much to a being who could fly faster than most aircraft.

Something was tugging at Gwen's mind now she had surfaced and faced land. A more civilized and less primal urge was trying to get her attention. It was her inner voice saying to her that she could use a hot bath, a soft bed and a very large glass of Chardonnay. Agreeing with herself about all three, Gwen morphed once more, from the sea bird she currently was into a grey seal and powered her way towards the rocky coastline. It was late afternoon by the time Gwen reached the rocks. She knew this because of the time of year and the fact it was starting to get dark. She guessed at it being about three in the afternoon. Gwen found a good solid looking flat rock and flopped herself up on to it. Retaining her seal look in case of prying eyes. A petite blonde girl down here would be just *too* suspicious. Though she didn't feel the cold as such - an advantage of being what she was, because she hated the cold really, which was why she moved to the desert in the first place - Gwen shivered all the same. There was a dank and clammy fog clinging to the coastline like some gigantic amorphous parasite. Leaving everything it touched wet, slimy and somehow...violated. It seemed to pulse and flow along the coastline. Probing and sucking at the cliffs as if its mere presence could pull the land and the rocks back into the sea. It was bad enough that the ocean seemed to have similar thoughts, but it had those desires about all land masses. It seemed to want to pull them back into its depths as though it begrudged them ever breaking free from its merciless grip. Though no-one could fault its persistence. Wave after wave crashed upon the rocks as they had done for millennia and would continue to do for eons to come, all being well. For there was little to match the patience of the oceans. They knew they would win eventually. But Gwen's contemplations on the elements and weather made her curious about this particular fog. She had felt something disconcerting when she arrived but had no idea what to ascribe it to. Now she wasn't so sure. Had her shiver been one of prescience? She had heard about the inclement weather of the Emerald Isle, but there was more to this fog than met the eye. It didn't take a meteorologist to know that on this evening, there was no actual wind. But the fog was swirling like a gale was blowing. It oscillated and danced like a living thing, searching, seeking and probing? It may have been her over-worked imagination struggling overtime and playing her for a fool, but she could have sworn it moved with an intent; A deliberate purpose.

Gwen resumed her sea bird form and with little effort, floated her way up the rocky escarpment, her mind still conscious of the menacing fog and her senses keen for any changes or imminent danger; instead, all she saw were half a dozen small stone buildings, looking like large stone beehives jutting out from the rock face. *What a bloody ridiculous place to build something.* Gwen was astounded at the dwellings perched on a ledge in the middle of apparently no-where. But it wasn't until she drifted over them, letting the odd air currents pull her where they will, did she see the great stone stair case that led away from the strange habitation. Wondering who would want to build something out there like that, let alone live in it. She saw as well, something further to dispirit her. For it was only then did she realize she hadn't actually quite made it to Ireland, her original goal, but instead, she had turned up on a rocky island, one of apparently three just off shore. Her bird's vision, now that she was above the fog a little, showed the other two slightly smaller islands a little ways off. Her vision also showed her that both islands were covered in roosting sea birds. So too was the one she flew over. She was no ornithologist, but she did know a Puffin when she saw one and she wasn't entirely sure, but she thought the others might have been Petrels. And Gwen would have been right, as she flapped her gull's wings and set off for the mainland. She had inadvertently drifted out to a collection of small islands known as the Skelligs. *I don't know how I've managed to get this far and do what I have already, I get lost in my own damn house some days. How I'm supposed to scoot all around the bloody world and find this tree when I can't even find a bloody great island without landing on the wrong bit is a fine way to carry on.* It wasn't that she was stressed, she had always been lucky that way, but there was an element of frustration that built in her when things didn't go as smoothly as she expected them to and that made her grouchy. She soared over the roosting birds, disturbing one or two and having to flap off a bit faster as they swooped at her, oblivious to who she was to them. All they saw was another bird who shouldn't have been there. She didn't have the time or the patience to explain it to them, so she just took off a bit faster and put some distance and air between her and them, flying upwards to both avoid any further harassment and to get a better view.

Gwen didn't notice at first, but the fog was suddenly conspicuous by its absence. She glanced back and saw it clinging nastily to the two islands, or trying to. It was as if something held it just off, a force field of some sorts, Gwen shrugged mentally not really having any other explanation. *Too much sci-fi Gwen me old girl.* The fog was squatting over them like an obscene bleve. It was an odd thought that Gwen had, having had a gas cloud described to her once, and of how it hung in the air just waiting to explode. It was an appropriate choice of word as a gaseous reference to describe the fog, for Gwen didn't know it, but the word gas originated from two other words, one being the Greek *Khaos* and the other, the old English Chaos. This Chaos was a reference to several things that lent it credibility as a menacing entity. Two being, the Void and the Abyss. Both had infernal connotations. Yet unbeknownst to Gwen, the fog, as she flew through it, had sensed her too. It started to follow.

Gwen knew nothing of the region below her as she flew on oblivious, as far as she was concerned, she could have been anywhere on the West coast. She needed to take stock and that meant finding someone and getting her bearings. Her book worming back at the store had implied that Ireland was a good candidate for the First Tree. It was steeped in natural mythology and the home of the legendary druids. *Weren't they guardians of trees and groves after all?* It made sense to Gwen. Avalon was another candidate, though not in Ireland, it was close and that had a fabulous tree by all accounts. Gwen didn't know exactly, but then who did and after all, if Arthur sailed west from anywhere near or around the West Country of England, where might he end up? Ireland? Or one of its little isles. She knew it was tenuous, but what choice did she have? She wasn't exactly brimming over with viable alternatives. People far brighter than her had spent their entire lives looking for fabled and long lost things and never found them, she probably had days at most to find something that no-one had even looked for. *Easy Gwen girl, never say never. Just think, this time last month you weren't a bloody big green dragon, shit happens in the weirdest way if you let it, so breathe and see what appears, it's all you can do.* She knew she was talking to herself, she also knew she did it all the time, *always had, always will I suppose.* Gwen was happy with herself and who she was and had become so therefore trusted the answers she gave herself when she was in a fix.

Gwen swooped down and landed on a vast stretch of beach as night fell. It wasn't the brightest of moons that night and it cast a surreal haze across the beach. The tide was out and she stood upon a vast sandy expanse, one lone sea gull in the moonlight wouldn't attract too much attention, even if there was anyone to see her - but there wasn't. Not even a house light. *Bloody marvelous, I must have picked the least inhabited bit of Ireland I could find.* But for all that, it felt good beneath her gull's feet to be on solid ground once more. With another glance around her, Gwen risked a transformation back to her own form. She felt the rush of enjoyment as the cool air brushed across her skin and the salty air brought a million miniscule droplets of ocean spray and flecked her body with their touch, almost a parting farewell after cradling her in the depths for so long. Gwen no longer felt the cold and she was equally no longer embarrassed by her nakedness, having come to terms with who she was; but it hadn't stopped her noticing the little things about what happened to her body. Though she no longer felt the extremes of heat and cold in the same way she had, she couldn't help but notice how her breathe plumed before her, like standing in a chiller. Though it wasn't *that* cold, even here, on some remote Irish beach in the early hours of the morning during mid-winter. It was too wet and salty to freeze, but the more she looked, the more she saw inconsistencies with the weather patterns. The sand beneath her bare feet, wasn't just wet and hard packed, *it was frozen.* Gwen knelt down and knocked it with her knuckles. It gave a hard solid *thunk*, definitely *not* like sand. She stood and turned about, her hackles had risen at this unnaturalness and she sought the cause. Though there was nothing immediately obvious except for one thing, the fog. It was creeping inexorably closer. Snaking its way across the water like a living thing. Floating a few feet above the chasing waves as if it was loathe to touch it. *It doesn't seem to like salt water. Hmm.* This little revelation allowed Gwen to make a leap of assumption, for when she had flown up over the Everglades and begun to track north, a small group of deminions had followed her, but they wouldn't leave the land and attack her out at sea. So she had stayed off shore and they eventually gave up chasing her and swept inland. They didn't seem to want to venture over salt water either, it was an interesting little fact to store away. The fog was definitely unnatural enough to be a weapon of the Adversary. But how do you fight a fog? She knew she didn't have long as it oozed, undulated and unfurled ever closer. Placing her hands upon her hips she set her jaw and watched it for a few moments as she organized her thoughts. Then, much to the consternation of whatever might have been behind the fog, she laughed. She had gotten a mental image of what she must look like to any observer. A tiny naked woman, standing defiant on a vast frozen beach in the middle of the night on a deserted Irish coastline, attempting to mentally halt and or prepare to fight a creeping fog. *Good girl, that's the way, keep your sense of humor.* With a reality check, she controlled herself and recalled her situation. This sobered her slightly. Gwen knew she couldn't stop a fog and it wasn't like it was moving overly fast, so turning on her heel, she strode away from the sea shore, leaving it skulking behind her and headed inland. A quick shimmer and she was a creamy pale owl, ghosting silently away. No sooner had she transformed and gained a little height, she saw an old monastery. Hoping for a friar or a monk awake at this hour, or whoever lived in such things. She would have been happy to see anyone really, at this moment in time. Any human face would have been a joy to behold about then. It wasn't that she had missed humanity particularly - quite the opposite - but when she needed information about where she was, it was typical that there wasn't a bloody soul to be seen. But she banked round and headed in the Abbeys direction. But swooping down and circling it once, Gwen dejectedly saw no signs of life, in fact, she couldn't even tell if it was even inhabited at all. *Tonight is just getting better.* What to do now Gwen pondered. Seconds later, the answer materialized out of the darkness. A road. It was the first bit of what Gwen thought of as proper civilization she had seen that didn't look like it was out of the dark ages. *Now that's more like it.* Her owl silently winged along it for a mile or two and was rewarded with a sign, but upon closer inspection, it just read the R566 and was no help at all. It didn't say where it went or where it had come from. Alighting upon the useless thing, she ruffled her smoky white feathers and thought about her next move. She hadn't seen any cars on her way, not coming or going, though for the life of her, she couldn't imagine why anyone would be going in the direction she had just come from, there was sod all there, just a bloody huge beach, a malevolent fog and an old monastery. After half an hour of sitting there, she was still alone, not one car had passed her either way. She wondered whether it would be wise to find some tree and roost for a bit, wait till daylight and see if things got any better. *They sure as shit couldn't get any worse.* Gwen discovered then, almost as soon as the last resonant syllable faded from her mind that saying those words was not dissimilar to waving a red rag at a bull, whilst wearing a red jump-suit then poking it up the arse with a cattle prod beforehand-cuffing yourself to its nose ring and chewing on its ears. It was never going to end well.

Somewhere in the darkness, back in the direction of the beach, came an unearthly screech. Her every mortal fiber and Drakarim's intuition told her emphatically that it was truly unearthly. *What the bloody hell was that?* Gwen growled to herself. The owl's massive vibrant eyes fixed on the inky skyline where she sensed the sound had originated, but even with her supernatural sight, she couldn't pierce the oily blackness. But her skin had begun to crawl with a sense of dread and anticipation. It was like a thousand ants running over her flesh - an image she quashed as soon as it popped into her head. But it was followed by yet more gruesome images of her flesh being swarmed over and devoured in the most graphic and horrendous ways possible by every manner of creature from crabs, through to beetles, then worms, rats, slugs, scorpions and a plethora of equally nasty species. Were it not for the fact that Gwen was more than she was, her mortal mind would have been overwhelmed by the sheer horror of what she was experiencing. It took a moments exertion of her will power to banish both the images and the sense of terror and dread that had accompanied it. Her mind fighting the urge to brush at her skin to remove any last vestige of whatever had been crawling over her, but it was then she remembered that she was in owl form and that might have been a bit difficult anyway. In a shimmer of emerald green sparks, Gwen was herself once more and subconsciously clothed in her clinging dress of tightly woven green leaves that seemed to emerge from her very skin and flow over her body. Her hair lifted slightly from her scalp as though a slight electrical current toyed with her and framed her face with a corona of gently waving golden hair. Power began to course exponentially through Gwen as the feeling of dread increased. It descended on her like a hail storm, slamming into her and crashing over her like a wave over a rock. Again the screech and Gwen grimaced involuntarily. Shaking her head to clear the sound, it was reminiscent of an infernal fusion of finger nails down a chalk board and a rusty nail over glass only ramped up through the decibel range for maximum effect. She knew then what she faced. Deminions; demonic foot soldiers much like the ones she had encountered before, only this time they were between her and the ocean prohibiting a swift exit. Another bone chilling howl, and this time it was accompanied by the tell-tale tendrils of the creeping fog. *So then, it was connected to them after all, shoulda guessed.* But before Gwen could beat herself up about not putting two and two together, she felt another wave of the fear and terror that these creatures clearly emanated wash over her, casting it ahead of them like a weapon to unman their prey before attacking. Grimacing at the slick oily touch of their essence, Gwen knew she had to do something, standing in the middle of the road waiting for it to come to her wasn't going to accomplish anything. At that moment, Gwen was truly glad that there were no people around. It was bad enough her having to confront these creatures at all, but it would have been devastating for Joe public to have to witness it. She imagined what humanity must have felt in the dark and less enlightened past when these creatures made impromptu appearances. They screwed with the mind first before destroying the body, it had to be awful beyond imagining. The total opposite, she guessed of meeting one of the Celestial host, weren't they supposed to be all love and light? Whatever they were, it had to be better than what was coming from these fiends. Another screech, no two. Separate. They were closer than ever and Gwen sensed they had split up to come at her from either side. At least that was how it sounded to Gwen's now supernaturally sensitive ears. But instead of fear, Gwen found a spark had ignited within her, slowly smoldering into a small flame. It was the flame of righteous and indignant anger. This was *her* world now, she was responsible for its safety and well-being. And like the cells that protects the body from damage and infection, she felt a rising urge to swell up and eradicate this demonic infection from her body. The more she thought of it, the brighter and hotter the flame within her became until she could contain it no longer. It began to cloud her vision and with no conscious thought, Gwen threw back her head and screamed herself, venting the rage that manifested within her in the only way she knew how. The way her arms were flung wide and the increased wind that had rolled in with the fog plucked at her leafy clothing and hair as if it would tear her from the ground upon which she was literally rooted. It had no chance of doing that, though it tried. She looked - again, had there been anyone to see - like a true queen of the Banshees, clothed in flowing green, her emerald eyes aflame with iridescent viridian fire, she leant into the rising wind and roared at the encroaching fog with such force that it balked. It actually hesitated, even the Morrigan herself would have hesitated at that. Where the tendrils and fronds of the foetid mist were undulating around and over everything in its path, obliterating visibility within its grey confines - at the sound of Gwen's fury, they actually retreated several yards.

Gwen's present consciousness returned to her as the roar cut off. She was breathing hard, her chest rising and falling as though she had run a marathon. Righteous anger coursed through her veins, pumping adrenaline around her body like a hydro-electric dam and power flowed through her being until she fought to both control and contain it. Reason returned to her with a jolt and she knew that she had to put an end to this abhorrence once and for all. In order to that, rather than stand and wait for them to attack her on their terms, she would find them first and meet them on hers. Gwen grinned evilly as she turned briefly, ran a few steps and leapt into the air, arms outstretched as though she were cliff diving, but a jade shimmer later and the hawk was powering skyward. Her beating wings sending her straight into the heart of the fog. If they wanted her, they would have to catch her. She sped off, twisting and diving with all the acrobatic skills available to her. And it wasn't long before she sensed that the fiends were following her, then another soul wrenching screech split the night sky and confirmed it. *I really wish they would stop doing that, it's getting on my nerves and my bloody ears are bleeding.* They weren't, but she felt as though they would be if they carried on howling like they were. She needed a plan. Just being angry at them wasn't going to do it. Diving amongst a cluster of abandoned slate roofed cottages, she scored her talons along one ridge tile and banked upwards, angling sharply left to help alleviate her growing uneasiness that they were right behind her. She almost imagined their foul breathe, spewing their noxious vapors on her neck. Fangs and talons just about to reach for her and rend the life from her body. *Think Gwen think.* She considered the dragon form but worried that seeing a bloody great big green dragon might be just as terrifying to the populace as these new flying deminions evidently were with their emanations of fear and horror, totally unaware that her own brother, Major Tomas Walker had felt the very same thing when he dispatched his deminion, the same fury sloughing off the magical dread as his own power took charge. As if the good people of Ireland weren't going to have enough nightmares to last several lifetimes as it was if these foul denizens were ever seen Gwen was unsure whether to add to that burden. Another screech made her mind up though. What options did she really have? She was built now to fight creatures such as these if not particularly trained in how to do so; *sod it,* she wasn't designed to fight anything as a girl, she was no bloody soldier; worse still was that she didn't have any sort a weapon, nor any clue as how to use one even if she did. *Probably do myself more harm than whatever I was aiming at.* Gwen ducked, dived and spun several more times but she still knew that they were gaining on her. She made a choice. *Dammit! I'm in Ireland after all and don't they have those little green people anyway and more myths and legends about fantastic creatures than you could wave a shillelagh at. So what if they saw a dragon, I am bloody green, what more do they want? Perhaps they won't be as disturbed by it as all that.* Happy with her rationale, Gwen picked up the pace and dived for a small copse of trees just ahead of her and the fog. She burst out of the damp, clinging mist and ploughed straight into the little wood. Weaving expertly between oak, ash and birch, taking full advantage of her lithe and muscular hawk form, until the moment when she exploded out the other side, spinning like a bullet from a rifled gun barrel. She knew she only had seconds, they were that close. The moment her wings cleared the foliage, Gwen made the transition in a dazzling double helical shower of incandescent green sparks. Snapping her majestic and massive draconian wings outward with an audible slap, like great sails on a galleon catching the wind, Gwen spun her reptilian self just as the deminions - visible now that they were outside the concealment of their insidious mist - burst clear of the trees, sending roosting birds and leaves in all directions. Their talons outstretched and overly wide mouths stretched to almost tearing as they screamed their impotent rage at their quarry. It was a scream that changed tune almost immediately, from rage to a terror of their own. For instead of finding some small feathered bird, they were met full on with a thunderous crash of bone, chiton and whatever else went into these deminions, as they connected at full speed with several tons of very angry, very fast moving and heavily spiked, scaled and armor plated green dragon tail. The effect was reminiscent of tossing a couple of melons into the path of a speeding express train. It was all over in heartbeat. As Gwen landed, quite delicately and surveyed her handiwork - shaking deminion remains off her tail - she was slightly disappointed that the mist didn't immediately dissipate with their demise, it merely retreated back beyond her visibility, back towards the coast. Gwen had no more time to spend on it though, she had other matters to attend to and one such task was to clear the tenacious and sticky remains of the deminions off her tail. She flicked her long powerful tail, whipping the mess that remained clinging persistently to it, in a spatter of gore and slimy bits. Distracted as she was initially by her draconian hygiene, Gwen didn't hear her worst fear realized. Excited, but not in a good way and slightly panicked voices filtered through to her as though she had sponge in her ears. They seemed distant and muffled but they became clearer as her mind focused on them, realizing them for what they were. Gwen was horrified. Whipping her massive reptilian head round on her long muscular, serpentine neck, Gwen levelled her car sized head at them, with her sparkling, bejeweled and multi-faceted eyes just a few feet away from the three people who were standing there, as rigid as statues with their own fear filled eyes as wide as saucers, standing next to a beat up and dilapidated range rover. They were gesticulating wildly at her until her head drew even closer to them, then they stopped all movement as if they had been frozen. The only indication that they weren't statues was the way their clothes and hair wafted gently back and forth as Gwen breathed softly in and out on them. The tableau was likely to be indelibly printed on their DNA for lifetimes to come as the three men, two of middle years and rough attire, unshaven in various shades of green themselves, heavy waxed waterproof coats with a brace of rabbits feet poking out from an overly deep pocket hinted at the tale of why they were out at this unsociable hour. The third was considerably younger; no more than his mid-twenties with features that would ensure him an interesting future. Rugged and lightly tanned, from time spent out in the open but tempered with youthful good looks, black wavy hair that he had pulled back into small pony tail, full - if quivering - lips and startling hazel eyes. *He'll have no trouble with the girls.* Gwen studied the three men before her, who must be so far beyond terrified they were in a whole new place. To one of the elder men's shame, Gwen saw the tell-tale darkening of his trousers and smelt the pungent waft of ammonia, but he paid his embarrassment no mind, refusing to take his eyes from the beast before him. Fully expecting it to swallow him up any second. She saw the other man, mutter from the side of his mouth, trying to speak and not look as though he was. And making a poor show of it. He sure was no ventriloquist.

'Don't move boys. I've heard o' these beasties, they can't see you if you don't move.' They didn't move and it had little to do with their companion's sage advice. Encouraged by their lack of movement and the fact he hadn't been munched upon yet, he continued his life saving suggestions in the face of a giant green dragon.

'If we stand still long enough, maybe it will just go away, it'll be dawn soon and they don't like the sun, or so's I've heard at least. T'was a tale me da tol' me when I was nought but tadpole meself.' Without looking at him, pant wetter whispered back just as badly.

'Will you shut ya face, ya ruddy gobshite, it can probably hear you shooting ya mouth off, Mary Mother of God, you've no got the sense yee were born with, our Daniel has more sense than you, at least he's not blabbing like an old woman.' Gwen was sure a full blown punch up would have ensued before long, whether she was there or not as they continued to berate each other about how they should behave in front of the dragon. What was she going to do with them? Of all the places to find people, right when she was in mid transformation. They had seen it all. Gwen figured she wasn't going to get a lot of sense out of them if she spoke to them, certainly not as a dragon. Even if she resumed her own form she thought it might be hard work. Gwen snaked her head a bit closer and on an in breathe she caught the familiar smell of alcohol. Lots of alcohol. They were a trio of half cut poachers, so who were they going to tell? And if they found anyone, who would believe them. But as Gwen moved closer, her choices were taken from her as one of them, the young one they called Daniel, promptly fainted dead away at their feet. They stopped their outrageous debate and both turned to look at their fallen companion, then they looked at the dragon. She could almost see the thought going through their heads. Run or tend to their friend; Run, friend, run, friend. Or as Gwen discovered, there was third option, fallen friend distract dragon, then run. They apparently liked that one, for without a backward glance, as though they shared the same thought at the same time, the two men spun and scrambled away as fast as they could. One tossing his rabbits over his shoulder as he desperately tried to get his legs to co-ordinate with each other, possibly in the vain hope the rabbits would distract said *beastie* from eating them. *Nice friends*, thought Gwen with barely restrained amusement as she looked down upon the prone man sprawled in the damp grass.

Gwen wasn't quite sure what to do next as she morphed back to her own form. Complete with denims, hiking boots and quilted jacket over a roll neck sweater, adding to the ensemble one of those quaint and quirky woolen hats she saw the skiers wear as they went up the mountains back in New Mexico for the skiing there. Her quandary was either follow the men and see where they went, for there had to be a town nearby, the men had to come from somewhere and hopefully that was where they were fleeing back to; Or, tend to the fainter, seeing as she was responsible for his predicament and she couldn't leave him to the mercy of any more of those deminions just in case they had friends in the area who came looking for their chums. It was a tough one as the call of civilization beckoned invitingly to her - civilization which was bound to have a public house and even a bed and breakfast with real beds. Gwen sighed and scrubbed her hand through her unkempt yet lustrous hair under her hat as she realized that in all the excitement of the quest and the series of tumultuous events that had led to her being here, she had no money. And a bed and breakfast was going to want paying. All powerful Drakarim Avatar of Nature, Immortal by all accounts and as magical as they come but didn't have nickel to her name. How embarrassing, yet fitting and Gwen laughed at the irony. Quickly she shoved the guilty thought from her mind about seeing if the fainter had any money on him. She was just being weak and pathetic. Home comforts would have to wait – it wasn't like she really needed them now - but she couldn't leave him to the mercy of the oncoming night, lying unconscious in a wet field. So squashing her hat back down, Gwen picked him up, recalling the ease in which the girls moved Dolores and found that she too had strength she didn't have before. Giggling to herself at her new found abilities she easily lifted the prone man and placed him in his car - at least she assumed it was his car. She assumed correctly as she did in fact rifle through his pockets and upon finding a bunch of car keys - which, to her relief, fitted - she started the car. Placing him in the passenger seat, Gwen jumped in the driver's seat and fired it up. The dilapidated heater kicked in and after belching out some foul smelling cold air, finally started to warm up. Something that passed for music grumbled out of the stereo. Which looked newer and in better condition than the entire vehicle. *What is it with boys and their car stereos? As long as they have music while they drive, they'll take any old crap out on the road and be happy. Seems our boy here is no exception.* Changing her mind about driving him away, she wondered how he would take it when he awoke and found some strange woman driving him in his car when the last thing he recalled would be staring into the jaws of imminent death in the form of a massive green dragon. No, that wouldn't be fair on him. Instead, she leant over and kissed him lightly on the cheek, which elicited a small groan signifying he was coming round. Her kiss also suffused some color back into his cheeks, as though she had kissed a tiny healing spell onto him, she was an Avatar of nature after all. *Wow, I'll have to remember how to do that again whatever I did, still, good enough for now, he should be okay, or at least I hope so, I can't stay with him all night.* He'll probably be too hacked off at his friends for doing a bunk and leaving him to worry about how he got in the car. Smiling to herself as she climbed out, she closed the door quietly and took a few backward steps away, watching to see if he woke. When he didn't immediately wake but began looking though he was about to, Gwen sparkled into her owl form and ghosted away on silent wings, content enough for now that he'd live.

# Chapter 8

## Smaragaid

Back to Gwen's matter at hand, which was getting herself some sort of bearing, she ghosted back towards the road and relying on her heightened instincts, she drifted towards the right and with only a vague directional feeling, she headed east. After gaining a bit of height, she saw houses off in the distance. *About bloody time.* But like the few cottages she had flown over earlier, there were no lights on. *Maybe they are just being cautious, or prudent, or even guilty about their carbon footprint.* Gwen was hoping for a rational explanation, but in her gut, she just knew that wasn't going to be the case. She landed and adopted her own form again. Manifesting her hikers gear back on, she stuffed her hands in her pockets and thought she would look better to walk into town in case they had watchers monitoring the roads. Again Gwen assumed the conflict had reached even here and she behaved as though it had, as though it was a war; which of course it was, but the only war Gwen knew about was what she watched on TV. That was her only training about how to behave when entering potentially hostile territory. For all she knew it could be overrun with the Adversary' forces and everyone dead. But that didn't explain where the fainter and his companions had come from. Too many questions and too few answers, the whole thing was giving her a headache. Guessing the time at stupid o clock in the morning, she doubted there would be much open or happening anyway. *So much for my warm bed and wine.* Gwen chuckled to herself as she thought that she was whining plenty to cover that aspect. She passed a sign that for the first time, gave her an idea of where she was going. It had two names on it and Gwen figured that one of them was the Irish for the other. It said An Snaidhm and underneath it, it had the word Sneem. *Three miles. Three bloody miles? I'm not walking that, bugger me I thought I was closer than that. It hadn't seemed so far away as an owl.* It was the different perspective between flying high above with the birds eye view and pounding the tarmac on two legs that she was going to have to get used to. But just before she resumed her owl form, she heard a sound that had been absent since she had made landfall. That of an oncoming car. Instinctively, Gwen stepped to the side of the road to avoid being hit, naturally assuming that they drove on the same side to what she was used to. But she had forgotten where she was, this wasn't America but more like Great Britain, albeit Ireland. The place she had left many years before. And what she didn't take into account was having gotten so used to American roads was that the Irish drove on the opposite side to them. So she virtually walked out in front of the oncoming car. All she saw were headlights, and the sound of squealing brakes, with incapable tires desperately gripping to anything beneath them trying to stop the forward momentum of the car on a mist slick road, screeching on the aged, gravel strewn tarmac with a smell of burning rubber accompanying the sound. Gwen disjointedly and somewhat randomly noticed that one light was dimmer than the other as though a bulb had blown and with an instant recognition, she knew who this was. It was the Fainter, now awake and in flight.

The car, with no hope of actually stopping skidded straight into Gwen, but she bounced casually backwards with it as it slowed, slamming her hands onto the hood of the car to stop it going over her. Gwen hadn't counted on her own increased strength and density as instinct took over. She moved only a couple of feet and the car was brought to a dead stop with the rear wheels rising a few feet off the road before dropping back down with an unhealthy sounding bump. Gwen also didn't notice at first the pair of delicate hand prints she had left on the hood. Gwen squinted through the grimy windscreen as the glare of the lights, poor as they were prevented her seeing clearly inside, so she covered her eyes with one hand and walked around to the driver's window, as she did, Gwen heard the tell-tale squeal of a window being painfully wound down. Once out of the glare of the one mostly working head light, which even that gradually died as the car gave up any pretense of running, her vision settled itself again and she saw the familiar yet pale, haggard face of fainter. He wore the expression of one who had just had something fundamental happen to him but at a total loss as how to explain it to himself, let alone anyone else.

'Hi there.' Gwen thought she should start friendly and see how it went. 'That was a close thing, silly me getting in the way like that, what was I thinking?' Gwen smacked her forehead as if to say *Duh*. Fainter looked at her as though he had seen a ghost, but couldn't work out how or where or why. Instead, he just shook his head and wiped his own moist forehead, grinning lopsidedly as he did so.

'Luckier than you know gal.' He spoke with that cool and lilting Irish accent that gave women the world over weak knees and even in his distraught state, his voice was still melodic if a little higher pitched than it should have been.

'The brakes on the car aren't what they were and don't always work. 'Especially not in the wet. Musta picked a fine time to do what they shoulda, else you would have been road kill I suspect.' The subject of killing things brought his recent memories back in a rush and the color drained from him all over again.

'You okay?' Gwen asked innocently, 'you look like you've seen a ghost, are you ill?'

'You have *no idea* what I've seen gal. It was the bi…' He cut himself off and stared right at Gwen as he rethought what he was about to say. 'There's things out there that have no business being out there is all, and I have had the misfortune of seeing one o'them, but thank the Virgin Mary Mother of God, I was spared, but I've no idea what happened to Kieran and Barry. We were altogether, then I woke up in me car on me own…' at this point he whispered conspiratorially '…then they were gone. I so hope they weren't eaten' He crossed himself automatically in that time honored good old Catholic way Gwen had seen her mother do a million times.

'Sounds scary,' Gwen agreed 'but maybe they just ran away. You seem alright now though, so whatever it was has gone has it?' He nodded. It was then that Gwen spotted the six pack of beer in the passenger foot-well, as well as a few empties. 'You sure it wasn't little green men coupled with a few fermented ones and an over vivid beer dream?' She inclined her head towards the cans, indicating she had seen them and put two and two together. He saw what she was looking at and scrubbed his hands over his face and hair again, groaning as he did so, slumping his head onto the steering wheel with an audible thud.

'I don't know, I can't be sure of anything right now, but it was so real.' Gwen nodded sagely, reaching in and putting a supportive hand on his arm.

'Of course it did, they always do. Now, I've got an idea. Why don't you do the gentleman thing and offer me a lift to town, where I can find a hotel and you can find your friends, I'm sure they'll put your mind to rest and you'll all have a good laugh about it.' He sat up suddenly, frowned and seemed to be concentrating on something that eluded him. Turns out, it was making a decision. He leant over and opened the passenger door from the inside. Turning back to her, he smiled weakly at her and explained that several things didn't work on the battered old car, the door was one of them. Gwen walked around and climbed up and settled herself in, reaching across with her hand extended, Gwen introduced herself.

'Hi, I'm Gwen and at two in the morning walking down a dark and wet country road, it's *really* nice to meet you.' Daniel looked at her hand suspiciously, weighing up her words - and the slight to Gwen - but clear American accent to fainter. For a few seconds longer than might be appropriate Daniel paused before grasping it and shaking it gently as though he were afraid he would break her.

'Daniel. Daniel Fitzgerald. Pleased to make your acquaintance I'm sure Gwen. Now, going to town are you? Strange time to be out and about though wouldn't you say?' Gwen was afraid of this, how to explain her weird nocturnal roamings. Gwen shrugged, recounting the first thing that came into her head.

'My bike got a flat a couple of miles back and would you believe as I was fixing it, I slipped, all girly like' Gwen made useless gestures 'and managed to put a hole in my tent, so there I was...' His expression said how the hell did you manage to do that? 'Don't ask' Gwen anticipated 'but I just thought sod it! A night in a hotel won't do me any harm and I'll face it tomorrow in the daylight and maybe it'll all be a bit drier too. So I left my bike and pack and started walking. But would you believe just how far it is to walk when you are used to riding? A long bloody way I can tell you. I thought Sneem was closer than that, but I've got blisters on my blisters now and I'm really fed up with this walking bollocks, so I really am glad you came along, my knight in rusty green armor.' Gwen quipped tapping the door and describing the cars condition to a tee smiling her most charming as she did so.

The smile and the tale weren't lost on him, but a shadow swept by and caused him to grab his rear view mirror and stare into it, he then hung out of his window and stared off into the darkness, trying to see something.

'What is it?' Gwen asked a little panicked by his behavior. Had more deminions found her again? 'We should go Daniel, come on, it was probably an owl. I've seen a few tonight.' Gwen hoped her voice sounded calm and level. He turned back to her, the haunted look had returned and he just nodded wordlessly, winding his window up and with one last check around and behind, he fired up the ignition once more and dropped the car into gear and tore off like he was pole position at some Grand Prix. Tires squealed for a second time as they fought again for traction and soon found just enough to launch them forwards with more spraying of gravel. The engine screamed itself from time to time as Daniel went through the gears a little too fast. In fact, he did everything a little too fast, which included talking but it was especially his driving that Gwen was paying the most attention to and she had been driven through New York, but this was something else entirely.

'You do know *how* to drive I take it?' the note of panic took on a genuine tone as she reached for the seat belt and buckled herself in. Just in time too, for he took a sudden turn off the main road on to what could only be called generously, a horse track.

'Of course I do, I've been driving these roads since I was ten. You just sit back and enjoy the ride.' Gwen grabbed the dash then with both hands as the four wheel drive was pushed to its operating limits over the bomb site that passed for a road. She tried to see the expression of boyish glee that came over Daniels face as he whooped and grinned as the car was thrown all over the place. Hurtling along in the dark as the car bounced up and down, suspension working at full capacity as hole after hole put it through its paces. And in between preventing her head from bouncing off the roof, Gwen tried ask where it was exactly they were going.

'Oh, we're going to my sister's place. It's just outside town.' Gwen tried a why? As the car hit another series of pot holes but the single word came out as a strangled word with several syllables. 'Wh-huh-huh-hy?' Daniel laughed some more as he threw the vehicle into top gear and jammed his foot down on the gas as far as it would go. The vehicle picked up speed and to Gwen's consternation, began to then head downhill too.

'Because me little blonde wanderer' Daniel explained gleefully 'you have no chance what so ever of finding a hotel open in town at this hour and even less of a chance since the troubles started.' Gwen was immediately interested, even to the extent of taking her eyes off the road to stare at Daniel. She asked what sort of troubles and he turned to look back at her.

'I don't rightly know lass, but it's had people disappearing gradually over the last couple of months. Shops have shut and not opened again, the same with the hotels and worst of all, the pubs have all shut. I can live without food, but not without me beer.'

'*Will you watch the bloody road!*' Gwen screamed at him. Daniel casually looked forward and made a show of peering into the night, trying to see with the insipid illumination provided by the one and a half dodgy headlights.

'What? Why? What have you seen?' Gwen was gob smacked. She couldn't believe the blasé way he was treating their break neck early hours journey through the Irish countryside.

'What have I seen? The bloody road you dullard. Keep your goddamn eyes on it, I have no intention of dying in the middle of nowhere least of all in this mechanical death trap, you know it would actually help if you used the brakes every now and again.'

'How can you say such things about my baby, she's a bit shy of the working parts, some of them even vital but it keeps on going and regarding the brakes, well sure enough I would use them if they actually worked like they should, you saw how badly they function first hand.'

'What do you mean if they worked?' Gwen stammered incredulously, taking a quick glance at the speedometer. Which she wasn't entirely surprised to find it not working either but could only guess that by the way the foliage and terrain was hurtling by them in a nocturnal blur that they were bombing by in the area of fifty to sixty miles an hour easily.

'Just as I say. They're fickle alright.' Daniel looked at her again as he spoke. 'But you have nothing to worry about, I know this road like the back of my hand, you see I was born out here. Me sister is living in the house we were both born in, so I grew up out here, in fact I probably put a few of these holes in this blessed road meself, so I ought to know where I'm going. The bloody car is probably on auto pilot anyway.' He laughed at his own joke, but Gwen was having trouble seeing the funny side. She was in less danger from the deminions than from this loon and his excuse of a car.

'We're nearly there anyway, just a few more bends and the little hill then Bob's your uncle and fanny's your aunt.' Gwen's mind raced and her imagination envisioned several scenarios involving burning car wrecks. *More bends and a hill? We're dead meat.* She even tried closing her eyes but that made it worse. Slung around and not seeing where she was going made it worse than any fairground ride. But what made it worse for Gwen, was the fact he drove one handed, the other rested nonchalantly on the gear shift. Then he had the nerve to take it off the wheel completely as he pointed out the dim outline of some distant building.

'There! You see that? That's me sisters house god bless her. She'll put you up for the night and it won't be so far back to your bike, not as the crow flies anyway, we can do the short cut tomorrow – if it's not raining. You see, she offers it out as a little bed and brekky, but off the books you understand, it's not official and all, but it helps with the bills occasionally. We get a lot of tourists round here you see and not all of them plan too well in advance so there's plenty to go around.' Ignoring her wide eyed look of horror, Daniel carried on chatting as they navigated the bends and started thundering down yet another hill.

'But things have been a bit quiet lately' Daniel continued, 'as I said. There's been no people coming for a while; In fact gal, the more I think of it, you're the first I've seen in months. And you *didn't* see the bloody big beastie that was out there earlier? Don't ya think that's a bit strange? Cos now I come to think of it, I do. You, a lone girly wandering the countryside on the self-same night I have me experience...' Gwen, in between hanging on to the car for grim death, was desperate for them to reach the house before he began making sense out of what shouldn't be made sense from. They hit the bottom of the hill in a spray of water as they forded a small stream that meandered across the road thankfully slowing them considerably. At a much slower speed, the car began to rumble up the incline that was on the other side of the ford. The event distracted Daniel momentarily as he felt the need to explain what just happened.

'...that was why I had to go so fast down the hill; if you don't get enough speed up, when you hit the water you don't have enough oomph to get up the other side, 'specially when both the gas *and* the brakes lock up after the water.' Gwen shot him a concerned look, one that implied that she would probably have been safer outside with whatever he thought was out there.

'So you're saying you didn't see or hear nothing?' Daniel suddenly asked and Gwen shook her head, but knew the gesture for the futile effort it was, so she backed it up by telling him no too.

'I'm sorry, I didn't hear or see what you did, but it's a big place out there and I can't help coincidence. I'm sure you believe what you saw but can you hear yourself? Don't you know dragons don't exist? This is Ireland I know and you're full to the brim with mythology, but this is the twenty first century and we don't have those sort of things anymore. They're all crocodiles and Komodo dragons now, big lizards and the like.' Daniel, with the disconcerting habit he had of watching her instead of the road, stared at her with a mixture of expression and obvious thought going through his head, ranging from belief, agreement, confusion back to disbelief and distrust. She was even sure she saw fear flit through there somewhere. A fear in his eyes as he looked at her as though she was about to turn into something there and then and ravage him. But their impending destination stole the moment from him and he was distracted instead by stopping.

The car was slowing and Gwen spared a glance ahead - not entirely sure she wanted to see what they were going to plough into - but she saw, to her relief that they had slowed to a crawl as they crested the little rise and were coasting towards a large tree about fifty feet from the house. She anticipated what was about to happen as she saw the groove in the bark a few feet from the ground. The car bounced gently off the tree and came to a whirring halt as the engine turned itself off.

'There you go!' And there she went. Climbing from the car, and placing her shaky legs and feet on the ground Gwen pushed herself out and walked, albeit a tad wobbly around to Daniels side where he had wound the window down again. Still watching her suspiciously. She alternated looks between him and the picture postcard cottage a short walk away. It was at first glance a stylized romantic looking cottage. Slate roof, dry stone brick wall surrounding the building with ivy and climbers and another tree forming one side of the gated entrance through the wall. There was one main door Gwen could see - big and green - central to the building with a window above and two more, one either side, top and bottom. *Ironic* Gwen thought. But after the initial impact wore off, Gwen could see the paint was faded, peeling on the windows and doors and some of the wood even looked rotten. Patches of render had fallen away from the wall exposing the brick beneath. Time and weather had taken its toll without anyone keeping up repairs. *Shame. It could have been lovely if they'd bothered.* Gwen turned back to Daniel and asked if he was sure his sister wouldn't mind? It *was* still late. Or early, depending on your point of view. But he just shouted *yeah yeah, it'll be fine* as he fired the engine up once more and began reversing round so he was pointing back the way they had come. Hanging from his window he offered a parting comment.

'You'll be fine, just say I said to give you the family rate, she won't mind. I've got to find me mates and see if they're hale and what they saw, cos I don't believe your tale, no offence gal but it's too weird, too wrong even for me what with all that's going on and all and to cap it all, I never mentioned the word dragon once...until you did.'

'What *is* going on then? You haven't really said.' Gwen tried to ask as he started to pull away. But all she heard was a *never you mind* on the wind as he tore off, bouncing and rattling until his tail-lights vanished in the encroaching early morning mist. She turned a three hundred and sixty degree circle, taking in just exactly where she was. But other than the dirt road and the cottage, she could have been just about anywhere again. She sensed hills and woods and mountains close by, but little of the people who lived amongst them. The cottage was fairly isolated, even for here and Gwen wondered just how much business it ever got. *Guess there's only one to find out Gwen me girl and that's to go knock.* She was reluctant to do so, but her options were fairly limited. Plus she had had quite enough of roaming round the country for a bit. Her need for a hot bath, warm bed and glass of wine reasserted itself. That was the prompt she needed; walking, slowly but purposefully - the theme tune to the Twilight Zone echoing in her head - towards the door, Gwen didn't see the big wind chime hanging from a low branch, so intent on the door was she. Suddenly it rattled like a fire alarm. The silence of the night making it even louder to her ears. *Bloody hell, that's done it. That'll wake the entire sodding island.* Gwen had jumped to one side, one hand going to her mouth, the other to her heart where it had made her jump, and was staring at the swinging and clanging tubes as though they would still under her glare. But it was as she watched them swing slower, though no less noisily, she saw the run of string that came from it and tied off across the entrance.

*What? Is that some kind of booby trap?* No, Gwen realized then, *not a trap, but an alarm, an early warning system.* But she had no time to think on it as the main door slammed open and a terrifying visage was silhouetted in the doorway. Wild hair billowing about its head and tattered clothes flapping in the sudden breeze and the most incongruous thing of all, was the double-barreled shot-gun that it waved in her direction. The wraith with the gun stepped out of the doorway and Gwen got a better view. It was a girl, dressed in gypsy skirt and top, a shawl over her shoulders and her mane of red hair falling unkempt way below her shoulders.

'Get away from here! I've told you before. I'll shoot!' Gwen stumbled backwards a few feet in surprise and raised her hands in a gesture of peace and defense.

'Whoa there lady, easy. My name is Gwen.' Gwen spoke fast in a hope she could say what she needed to before being shot. 'Daniel said I might find a room here? I'm a little lost and he found me, just gone in fact and he said something about the family rate?' Gwen took a breath then and waited. She had stopped backing up and now stood a few feet from the big tree by the gate. The woman with the gun, who Gwen took for Daniel's sister, stepped out a bit further and checked left and right, as though there might be others lurking nearby.

'What sort of car was he driving?' she shouted out.

'A battered old green and rusty Land Rover, but I wouldn't call what he does with it driving, more like pointing in the general direction he wants to go and hanging on. At least that's what I did.' Gwen felt a momentary relief when she heard the woman chuckle to herself at the description. *All this for a glass of wine, jeez, I must have a bigger problem than I thought.* Gwen mused 'Look, if I've caught you at a bad time, I'm sorry. It wasn't my choice nor my intention to upset you, but he said you wouldn't mind. He didn't however mention the shotgun reception so if it's too much trouble, I'll be on my way. Sorry to have disturbed you.' Gwen backed up a little more and turned to go.

'Wait!' The lilting Irish voice wasn't so aggressive now, it had softened from its earlier warning tones. 'It's me who should be sorry, I don't usually greet everyone with this old thing, but things have been a bit hairy of late, hence the chime alarm. Long story but not one for standing out in the chill morning letting the dew settle on us.' Gwen heard the familiar sound of a safety being activated on the weapon. She recalled how her dads did the same. It was a sound from long ago, from when she was a little girl and she would sit with her father as he cleaned his weapons. He was meticulous about them. Every Friday, he would unlock his cabinet and get all seven out, and she would curl up next to him as he went about cleaning each and every one. Telling her tales of his adventures as he did so. She recalled the smell of the oils and cleaners he used and it brought a lump to her throat as a rush of emotion of times past and the massive fact that he was gone and she would never see him again.

'Get yourself in here' Daniel's sister ordered 'and you can tell all about why my brother is picking up waifs and strays and depositing them on me doorstep in the wee hours. I'm also guessing you could use a drink, because let me tell you darlin,' I certainly could.'

'Now you're talking my language.' Gwen piped up 'Make mine a double of whatever you're having.' Gwen stepped over the string and walked up the path. Yet the moment she put her foot on the path proper, she stopped. Waves of icy coldness washed over her like repeating breakers from an ocean. Her skin tingled and she saw goose bumps rise on her arms. An electric current seemed to be coursing up her legs. Though through all this, Gwen was unharmed. She looked at the woman who had invited her in and saw an expression of curiosity mingled with fear and she took a back step again, closer to the door way. She also raised the shotgun a touch higher too and the safety came off once more. Gwen took two more steps towards her and the feeling passed. She looked back and caught a glimpse of a feint silvery light running through the stone

266

wall, around the tree and across the threshold of the garden path. She Gwen concentrated then, she saw it go seemingly all around the house. A protective circle? Gwen mused. Kneeling, she placed her hands on the ground and let her mind reach out. Fingers in the soil, she felt the barrier pulsing and it did indeed go all the way around. It was pretty strong too, similar to the one at Earth Angel.

'How did you do that?' The woman with the gun asked, a tremor in her voice.

Gwen stood up and walked closer to her, as she did so, hands open and spread wide. Gwen noticed the vibrant green eyes and wild red hair, her pale complexion setting both off vividly. Her strong, yet feminine features gave her an ethereal beauty, just like one of the imagined goddesses of Irish legend.

'Do what?' Gwen asked innocently, fishing for the reason behind the question.

'Pass through the barrier of course, don't play me for an eediot.' Gwen looked shocked and with mock horror she looked around, but seeing nothing, she looked back at the woman before her.

'What barrier?' The shotgun came back up and the woman looked angry now rather than fearful. Gwen knew she was on tenuous ground and had to play this carefully.

'I think you know what damn barrier I mean, now how did you cross it? No-one has been able to yet but Daniel and meself, what are you? And I suggest you talk fast.' Gwen slumped her shoulders in resignation. She was running out of options here. She didn't fancy getting shot, there was no point testing her new supposedly bullet proof powers unnecessarily, nor did she want to leave so soon. But this encounter had intrigued Gwen more than she knew and she wanted to find out more about the protective circle and who put it there.

Gwen folded her legs beneath her and sat on the path, cross legged, watching the woman with the gun, who seeing her sit had come a step closer. Gwen watched her look up and look around. Following her gaze, Gwen noticed that the mist that unbeknownst to Gwen had annoyingly followed her and Daniel had made it as far as the threshold but not any further.

'See that?' Gwen began. 'That mist out there?' not waiting for an answer Gwen carried on. 'Do you feel anything from it? Any sort of unease, fear even?' The woman nodded that she did indeed feel something and she didn't like it either.

'Notice how the mist seems incapable of crossing into your garden, unlike me. Your barrier is strong enough to hold that at bay, but not me. Not because I'm stronger than that, though I might be, but because it is malevolent and if I can use the word without sounding off my trolley - Evil.' Gwen paused for effect before continuing.

'I on the other hand am not, I'm one of the good girls I assure you. That's how I got this far, though I did feel the energy as it tested me, strong and old I sense. It's not something you did am I right?' The woman just nodded, not yet taking her eyes from the mist beyond them.

'Thought so.' Gwen smiled 'I'm tempted to say your mother, but no…' Gwen screwed her face up in concentration, she was getting images and some of them made no sense. Pale faces, bloody and torn throwing themselves at the barrier and being repulsed. But they were too fast and too jumbled to make any real sense from, so Gwen just concentrated on the here and now. 'It's older than that even.' Gwen spoke slowly as though she were hearing something talking to her, telling her details. 'Nah it's older than a mother isn't it? A Grand-mother perhaps or even her mother. It's definitely feminine and I can only imagine, once, long ago, it was even stronger than it is now. Though It still seems powerful enough to hold that back…' Gwen thumbed at the mist behind her. '…which right now is more than enough to make me happy. What about you? Was that answer enough to let us carry this chat on indoors? I'm gagging for that drink you teased me with.' As though waking from a dream, the woman turned to the sitting Gwen and saw her properly for the first time it seemed. It was as though a spell had been dispelled from the feisty Irish woman and she found herself actually seeing Gwen as though never having seen her before and she suppressed a little gasp as she took in her features. Her own emerald eyes going wide as she took in Gwen's face and the slightly wavy hair that framed it as Gwen tugged her hat off. Then that moment too passed by and she smiled even if it was a bit strained and crooked. As she did so, the tiny crinkles at the corner of her eyes became slightly more pronounced making her eyes sparkle all the more; Even so far as looking a bit abashed at what she had done and how she had behaved. Reaching a hand towards Gwen she helped the slim woman to stand whilst propping the made safe shotgun against her midriff, butt down in order to free up both hands.

'I am *so* sorry, but there is so much I need to say to you, and I don't know where to begin; but, let me at least start over.' Taking advantage of the hand Gwen held out, Tara took it in both of hers and shook it warmly, though she didn't immediately let go either. 'Hi there. My name is Tara,

Tara Fitzgerald and won't you please be welcome to my home. Come on inside and pay no attention to my mental state. I think me medication is wearing off,' Tara shrugged as though it were a normal thing. 'But, it just so happens I've got another bottle of medicinal Merlot that should just about be room temperature by now, having hopefully breathed its last; can I tempt you?' Gwen smiled back that she definitely could and still hand in hand, the two women walked back up the garden path towards the cottage and went inside. As they closed the door they didn't hear the anguished and agonized screams of more deminions echoing in the distance, nor the tortured howls resounding in the mist. Sounding as yet far off, but seemingly drawing ever closer as they left the burgeoning dawn outside.

Comfortably seated on one of the two sofas that dominated the lounge, strategically placed before the fireplace for optimum warmth, Gwen began to take in her surroundings with a touch more detail. She had dematerialized her boots when Tara wasn't looking and curled her feet up beneath her like a cat. The room was as worn and tired as the outside with faded walls and furniture that seemed derived from the nineteen thirties. The massive fireplace almost filled one wall and the stone that comprised it seemed older than the cottage itself. It was so big in fact, Gwen reckoned she could have stood up inside it. Oddly, Gwen thought, the more she looked at it, the more it looked like a small Henge rather than a fireplace. A Henge that had the cottage built around it and a wall put behind it to enclose it. The floor was old too, but unlike the stone walls and fire, it was just aged and smooth boards with several rugs scattered over it for warmth. Yet for all its shabbiness, Gwen could feel the history in everything there. She felt that familiar familial sensation of Christmas's past and gatherings of relatives at birthdays and anniversaries. This was a well-used family room and it made Gwen miss her own. Just then, Tara walked back in, equally barefooted and Gwen took another moment to assess her now genial host. She reminded her of her old art teacher. For she too frequented the baggy sweater, several sizes too big, floaty skirts and bare feet. No doubt she thought, many a night too curled up with her knees tucked inside her jumper, Gwen understood this for she had a baggy fleece that had gone the same way for that very reason. Moving beyond her clothes, Gwen saw that not only did she look like her art teacher but there was actually paint smudged on her cheek too. *Now that's too spooky.*

'Doing a bit of painting then are you?' Gwen asked innocently. Tara's hand went automatically to her cheek after she put down the wine and glasses, touching the blue smudge.

'Or are you doing the woad thing, you know, lime in the hair, paint yourself blue and run screaming over the hills?' Tara laughed, probably the first genuine humor she had experienced for some time, judging by the way it exploded from her. But she calmed quickly and Gwen could see her trying to come up with a reason why she had missed the canvas and indulged in a bit of impromptu face painting.

'No, well yes sort of, it's hard to say and even harder now you're here. Look at me, I don't know where my brains are these days.' Tara ruffled her fiery mane with the end result that it looked no different than it did before - wild and untamed.

'I'm just glad mine are still in my head.' Gwen tilted her eyes towards the shotgun that stood propped by the door, in easy reach if the need arose. A thought that had troubled Gwen since she arrived. What need could be so dire that folk had to answer their door armed to the teeth. That and the myriad of flashing images she had gotten from the barrier, of the pale and disfigured people screaming and howling. Some mutilating themselves even as they stood at her gate. Gwen feared the worst.

'It's funny you should mention painting though. Have your wine, warm up a little and I'll put some toast on; then there's something you need to see.' Sipping her merlot, Gwen was intrigued now. It smacked of mystery and fit in with the ancient and myth filled land she found herself in. Gwen had half finished her glass when Tara came back in with a plate of steaming toasted bread with what looked like fresh yellow butter slathered upon it. Gwen didn't feel hunger as such anymore, but the sight and smell of the toast made her mouth water all the same and she tucked in hungrily. Making cooing noises and pulling contented faces as she swallowed the slightly salty butter moistened bread. Washed down with the last of her wine, she sat back eventually, sated and replete.

Tara popped her momentary bubble of contentment when she spoke. For it wasn't so much the words themselves that ensorcelled her, but an underlying feeling of power to them. They held the weight of prophecy and an ancient magic that wrapped itself around the listener and the way Tara delivered it, they captured Gwen and held her in a grip that no amount of chain could hope to match. She was riveted, staring straight back at Tara, unable to look away even if she wanted to.

'*White phantom, she of the ancient name,*
*Bearer of light and the blood of kings,*

270

*Mother, sister, summers daughter,*
*By wave and wind embraced by three rings.*
*Take three to four heads of water,*
*From wood she calls life, not once but twice,*
*To his death from above, his destiny calls,*
*She to become two as his mistletoe wife,*
*Life giving spark, to her summons she calls.*

Gwen just sat there as the words reverberated through her every molecule, echoing in her skull like she was in a concert hall.

'What was *that*?' Gwen finally managed to ask as the words of power faded away, though not without leaving an indelible imprint on the inside of her skull. Gwen closed her eyes and saw the rhyme blazing in letters of blue fire. *What did it mean? What did any of it mean?* Gwen couldn't even begin to figure it out. She was useless at riddles at the best of times, always skipping to the back of the puzzle books that Jen left laying around, seeing what the answer was before attempting it.

'Come with me, remember that something I said I had to show you? Well, maybe seeing it will put that rhyme into perspective. Not that it did me, but then again, I'm not you.' Gwen was truly lost now. *Not me? What the bloody hell is she on about now?* But a part of Gwen's awareness was telling her that she was part of something much bigger than herself now and all choices had consequences. *Was it even my choice to beach here of all places?* Or was there an even greater power afoot. Was the Earth reaching out with what little power remained to her and influencing her direction? That was just all too big a question for the present, for she was having enough trouble barely clinging to what little part of reality she still had remaining. *And my bloody fingers are starting to ache.*

Again, Tara held out a hand and as soon as Gwen grasped it, she felt another jolt. This one more physical as though she had stuck her fingers in a socket and flicked the on switch. The girls looked at each other wide eyed as though the other was the cause, but neither let go of the other for all that. They just chalked it up to yet another strange occurrence. Tara led Gwen up the creaky wooden stairs and along an equally groaning landing, to a small back bedroom which Gwen could see past Tara, acted as her studio. She could see canvas and paints everywhere. Sensing where Gwen was looking, Tara offered a hasty explanation.

'I do landscapes usually, and sell them, or at least I used to, up at the craft shops in Sneem, Kenmare and Killarney. One even went back to the states apparently.' A note of pride crept into her voice at that admission.

But there was no time for any well-dones as they made it to the door and Tara stepped back to allow Gwen to enter first.

'To your right, you can't miss it. I didn't have a canvas big enough so I had to use the wall. You see, I was going to leave about a year ago, just pack up, take Daniel and head north; there are just too many hotels around here for a little two room effort like this to make it, especially just out of town like we are, but that was when the dreams started along with the voices; then came the painting. From my art which I had never thought of selling before, don't know why, but I made just enough from them to keep me here, now I see why.' At that precise moment, so did Gwen.

It did, as she said, cover the entire back wall. Floor to ceiling and wall to wall. And it was so vivid and realistic, Gwen was sure that if she tried to step into it, she would feel the grass that was portrayed beneath her feet. But it wasn't the grass or the trees and animals that abounded in the fresco, it was the figure in the center. Looking back at her with vibrant and almost living, emerald green eyes. It was so lifelike, it was like looking into a full sized mirror and looking back at herself. It was - in all its uncanny likeness - an image of Gwen.

Gwen had no words to describe the feelings that flowed through her as she gazed upon the incredible piece of art. She was no art critic, but to her, it surpassed many of the pieces she had seen both modern and ancient. Michelangelo himself would be proud of something like that. Gwen reached out a slow, tentative finger to touch herself, to touch the leafy dress she was wearing because they looked as though they were actually rustling in a non-existent breeze. If to just to convince herself it was flat and two dimensional because it looked so real; Gwen half believed that it was actually rendered in *three* dimensions. With her finger tips just centimeters from the wall, Tara coughed lightly behind her and made Gwen start, the spell broken. Withdrawing her fingers swiftly like they were burnt. She turned to look guiltily at the red head, like a child being caught by its parent, who snap out almost automatically *don't touch!* Gwen knew that there was a lengthy discourse pending about how and why and when such an undertaking had been done, but all she could manage was *You have got to be kidding me!*

'No, sorry, I'm not. Now you see why I looked at you gone out when we first met and after I got an even better look at you in some light. I just couldn't believe you were there, before me, like you had just climbed off this wall and started wandering around in the garden.'

'But that's *me!*' Gwen thumbed at it, stating the obvious a bit lamely. Tara nodded her agreement, taking the revelation considerably better than

Gwen. Though she supposed the artist had spent a longtime with it to get used to it. Gwen was in shock. Part of the fresco included several lines of text, rendered in the same beautiful style as the rest, portrayed as an engraving on a rock at Gwen's feet and it was the strange rhyme that Tara had come out with earlier.

Gwen looked at the detail again and it was simply amazing. She could look at it for days and still see things she had missed. There were birds and trees, fantastical creatures, a starry sky with a large, silvery moon that looked almost photographic. There were sparkling stones and crystals all over, animals and plants. Several weapons including fantastically ornate swords and daggers and amongst it all, were no end of symbolic depictions. Quite a few keys, astrological symbols, runes, spirals and elemental references. She was put in mind of an artist friend of hers who now lived somewhere in Cornwall apparently, who used to do similar work, she loved that and had a few originals but this transcended anything she had seen before. Gwen couldn't take her eyes off it.

'I thought it was me at first.' Tara spoke quietly, softly respecting the moment and not wanting to interrupt Gwen's absorption of the image. 'You see, the green eyes and ancient name bit, well, my name is Tara. Tara used to be the seat of the ancient high kings of Ireland and I've got green eyes too, there are six gems at her feet which I took for the bracelet my mother gave me.' Tara held up and rolled the six massive moonstones that made up her jewellery around her wrist. 'And I live here in Kerry, which has three rings.' Gwen turned to look at Tara and mouthed her question *what three rings?*

'There are three rings here, though not all are known about. Though they are not actually rings as such, but areas of beauty that became known. The Ring of Kerry, the Skellig Ring and the Beara Ring. So you see why I thought it was about me, but the face was all wrong and no matter how many times I tried to change it to me, it always seemed to change back. It's been there about seven months now and I look at it every day. That's why I know the rhyme almost by heart. You're the first person I've shown it to, not even Daniel has seen it. It scares me a little if I'm honest.' Gwen was stunned.

'A little? If I had done this based on dreams, seeing stuff in my head and hearing voices you say? I reckon I would be more than a little scared. I'd need to be changing my underwear.' Tara laughed at Gwen's admission, but added a little gem that made Gwen shiver all over again and stare once more at the fresco with new eyes.

'If only that were it, but since I've finished it, each time I come to look at it, there is something new added, the animals have changed places or the trees have moved. I even think her expression changes ever so slightly too. As though it is trying to communicate with me somehow.' As she was still gazing at the picture, looking for any of the changes Tara had mentioned, Gwen offered her contribution to the riddles possible direction.

'My name is Gwendoline, it was a concession to my mother, by my father, who wanted to call me Gwenhwyfar after the Arthurian tradition. Plus, somewhere in my dad's lineage there was some Celtic in there, hence the green eyes I guess, and I think he wanted to pay tribute to it somehow. As for the rest though, I don't know. I have a brother but I don't have any kids, thankfully, don't really want any either. It isn't like we have a shortage of them. There are plenty of happy breeders out there who are more than welcome to my share. For the love of me, I can't see what the fascination in them is. Noisy, smelly, expensive and above all time consuming. And I sure as hell don't want the rest of my life taken up with funding them, worrying what they are into and bailing them out of trouble until I'm old and toothless. Then there's all this bloody babysitting crap when they have brats of their own. No sooner have you gotten rid of your own than you have another load foisted off on you, I don't bloody think so.' Outside, as they spoke, thunder began grumbling its presence, accentuated by the occasional flash of lightning.

'Oh no!' Tara said, her voice nervous as she heard the thunder for the first time.

'What?' Gwen asked, concerned about the sudden change in the woman.

'Storms. It always seems to stir them up. We had better go down and make sure all the doors and windows are secure in case they get through the barrier.' Tara turned and hurried off. Dragging her baggy sweater sleeves a little higher as though she meant business, only for them to fall back to the position they were in before. But it was the ritual that mattered more, doing so made her feel all business like. Gwen quickly followed and helped her do the rounds checking locks and even propping a chair or two against door jams. When Gwen finally caught back up to Tara, she was busy checking the shotgun was still loaded. Gwen was astonished at this turn of events and a touch worried.

'Who exactly does it stir up, you said them, who's them?' Gwen followed Tara to the main lounge window and stood next to her as she

274

drew the curtains and took a sly peek out, trying to see if anyone had appeared. She wasn't disappointed.

# Chapter 9

## Sinscar

'There!' Tara pointed warily 'Take a look, but be careful, don't let it see you. If they think you're looking at them they scream and trust me, it's horrible.' Gwen teased the curtain just a fraction and took a look at what Tara was referring to. There were three people standing by the tree and one directly in front of the entrance to the garden path. She watched it try to enter but it seemed unable to do so, held back as though it were walking into a wall. But the most disturbing aspect of the scene before her was these people, bore a horrific resemblance to the images she had received when she too walked into the barrier. They were pale alright, but that wasn't the half of it. All three, as far as Gwen could see, had raked their eyes out and their faces were a mess of gory scratches beneath dark, bloody eyeless sockets. The one trying the entrance looked angry too, its mouth was open and it was mouthing obscenities as it failed time and time again to gain access. Gwen could see its mouth was all busted and half the teeth were missing, blood had congealed down its chin and drenched its clothes at the front. Tara was right, they *were* horrific but she had seen them before. Back in Santa Fe. These were the possessed, and they were certainly getting around.

'Does this happen every time there's a storm?' As she drew the curtain closed again and moved to stand near Tara, who had - if at all possible, for she was already pale of complexion - gone even paler and started to tremble slightly.

'Every time for the last few months. You'd think I'd have gotten used to it by now, but I haven't. It scares the beJesus out of me every time.' She held her hands out. 'Look at me! I'm still shaking just from knowing they are out there. What do they want Gwen? What's the matter with them and why are they doing this?' Gwen took Tara's hands in her own, which Gwen was inwardly pleased about, were not shaking. And she led Tara to the sofa and guided her to sit down.

'Looks like they are still having trouble getting in, so forget them if you can for a moment at least and tell me about these dreams you're having. I'm not saying there is, but maybe there's a connection and a fresh set of eyes and ears might help.' While she waited for Tara to start talking, keeping her eyes on the woman, Gwen picked up and topped up the wine glasses from the half empty bottle standing it on the pine chest that doubled for a coffee table. Handing one to Tara, hoping that the alcohol would calm the Irish girls nerves a bit and the glass would give her hands something to do other than tremble. Gwen waggled the bottle then, signifying it was empty. She mouthed that she would just nip to the kitchen and get another one. Leaving Tara sitting alone and hugging her glass, staring into its swirling crimson depths, wondering where to begin. Though she had organized her thoughts as much as she was going to when by the time Gwen returned, for she barely had time to sit and make herself as comfortable as she could before Tara launched into her tale.

'Other than you obviously, I see fire. All sorts of fire blazing in all different colors. Sometimes the fire is spinning like a huge buggery wheel. Then there's the tree.'

Gwen felt the cold chill of prescience tingle over her flesh at the mention of the tree.

'It's the biggest damn thing I've ever seen. At its roots are things like the Eifel tower and the pyramids and loads of other gigantic landmarks, but they are all tiny by comparison.' Tara paused, looking fretful, as though inwardly wondering how she must sound but too far past the point of caring now. She took a sip of her wine, then another and then proceeded to chew on her lip for a bit before speaking again.

'What is it Tara? There's more isn't there?' Tara just nodded.

'There's a man.' Gwen wanted to sigh and say there's always a bloody man, but she held her tongue, not wanting to cheapen the woman's dream by some seedy connotation.

'He scares me though, every time I see him. I'm drawn to him and petrified of him both at the same time. I want him in ways even I'm too embarrassed to discuss, but I know that it would kill us both if I did have him, yet danger aside, I feel driven to possess him. One half of him is golden light, so bright and dazzling that it hurts me to look at him for too long, then the other half is darkness. Thick and tangible, like how you imagine a black hole is, sucking at the light, trying to absorb it or extinguish it. Waves of cold emanate from that side so realistically that when I wake sometimes, my breath is coming from me in frosty clouds, like I'm sleeping in the fridge. The entire room is perishing. How can a dream do that? They can't affect the real world can they?' Gwen had no answer for her, the jury was still out on dreams. She had read a fair bit and when she did her Parapsychologist's diploma during her first year at

277

the store, she covered dreams and the many cultural variations on their import. From Australian natives, the Aborigines and their Dreamtime mythos, through the Aztec ideology up to and including Freud and Jung's interpretations. There was still no real definitive answer, just lots of theories based on where you were in the world and what culture you are brought up in. Astral travel was another by product of these dreams and she found that the body grew a small amount and lost a minor amount of weight each night when the body slept. It was widely held that this was the astral-self leaving the body to venture where it would. Travelling to different lands, but she hadn't heard of those different lands coming back and affecting the sleepers world like the way Tara described.

'Then there are these rivers,' Tara continued 'sometimes there's four, sometimes more and they all merge into one big one. Raging and bubbling with all these people standing on both sides of the embankment. They look incredibly sad but I don't know why. Then what I thought was my own Catholic upbringing casting overtones on my dream turns out not to be really, because I see a sky filled with angels and demons fighting. They don't look much like the Church portrayal of them but more like flying knights fighting flying animals, but their screams are terrible and there's blood everywhere. I see them falling from the sky like rain, dead and torn. Smashing into the ground and falling into the river. The screams get so loud they fill me with their pain until I can't take any more; that's when I found that I was even waking myself up screaming.'

'No wonder you've got no bloody guests.' Gwen laughed a weakly, in an attempt to alleviate the mood before it got too heavy. Tara joined in weakly as she pictured the scene, her eyes were moist and slightly red from the contained emotion.

'Yep, that'll do it alright.' Tara agreed weakly 'It isn't the most socially accepted alarm call is it, a hysterical woman screaming her lungs out first thing in the morning or during the middle of the night either for that matter.' Outside, the storm had picked up and along with the intermittent thunder and the odd scream from the possessed, they could now hear packs of dogs barking and howling. Adding their canine chorus to the cacophony. Tara spared her lounge window a look of anguish just for a split second, so distraught by what she could hear outside, she put her wine glass down too heavily, splashing a little scarlet drip over the rim like flying blood droplets to land onto the pine box. Gwen wondered if she was going to slam her hands over her ears and scream back at them all to be quiet. But she didn't, after standing and staring at the curtains for several minutes, her imagination fueling her vision, she just sighed and sat down again. But she was at the limits of her strength, Gwen could see the strain starting to show. Tara took her seat once more.

'Who are you Gwen? Really?' Tara turned to stare at Gwen. The intensity caught her unawares at first. Gone was the down trodden expression of someone caught in the web of something world shattering. Gone was the look of the victim that Tara had worn when Gwen started to discuss the dream with her. Speaking of it had some sort of cathartic effect on the previously wary Irish woman. It seemed as though Tara had reached a point of acceptance and a great burden had been shed in doing so; she even sat a little straighter and her eyes sparkled with a curiosity that had been absent before now though they still retained their weary seen too much look. Gwen tried the innocent tack once more.

'What do you mean? I've told you my name and I'm here cam...' Tara closed her eyes and shook her head sadly, holding one hand out in the halt gesture.

'No! Not the story you fed me and no doubt Daniel as well. There is more to you than you're letting on. Firstly you get through the barrier as though it wasn't there. I don't know how you did that, absolutely no-one has made it through that without Daniels or my help. Only he and I can pass through it for some reason I am eternally grateful for. It's been that way since these troubles started. It just sprang up one day, I know because I can see it, the same way I can see the aura blazing off you, which by the way, I don't know if you can turn it down, because it's getting brighter as we speak, you must be getting excited...or something, not angry I hope. And let's not forget the bloody wall upstairs, that's you plastered all over it remember?' Gwen went perfectly still as she listened, all joviality gone. Tara was all business now and Gwen dropped her pleasant façade along with Tara. She tensed and prepared her mind for immediate action should matters take a turn for the worse. Had she been lulled into some sort of trap by this person? Was this it being sprung? Her heart rate quickened as the adrenaline began to flow through her. *Shame, I quite liked her too.* Gwen thought sadly as her eyes took in the door way and the window, searching for the nearest exit just in case.

'Since you arrived, which even you have to admit, is damn strange by any reckoning, there has been a mist or fog out there pushing against the barrier, I can feel it relentlessly driving at it; and then there's the storm. There was none forecast and yet there it is, lashing down and blowing a hoolie. But tonight it's different somehow, those people turned up much faster than usual, shortly after you actually, and there are still more arriving; and then there's the dogs...what have you brought here Gwen?

What has followed you to my doorstep?' Tara didn't sound so much angry at the prospect of what she may have brought, but more resigned to the inevitable and weary from the wait, it was as though she sensed the end to her perpetual nightmare was imminent. Gwen could see no real option at this moment than to share what she knew and see how it was received. But first she needed to know Tara's affiliation and she thought she had a way to do that. Gwen recalled when she had kissed Daniels cheek. As much as she passed something to him, she in turn got several impressions back from him. One of them had been his heart. Telling her it was in the right place and there was no real malice in him, none intentional anyway. Mischief yes, and something of the scrapper but nothing dark and overtly violent. In essence, he was a good guy. Gwen hoped she could do the same with Tara and that the familial gene ran true. She didn't know how she had done it last time, it was an unconscious thing, but now she wanted to do it fully aware. That would be a different story, but it was worth a go. It would either spring or confirm if it really was a trap as well. Gwen took a breath and made her choice.

'Sit down Tara and give me your hands.' As Tara had been standing and sitting in equal measure as the adrenaline picked up within her. Gwen spoke with as much authority as she could muster and Tara duly sat holding out her hands. Gwen studied them briefly. They were fine boned and long fingered. Artists hands alright. She took them in her own and closed her eyes. Concentrating on the woman before her. A deluge of images poured forth and Gwen gasped. She wasn't expecting such a bombardment. Gwen thought she would get images of her daily life, much like she had from Daniel. Oh no. This was more like an epic movie. One that spanned centuries, or at least that was how it looked to Gwen. She saw barbarous looking men, dark clothes and painted faces. They were in the midst of fighting ferociously with armored men and the death toll was monstrous. She saw white robed men and women, wielding wicked looking, curved blades. They looked like scythes and sickles and these people knew how to use them to gruesome effect. They fought against these dark men and held them back. The images changed again, and Gwen saw packs of hounds, some with red ears tear into the men from behind and savage them. Biting through calves and legs, tearing the throats of the fallen. But Gwen noticed that they left the robed people alone. The images flowed once more and Gwen saw a powerful looking woman, dark of eye and pale of skin, her shoulders were back as she moved, as though steel rods reinforced her back and she regally walked a path that was one half moonlit and the other as radiant as a summers day.

She emanated a power that felt familiar to Gwen but she couldn't place it as the images flowed by her. There was another woman with her, she too throbbed power, but unlike the first, who clearly differentiated light from dark, hers was a foul mixture of the two, a stygian twilight as though she were a doorway between light and dark and Gwen sensed the bitter taste of vengeance and betrayal. Again and again the images flowed and changed. This time though, along with images, Gwen felt emotion, bitterness and resentment, verging on hatred. She didn't know the source of this outpouring of ill feeling, was it the woman or the queen like figure? She didn't know, but instead, she saw thousands of men, women and children, slaughtered and crucified, dying as they hung from trees and stakes and anything else that would serve. The lucky ones already lay dead at their feet. Blood flowed freely from their many wounds, staining the ground and turning it into some tiny black river as it flowed away. In it, foul things squirmed, wriggled and slithered. Above them wheeled clouds of carrion birds, some were even brave enough to swoop down and pluck at eyes and stab at the raw and bloody wounds. Tearing gobbets of flesh off before flapping away to devour their meals. Gwen heard many a scream from the tortured before the weight of their bodies ruptured their lungs and they suffocated in abject agony. Once more the images flowed and this time it was through hundreds of births, mothers and their daughters, over and over. And Gwen saw a shining silver line of light, connecting each to the last as though the mother and infant were connected through time. And oddly, each seemed to have to fight for its life in the first few hours. Some were even still born, but through immediate intervention, life was found. Some were burnt, some stabbed. Others cut, slapped or shook. Each one had a birth mark shaped like a question mark. Wait, no. Gwen realized then it wasn't a question mark, but a sickle. Like what the robed men and women used. Druids? Or was it the Kore Megara Jen and Maddy had spoken of. They too were ancient and powerful. But she didn't think that druids fought like that. Or fought at all if she thought about it. It was as though they were martially trained. Gwen had always considered them men and women of peace. Odd. But then so much of what she saw was odd. The images flew by so fast and Gwen couldn't fathom many of them or much of what she saw. Only briefly did the vision somehow slow enough for her to see things clearly. There were knights, heavily armored and fighting other knights again, great battles with swords, axes and ballistae. Caves and deep underground chambers, rivers and doors. All this streamed by Gwen in less time than it took for the heart to beat twice. Her last image as she let go of Tara's hands was the strangest. For it was of the fireplace they sat before, only without the house surrounding it. Upon it was the woman she had seen earlier, the powerful one who was cloaked in light and dark. She lay bleeding upon the mantle. Another woman with flowing red hair, stood with her back to Gwen so she could not see her face. She held what looked like an egg above her hands, but Gwen quickly saw that it wasn't an egg, but a smooth stone. Flashing blue and silver, she saw it was in fact a huge moonstone. Twice the size of the ones that Tara wore upon her wrist. The woman sprawled upon the rock held out a hand, almost beseeching the other but to no avail. She ignored the plea and placed the stone upon her prone breast. The other woman sighed at the contact and sagged even further as though it took her strength. The woman with the red hair, then drew one of the cruel looking sickles from her hip where it had hung. There were no words or incantations or supplications. She simply raised it and swung it down upon the prone woman. Her head rolled clear and blood pumped out onto the grass. It ran in a crimson rivulet several yards, and where it pooled, a tree began to grow. It grew into a massive oak in a matter of seconds. Gwen recognized the tree as the one from the gate. The woman then plucked the stone from the corpse's chest and held it to the pommel of the sickle. There was a blinding flash and after the light diminished, Gwen saw the stone was fused to the blade and the corpse had gone. But just as the red head was about to turn and show Gwen her face, the image faded away. Gwen sat back abruptly and let go of Tara's hands and she just stared at the woman before her. Sweat had beaded her forehead. And Gwen idly mopped her brow as she watched for any reaction. But Tara just sat there, her hands still in her lap where Gwen had dropped them.

'What did you just do? That was the strangest feeling. Not unpleasant mind you, just strange. What were you trying to do?' Gwen looked up the woman.

'I wasn't trying Tara, I succeeded. But I don't understand half of what I did or saw. Suffice to say I didn't feel any malice or evil from you, which was what I started out to find; cos there's a few things I need to tell you and you're right about one thing though.'

'Oh? What's that then?' Tara asked shakily, Gwen sat back and poured herself a top up of wine, twirled it in her fingers before speaking again, taking a sip she moistened her throat and lips before talking again. Trying to formulate the words to make what she was about to say sound even remotely credible. Flicking an errant hair from her face, she began.

'It doesn't appear to be any accident that I'm here. I had an idea where I wanted to go, but that was about it. Maybe instinct or intuition guided me; or perhaps a larger and more powerful entity influenced my choice and trust me when I say that I don't mean God.' Tara's expression asked who that might be then. So Gwen, glossing over some of the more personal bits, and leaving out the other shape changing elements, told Tara her story up to the present moment they found themselves in. Including as much of her vision as she could remember.

Now if Gwen was expecting incredulousness or disbelief, she was greatly disappointed. Considering her own reaction to being told what she had just divulged to this almost total stranger. Granted, it wasn't actually happening to Tara, not in the way it was to Gwen, but still; the idea that there was a giant green dragon sitting in your living room wearing a human form still took some swallowing. Yet for all that, Tara took it pretty well really. She just sat back, sipped her own wine and studied Gwen for what seemed to be an age. But as Gwen waited for a reaction – maybe it was delayed - she wondered that maybe it wasn't the dragon thing so much after all, as it was more the prospect of the actual existence of demons and angels - she was in the middle of Catholic and Protestant land after all, where nearly everyone is weaned on the good book in one form or another, so anything to do with God or religion wasn't to be taken lightly – these celestial beings were fighting for the salvation of not only humanity, but their own worlds and continued existence. In this war though, humans were mostly just going to be collateral damage whilst beings of immense power were using the Earth as their own personal battlefield and once they had devastated this world, they would likely be moving on to the rest. Yet the battle currently being fought on this world was pivotal to the war as a whole, hence the necessity of humans having to - through the freewill clause as Gwen had come to think of it - offer themselves up to take a decisive stand, rather than just take a back seat and just hope they survived at the sacrifice of others…as she had. But it was a delicate course of action. The slightest mishap or one wrong choice could see everything lost. One such choice was being mulled over by Tara as Gwen sat silently waiting for her reaction. Both women sipped their wine and studied the other in deepening silence. Gwen was impatient at the best of times and this sort of waiting did her already frayed nerves no favors at all. So, to keep her mind from panicking, she went back over her earlier conversations with Tara. Checking for irregularities or anything that might give her a clue to how Tara was likely to react. One thing sparked up for her. Tara admitted to seeing auras. She had said hers was vibrant and too bright. *Damn, damn and damn again.* A penny dropped suddenly in Gwen's mind, resounding with an audible chink. *That's how they found me and followed me.* It had annoyed her at the time how those demons had spotted her and kept on her tail even as she adopted her hawk form. *My bloody aura must have shone out like a supernatural beacon everywhere I went.* Invariably, as her power was enhanced, so too had the brightness of her field. *Makes sense if I think about it. How many other stupid mistakes am I going to have to make before I get me or someone else killed?* She'd have to figure out how to turn it down sooner rather than later, surely it was within her capability considering all the other stuff she could do. She would have to figure it out quickly as well, before she was caught out by any more fiends and horrors. She'd dealt with the last ones well enough, but the next ones might well be another matter. It was a matter she would rather avoid. Suddenly, snapping Gwen back to the immediate Tara spoke, albeit quietly and deliberately.

'Suppose I believe everything you've just told me, what then? It still doesn't explain what the fuck those bastards out there want with *me*. Cos they were here before you.' Tara was primarily talking to herself as she gazed still at Gwen, so Gwen sat still and waited for her to finish. It seemed that Tara was organizing her thoughts by speaking them aloud. 'Unless it's not me they really want, but then how did they know you were coming?' Tara paused again and sipped some more before carrying on 'Maybe they didn't; maybe they were drawn by the barrier when it flared up. There are any awful lot of maybes Gwen. So, what do you reckon, you being a dragon and all?' Gwen shrugged noncommittally.

'How the hell should I know?' Gwen shrugged dejection evident in the move 'Didn't I just tell you that all this shit has only just happened to me? I'm definitely no expert. And I'm just making the majority of this up as I go, trying not to get myself killed in the process. Trouble is, since I touched you I've got more questions now than answers. One of them would be how much do you know about that fireplace?' That threw Tara right off.

'What the fuck has my fireplace got to do with anything?' Tara replied, caught off guard by the question and feeling she was being sidestepped. Gwen had told her briefly as best she could about what she had seen but she went back over it with as much detail as she could recall. It had been a bit sketchy but she had gotten the gist of it. Gwen was still amazed at how calmly Tara was taking all these world shattering revelations about her life and the world she lived in, even her house. She either knew more than she was letting on or she was going to implode later as her mind was overloaded by the enormity of it all. Inwardly, she hoped that it was neither, because any one of them could be potentially dangerous to her or anyone else. These sort of things always went south at the wrong time in the movies as Gwen recalled and she couldn't afford a meltdown at a crucial moment. Tara stared with undisguised resentment at the stone edifice that had been part of her life for so long.

'That explains why I've always hated that fucking thing. It gave me the creeps even as a girl. Now you tell me it's some sort of altar where some woman got her heed cut off? Marvelous, me mam always treated it like it was something special, now I know why.' Tara threw the last of her wine down her throat and almost slams the glass down. 'Damn it explains so many things.' Gwen could see Tara was upset, as the flood of memories Gwen had instigated kept triggering other ones. 'I always thought my mother went a bit off when my da died. Daniel was too young to remember it, but I do. It didn't occur to me till I was about fourteen and I heard of people who cut themselves. Kids mostly, it was their way of dealing I suppose, I thought it was just what my ma did. But she always did it here. Now I come to think about it, it was there, by the fireplace. She told me it was her favorite spot and her chair, the one you're sitting in, that was hers.' Gwen squirmed slightly in her seat and looked askance at the chair she was curled in as though she thought it might begrudge her sitting there all of a sudden.

'It was always placed close to the fire and I just thought she was cold. But she was slyly blood sacrificing wasn't she?' Gwen thought it was likely and told her so. But just as disturbing was what she did with her daughter. It could have significant meaning to her vision. But as much as part of Gwen dreaded the answer, she knew she would have to ask.

'Did she ever cut you Tara? Was your blood ever spilt on to this rock?' The way the blood left Tara's face gave Gwen all the answer she needed. Perhaps the red head in the vision was some sort of ancestor, but who was she and what did it mean for Tara? Or Daniel for that matter, how was he mixed up in all this?

'I was born in this house Gwen. But according to me ma, I wasn't breathing when I popped out; I was sorta going blue and everything. So...' as she spoke Tara stood and pulled one side of her jeans and pants down, revealing one of her butt cheeks, Turning her hip so Gwen could see it, Gwen could indeed see an odd shaped burn mark.

'To kick start me so to speak she said; she says the mid-wife grabbed a brand from the fire and pokes me on the arse with it. The shock apparently got me breathin' Gwen's heart felt heavy at the story, but what confirmed her suspicions more than that, was the sickle shaped burn mark glaring red at her from Tara's rump. But Gwen just smiled at the woman, in an attempt to alleviate the mood that was rapidly degenerating.

'Nice one. At least its somewhere that should someone see it, you want them too, if you know what I mean.' Tara pulled her skirt back down and sat again, smiling at the implication, humor warring with her own confusion and fears. But it didn't last long.

'It means something doesn't it?' Gwen could only nod, though she didn't have the answer to what it actually meant, she did feel that it didn't bode too well in the grand scheme of things. But she kept her suspicions to herself, they had enough to contend with as it was without adding further mysteries to their woes. Gwen lost herself momentarily in her own thoughts and she was only barely aware of Tara rising to peek through the drawn curtains once more.

'They're still there and there's even more of them now. There's got to be at least twenty of the buggers just standing there.' Gwen's mind switched from the esoteric to the mundane and she asked with genuine curiosity how Tara managed to get out shopping. Considering the wine she held in her hand. Tara turned from the window, and Gwen saw a look of concern there.

'Daniel had been delivering them since the barrier went up. I haven't left the house, well the grounds anyway. I did go out once to see who was standing at my gate, just after it went up and I hadn't seen their faces up close till then. It was a man; I didn't know him and his face was hidden in the hood of his coat at first, so I couldn't see what he had done to himself. But as I drew nearer, he flung it back and screamed at me. Lunging towards me as though he was going to vault the wall and attack me, but the silvery flash sent him sprawling backwards. I haven't been that close since then. That has to be near to three months ago. But I don't know how he's going to get in now with that lot out there.' Gwen tried to reassure her but didn't think it did any good. Her own heart wasn't really in it because she thought the same thing and what it meant to the continuation of her quest. She couldn't stay here for much longer, but neither could she leave Tara and Daniel to the ravages of the possessed. Were there more coming? If so, how many more would it take before they were unable to leave? Gwen was okay, she knew she could shift to bird form and just fly off, but Tara couldn't do that, nor could Daniel. He was the next problem. Where the hell was he? Because Gwen had the distinct feeling that Tara wouldn't leave without him. *It's just one bloody problem after another these days, why is nothing simple.*

'You know we are going to have to leave here, quite probably tonight before that rabble gets any bigger or that barrier fails or any other number of horrible alternatives.' Tara sat down as though her legs had suddenly had the bones removed. Apparently the thought of leaving hadn't occurred to her and the prospect terrified her rigid.

'Has Daniel got a cell?' Tara's expression said *a what?* 'You know, a mobile?'

Tara shook her head glumly, explaining that he lost anything that wasn't attached to him within days usually and that even that was no guarantee. But, she continued thinking and blurted that he usually turned up for breakfast about mid-morning if they could wait that long to see him. Gwen accepted they didn't have much choice as she saw it. So with a bit of persuasion, she sent Tara upstairs to pack a few belongings while she kept a look out for the possessed. If she rationalized things, she knew she could inflict considerable damage on them in her dragon form, so she had little to fear really, but it was just the idea of them that creeped her out and the effect they had on normal people. It was odd how humans accepted evil monsters that looked like evil monsters easier than evil that actually looked like them. As she watched, several more arrived. Women and children alike, torn and sundered by the unimaginable presence of some deminion inhabiting and corrupting their bodies. Gwen wandered around the house then, checking every window and looking out into the night to see if they had surrounded the house. But, to her relief, she only saw them at the front gate and wall area. Though that was not to say they weren't lurking out in the darkness somewhere. A quick check told her dawn wasn't far away and she hoped the rising sun would banish them to whatever dark rock they had crawled out from under.

Gwen kept watch as the sun rose – breathing a sigh of relief as it did so - and Tara busied herself with putting the house in order to leave it and flitting about, shoving objects in and out of her pack. Changing her mind about what she needed or thought she needed. And yet more possessed arrived. There were nearly fifty gathered along the wall and by the gate now. Eerily silent and standing still as statues, just watching. Though watching was the wrong way to describe it as they all had the torn and ruined eye sockets, where nails had gouged them away, leaving bloody empty holes. Yet they all unerringly faced the house. The fog had dissipated as the morning took shape, but the sky still held a steely menace as the thunderclouds looming above continued to build. A light, icy, sleety rain was falling too just to add to the gloomy atmosphere, which only threatened to grow worse as the day wore on. A distant rumble of thunder emphasized Gwen's fears and she saw several bolts of fork lightning illuminate the horizon beyond the indifferent possessed who continued to watch them.

Turning back to the fireplace, Gwen saw that the ancient markings that hadn't been overly pronounced earlier were now in fact glowing a faint blue. *This can't be good* Gwen groaned to herself as she stared at them. She moved closer as her heart rate skipped up a beat. *What now?* She wondered. Reaching out a tentative hand, Gwen felt the rock thrumming gently beneath her fingertips. Vibrating and resonating like a living thing. Simultaneously, all around the world, standing stones and megaliths of all shapes, sizes and proportions began to vibrate and glow an ethereal blue light. Those people who sought sanctuary within their stony circles and sheltered in their vicinity - having fled from the minions of the Adversary - found themselves reassured by the phenomena rather than scared by this sudden occurrence but they didn't know why nor did they question it. Dormant for thousands of years, their purpose shrouded in the mists of time, the ancient stones had still drawn souls to them, much the same way a lodestone drew iron. Kindred spirits who felt the old world touch of magic had flocked to these ancient protectors in the same way other religions flocked to the temples and sanctuaries. With one exception. Where they were abandoned by that which they were built to worship, these stones were not. It was a faith that pre-dated known religions and it had endured. Endured where lesser, more recent ones had failed and were failing still. Even the Four Horsemen, who were engaged in several conflicts across the Earth, paused briefly to wonder at the phenomena and what new sequence of events had been set in motion, or, unbeknownst to them and the world, what had been released.

Gwen had no way of knowing that her mere presence beside the altar stone would imbue it with enough energy to perform its last charge. Being a thing of Earth, it absorbed Earth energy. Gwen was now a font of that particular power. And it drank heavily. And somewhere, veiled by time, a woman with flowing red hair turned to look over her shoulder. She felt a touch of power, subtle and distant. Smiling, she knew that the enchantment was complete and that the connection had been made, past to future. Now it was just a matter of time, literally. Returning her attention to the prone woman before her, she smiled cruelly at the beseeching hand that was stretched out towards her. Hoping in vain that it could touch some vestige of humanity within her. It would fail, there was none left. What little remained to her she had willingly given to the Adversary hundreds of years before when this woman, who lay weak and helpless before her, refused her supplications for more power. Hadn't she served her long and faithfully as her priestess for her entire life? Sacrificed her family for her? Still, it mattered little now. The dye was cast and she had made her choice. There was no returning or forgiving now. Mercy was no longer an option even if she wanted to extend any to the woman before her. The enchantment was too powerful and for it to achieve its goal, she needed the life essence of one of the immortals. Who, as it turned out, weren't so immortal after all; it's just that humanity didn't know what it took to kill them. She did now. Lifting the iron sickle from her belt, she gripped the handle firmly in both hands and swung down.

The storm was picking up apace, booming and crashing outside. Lightning flashed its jagged signature across the sky and over the land, trees and rocks succumbed to its awesome power. Exploding timber and stone with apparent ease. Gwen could feel its power tingling over her skin and she knew it was unnatural, but she knew also, she had no power over it. Maybe Jen or Maddy could have dealt with it, but they were not here, she was. Gwen felt her solitude and their absence was like a cold rock in her gut. So powerful, yet so powerless at the same time. But what she didn't know about the storm, was that it wasn't just targeting random trees and rocks. No, the lightning sought ancient oaks and stones of power and that the raging maelstrom was heading straight for them.

The fireplace, with its strange glow and increasing vibration was still - for all that - just a fireplace. And the fire from last night hadn't quite yet gone out. As Gwen watched the last vestiges die down, as though it did it on purpose to taunt her, a burning ember leapt out and flew unerringly to Tara's mother's chair that sat close by. To Gwen's astonishment, the chair instantly went up in flames and Gwen screamed. Panic over rode her mind, just for an instant before she ran to get water and wet towels from the kitchen. Tara, upon hearing the scream, rushed downstairs and into the lounge to see what had happened. She skidded to a halt before the blaze and flinging her arms up to protect her face from the sudden and searing heat. Gwen came hurtling back in with a bowl of water and threw it over the flames. They hissed and spat, sending clouds of black smoke roiling up. The flames diminished only ever so slightly before flaring up once more with renewed vigor. The crackling and snapping sounding to Gwen too much like diabolical laughter. Angry that her efforts were so pathetic, Gwen found herself walking towards the burning chair, initially with the intent of kicking it into the fireplace where it could do less harm, but instead, she found herself wanting to actually extinguish it. From where her clothes formed about her arms, Gwen grew a cloak of thick dark leaves and she swept it up and over the flames. Smothering both the fire and containing the thick choking smoke. She felt a tingle on the underside of her arm but that was it. Withdrawing the cloak and standing up, she saw that the flames were gone and the smoldering remains of the chair could be seen clearly now. All that was left was the basic frame and a few springs. And something else. Something that wasn't part of the chairs design. It looked like a stone tube with several crystalline rocks attached to it and bound around with gold wire. For all the inferno it had to have been in, it appeared unscathed. Both Tara and Gwen exchanged puzzled glances at seeing the object. But it was Tara who moved towards it first.

'Not gonna find out what the hell it is by staring at it are we.' She said as she reached in and plucked it from the chairs wreckage. Surprisingly, it was cool to the touch. Another shock to add to Tara's growing collection. She looked it over, turning it this way and that.

'Don't know, I mean I have no idea about this whatsoever, take a look yourself.' She proffered the tube to Gwen and turned it for her to see. 'There's nothing special about these gems that I can see,' Tara observed as Gwen looked it over 'they just look like regular quartz and amethyst fragments. Okay, that one's smokey quartz and that other one is rutile, but for all that, I don't know what they do.'

'Well at a glance, I'd say they protect it from fire for a start.' Gwen said, and Tara gave her a look that said *smart arse.* 'You see the thing with quartz is that it is good for receiving and transmitting frequencies. All sorts of frequencies. Radio is the most widely known, but when the new age movement got their hands on them, they found out or someone did, that quartz had an effect on humans. Much more of a subtle effect, not the wonders that they profess now, but as you see auras, what you're seeing is the color of the myriad of frequencies all living things generate whilst alive. Magic, though not as we know it now, but great enchantments were probably amplified and contained in quartz. That type of magic was the mystical connection between all living things and the ability to manipulate it is an ability humanity has lost over the centuries, or at least the majority of people. I suspect your family still has a connection, your mother certainly had one if this is anything to go by, her mother too no doubt so on and so forth. I expect, for better or worse that you have it too.' Tara rolled the tube around in her hands once more, examining it with new eyes based on what Gwen had said. It was during a twisting motion that the tube came apart. Neatly separating into two equal sized halves. A cleverly designed screw thread could be seen at the join. A masterful piece of work because when it was together it was impossible to see the seam. Rolled inside it was a piece of parchment, equally untouched by heat or fire.

'What's that?' Tara asked looking at the protruding scrap of paper.

'Well why don't you take it out and look at it, that way you'll know what it is won't you.' Tara raised her eyebrows at the obviousness of the statement and the stupidity of her question and then took the scroll out. Placing the two stone tube halves down, she went to untie the scroll when she gasped.

'What is it?' Gwen asked, instantly concerned. Fearing the worst that maybe with their haste they had tripped some sort of mystical trap. Gwen was at her side in a shot.

'It's my mother's hair ribbon.' Gwen heaved a sigh of relief, but not before punching Tara on the arm for putting her through things like that.

'Ow! Easy gal, sorry to have scared you though, but it was a shock that's all.' Tara rubbed her bruised arm and undid the scroll, sniffing the ribbon, in the hope she could get some essence of her dead mother, then tucking the ribbon in her jeans pocket she undid the scroll fully and began to read.

'C'mon, out loud.' Gwen whined. Disappointed at missing out on the discovery.

Tara had by then scanned the contents and she looked over at Gwen, her expression unreadable. But she began to read out loud as Gwen had asked.

Dearest Daughter,

I was hoping to be able to tell you all you need to know in person when you were old enough, but if you are reading this then it means I wasn't able to do that and I am probably dead. We spoke of many things when you were young, I don't know how much you can remember but whatever it is, it isn't near enough to help you with what you must face. I fought against our destiny in the vain hope to prevent you succumbing to the same fate as the rest of our line. It seems I failed and have paid for that failure with my death. If the fireplace ever glows blue, you need to place both hands upon it and repeat these words. *Hecate guide me, Hecate protect me, Hecate grant me the sight to walk the world between worlds. Hecate, mother, sister, daughter, threefold guardian, I am your servant, grant me what is mine by blood.* This is a double edged sword and may cause you more harm than good, but you will need the power it grants to survive. I hope that you are strong enough to bear it my daughter. Seek safety in the stone circles for they are the crossroads of the earth. Walk in the light but respect the darkness and only do what is right. I must leave you now for there is no more time. Grace be with you my child. Beware.

Eternally, your loving mother

Riganmor Fitzgerald

With a desperate look, both women turned to see the fireplace was indeed still glowing, Tara took a step towards it. Wringing her hands and chewing her lip as she did so.

'I'm terrified Gwen, but this is from my mother, what harm can it do?'

'I'm as scared as you and I hate to say it but it could do a lot of harm based on what I know of Hecate. I know it was your mother and you miss her. You are hoping this will connect you to her, and I understand that, but think about what I saw in my vision. Sacrifice, beheading and the blood. Crap, I don't know Tara. I wouldn't, but it's your call.' Tara nodded once then placed the scroll on the mantle. The moment she did it caught light. Panicked now, she slapped both hands on the rock and quickly read the words before it all went up in flames.

Distracted by the blaze, they hadn't noticed the storm creep up on them. Thunder crashed right on cue as Tara spoke, and lightning raged outside in the most awesome pyrotechnic display Gwen had ever beheld. Even the desert storms would have been hard pressed to compete with this one. Tara was oblivious to it as the blue light began to envelope her and suffuse her entire body with the blue light. It blazed from her eyes like car headlights and she mouthed a silent scream, light pouring from her open mouth. Gwen couldn't have heard her anyway. The storm took all sound and annihilated it. Gwen ducked involuntarily every time a concussive lightning bolt struck something. She wondered in between explosions that this must be what it was like in Bagdad or anywhere else in the Middle East when they rained missiles down on them. But just as Gwen was about to check on the storm through the window, a mighty thunderclap, followed immediately by a lightning bolt of such magnitude struck, and blew out the lounge window and half the wall along with it. Sending shards of glass and chunks of masonry hurtling into the room. Was it anyone else in there but Tara and Gwen at that moment, they would have been pulverized and shredded in equal measure. As it was, the shrapnel and debris simply vaporized as it hit the blue aura that surrounded the oblivious Tara and for Gwen, all she had time to do was throw her arm up to protect her face as best she could. What she didn't expect was that as her arm came up, so did a wall of root, bursting from the floor and cocooning her in their protective embrace. Again, she realized, something else done on instinct and without thought had come to her aid. If only she knew what she was capable of, life might be that much easier she thought, piqued at her trial and error learning curve.

The storm continued unabated and the rain now saturated the lounge as it hammered into to the room, effectively amplifying the sound which was even louder now as Gwen emerged from her root built shelter. Tara was slumped now against the fireplace, which had reverted to its original stone look once more, the light gone. Whatever coursed through it, had either simply gone, or it now coursed through Tara instead. Only time would tell that one. Gwen picked her up and carried her to the protective barrier and placed her gently behind it. Then she went to see what was happening outside.

Stepping out into the rain Gwen felt its touch as something to be welcomed even for all its unnatural origins, she embraced all the elements now and headed towards the smoking ruins of the oak tree. It had taken several hits and was nothing more than a charred stump now. Of the possessed, there was little remaining either. Their blasted bodies were strewn everywhere. Twisted and burnt almost beyond human recognition. *Even a demon can't inhabit a body that's destroyed to this extent surely.* Gwen hoped that was the case at least. Several more lightning bolts slammed into the Earth and she felt each one resonate through her bare feet as she trod the wet grass near the tree. Another hit the house behind her making her duck again. Turning on her heel, she ran back in concerned for Tara. Gwen checked Tara first, and she was fine; protected by the roots. Only then did she notice the fireplace had been sundered in two by the last strike.

*Too late. Whatever you tried to prevent happening has already happened. Tara has her heritage, for good or ill is yet to be seen but at least she'll have the choice.* As if sensing that very fact, the storm blew past and even lessened somewhat as it moved beyond the smashed and wrecked house, expending the last of its energy out over the mountains. *At least it got rid of the possessed. One good thing to come from it I suppose.* Thought Gwen as she sank down on the soggy carpet, beneath the root shelter. She sat beside Tara and gathered the unconscious woman into her arms. Affording her some rest and protection until she awoke from whatever held her unconscious mind in its thrall. Light still seeped from her closed lids, but the eyes that flicked beneath the skin showed her to be deep in rem state. She slept and Gwen would be there when she woke.

Daniel had seen the storm from town. Since most of the people had vanished, leaving shops and business's abandoned, Daniel had taken to acting like some impromptu caretaker. Of course he took what he needed as payment, but he made a note of it, with the full intention of paying them back if they ever returned. One of the last bastions of the townsfolk had been the pub, but even that was gone now, smashed to rubble by the lightning storm. The desolated populace fleeing in all directions in an attempt to escape the carnage wrought by the storm. Daniel had seen several not make it, or what was left of them at least. He still hadn't found his companions from the nights earlier adventures, but he was gratified that he hadn't found their bodies either. It was all like some horrible nightmare he couldn't escape. He had leapt into his car and made the best effort to get back to Tara's but he was thwarted, as there were so many fallen trees blocking the majority of roads. Off road in the dark and the storm would be tantamount to suicide, but he knew he had few options remaining open to him. Resigned, Daniel hauled on the steering wheel.

Setting off across Gilley's field saw him vanish into the night, one tail light was all that gave him away, then that too was gone. He'd had to abandon his car six miles from home, as a bolt of lightning tore up the ground in front of him, leaving an enormous crater which he promptly drove into, not having the most reliable brakes. Stuck head first, he clambered out into the smoking mud and clawed his way back to the surface. It had been a wet and terrifying trudge, dodging lightning and several of the running possessed as he went. They seemed too focused on something else other than him, a fact he was immensely grateful for. Though to be fair, Daniel didn't know they were possessed at the time, he just considered them mad. Mentally ill. Something in the water perhaps? He had no idea what had turned the people weird as he considered them, all he knew was that several had become violent and totally unhinged. What did it for him was watching Sean the grocer grab his dog and savage it with his teeth, it screamed and howled as he ripped its throat out with his own mouth. There was blood everywhere and he held the twitching corpse for long minutes as he swallowed the pumping claret. That was more than enough for Daniel; swallowing back vomit, Daniel had run far and fast away from the sight before he couldn't take it anymore and he stopped to spew his guts behind some bins. Something had definitely happened to the gentle townsfolk and he didn't like it, no sir, not one bit.

By the time he reached the cottage, the storm was then leaving. He had come up the back way, as he usually did. There was an old track that few knew about, it meandered through some rough ground that at first glance was totally impassable, unless of course you knew about the path, which he did. He had used it to great effect these past months, slipping past the freaks at the gate who stood and watched the house day in day out for some reason that was lost on him. All he knew was he intended to avoid them at all costs. Whatever they had he wasn't catching if he could avoid it. But as he drew close, he saw that something was wrong. He could see the front garden through the kitchen window. Creeping in the back he worked his way to the hallway and down towards the lounge door. Peering in carefully, making sure he wasn't seen, his mouth dropped open at what he saw and all thoughts of stealth left him. He strode in and looked left and right, taking in the destruction of what used to be his home.

'What the bloody hell happened here? And what happened to the wall?' He was gazing at the ruins of the front where the garden became one with the front room, complete with newly built rockery. The man's voice had startled Gwen from her reverie and she eased out from under the still comatose Tara and grabbed a piece of the exploded window frame. He for his part hadn't seen the women behind the screen yet so she took advantage of the surprise and moved to intercept him as he crunched through the broken glass towards her. Timing her leap she jumped out in front of him and brandished her timber. Swinging it for all she was worth. It was only his own defensive instincts that saved him from losing his head as he fell backwards as the piece of frame flashed before his eyes.

'Whoa there, friend! Peace! It's me Daniel.' He all bar screamed as he back-pedaled towards the doorway and safety. The lump of frame bounced harmlessly off the root screen as the momentum swung Gwen round. Realizing who it was and glad she hadn't decapitated him she dropped her make shift weapon and brushed her hands together. Looking at the filthy man who stared at her wide eyed and obviously terrified.

'Sorry about that, just that it's been something of a strange night and you took me by surprise that's all. Tara did say you were coming but I must have lost track of time.'

'You! What are you doing here? Is this your doing and where's me sister you... you...' Gwen held up both hands in supplication sensing where this was going. He held her responsible for this carnage based on his last discussion with her as he sped off, thinking she was some creature of the night. Of course he hadn't thought that at the time that he was leaving her on his sister's doorstep.

'Easy Daniel, your sister's fine, I think, she's sleeping anyway, just there.' Gwen pointed to the shelter. 'Look for yourself. This though is nothing to do with me; well, not directly anyway.' Gwen gestured at the ruins 'I think something wanted your sister and your fireplace just as bad. I'm sorry to say that I might have triggered it but other than that, all I can say is sorry about the mess.' He didn't know what to look at first. His sister or the little blonde woman standing bare foot and uncut amidst the array of broken glass and smashed brickwork. Fortunately for him, his choice was made for him as he heard his sister groan from behind the screen. That swayed him, and he ran towards her, though without taking his eyes from Gwen, in case she did something to him. It made for an amusing spectacle as he navigated the ruined room to get to her. He was like a puppet with his strings tangled as he lurched and skidded his way to his prone sister, who was now sitting up and rubbing her head, groaning much the same way Gwen remembered groaning after a heavy night out on the tiles. She watched as he hunkered down beside her and checked her all over for wounds, fussing like some mother hen until she swatted him away and said she was fine, just a headache. But they hugged anyway and he helped her up. Gwen just stood and watched, her arms folded across her chest and her finger absently tapping her bicep. Supporting Tara, Daniel tried to edge them both around Gwen but Tara saw what he was doing and gave him an elbow in his ribs.

'What the bloody hell are you doing Dan? Gwen's no threat to us, quite the opposite actually. Were it not for her I might not be standing here now to talk to anyone, though I am still a bit hazy on what we did at the fireplace.' Tara turned to Gwen for some help and was about to ask her to fill in some blanks when all thought of conversation washed from her head. Instead, her eyes were drawn beyond Gwen to the gaping wreckage that was her front wall and window. For heading towards the house was a mob of people, and they weren't walking casually. They were running and Tara could see that their eyes had been ripped from their heads and mouths were drawn up into snarls, with hands reaching ahead of them as though they could get them there any faster than the rest of them. Tara just pointed. Fear locked her vocal chords, freezing them in terror at the sight of the charging horde of possessed. Gwen turned to see what had affected her so and she too gasped at the sight. Though that quickly turned to anger, for enough was enough. Gwen closed her eyes and concentrated for a second, remembering the bramble wall that

296

protected her grove back home. With a ferocity and a speed that amazed even her - and she was doing it - bursting from the ground before and around the horde sprang a thick and entwining wall of thorny bramble. Like organic razor wire, it ensnared and tangled the charging horde. Tripping and binding them within its barbed embrace. Yet still they fought. Tearing and slicing their bodies beyond human endurance in their desperation to break free and get to their quarry. Flesh was shredded and ripped hideously and their blood flowed freely from wounds that would have been fatal to normal people. But these were not normal people anymore, they were deminion driven and they cared nothing for the damage inflicted on their mortal transport. The trapped soul of the innocent felt everything that happened to the body that it no longer had any control over though, screaming in impotent agony until it too eventually died. The demon then sought another host and continued its diabolical mission.

'That should hold them for now but I don't how many more there are out there.'

Daniel was stunned, he couldn't take his eyes off the entangling wall of thorn and its struggling occupants.

'Did you just do that?' he asked somewhat shrilly and Gwen rolled her eyes in exasperation, now wasn't the time to explain things to him and Tara knew that too. She poked him in the ribs again, getting his attention.

'Daniel, we have to go. Now. Before anymore come. Now how did you get here without being seen? I don't see the car.' This brought him back to the surreal world.

'Ah, well, I had a little accident with that. It's in a hole in a field somewhere. There was this bright flash and then there was this hole, you know how temperamental the brakes are…well, long story short, the cars out of the question.' Tara scowled her disapproval at his recklessness.

'We're never going to out run them, we need another car.' Daniel looked thoughtful for a moment before speaking. Gwen thought that might have been a first.

'There's plenty of abandoned cars in Sceem, but it's a good six mile hike on the best of days. This sure as shit doesn't qualify as one of them. We'll have to take the scenic route to avoid that bunch of nutters and any of their friends out a wandering. You say they are probably looking for us?' Gwen nodded, frowning herself. *How the hell am I going to get them out of this? I need to think and there's no time for breathing hardly, let alone thinking. First thing was first, get away from here, it must be like a beacon to the possessed after last night's events.*

'Okay, out the back. Daniel, you lead. You obviously got here unhindered and I know you know your way around without being spotted, so let's go. Tara, can you run?'

'Like a gazelle normally, but at this precise moment I feel like a new born, but I'll do my best. Dan'll prop me up till I get me feet. Won't you Daniel Haden Fitzgerald?' Like most people, they knew they were in trouble when their full name was used, usually it was from one irate parent or another, but in this case, he knew better than to cross his sister. She had a fiery temper, much like her mother and though it was a dim memory for him, he had heard enough stories and seen Tara in action himself more than once to even consider crossing her when she used his name like that.'

'But of course sister dearest. I wouldn't even think about leaving you to struggle. I'd sooner stick sharp sticks in me testicles than abandon ye.' She glowered at him and he smiled his ingratiating and even somewhat charming smile at her as he spoke.

'Take the piss like that Daniel and I'll do it for you, now let's move. The nearest stone circle is in Kenmare, that's where we have to get to.' Gwen smirked to herself despite the seriousness of the situation. Such humor and banter was important considering the severity of what they faced. The old adage of smiling in the face of adversity was never more apt. Gwen took a last look out at the possessed and sent her awareness a little further. Utilizing the eyes of the carrion birds that circled the possessed, scenting the blood. What she saw made her heart sink and a cold knot of fear lodge itself in her gut. There had to be hundreds more running towards them, intent on one thing. Their deaths.

'Out the back, go now!' Gwen ordered with a tone that was almost otherworldly. There was no more banter as she propelled them out, arms wide like a mother herding her recalcitrant children out. Gwen grabbed the stone tube on her way out, picking it up from the ruins of the fireplace where Tara had dropped it when the light overcame her. Figuring it might be useful to her later. With that, she took off behind them, through the house and out the kitchen. Gwen caught up to them at the head of the concealed path at the end of their garden, leading out into the wilds beyond. She saw that Tara still had enough foresight to have grabbed her shotgun and her coat as they made good their escape. Slipping into the undergrowth behind them, which Gwen turned back to and thickened the foliage with a thought, filling it with yet more briar, bramble and thorny vine she could recall, effectively concealing their direction and hopefully slowing any pursuit. They ran on. But they couldn't outrun the screams of the possessed as they howled their frustration and the cries of those who ran to join the hunt. It was a chilling sound and Gwen could tell it was drawing closer by the second; she knew also, they wouldn't give up till they caught them. Six miles soon began to feel like six hundred and that was just after *six hundred yards*.

# ACT 3

## Chapter 10

### Ragnor

Seb had been having a bad feeling for several weeks as his current investigation ran on. There were more Hounds than ever on the mortal plane than there had been for decades. Seb knew this because he made it his job to know this. Since they had destroyed the order back during the sixties, Harry and he had tracked Conmore's cronies down and wiped them out wherever they raised their shaggy heads. All they had come across since were the mutated wild hounds of Fenris, his pawns in a larger game being played. None had gathered so readily though in one place – New York – since Gwen came on the scene and it bothered Seb to the point it made a permanent itch beneath his fur. But Seb tired of chasing them, so he had changed tack. A way to corroborate his theory too, Seb had begun hanging around known haunts asking for the whereabouts of the order, quite blatantly drawing attention to himself. A few scuffles later and now Seb reclined upon a reconstructed bench in Central Park and waited for the breadcrumbs he had left to be followed to his feet. He didn't have long to wait, he'd ruffled their fur good and proper. Which was bad, as it solidified his theory. 'You took your time, I've been here ages.' Seb taunted as he counted. Sixteen he could see and another dozen he could smell. They were Conmore's for sure. They walked calmly towards him in their human form. Long heavy and hooded coats concealed some of their features but Seb's eyes were better than theirs and he saw they were in part transition, poised for the fight they came for. Another tick in Conmore's box as Fenris Hounds had no human form anymore and only the very powerful could control the switch and the pain that went with it. But these even dressed like the quasi-religious zealots they were the same as those they took out in Cerne Abbas that night. 'I thought there would be more of you or at the very least, someone higher up the food chain than just you scum.' One of the hooded wolves raised a fist and they all stopped and he took another step closer before stopping. *Hmm, military trained, militia I wonder.* Seb filed the idea away for future exploration. 'Other than the fact you've been poking definitely where you shouldn't, you've proven to be quite the thorn,' the spokesperson for the wolves growled 'you and that black mongrel you hang around with.' *Uh oh, Harry isn't going to like that.* Seb mused before responding glibly. 'We're good at ferreting out trash' Seb took a moment for the insult to register 'especially trash that shouldn't exist anymore, so it's interesting how you roaches all scuttled back together and whoever is yanking your leashes these day; I've an idea, but I wanted you pups to come out and play to confirm it for me.' The leader of the wolves laughed an abrasive sound and Seb knew then he was dealing with arrogance instead of experience. *You found them all Harry?* Seb and Harry were magically linked to communicate with each other over distances. They had to be, as standard wired ear pieces wouldn't work when they transformed and their supernatural senses heightened. *I have, I'm quite astute for a mongrel.* Seb chuckled and the leader saw the smirk. 'You think this is funny?' Seb leant back all the more and bared his teeth, displaying a humorous visage but there was no joviality there to be had. 'Oh yes.' Seb answered smoothly 'There is a phrase by Einstein I believe that says only a fool repeats the same thing over and over expecting a different result. I'm guessing by your rash behaviour at following me here, Conmore isn't calling the shots here? For fancy leaving imbeciles in charge of themselves...' The leader threw back his hood, showing he was indeed part transformed, red eyes, lupine ears, fur and semi protruding muzzle. 'I Jurgen command here in the absence of the Lord Conmore, and as such I am more than capable to ensure your demise so to present my Lord with your heads upon his return.' Seb pressed for a bit more while he could, ignoring the threat like he had never spoken. 'Surely he wouldn't go far leaving you looking after his interests, he must be in the USA still, as your leash couldn't be that long, you're too stupid.' Harry during this diversionary chat was systematically taking out the dozen not so well hidden back up hounds, and as he took out the last one with a brutal neck snap then decapitation – he didn't want any sudden regeneration joining the fight about to take place- Harry placed himself ready for Seb's signal. 'Goad me all you will Collective' Jurgen sneered 'your days of thwarting our destiny are over.' Seb laughed properly this time as Harry confirmed the all clear. 'In that case...' Seb probed 'telling me where Conmore has gone at least won't matter if I'm dead with that knowledge, here...' Seb tossed the leader a phone, catching him on the hop he fumbled before catching it. 'Look, I can't call anyone, you know I'm not wired as we can't function with that modern tech, who am I going to tell?' But it was a ploy albeit a casual one to make life easy, but Seb didn't believe fully they were really weren't that dumb as to just give it away on that ploy...were they? Jurgen was however dim enough not to check Seb's phone for explosives as he caught it, for they wouldn't be able to smell the explosive inside, it was a proprietary odourless and incredibly powerful version of C5, magically enhanced by the Archives sorcerers. The DNA trigger however meant that anyone other than Seb handling the phone, activated its countdown. And it just ran out. With a concussive blast that removed the leader's upper torso messily and took another three besides, Seb and Harry took that as their cue. Harry was already in his hound form and crashed through the foliage where he had been secreted and engaged half a dozen of the Order, Seb burst into his golden wolf form and with arms wide threw himself at the rest as if to engulf them. It was a brief fight for even eight each was little match for Seb and Harry. 'How is it we're responsible for making a bloody mess in this Park again?' Harry asked as he piled up the bodies to a central pyre shortly after and back in human form. Once all the bits were stacked Seb gave the magical command and green fire sprung up like a rocket was taking off beneath them, roaring emerald flames blasting skyward hungrily. But within minutes, the carnage was a pile of ash and even that blew away on the breeze.

It took another two days of revisiting the haunts Seb had antagonised and going through what few hounds remained to find what they were looking for. Logged flight plans to Norway under Conmore's name. Seb didn't like it at all and when he reported to Ted, the old man went quiet. He had been filing his suspicions away over the years in case of a re-emergence, praying it never happened but prepared for it all the same. Seems his preparations were founded after all. Norway wasn't the end goal Seb knew, he also knew what was just a short helo ride away. Dispirited, Harry and Seb torched what they safely could, what they couldn't they had Summer magically translocate back to the Archive. There were boxes full of ingredients and grimoires that served no other purpose than to summon revenants. It was a disturbing day when Hounds were calling upon the possessed and that idea sank their spirits lower still as they headed back to the diner that was to be their RV point if things went swirly, which for a change, they didn't but even that couldn't raise their spirits against the prospect of what was coming.

Seb and Harry genuinely thought that would be an end to the incursions into New York by the Revenants once Gwen was gone, they also hoped the same for the Hounds, but in that hope they turned out to be very mistaken. The chaos had taken months to clear up in the aftermath of the dragons and the Kore-Megara, construction crews were working around the clock, seven days a week. But for commercial normality to return to the usually busy area, that took another eighteen months. Harry and Seb left the city occasionally but what grew more curious were the threads that kept bringing them back, albeit different parts of the city, Manhattan, New Jersey, Queens and many more and over the ensuing months a pattern began to emerge; one that had been cleverly hidden and clearly built upon over a very long time and the more the two Collective wolves discovered the more their hearts sank. The discoveries were fast becoming familiar and the scale, as well as the audacity was beyond belief.

'I thought we'd buried these bastards years ago.' Harry growled as they sat in a diner nursing cold coffees and uneaten food. Harry was angry where Seb was disappointed. Between them railing at the possibilities the food and drink they had before them to maintain their pretence simply went cold and untouched. 'We did Harry, don't beat yourself up about the past. They're like cockroaches, squash one and you miss the twelve you don't see.' Harry looked long and hard at Seb before asking the question they had both put off. 'Do you think he's still alive then?' long excruciating minutes dragged by before Seb answered 'I do. Malcolm Conmore survived and I'm more and more convinced he is behind this.' Harry looked into his coffee with a troubled expression, hoping maybe the answer was swirling in the dark unsettled liquid. It was not. 'Why do I think that Conmore has teamed up with the legion? And, if that is even remotely true there is a maelstrom of shit coming that really doesn't bear thinking about.' Seb frowned uncharacteristically with genuine concern and looked at Harry to elaborate as he hadn't made that leap quite as definitively as Harry had seemed to. 'You were in Chicago at the time but I was here, six months ago or there abouts I suppose, but you recall after the shit hit the fan with the Legion that first time?' Seb nodded 'When they took all the OB's out?' Seb recalled it vividly, there was nothing they could have done, and it was a well concerted attack timed for when all those who might have stopped it were diverted elsewhere. 'Well...' Harry continued '...remember that nasty little Drakul Corben briefed us on and put the BOLO out for?' again Seb nodded, this time encouraging Harry to get a move on as his patience what it was after their discoveries these past months. 'Okay, okay keep your fur on, you know who I mean...Stryfe. That was his name as I recall, well I'm better with faces and scents than I am with names. Names are easy to change, your face less so but your scent…well, that takes magic and even that smells.' Seb widened his eyes as he was about to lose patience entirely and Harry took the hint. 'Basically I've seen Stryfe here, in New York-more than once-and as he is the stiletto of the Legion, there I am just putting two and two together…' Harry shrugged as if to signal Seb to draw either his own or the same conclusion.

'It wouldn't surprise me if I'm honest. Conmore was a piece of shit…' Harry butted in with a demoralizing '*is* a piece of shit Seb, we hoped *was* but it's an *is* for sure.' Seb sighed and finished his observation dryly 'so it doesn't come as shock he'd get into bed with lizards to get his own way.' Harry and Seb were silent for a moment as the implications ran around their ever scheming heads. They thought like the enemy they chased making them extraordinary at what they did but the avenues for chaos and mischief when presented with an alliance of that magnitude silenced them both. 'Do you think he still has the same bug up his arse that he had at Cerne Abbas back then…you know when we got… this?' Harry held up a suddenly taloned finger and flicked his eyes golden to demonstrate what *this* was.' Seb nodded but said nothing, his own troubled eyes spoke for him. Harry studied his friend and after decades of working together, sharing the same curse Harry instinctively tuned his thoughts to where he suspected Seb was directing his. 'How many of the hounds that we've fought are Conmore's and how many belong to that whiny son of a bitch Fenris? You think Conmore has had more of a hand in these attacks than we thought?' Again Seb nodded, still not wasting energy talking as his mind was tracking off several different directions taking scenarios to their possible conclusions in a bid to discern Conmore's motive. They all came back to the one objective and he disliked it so much he tried another tack and another and another, but logic kept him presenting the same answer to himself. 'They're hunting Gwen!' was all Seb finally said and Harry virtually deflated in his chair, as that statement woefully corroborated his own suspicion and when he and Seb agreed like that, it was usually ninety nine point nine percent certain. 'Damn, I hoped it was something else.' Seb frowned and shook his boyish mane of blonde hair. 'As do I, but no matter how you shape it, that's what they want. The Order of Ragnor were obsessed with one thing if you recall, creating sentient and unburdened hounds – like us. Using the ring…' Harry butted in again 'Did you know the archivists named it after we brought it back? They called it the Fenring, catchy eh?' Seb sat back and spread his hands 'How is that relevant?' Harry shrugged and grinned briefly, he was irrepressible and didn't stay despondent for long 'Just saying, if you're gonna talk about it, call it by their name for it.' Seb rolled his eyes and carried on 'The Fenring was Conmore's methodology, it would be his seat of power but as he can't get that out of our vaults…ever, all being well; he will need an alternative. Now I don't do coincidence, you know that, so how do we have the Legion here with their master assassin and where he is there will be those who give the orders, on top of that we have Kore-Megara, a sect of witches thought extinct but clearly not. On top of that again we have demons…actual bloody demons walking and talking here where they should not even be. Too many powers with too many revenants at their disposal, all coming together where Gwen is…was. Now you were in New Mexico with that truly scary woman…what was her name again…?' Seb left it hanging knowing Harry would oblige, smiling when he did like a schoolboy letting slip his school crush. 'Ah yes, Madeline. Maddy. That was it. Don't suppose she let on to you what they wanted to keep Gwen safe for? We all know what from, but that's some array of enemies for a mortal woman.' Harry was about to speak and when he opened his mouth to do so, a woman's voice answered. 'Think I can answer that for you.' Harry checked his throat and sighed in relief as he looked back and saw the reason. 'Well hello Bex,' Harry chirped cheerfully 'how did you know we were back in town?' Seb said as sidled over to allow Bex to sit and as she did so, Seb ordered fresh coffee in that silent hand waving practise of diners the world over. 'Hello boys. As to how I found you, well you know I have some power right?' They nodded in concert 'Then don't ask stupid questions. I keep my fingers on the pulse more now and I've learnt something very exciting and at the same time terrible, which sounds like the direction you two were going when I came in, so I thought I'd save you some brain power, and time.' Harry relaxed back against the wall, pulling a packet of cigarettes out and offering them around before taking one out after Seb and Bex refused. Popping it in his mouth and was about to light it when the waitress retuned with the coffee and snapped at him.

'There's no smoking in here…sir.' The delay conveyed the necessary contempt for his behaviour and Harry grinned guiltily and spat it out, deftly catching it and slipping it behind his ear, just as he did during the war when he and Seb were fighting in the Ardennes offensive, just before Christmas, 1944. They weren't Harry's fondest memories. 'So then Bex…' Harry started, effectively dismissing the waitress and trying to regain some equilibrium '…what do we need to know?' Bex looked at them both then and asked one question. 'Did you feel that shockwave a while back? You'd remember it.' Seb and Harry looked between them and nodded imperceptibly. Bex was super vigilant and caught their subtle communication 'Good, well that was Gwen.' You could have heard a pin drop and Bex was inwardly amused at the fact in all the time she had known the two incorrigible hounds Seb and Harry were, she'd never seen them both quite so dumbstruck. 'Crikey, silence. Let me elaborate as you close your mouths. You recall the dragons?' Bex's question was rhetorical as she pressed on before they could answer 'Well, Maddy and Jen are if you recall Drakarim, ancient by human terms but as you see, still young dragons who were part of the Kalithine War Drakarim support. Once they arrived here on Earth, she took them…the Earth if you're confused, this is a summary so no details boys, but they were to be the Avatars of the Earth, her voice and will. Very, very long story short but should there be such a crisis, one as apocalyptic as we uncoincidentally find ourselves in, then another would be called to create the Trinity. Rumours existed on my world long before I left it about this, a thing beyond prophecy and beyond legend for it had never happened anywhere at any time and even the Absolutes had no such knowledge of it ever happening before. Never three' Harry leant forward at that and sought clarity 'Did you say The Absolutes?' Bex just nodded, slowly. 'The actual four horsemen?' Harry reiterated slowly, unsure almost of what he was saying. 'The same' Bex answered coolly. 'I'd read as much of the histories as I could handle' Harry moaned 'during that sojourn at the archivists but It's hard to imagine…I mean I know what we are and what we've seen but those four…it's just hard is all to accept them on top of all this.' Bex smiled and patted Harry's hand, knowing how daunting their presence could be and simply knowledge that they exist is a weight few should or could bear. 'They're real and they're struggling like the rest of us right now which is another reason why The Earth called for Gwen.' Seb, who had been silent leant forward and steepled his fingers as he folded his hands together upon the table. 'So Gwen is an Avatar now?' Bex again nodded and knew that her next words would have an equally devastating effect upon them. 'As well as being the Avatar of Nature now, Gwen has been…changed. On a molecular level, right down to RNA, DNA, musculoskeletal and a chromosomal level Gwen is now a green dragon.' Seb said nothing but picked up his previously ignored coffee and downed it in one. Harry just stared agog at Bex, eyes widening beyond their normal capacity until Bex was worried they would simply fall out and roll off across the table. It was Seb who spoke first though. 'A green dragon? An actual giant lizard like those two that melted Fifth Avenue?

747 sized, flying fire breathing, scaled and teeth and all dragon?' Bex smiled and nodded to every reference. Harry just said 'Holy shit.' But it was Seb who had taken several steps ahead of himself and answered his own quandary. 'So that's why they want her. Her blood fused with Conmore's blood will create an army of hounds the likes the world has never seen, allowing him to even take on Fenris I suspect if I read his madness right. There are sorcerers aplenty now too I'm guessing, what with the Kore-Megara skulking around once more to make him another Fenring and then there will be little to stand against his ambitions.' Seb looked at Bex, studying her as his thoughts processed themselves into some sort of order. 'Have you been in any trouble since we left you effectively alone here?' Bex was touched by the concern but she had been alone for centuries, recent events although more hands on were no more than she could handle. 'I've been fine Seb, but thank you for your concern.' Seb nodded, accepting that at face value 'What about the hospital? Nothing weird there? We're not fans of habit and repetition, makes you vulnerable to the enemy and you're nothing if not repetitive there by turning up regularly…' Bex was about to argue she had stepped down but Seb beat her to it '…even though you are only consulting, it's still a pattern. Why don't you come back with us or let me call Ted, have him induct you officially into the Collective? You would have at least some back up to call upon if things got sticky here or anywhere for that matter.' It was an interesting thought and one Bex hadn't seen coming; it might be nice to not be so alone for a change. 'I'll think about it if that's okay?' Seb saw an opening and pressed it 'You think about then, I'll make a call, if Ted is there, you two can meet, he'll be ecstatic to meet you I know, have a chat and dinner here on us as we have matters to attend to elsewhere but how about we catch up for breakfast at Hannigan's tomorrow, you can tell us all about it?'

'You're not going to let this go are you?' Bex asked, pretty sure of the answer 'No, I'm not. I didn't like leaving you here before but things have just gone swirly and that usually means hazardous and messy follow, be good to have some support here as if I think is about to happen happens, we need to be on a plane to Scotland asap.' Harry chimed in then as he picked up the thread Seb left hanging like a twin finishing his twin's sentence. 'Too many years ago, matters escalated into almost all-out war with an order of werewolves, to call them Hounds implies they were affiliated to Fenris but these were battle wolves, turned and corrupted by who we thought was the late Lord Malcolm Conmore and head of the Order of Ragnor and before you say it, no they were not very imaginative in the naming of their group. Anyway, it all kicked off and long story short Ted and the Collective and us of course won the day and Ted took possession of the stately home known as Whitespire – formerly owned by Conmore. I suspect as an opening salvo, Conmore is going to want it back – or try at least.' Bex was slowly piecing their story together as snippets of information still filtered their way to her over the years and this was familiar, though not enough to contribute. But Bex guessed that as Seb and Harry were going, they wanted assurance she was not alone again. She acquiesced. 'Okay, call him and I'll talk, here you say? How long am I going to have to wait? Didn't you say he was in Scotland or some such?' But whilst Harry talked, Seb had called and the male voice that spoke next was neither Harry nor Seb. To Bex's ear it was aged but strong, confident yet warm and radiated power that one such as she felt like a heat source drawing closer. Bex turned from her seat and looked back to see a man, well dressed in a three piece herringbone suit, dark brown, immaculate white shirt with a subtly striped yellow tie tucked in to the waistcoat and highly polished brogues. But it was the shock of bone white hair that sat upon his head that drew her gaze. He deftly checked the pocket watch that hung at his waist as he spoke 'You won't have to wait long at all young lady.' Ted reassured Bex as he drew alongside their booth 'you two were now leaving did I hear?' and with that both Seb and Harry grinned like schoolboys as Seb sidled out and Harry deftly sprung over the seat whereupon Bex slid in further and Ted took Seb's seat opposite. Ted looked up then and gave the two wolves his parting words 'There is a plane fuelled and ready at JFK to take you direct to Edinburgh, you can make your way to Whitespire from there I take it?' Seb nodded curtly and Harry mock saluted and with that both were gone, only the door slowly closing behind them remained. 'They're definitely the good guys those two.' Bex stated as she sensed their presence fade fast, knowing the supernatural, lupine speed they possessed, they'd be at the airport in minutes. Ted meanwhile watched the woman before him for those few minutes as he weighed her up before speaking 'Yes they are, I've known them a very long time and there are few people I'd trust my life with, but those two are high on the list.' Ted briefly ordered some food and a very confused waitress came over, looking at who sat in the seats now and took Ted's order, after she had gone to set wheels in motion he explained his plateful 'I don't actually get to enjoy the places I visit very often, there is usually some crisis to be averted then on to the next, sadly my role isn't all I would often like it to be.' Bex cocked her head birdlike as she asked innocently 'Oh? And what role is that?' Ted smiled, all teeth and rugged tan, teeth almost as white as his hair, and on this day, Ted sported a thin, pencil style moustache that just sat upon his top lip, as white as his hair and Ted carried it off with suave sophistication like a man born to it – which he was. 'You look like you could have been Clark Gable's dad.' Ted smiled and winked ruefully 'I'm old enough to be Clark gables dad as it goes and weirdly you mention him, I was at the Presbyterian Hospital the day he died there, though they still debate whether it was a heart attack or a stroke that claimed him.' Bex leant forward and put her chin in her hands with interest 'Why were you there of all places?' she asked interested as Ted's expression turned sour at the memory then, 'Revenants. They get everywhere you know and hospitals are good sources of weakened bodies to inhabit, you'd be surprised how many originate in them.' Bex chuckled at the irony and told Ted of her history at Saini and how Bex had been there for several decades in different roles. At which point, both regarded the other with an increasing awareness of supernatural status. Seb hadn't mentioned too much, he knew Ted liked to formulate his own conclusions and Bex was also fast concluding there was something more than human about Ted. 'Seb tells me you are considering joining us at the Collective?' Ted asked between mouthfuls of food 'Why?' Here it comes Bex thought 'What do you know of me Ted...can I call you Ted?' Ted mopped his lip with a napkin and sat back 'You can call me whatever makes you happy to be honest, I'm not a one for standing on ceremony unless it's called for. I'm known by many names in many different places, it depends on where and who you are I suppose. But I like Ted, it's less intimidating than General or Sir.' Bex was warming to the man before her like few she had ever encountered and she realised then it was because he was an old soul, like her, out of her time like a visitor to the future, she adapted but was at heart more comfortable with history and those from it. 'To my question, what do you know?' Ted looked at Bex then not with the kindly gentleman eyes but with those of the demi-god he now was, his eyes lit vibrant blue as the Shard's energy flowed through him and for an instant, Bex thought she saw the stereotypical Odin image superimposed over Ted, mane of hair, furs draped across broad shoulders, patch over one eye, twin ravens perched upon each shoulder and wolves at his knees, grasping a vicious looking spear, then it was gone and Ted remained. 'What would you have me say Bex, or is it Rebecca? You are far more ancient than I, even more so than my colleagues at the Collective, the Drakel who hearken back to the dawn of human time. Benevolent, that much a blind man could see but you are not one of the celestial host - the Angelics, nor are you of the reptilians. A mystery for sure but one that would be welcome at the Collective, The Shard is a perfect judge of character I've found.' Bex lowered her eyes demurely at the compliment even as she named her ancestry 'I am of the Unc'Anharaphim - one of the last - as many of my people were hunted to almost extinction and I've been in one form of hiding or another since the Kalithine war ended. Truly, I've only really come into my own these past couple of years since Gwen appeared.' Ted nodded as he knew all about that 'Ah yes, Gwen.' He sighed almost 'The daughter of a colleague of mine sadly no longer with us thanks to this war and it is in that spirit we look favourably upon all potential allies in this war, for make no mistake; that is what it is…a war unlike any other.' Bex agreed and in doing so, felt a kinship she hadn't experienced in an age. That of Kindred souls, of an age where she could be herself and it felt invigorating. Almost like someone had invited her home, her home. She made her choice.

'I'm in. I'll join your Collective if you'll have me.' Ted beamed again and held out a hand. The one Bex shook however was not cold or feeble or limp or weak, like many of her elderly patients at Mt Sinai who resembled Ted in appearance had. Bex knew then it was appearance only, steel existed within this man and soon enough would she discover it was the steel of The Shard. 'Excellent.' Ted exclaimed with genuine satisfaction. 'Well there are a few formalities which we cannot do here. I'd like to bring you to the London office where Summer can process you in, then after lunch we'll meet with the Council at the Archive where Clare, Bernard and Angela will walk you through the details, you'll like them.' Bex mentally evaluated what she was hearing and what she would need but Ted was way ahead of her. 'Don't worry about passports etc. ever again for that matter, we don't adhere to the conventional rules of international oversight.' Ted reached into a pocket and withdrew a hundred dollar bill and left it upon the table 'That should cover everyone, now would you care to take my hand once more?' Bex did, shyly almost as Ted's charm was quite disarming for one of her heritage. Ted gave a quick warning then 'You may need to take deep breath if you're in anyway unfamiliar with…' Bex was so intent on what Ted was about to say she was totally unprepared for what happened next, which was Ted's plan as they both just winked out.

'…this mode of travel.' They stood in the recreation of Ted's wood panelled office, relocated to a top private suite in the newly constructed Collective Towers, a work of magical artistry and so spell woven it was virtually undetectable as what it was by any supernatural entity and ironically being located only half a mile from The Shard itself. Ted loved irony.

'Welcome to London Rebecca.'

# Chapter 11

# Elementum

ow long?' In a voice devoid of all emotion, Daniel asked the now suddenly distanced doctor, who himself had adopted a regularly practiced, sad expression of helpless sympathy - one that Daniel figured must have been ingrained in to them during their medical training. Grimacing inwardly at doctors everywhere for their pity Daniel found himself suddenly annoyed by the insipid, pale and pasty face before him as though he had never seen it before. How long was the question Daniel reasoned that just about everyone in his predicament must have asked when their mortality was handed to them with an expiry date. The unfairness of it stripped his rationality and colored the world he thought he knew in dull, lifeless shades never before imagined. He was going to die. And not even because of anything he had actually done; a serial killer on death row must find it easier to come to terms with their impending doom because at least they knew why. Or at least Daniel assumed they did. His mind was too busy scrambling for the implications of what he had just been told to bother with such trivial things as details and the overall moral viewpoint of perspective.

The actual voice however that spilt from his head - which Daniel distractedly noticed, was at least coherent and steady- was like a rational version of himself that seemed to be acting on auto pilot for him. Speaking the words in his stead and asking the questions that he needed answers for instead of the high pitched scream of abject disbelief that he wanted so badly to set free, whilst simultaneously absorbing the cataclysmic fact, that all bar the shouting, his life - as he knew it - was essentially over.

'Two years at the absolute most Mr. Fitzgerald,' the doctor intoned 'more likely eighteen months if we are honest with ourselves.' *We? What the fuck is this we shit?* Daniel wanted to throttle the superficial look of pity right off the face of the man before him; The same man he recalled bitterly who had given him the only hope he had to begin with, some thirteen months earlier but then cruelly, yanked the rug from beneath his flailing feet by explaining - as though he were talking to a child - that the tumor in his head, nestled cozily in his grey matter, had spread like an evil octopus and was now totally inoperable. 'In fact Mr. Fitzgerald, it's a miracle you're even still standing at all.' The doc added.

'But you said there was a chance?' Daniel grasped for the final straw as it drifted, dreamlike further and further rom his grasp. 'That there was a new experimental procedure that might be able to reach it, what the fuck happened to that?' Daniel stopped talking abruptly, conscious of his now rising voice. If he continued talking he knew it would degenerate into a screaming hysteric. Not yet, he needed to remain calm for now, to get all the facts before he figured out what he was to become next, something other than dead.

'Now Daniel, if you remember…the doctor employed his best patronizing tone '…we said that it was only a slim chance, so slim we shouldn't get our hopes up, we…' Daniel couldn't take it anymore, not known for his patience at the best of times, which these really weren't. A tiny part of his mind knew it was the frustration getting the better of him and he should be more understanding, but the greater part, the part that had just been told he was going to die overrode that and with a popping like sound in his ears, Daniel stood swiftly and grabbed the edges of the doctor's desk and leant over it as he shouted at the pasty man in the white coat opposite.

'Will you stop saying we.' Daniel shouted suddenly, causing the doctor to flinch involuntarily stopped from flying backwards out of his own window by the back of his own chair. Daniel instantly calmed again and his tone was placid as he added. 'It's not you who's got a fucking lump in his head which is going to snuff him out like a fucking candle without a moment's notice any time soon is it?' He didn't wait for the now paler man before him to answer. 'No, it's not. So quit the fucking empathy will you, it's not working. You can't just blurt out that I'm going to die within eighteen to twenty four months and expect me to act rationally can you for the love of God. It's not we, it's me, got that? Me! Alright? Me, me, me, fucking ME!' The doctor blanched even more in the face of Daniels outburst and Daniel secretly took a little guilty pleasure from his fear and trepidation.

Though it couldn't be easy, Daniel mused disjointedly as though he was having a lesser conversation with himself inside his head while the rest of him went in to meltdown, having to be the one who broke the news to people that they were going to die. It had to be an integral and fundamental part of their job. Mainly because they were on to a loser to begin with. Death came to the greater majority of his customers first and regularly; though he comes to us all anyway Daniel reasoned logically, sometimes it came prematurely and often painfully, with little dignity. Others, like his case, where the tumor was just going switch him off one day, much like a walking organic light bulb were unobtrusive and comparatively pain free, though the head aches when they came totally pole-axed him and sent him crawling for his bed in a very dark, cold and quiet room with more pills chundering down his throat than were really good for him. That tiny part of his consciousness that kept him going through it all and not hurling himself off some bridge tried to keep him sane, and that same small part of Daniel that still had its diaphanous grip on reality, actually felt sorry for the little man in front of him whose eyes were darting left and right looking for an exit; But then again, he argued with himself, it was that self-same man who was going to go home to his invariably comfortable life after ruining Daniels and relegating his ailment and problems to just another case file. To be forgotten and boxed after he left the office. Relegated to the status of just one more distraught victim of the dreaded, ever present specter of cancer. It was a terrible job really, but it was one he chose and got paid very well for no doubt, but at the end of the day, however much of a shitty job it was, somebody had to do it, so why shouldn't he earn his bag of thirty silver pieces.

The rest of the conversation hadn't gone too well after that and Daniel stormed out of the doctor's office slamming several doors on his way out. Even rattling many of the ridiculously thin panes of glass in their frames, almost daring them to smash and shatter onto the thin, well-worn carpet. Catching sight of the receptionist as he stomped past, Daniel caught sight of her watching him in turn with a mixture of pity and wariness before going back to her nails and typing, whichever she thought the more important. Daniel had turned away hoping she hadn't seen, but he knew in his heart she had spotted the tears that now flowed freely down his ruddy cheeks. And knowing she knew just made it worse. He resented her the life that should have been his. In fact, by the time Daniel had made it outside to the suddenly chill air of the street, after the claustrophobic and slightly warm antiseptic air of the doctors consultation room, he resented just about everyone their life.

He hadn't told Tara about the increasing headaches that escalated over the last couple of years, blaming them on hang overs. Nor told her about the equally increasing number of visits to the doctor, all of which culminated in the MRI scan and capped it off with the eventual diagnosis of his cerebral cancer. They had been optimistic during those early days as it had been quite small, but suddenly, the little bastard had begun to grow at an alarming rate. A rate that was unconcerned with NHS waiting times and the availability of consultants who were probably too busy on the golf course to bother themselves with no hopers like him. Daniel's cynicism painted a very harsh reality, one where people he despised were cruel, cold and complete wastes of the polluted and disease filled air they breathed. But test after test and poking and probing they still said it didn't look good.

That was what he had been told anyway and he was to prepare himself for the worst case scenario. He had; or at least he had tried. But how do you ever prepare for news like that. Numbly, Daniel went about his life, what he considered was left of it anyway. He seemed to those who knew him, to adopt a certain recklessness that came across as irresponsible and deplorable behavior. Daniel cared less and less, but it wasn't until after a blazing row with his two best friends, Kieran Doyle and his cousin Barry that Daniel realized how much of a prat he had become.

As they had after his every visit to his oncologist, they both found him and eventually left him draped over the bar where they had propped him to continue to wallow in the personal misery he dwelt in, a private hell of his own making while they went off to plan their regular fishing come business trip without him. Though it was always more business than fishing. The only thing they caught were the two dozen watertight drums filled with some two hundred and fifty thousand cigarettes which the helicopter had dropped off on the west side of the Ballinskelligs. All the cousins had to do was snag on to the weighted drums by the hook with the flashing light attached and pull them aboard. A bit like a larger scale version of the fairground attraction, only this time the prize wasn't a goldfish, but an easy few grand on the not so much black, but more of a nicotine colored market. It was a dubious and dangerous pastime in those waters, but they cited needs must.

That fateful morning of his last consultation, where he was handed his final timetable had been the day he really blew up at his friends. After stumbling out of the doctors, Daniel had found the nearest bar and dulled a lot of pain there. They had eventually found and subsequently left Daniel there, as he was in no shape for anything except draping over his bar stool like he was made of wax in room too hot. Eventually though, he had stumbled out of the bar- more because it was closing- barely able to walk let alone drive, finally falling into his death trap of a vehicle – once he found where he had left it-and after ten minutes or so of rummaging through every pocket at least six times, he finally found the keys and fired the battered old Land Rover up. Smoking like it ran on steam, Daniel was soon gunning the muddy green and slightly rusty four by four away from the curb and nearly running over a couple of errant revelers in the process, he swerved off to a hail of abuse from the lucky to be alive pedestrians behind him. Daniel waved the middle finger of his right hand out of the window at them to tell them he couldn't have cared less and proceeded to grumble his Landy out of town. He found the N70 almost by accident rather than by design and set off southwards. He originally intended to stop at Tara's and spend some time there, it always calmed him somehow, but he was too full of drink this day-common sense prevailed even through the whiskey haze to not upset Tara- and knowing somehow that he had plenty of supplies on the back seat to ensure he stayed in his cups for at least a week, his choice was made for him.

Daniel vaguely remembered there being a Wednesday; And there was also a Friday involved when he was due to be going with the cousins on one of their fishing excursion, which gave him - to his alcohol befuddled mind - two days to decide whether he was going to throw himself overboard and beat death to the punch line before he got him. Or, take out the biggest loan he could find and blow it all on all the things he knew to be bad for him, but fun. It wasn't like he was going to have to pay it back was he. Passing Sneem at something close to ninety miles an hour, he navigated the roads with an almost inhuman ability with the car occasionally cornering on two wheels and squealing its displeasure at such treatment. Protests that this day, fell on very deaf and totally intoxicated ears as he exhorted it to greater feats of mechanical acrobatics.

He didn't know how long he drove for, not that he cared much anyway, but it was getting dark and his tear filled and booze swamped eyes were struggling to see more than a few feet past the dent filled and cable-tie supported bonnet. So he pulled off the road at the first muddy track he saw and parked the thankful - and if it could have - sweating car close to a small copse of oak and ash trees, about three quarters of a mile off the main highway, and summarily passed out.

Daniel woke slowly. A sickly grey light filtered its way into the dim interior of the car, and it was this that told Daniels tender brain, that it was at least if nothing else, day time. But the light was so nondescript, that the actual time of day eluded him totally. It could have been anything from early morning to just before sunset. Daniel took in his position within the car before moving his limbs, rolling his eyes only which was painful too but easiest. He was sprawled across the back seat with one leg hanging over the passenger seat, the other propped up on the rear door with the base of his boot pressed firmly to the glass. Daniel absently realized his right leg, where it was draped, had gone to sleep too and had stayed that way upon his waking. He knew that when he dragged himself together, his foot was going to give him merry hell as sensation came flooding back into it. The stench of vomit assailed his nostrils then and he almost gagged before he realized that it had been himself that had done it. Some point during the night he had rolled over and thrown up all over himself. Then he caught a whiff of his own breath and decided the vomit was preferable. It was as though the entire population of Kerry's seagulls had taken turns in swooping in and shitting in his mouth – or so it tasted. Painfully, as his neck had constricted due to the awkward angle he had found himself laying in, he turned to survey his handiwork of the previous night. There were several empty bottles and heaps of cans along with what looked like ancient discarded pizza boxes. In disgust, Daniel realized that at some stage during the night, as he poured unhealthy amounts of booze into himself, he had gotten a nasty case of the munchies. Apparently, as the evidence before him substantiated, he had discovered a some weeks old abandoned pizza and a few old cartons of Chinese noodles that had been carelessly tossed and subsequently forgotten a week or two earlier. In his haze, Daniel had ignored the patches of soft, velvety blue fur that had cultivated itself on the material formerly known as food, along with the fag ash and mud from the rear foot well where he had retrieved it from and shoveled it down his neck. Like all things alcohol glazed, it had seemed a sound idea at the time and had even tasted pretty good too. At least that was what his fogged memory told him, but in the cold light of day, or something that loosely resembled it, he realized that even the damn seagulls would have wisely left that alone. This memory alone promptly had him lurching up and throwing up once more, this time over the dead leg as he couldn't move it to reach the door. 'Feckin hell.' Was all Daniel managed after as he contemplated his state of being right there and then.

## TRINITY

Daniel was a big believer in not remembering things when he had gadgets that could do it for him. So with a Herculean effort and no small amount of contorting, he managed to extricate his phone from his coat pocket. Amazed that he had managed to hang on to this one for as long as he had. He was notorious for losing them. Flipping the thing open he struggled to focus his bleary eyes on what it was telling him. When he did, he couldn't believe what he was seeing for several minutes afterwards.

'*Feckin Saturday?*' He looked at it again as if it was going to say something different the second time around, but it didn't. The little word kept glaring at him as if defying him to disprove it.

'How the hell did that happen?' Daniel knew it was rhetorical as he knew full well how it happened. 'What did you drink Daniel? That's two feckin days you've lost, you complete utter and total imbecile.' As he was berating himself, he tried desperately to haul himself upright, eventually doing so, then with more effort than should have been required, he opened the rear door. Fully intending to stumble out and park himself back in the driver's seat. The door crunched open and he gazed upon an alien world. It was only after several very confused seconds that he cottoned on as to why the light was so diffuse through the glass of the car; it was frosted over as though it had been etched opaque. The copse nearby, the surrounding fields and just about everything else he could see was a dazzling, stark and icy white. Words failed him as he slowly got out and turned in a deliberate –slow- three hundred and sixty degree circle taking in the fantastic vista he found himself in. Daniel inadvertently put a casual hand on the roof of his car and had to snatch it back suddenly as though it had been burnt. He looked confusedly at the red patch of skin on his palm then at the icy spot on his car where the intense cold had seared him. He drew a deep breath and almost choked as the biting cold air tore into his unprepared lungs. He had been temporarily protected from the extreme climate change when he first emerged from his cocoon by the two day old bubble of warm foetid air that clung to his clothes and skin. That soon evaporated under the frigid wind that howled across the land, ripping and tearing at everything, including him, with icy fingers of razor wire. He tried to breathe again but only ended up coughing as the chill air was too much for his body to take.

'What the bloody hell happened?' he asked himself lamely as he could see exactly what had happened, but the why and the how were lost on him completely. Kerry, or certainly the part he was in had turned into a wintery nightmare land and he had been asleep in a drunken stupor the entire time and missed it. 'This isn't good and it's certainly not feckin good for me.' Daniel started to shiver as the dank sweat that had cloyingly covered his body beneath his still vomit stained clothes began to freeze on his skin. 'Sod this shit, I'm not freezin' to death out here with that hyperthermawhotsit and wastin' me life in the damn middle of nowhere' Galvanized into some sort of action plan, Daniel staggered about like he was still blind drunk, hampered by the dead leg that was slowly regaining blood supply and true to prediction was hurting him like a mad thing and trying to get himself into the driver's seat one legged. Eventually managing it and with a prayer and promise to go to church more often, which was the same one he uttered every time he tried to start his car, it was also the same one he knew he would never keep, Daniel turned the key. Much to Daniels intense joy, great relief and total surprise, the Landy roared into life first time. He wasted no time in wheel spinning the vehicle out of the field and back onto the road, gunning the engine as hard as he dared, Daniel headed back to town.

The next couple of weeks were as surreal for Daniel as any movie or novel could have portrayed them. He had arrived at first to find the town deserted. It was picture post card beautiful, all white and frost coated but at the same time it was creepy beyond belief.

## TRINITY

Over the following days, Daniel found more and more equally confused people but one fact came to light, as each recounted their tale in the bar Daniel usually frequented, but was now deserted by the former owners, where they had gone was only speculation but no one Daniel spoke to had seen them. So, they had chosen it as a meeting place and rallying point for any other survivors he found. The thing that bound them together in a common goal was the fact they all had been out of town at the time of 'the big freeze' as it was simply referred to. Well out of town too. For it seemed that the worst of the weather had centered on the areas of civilization and the towns themselves were affected more than buildings in the outlying countryside. A fact that no-one had any explanation for. But it was one Daniel was grateful for, seeing as Tara lived out on the periphery. Daniel visited her often after that, taking groceries and anything else she needed and because of that, she was fine where she was, if a little confused by it all. She tried to calm her younger brother initially as he tried to explain how it was out there but Tara hadn't experienced it, so was sensibly skeptical and just tried to reassure him that it was all just a coincidence and everything would be fine. Tara tried blaming it all on global warming, but she soon gave that up for the obvious reasons. One, it sure as hell wasn't warm. Two, it didn't account for the missing populace Daniel reported and three, why wasn't it mentioned anywhere on the TV about any freak weather phenomena or missing people in and around the Southern Ireland region. The news was filled with the usual stuff about terrorists and how badly off the rich people were because they had lost a few million quid in a stock market glitch but soon enough even that went off and the screen was blank on every channel. Poor them, Daniel drove away from Tara's that last time, leaving them both with plenty to think about but safely out of the way all the same. Tara's cottage, formerly their mother's cottage after their father disappeared early in his life, was always a safe haven from trouble as they grew up. Somehow, misfortune seemed to slough off it as though it was mysteriously Teflon coated. Daniel crossed everything he had that it stayed that way too.

The evening Daniel had found his two friends again - after their fishing trip had run into a few problems and they had been forced to take shelter on the Skellig islands for a while - was the same 24 hours in which Gwen had arrived. Not that Daniel knew it was Gwen of course back then, but a massive green dragon was something of a memorable sight all the same. Kieran and Barry had fled. Sensibly really, while he had stupidly passed out. Shock, and a little too much afternoon vodka had overwhelmed his already stressed synapse and maybe with help from his tumor, he switched off. Matters had just gone downhill from there. As if they weren't bad enough before, the shit had really hit the fan the moment Gwen had arrived at Tara's which Daniel cursed himself as responsible for, but what else was he to do? He felt caught between the hard place and the Skellig rocks for was Gwen the catalyst? Did he set things in motion by delivering her to Tara? Could all this have been avoided if he hadn't? Within what seemed like just a few hours after leaving Gwen at his sisters, the populace had started returning. But on seeing them close up this time- for he had encountered wandering people before but had avoided them as he had been busy doing something or other, Daniel wished with all his might this time that they would just fuck off again. Gwen had explained as best she could that they were possessed. *Fucking possessed?* Daniel had a tough time getting his head around that one. At least until he saw them right up close. That did it. He put two and two together and came up with the Exorcist on steroids. He never did like that film, now he knew why. They were a mess alright and it was a miracle that they could even stay upright let alone run and scream the way they eventually did. But it was when they started turning up at the house shortly after *the troubles* as he called it all started that Daniel knew something was truly not right. It was just ones and twos at first and Daniel paid them no attention and slipped past them easily enough over the ensuing weeks as he brought Tara's supplies to her. For some reason he noted more in hindsight now, they couldn't get past the front gate, it was as though some invisible hand held them back; a fact that got no complaints from Daniel, nor Tara for that matter. It was that fact that kept her inside and Daniel was glad about that, at least she was safe for now. But it still gave him the creeps.

Now, as he ran for his life from a howling mass of these possessed, they gave him more than the creeps. He had seen them in action and they scared him witless now. It was pure adrenaline that powered his limbs now as his mind came to terms with the fact that the world he once thought he knew, no longer existed. He was living some fantastic nightmare, ripped from the pages of some far too graphic novel, like the sort that Kieran used to read and Daniel used to scoff at. *Seems he had the last laugh after all. Bastard*! Daniel knew they were never going to make it to Sneem, not in a million years, not running anyway. His mind raced as his legs pumped. Sparing a glance behind him, he saw that the undergrowth they had just ran through had mysteriously thickened considerably, hampering their pursuers. *How the bloody hell did that happen*? Then he remembered Gwen leading the way and attributed that to her.

'Can't you do anything else?' He panted loudly as he ran, which was more resembled continued, perpetual stumbling. Talking *and* running took more out of him than he would have liked. He wasn't the most energetic of sorts at best. Multi-tasking like he was doing took more out of him than he had spare. Gwen seemed to see this as Daniel slipped and ended up in a heap, so she slowed the little fleeing group allowing Daniel to get up, catch his wind and catch up. Gwen though cast several concerned looks behind her and beyond Daniel to the horde. The screams hadn't stopped but the pursuit had, at least temporarily. They were tangled in Gwen's mystical briar and out of sight in a crunching and contorting morass of deadly thorns and bramble. Daniel envisioned the barbs shredding the flesh of the possessed but knew it somehow wouldn't hold them long. He looked to Gwen and Tara hoping that one of them would have a suggestion that got them out of their current predicament. He wasn't expecting the one Gwen came up with though. Able to concentrate now without running and distractions, Gwen asked them if they knew how to ride.

'Ride what?' Daniel asked, a look of trepidation creasing his face, knowing as he asked it that he didn't really want to know. He had seen enough weird shit in the last few hours to last him several lifetimes and he knew also that innocent questions like his last one were likely to have answers he didn't want to hear.

'Horses silly.' Gwen responded as though it were the most obvious thing in the world. 'What else is there out here to ride? I can't see anything, can you?' Gwen held her hands wide demonstrably and Daniel scowled and looked purposely to either side as he answered her.

'No I don't, but I don't see any bloody horses either, so easy with the smart answers me gal, I'm a little fraught about now as you might have guessed what with all that back there.'

'Well? Be that as it may, can you?' Gwen ignored the veiled threat in his answer, putting it down to stress.

'Can I what?' Daniel snapped, clearly not keeping up and his headache was coming back just to add insult to his already long list of woes.

'Ride a horse Daniel, ride a bloody horse.' It was Tara who answered for them both.

'Yes Gwen we can,' Tara answered for them both 'though not well, we aren't likely to fall off easy either.'

'Good. Now that I've got a few seconds to get my breath back and get my thoughts in order, I'm going to get us a horse. That should make the trip to Sneem a little easier.' Again Daniel looked around him, only this time instead of wariness, scorn colored his words.

'Oh yeah, there they are! There's that herd of tame horses that always appears when there's trouble, how silly of me not to have noticed.' Tara smacked her brother smartly across the back of the head, shutting him up abruptly as he yelped and his head flopped forward, as much in surprise as in any sort of pain, though that was coming.

'Less of your lip my lad,' Tara scolded 'Gwen is trying to save your sorry excuse of a life, try having a bit of faith. Just look behind you, you have no concept...in fact *we* have no concept what she is capable of so unless you have any better ideas..?' Daniel shook his head sulkily, but silently. 'I thought not, so let's hear the gal out.' Tara turned to Gwen expectantly as did Daniel after a few seconds of rubbing his smarting and now throbbing head. His thoughts a jumble with their current predicament but he couldn't help but wonder what sort of effect Tara's smack had on his brains unwanted passenger.

'There are a few things I haven't told you...' Gwen started warily, looking straight at Daniel and I'm not sure how much you can remember Tara about our little chat last night but there are one or two things I can do that might test your sanity more than you really need right now, but needs must, so please, don't be scared or do anything stupid.'

'I'm way past doing something stupid now.' Daniel grumbled 'I should have done that ages ago, I wouldn't be in the middle of this shit right now.' Tara frowned at the cryptic comment but didn't press it, though her gaze did linger on his face for a while longer, searching for something, anything that would provide her with a clue as to what her little brother was keeping from her. She knew he had a secret, but he had been uncharacteristically good at hiding it from her. Normally she could ferret out anything he tried to keep secret, but this was something else. Her thoughts were interrupted when Gwen spoke next. Not by the fact she spoke, but by what she said.

'Okay, right then, there's no easy way to say this. I'm going to turn into a horse.' Daniel burst out in sudden and uncontrolled laughter. It was an explosive release of sound that startled Tara at first and made Gwen scowl. Tara turned to rebuke him for scaring her, but as she turned, the air shimmered before her and Daniel. On seeing what was before his disbelieving eyes, he shut up as abruptly as he had started. Both brother and sister stood dumbly staring at the massive golden mare that stood before them. At sixteen hands to the shoulder, Gwen made quite an imposing sight. Rhiannon herself would be impressed by the form Gwen had assumed. She was easily as big as the Clydesdale horses that pulled the Budweiser wagons that she had seen at SeaWorld, recalling one of her earlier trips before settling New York and then in Santa Fe.

'We don't have all day, get on!' Gwen the horse said as she bent a foreleg so they could mount easier. That did it. A talking horse broke the spell that transfixed the pair and they shared a glance with each other, just briefly, before clambering up on to Gwen's back. Daniel straddled Gwen's wide back first, followed by Tara who encircled Daniels waist with her arms. Daniel entangled his hands into Gwen's mane as she stood and he gripped her ribs with his thighs to hold himself in place.

'Are we sitting comfortably?' Gwen's voice issued from the horse's mouth and she turned her head gently to look at them, flicking her ears slightly as she did so and not wanting to dislodge Daniel's grip in her mane. They just nodded, but that was good enough for Gwen. Her equine eyes took in the possessed beyond them, still trying to get through the briar barrier. They were tearing furiously and several were close to breaking free. *Time to go* she thought, and bunching her powerful hind quarters, Gwen leapt away. Muscular legs began to pump as she built up speed. Her hooves pounding untroubled on the hard frozen landscape as the scenery began to blur by for her riders. Icy wind made Tara's and Daniels eyes water so their view of the world became somewhat distorted and surreal. They leant forward into the shelter of Gwen's mane and powerful neck as she thundered on.

Daniel gave directions as best he could and soon enough Gwen was galloping through the fields that ran parallel to the road. But even as they ran, they could see possessed running towards them across the barren landscape. Like they followed some uncanny and unwanted GPS signal, the creatures seemed to home in on them no matter where they were. Had they remained on foot, they would have been overrun by now Gwen was sure of it. She desperately wanted to glance back at their pursuers but at the speed she was running at, she didn't dare. It was going to be touch and go even now she thought worriedly, to make it to Sneem, let alone Kenmare where Tara said the stone circle was. Gwen didn't fancy her chances running that far, not that she knew exactly how far that was, nor laden down as she was. It wasn't that they were particularly heavy to her supernaturally powered body, but in an unfamiliar form, it took more effort than she would have liked. Flight like this wasn't conducive to thinking and she needed to think about what they were going to do next, they couldn't just keep running, sooner or later they would have to stop, then what?

The sign that said they were now in Sneem, or at least the edge of it, came and went as Gwen slowed, satisfied that for the moment at least, there were no possessed in the immediate vicinity.

'Where to now?' Gwen asked over her shoulder. Daniel was scanning both left and right as though he were looking for something in particular. 'And you can let go of my mane a little, we've slowed down now otherwise I'm going to have the mother of all face lifts with you pulling like that.' Daniel grimaced slightly but released his grip all the same, the color flowing back into his white knuckles.

'Over there!' Daniel said croakily, the chill air drying his throat as he sucked in terrified lungful's. 'There's a house that's tucked away that I used a few times, I know it's empty cos the owners had buggered off to Australia, and it's been up for sale for ages. I found some old letters in a cupboard that's how I know.' Daniel added quickly to Tara's questioning look of how he knew so much. 'It made a useful crash pad when I'd had a few too many. I saw where they left the key once and it when I looked, well? Imagine my surprise when it was still there. So...' Tara dug him in the ribs. 'Ow! What was that for? It isn't like I broke in or some such.' Daniels voice had taken on a whiny, sulky tone 'I had a key and they weren't using it. No harm no foul I say.' He didn't like being told off. Much like a big child that had refused to grow up.

'You would.' Tara harrumphed behind him. Gwen stopped and let her passengers off, reverting back to her own form, she stretched and took a second or two to get used to two legs rather than four before heading across the street from their present position. Tara and Daniel did likewise, their abused bodies unused to the rigors of high speed bare back riding knew they were going to be sore later. Gwen though, strode over the empty pavement and desolate road like a queen, confident and assured. Filled with her own power still as she was from the transformation, her psyche adopted a form that her subconscious felt was more appropriate for one of her position and current predicament. Green was the color of the day and it took the form of a close fitting and figure hugging dress made from every type of leaf imaginable, over lapping so cleverly they looked like the scales of the dragon that she was or like an expertly crafted metallic green mail shift. One that fell to just below her knee where she manifested high, sage colored boots, tooled with intricate designs of vines and roses. Ivy wound its way down her arms and ended at her wrists, flowing around her and into her. At her throat hung a multi-faceted green tourmaline of such luster and clarity that it veritably shone with an inner fire as though it held its own star deep inside. But what made Daniels throat catch was Gwen's face, especially her eyes. For they shone like twin emerald suns. Blazing in a field of hazy green moss that air brushed itself across her eyes from temple to temple. The tiny blue spirals had re-materialized too, swirling and subtlety covering any exposed skin. Several danced across her forehead and across each cheek. Daniel thought that Gwen looked more like a goddess now than any picture he had ever seen of one. Long delicate fingers with equally long, deep forest green fingernails at their tips pushed their way into her hair which was alive with tendrils of ivy and small dark leaves.

'Wow!' was about all Daniel could manage as he took in the beauty beside him.

'What?' Gwen didn't notice at first how she must have looked to the others, but Daniels comment made her do a quick inventory in a passing window – one of the few that wasn't smashed. 'Oh, I see, well... Yes...Um, well it has a tendency to do that sometimes when I'm not concentrating. Even I forget who I am now, though it seems by this not so subtle hint someone doesn't like to let me do that.'

'Someone? Like who?' Daniel asked one of those questions again and regretted it.

'The Earth. She's who I answer to now you know. Long story, I'll tell you about it one day, for now though, let's get inside shall we? You mentioned something about a key?' Gwen looked wide eyed and expectantly at Daniel, her face and body language conveying more than words that he should get a move on and fetch it, getting the door open as soon as he was able; if not sooner.

They hadn't been inside for much more than a quarter of an hour. Tara had rechecked their packs and even reluctantly scavenged a few extra things from the semi empty house, Daniel had disappeared into the lavatory, complaining about the cold, his abused arse and his sore nuts from the back of some horse. He was going to check they were still intact and evacuate his bowels at the same time.

'Nice!' Gwen had commented. 'You're all class you know.' Tara had grimaced distastefully and added her own gripe.

'Thanks for sharing that Daniel,' Tara added 'I'm sure we really wanted to know that, but seeing as you're full of shit most of the time anyhow, it's no big surprise.' But the moment he got the door shut and thrown the lock across, he whipped out the flask that he perpetually kept tucked in his jacket and pulled several swallows of rough brandy that he kept in it. Convincing himself that it was purely medicinal purposes, to calm his shattered nerves. He was still repeating those reasons when the last drop slipped down his throat. He emerged a little happier than when he went in, the lopsided grin on his face gave testimony to that, but it also gave him away to his astute sister who had seen it before. Too many times before apparently as one look at her and he knew she wasn't happy.

'You've been drinking?' she rounded on him like fiery tempest. Daniel wanted to say something clever, but all could manage was 'Pain relief' a stupid expression and a shrug.

'How could you?' Tara railed, furious 'At a time like this, are you completely witless or is today an exception?' How could he answer that? Daniel wanted to, desperately, but he didn't know the words. He wanted to tell her about his cancer, about how short his life was, about how it felt infinitely shorter still with those possessed baying for their blood. He wanted to spill his guts about the dragon and the horrors that would haunt him until his rapidly approaching dying day and how he was struggling to handle any of it. But how could he explain any of that to his sister and make her understand that the alcohol dulled the ache and quelled the voices of regret and recrimination in his head. How it enabled him to continue putting one foot in front of the other day after day, for however many days he had left. He had always maintained that it was for her sake that he never spoke of it, but it probably wasn't if he was honest with himself. It was because he didn't know how to and if he did, that would make it even more real than it already was. He would never be able to take the pity and hurt in Tara's face once she knew. It would be all he would ever see again, every time he looked at her, he would see his death there. And it scared him far more than he could ever admit even to himself. So he drank.

Gwen had overheard the conversation and had come back into the room from tentatively exploring the ramshackle house. She had peeked in the odd cupboard and opened the odd draw, more for idle curiosity than the hope to find anything. But even these sly observations into another's past and life made her feel slightly uncomfortable at the idea of invading someone else's existence. Her conscience had obviously grown along with her power, *Bummer!* She thought lightly. She interspersed her investigations with brief looks out of the various windows, paranoia ever present in her mind now that there were or at least could be, enemies at every turn. But thankfully, they were still undiscovered though she knew in her heart of hearts that it couldn't and wouldn't stay that way for long. But she was interrupted by Tara's outburst and she sauntered back to see her ripping into her brother, who just stood before her grinning, a sort of guilty, lop sided grin of the partially inebriated. She had seen that look before too. Her own anger flared. They didn't have the luxury of supporting a half-cut Daniel when death could descend on them any moment. Everyone needed their wits, what ones they had left, firing on all cylinders. Gwen accelerated and strode right up to Daniel, almost barging Tara out of the way. With the sound of flesh smacking resoundingly against flesh, Gwen slammed both her hands onto either side of Daniels face. Her tiny hands gripping his reddening cheeks and ears in a vice like grip; and then she spoke to him. But it wasn't the kind words of Gwen the woman that issued forth, but instead, with the power of the position she now held, her voice took on a physical presence all of its own. When she spoke, it vibrated through every molecule in his body and he heard her words on more levels than he knew existed.

*'You will not drink alcohol ever again! You foolish man, do you know what it does to you?'* Daniel just gazed blankly back at her, too rapt by the power coursing through him, emanating from her rapidly heating hands. Her voice fizzed and snapped like it should have been throwing off white hot sparks and blue vapor began to issue from Daniels exposed skin, as though his flesh steamed as the alcohol was evaporated from within. Every pore was evacuating the accumulated booze from his system. Gwen unconsciously purged his body of all traces and effects of not only the brandy, but along with the remains of any excess that already permeated his body and accumulated over the last week. But as he began to shake, her hands gripped him tighter and a low moan trembled from his slackening mouth. Gwen pinned his eyes with hers as though she

could see into his very soul, drumming her message home into him as she concentrated on scouring him from the inside out, removing all trace and desire for anything remotely alcoholic. But quite suddenly, she encountered something she hadn't expected. It took her so much by surprise that she abruptly let go and took a step back, looking at Daniel with a wholly different expression, mostly one of concern. Daniel just juddered and dropped to his knees as though someone had turned off the current that he was plugged into. Collapsing to his haunches as though all his bones had turned suddenly to putty, Daniel put his hands on his knees and sucked in several deep recuperating breaths, finally, after several silent and tense minutes, he looked up. First at Gwen then Tara.

'I don't know what to say.' His own voice was quiet at first; quiet but clear and more importantly, sober. 'I don't know the last time I felt like this, I can't remember that far back, but wow. Gwen!' She looked at him questioningly as he said her name. 'You could make a fortune with a detox regime like that. I don't even *want* a drink now, how about that?' But Daniel lost his joyful expression when Gwen asked him her question.

'What's that in your head?' In fact, any vestige of expression he might have had but been unaware of left him then and his eyes narrowed suspiciously, anxiously flicking between Gwen and Tara.

'What are you talking about Gwen?' he asked steadily, as though testing where she was going with this but dreading the answer he knew was coming.

'That thing nestled in your brain, did you not know?' Gwen was concerned now, conscious that she had unearthed something he didn't know about and after saving him from one poison, only to draw his attention to another, much worse condition. Again, long moments passed before Daniel moved, only to slump even lower. As though all the will to live had drained completely from his person along with the alcohol. Tara moved faster than Gwen could have thought as she dropped beside her brother and threw her arms around him. Gwen watched silently as the brother and sister held each other. She saw Daniels shoulders shudder and she knew he was crying.

'I'm so sorry Daniel, I didn't mean...' Gwen began but Daniel just held up a forestalling hand whilst still looking down weeping. Eventually though, looking up at her with startling red rimmed eyes, he sat up ever so slightly, a little straighter than he had been and when he spoke, his own voice had lost the joyous spark that he had exhibited only moments earlier.

'I never wanted anyone to know, I just wanted a life. Until that is, it ended.' Tara sat back and looked at him curiously. Curious but with a shadow of the hurt she was now feeling at being excluded from a fundamental part of her brother's life.

'You don't have to say anything you don't want to Dan.' Tara started but again, Daniel shook his head and stopped the two girls from drowning him in consideration and sympathy. It was the one thing he dreaded almost as much as dying. Those looks, that tone of voice that said *How sad, what a waste, isn't it a shame and he's such a nice boy.* They had no idea. One day soon, he would be gone and they would all say the same thing except with a past tense. How meaningless was that, but Daniel told them both his story anyway. By the end of it, both Gwen and Tara had tears in their own eyes.

'That's why I kept it to myself Taz.' Using the nickname for his sister for the first time in Gwen's hearing. 'I didn't and still don't want all the worried looks and pitiful glances, nor the whispers behind my back. There's nothing to be done about it apparently. It's inoperable and has been for some time it seems. I thought it was a big deal until this shit hit the fan, now it seems fairly unimportant by comparison. Judging by the faces of some of them people back there chasing us, there's those worse off than me.' Tara spun to Gwen, a look of hope blossoming in her face as she recalled his detox.

'Can't you fix it? You can do incredible things Gwen, you can't you?' And Gwen's heart broke at the desperation in her pleading voice and the glimmer of life in Daniels eyes. She recalled her feelings when she had first discovered the mass there in his brain.

'No.' The word couldn't have had a more devastating effect if she had taken a Louisville Slugger to the pair.

'What do you mean *no?*' Tara spat 'I've just seen what you are capable of, surely a simple thing like removing a tumor should be a piece of cake to one like you should it not?'

'No, it isn't. Tara, you must remember, I'm almost as new to this as you are to what you've become and I simply don't know how to do such a thing. What I saw is so entwined and threaded through his brain firstly, it's a miracle he's even walking and talking as it is, secondly, if I touch it, I'm more likely to kill him rather than cure him. And I'd rather he live with whatever's keeping him going now than see him dead at my feet because I screwed up, wouldn't you?' But Gwen knew her reasoning had fallen on deaf ears, all Tara still heard was the No. Not the sense behind it. She saw it in her eyes. Tara's eyes had all the warmth of a shark for

329

the briefest second and Gwen knew beyond any shadow of a doubt, that whatever might have been between them had perished there and then with her refusal to help her dying brother. Tara took a long lingering look at Daniel, kissed his cheek and stood. Then promptly stormed off upstairs. Gwen heard a door slamming several times then silence. Gwen made to follow but Daniel stopped her with a simple 'Don't.'

'She'll be fine when she calms a bit.' Daniel croaked, his dry throat constricted by emotion. 'She's always had a fiery temper on her and she doesn't see the shades of grey that life really is, only the black and white of how she wants it to be, how she wants me to be.' Gwen stared at the young man before her and she couldn't speak for the understanding in his eyes. If she did, she knew she would break down and cry too. 'It's okay Gwen, don't feel bad. You've done one good thing and I've already been told I'm a goner once. I've accepted that, even if I don't like it. Now I know what they mean though when they say ignorance is bliss.' He stood, a little shakily at first, then gradually, straighter even than he was before.

'I might be a dead man walking, but I bet most of those who've got what I have don't feel this good about it, I haven't felt this invigorated for years, tanks for that.' That did it for Gwen, she swiftly drew him into a rib crushing embrace as she broke down then and cried on his shoulder, her emotions jumbled beyond her ability to control them, so she just let them sort themselves out. Daniel just smiled and silently held her back until she was finished, rubbing her back and hair as she wept.

'You want a cup of tea?' He asked after about ten minutes, when he felt her body begin to relax and the tears slow to soft snuffle. She leant back, still holding him and nodded weakly. Daniel then gently disentangled himself from her and slipped into the kitchen, leaving Gwen to watch his back and rub her eyes with the back of her hand.

But just as Daniel came back with a tray of steaming tea in a hotch-potch collection of mugs and cups, Tara came thundering down the stairs.

'They've found us!' She looked at both Gwen and Daniel as she spoke and Gwen got the distinct impression she was looking at a wholly different woman than the one who had gone upstairs only minutes before. 'They're coming up the damned street as we speak, what do we do? Stay here or make a run for it, there's hundreds of them.' Daniel threw the tray to one side knowing that tea was off the menu now, they had more important issues to worry about and he offered a solution to them even as he began grabbing their gear.

'I found some car keys here when I last dropped in. Never used them though,' Catching Tara's disapproving look again 'I had me own car

330

didn't I and it didn't seem right somehow anyway. I do have some principles you know Taz.'

'But using their house was okay?' she whipped back 'You have a strange view of priorities Daniel.' Gwen responded with a wan smile, trying to regain some levity in the face of the horror outside, that was by all accounts, hurtling towards them as they spoke

He just shrugged and gave his usual now this time sober disarming and lopsided grin he gave when Gwen first encountered him.

'Do you know which one it is?' Tara sensibly asked 'We don't want to be fannying around trying to find which car your key fits with that lot bearing down on us, we've only got minutes as it is.' Tara was gathering the belongings Daniel didn't pick up as she spoke and shouldering them for the off. Daniel just winked and plucked a bunch of keys out of a jar that stood on the discarded dresser in the dining room where they stood. He held it up and at a glance, Gwen saw it was black and tablet shaped, with four interconnected rings on it. Gwen looked as blank as she had before he pulled his automotive rabbit out of his ceramic hat.

'And? Is that supposed to mean something?' Daniel just rolled his eyes.

'Girls. What is it with you and cars, it's an Audi.' still nothing. ' It's got infra-red central locking, that means when I push this, it'll bleep, flash its lights and unlock the doors. Then we'll know which one to run to won't we, bloody hell and you thought I was the addled one.' The girls scowled at him and Gwen pushed him towards the door.

'Let's go then, stop being a smart arse and find the car.' They opened the door cautiously and Gwen instantly heard the screams of the approaching horde. They dived out and headed towards the parked cars, veering off as Daniel spotted the A4 estate several yards back. He held out the key fob and pushed the button. True to his description, it flashed its lights and they heard an audible click.

'Now I just hope it starts.' The trio skidded to a halt by the silver vehicle just as the first possessed hove into view. Gwen rounded on Daniel as she threw open one of the doors.

'What do you mean you hope it starts?' She yelled at him, not believing the possibility of what he said.

'Like I said' Daniel tried to explain 'it hasn't been used in some time, maybe it was part of the deal with the house, can't be easy taking a car to Oz, guess they musta bought a new one out there, and like I said, I never bothered with it. So who knows?' A shot rang out and both Daniel and Gwen spun to see Tara with a look of horror and disgust on her usually pretty features and the smoking shot gun held out before her. One of the possessed staggered slightly from the impact, bits of it spattering to the ground, but other than that it just kept coming.

'Get in the car Tara,' Gwen shouted at her 'I'm not sure that's going to be a lot of use unless it's up close and personal.' Having little choice but to agree as her target kept running, howling and screaming towards her, dripping and bleeding to boot, Tara dived in and slammed the door behind her. And the moment she did, she smacked Daniel smartly on the back of the head again without thinking.

'Will you get this thing moving for God's sake! Can't you see that lot heading straight for us?' Daniel took the slap the way a younger brother accepts such things from his big sister, that familial banter born over years of closeness, for there was no malice to their casual abuse of each other, just sibling rough housing but tumor wasn't so keen and simply turned up the pain on Daniel's increasing headache.

The Audi fired up first time though as Gwen dived in herself and with a dramatic wheel spin where the tires sought purchase on the icy road, the car slewed out into the street proper, slamming Gwen's door for her and nearly taking a foot off in the process. Unfortunately, all they achieved was to close the gap between the rampaging possessed and themselves as Daniel fought to regain control of the slipping and sliding car, as he did so bringing them closer by the second to that which they were trying to get away from. Time slowed as the possessed swarmed around the vehicle, screaming and howling as they tore at the car with ragged fingernails in their desperation to extricate its passengers. Tara screamed too as she saw the faces of people she knew ripped and tortured by the demon possessing their bodies, this being the first time she had been this close. Gwen too screamed, but not in panic or fear, but anger and directed it at Daniel.

'What the bloody hell are you trying to do? Are you actually trying to kill us?'

'I'm doing the best I can.' He wailed back 'You said drive, so I'm driving.'

'But you're going the wrong…bloody… way!' Tara added her holler to the escalating din both in and outside. Daniel looked on the verge of snapping as he scanned left and right with eyes that seemed to have trouble keeping up with the movement.

'How am I supposed to know where we're going? You didn't say and the damn car was facing this way anyhow. So this is the way we went.' There were concussive thumps which almost punctuated Daniels comment, glancing back he saw Gwen closing the door again after using it to slam the metallic shield into a couple of possessed who refused to give up and with her increased strength now, was quite effective.

'Turn us around now and get us out of these creatures before one actually succeeds in getting in here, Jeez that doesn't bear thinking about.' Gwen added more to herself than anyone else as her eyes took in the carnage outside the car. Bodies were bouncing and falling over and under the car as Daniel continued to plough into them. Conducting a flawless three point turn whilst battering possessed out of the way at the same time he spun them about until they were facing the way they had just come from. Gwen continued to use her door as a battering ram wherever possible without putting herself or the others in jeopardy as Daniel put his foot down. Again, the car fought for traction, finding it and leaping forward to smash and scatter possessed left, right and center but it was going to be a harder fight now, for the press of bodies had impeded their forward momentum of the car and the engine screamed back in protest. Gwen watched in horror as more and more began to beat on the sorely abused vehicle.

## TRINITY

'This is getting us nowhere fast.' Gwen stated the obvious, more for her own benefit than to voice the unnecessary. 'We need to clear a path.' Again, it was an obvious statement but it helped galvanize her thoughts and those of Tara, for she too had seen the imminent danger of being overwhelmed. She hit the electric window button and it dropped a few inches. She shoved the barrel of the shotgun out and fired.

'You were right Gwen, up close and personal is much more effective.' Tara shouted over the din. Ruined bodies and heads were flung back as the weapon discharged. Tara quickly reloaded and fired twice more. Loading again, Tara risked opening the window fully before they recovered and she leant out, Hollywood style, giving both barrels to the press of bodies impeding their way. It had the desired effect for the briefest of moments and the car lurched forward, gaining a little momentum. Daniel macabrely flicked on the wipers to clear the gore that had spattered there and gunned the Audi away. But just as they pulled away from the snarling horde and thought they were home free, another group of possessed came sprawling out of a side road. By rights, this should have posed little to no threat to the rapidly accelerating car, but

333

Daniel suddenly leapt on the brakes and brought the car to a screeching and swerving halt. His gaze was fixed dead ahead on the lead figure, who himself, seeing who was behind the wheel of the car grinned a flesh splitting grimace and leapt to the top of a nearby parked car and squatted down upon its roof doing a macabre impersonation of a giant wild and feral frog poised to leap from a metallic blue BMW lily pad. Daniel looked directly at his best friend Kieran, who now resembled something freshly dug up and hacked at with various edged weapons. His clothes were shredded and gaping wounds bled a dark viscous fluid from numerous parts of his emaciated body.

'Ddddaaannnniiieeelllll!' a voice like broken frozen glass grazed its way across the wintry and glacial air. 'Cooommme to ussssss Daanniieelll. Giiivvee yoursssselffff to the Daarrkkknesss you seeekkk in yourr hearttt. Commmee to meeeee!' there was almost a compulsion in the hideous screech that passed for his voice and Daniel looked torn between leaping out of the car and running to his friend. But it was Gwen's whispered voice in his ear that snapped him out of the daze he found himself in.

'That's not your friend Daniel, your friend is dead.' Her melodious voice wove its way through Daniels mind, severing the sticky, tenuous webs of enchantment that were carried insidiously in the demons voice. 'What occupies his corpse now has no right to be here on this world, certainly not in the body of your friend. Fight it Daniel, for the love of God and your sister, fight it. If those behind us catch us, we're dead.' Gwen had recognized Kieran from his moment of draconian advice the night she arrived. Fragments of an idea came to her as she spoke words of encouragement to Daniel. Why wasn't he petrified of her? Why was he out when the minions had been abroad and chasing her? In light of recent events that was two too many coincidences for her liking.

'*Daniel! Do something! Now!*' Gwen's tone changed abruptly to forceful dominance to spur him into action. But in truth, she was only hoping he would drive away, not reach back and grab Tara's shotgun from her hand where she was loading the last shell into the weapon. Daniel leapt from the car and ran to his friend who watched him curiously, still smiling, he cocked his head sideways, bird like. Even when Daniel levelled the weapon at his friends head, the Demon continued with its silent mocking expression. Perhaps it held the belief that Daniel had joined its cause and the web of coercion it had laid upon him had been sufficient, rendering the man before him helpless.

The demon that was Kieran had barely a micro second to register its error as the head it wore exploded in a spray of blood, brain and bone matter.

Daniel wept as he ran and jumped back into the car and hit the gas. Both girls were thrust back into their seats as Daniel purged his devastated emotions in an outpouring of deadly and nigh on suicidal speed. He had bounced off several other cars, cracked the windshield and virtually destroyed the hood as he ploughed through body after body of the possessed as they spilled out into the street, leaping at the car in some futile effort to halt its flight before he slowed his semi suicidal rally. But even as the emotional adrenaline rush subsided within him, they hadn't gone more than a mile out the other side of Sneem before their collective hearts sank. The deepest pit of despair still wouldn't have accommodated their depleted spirits when they rounded a corner and came skidding to a halt; for before them had to be close to a thousand screaming possessed. Pouring across the open countryside like a plague of humanoid, cannibalistic ants. If Gwen had foolishly thought the plague that infected these poor people was restricted to Sneem or the villages and locals in that vicinity, she was poorly mistaken, for it had spread voraciously. What was howling towards them had to be from somewhere much larger and invariably further away. Wondering what to do next. Tara prompted her train of thought by pointing across a field.

'This isn't good Gwen, as the crow flies, that's the direction of the Kenmare stone circle, which I needn't remind you, is where we need to be.' Gwen briefly considered calling out for help. Back in Santa Fe, when the Ogre Kachinas attacked, she called for the animals to help, but she didn't really want them to get hurt here by engaging these unfeeling creatures. There had to be another way to get through them. Then it occurred to her. Not through them, but as Tara said - as the crow flies - *we'll just have to go over them. This should be interesting.* Gwen got out of the car and closed the door behind her. As she did, the sounds of those possessed ahead and the distant cries of those behind reached her ears. It was an infernal, unnatural sound and she found herself inwardly raging at their temerity for even being here, let alone corrupting and desecrating those that called the Earth home. Someone would pay dearly for this, that much she promised, but to keep that particular promise, all she had to do was find the one who was responsible and that was a far more daunting prospect that facing its deminions.

Putting thoughts of retribution and vengeance behind her for now, Gwen tapped on the glass for Tara to wind her window down. Leaning in after, Gwen spoke swiftly. She didn't want this to become a lengthy convoluted discussion or give them too long to think about what she proposed. They were going to have enough trouble with this as it was without adding to their woes. The horse had been bad enough, and Gwen still felt their eyes on her when they thought she wasn't looking. Seeing a person actually change into another creature and knowing it wasn't some computer generated wizardry just had to do something to their sanity retention capacity. But that had only been a mere horse, a creature they were familiar with; Gwen hadn't used the word, but the implication hung heavy and Daniel had already been privy to a close encounter of the draconian kind and that had been enough to drive conscious thought from him. *Let's hope he fares a little better this time* Gwen thought wryly as she backed up a few paces.

'Oh by the way.' Gwen shouted to the car. 'You might want to put your seat belts on, this won't exactly be a regular take off.' Daniel spun and spoke to Tara, and with Gwen's exceptional hearing now, she picked up what he said and she sighed, apparently he hadn't been listening, or had simply blocked it out as some sort of mental defense.

'What does she mean Taz? What does she bloody mean by take-off?' Even Tara rolled her eyes.

'We are dummy, buckle up and hang on.' Watching his sister hastily pull the strap over her chest and click it firmly in the belt device at her side, Daniel swiftly followed suit. Concentrating so much on securing his own belt, he didn't see the crystalline, emerald sparkles that marked Gwen's transition to the small hawk form she first assumed. Powering upwards in almost vertical trajectory, she knew she needed room for the larger transformation and she could use a bit of gliding momentum.

Daniels last look stayed with Gwen for some time as she saw his mortified face peering up through the sun roof at the malachite underbelly of the jumbo jet sized dragon that swooped down over them. His gaze had been drawn upwards as Gwen had cast a shadow over the tiny car and he looked up to see the cause. Immediately wishing he hadn't. Again. Gwen's JCB like forepaws suddenly gripped the car on both sides, causing a disconcerting crunching sound within as her scimitar sized talons found purchase in the fragile chassis, and she could hear their screams of panic as the Audi was lifted off the ground faster than if it had been catapulted off the flight deck of a Navy carrier. Though she also heard the frustrated and malevolent howls of the swarming possessed beneath her, impotently waving their arms in a pathetic defiance as her sail like wings beat at the air and sent her soaring skyward.

336

*Hah! You ugly demonic bastards, you didn't see that coming did you?* But by feeling the amassed power of her dragon form flowing through her, she wanted nothing more than to drop the inconvenience she held in her forepaws and turn back to strafe the swarm with fire. Over and over she would raze the soil clean until she had eradicated them all. To purify the earth from their foul presence. But she couldn't. She had a mission. But even so, Gwen thought angrily, even with her hands full so to speak, she would give them something to remember her by. Swooping lower, she only intended to bellow a battle cry at them, but her own fury spilt over into something else and she belched forth a cone of fire so blisteringly hot, she not only took out a corridor of possessed and left a four foot molten trench in her wake, but the heat she generated peeled the paint off the car she held.

Daniel watched in wide eyed terror as the bonnet before him rippled in the heat haze and silver paint began to peel away as though the engine had caught fire and seconds later both he and Tara felt the blistering heat inside, turning the car into an oven. It was worse than being left in the midday sun for hours with all the windows shut. They were basically cooking within the car like an impromptu microwave. Before it got the better of them and they both passed out from the soaring temperature, but Daniel regained his composure first, coming too and with a herculean effort he grabbed the butt of the shotgun and smashed a window open. He sighed in relief as gales of cold, life returning air blasted through the car, reviving Tara as well. Though their pleasure was short lived as they both started to shiver then. Tara just looked blankly at Daniel, who just shrugged before they both ducked down into their respective foot-wells to get out of the now freezing draught.

Gwen inhaled as she passed the now floundering possessed and felt good in herself that she had at least struck a blow against the darkness. That was until she looked up. Gwen had thought the swarm of possessed to be impressive albeit in a diabolical kind of way, but that paled into real insignificance against the monstrous demon army that was filling the horizon before her. It was as though an inky cloud was rolling across the landscape, annihilating everything in its path. What it passed over, ceased to exist behind. There were no prisoners, no mercy, no nothing. Every animal, plant and human in the demon army's path was extinguished. And their numbers had to top several hundred thousand to create such an unholy spectacle. Her supernatural vision showed her far more than she really wanted to see and Gwen felt true fear touch her soul then with fingers of barbed steel for she knew that they had now seen her too.

*Oh Shit!* Was about all she could think of to say. Gwen recalled her recent encounter with just a few deminions and now there were just so many more. Gwen could do nothing but fly on and wonder if her passengers had seen them too. The only thankful thing was the fact Gwen could now see the stone circle and she knew she would be there long before the approaching army got anywhere near their position. But Gwen was no military tactician and she knew nothing of scouts who ranged ahead of the main body gathering intelligence for the commanders. Not yet anyway.

Gwen swooped lower and deposited the car just outside the circle in an adjacent field, she watched it roll a few feet and come to a juddering halt as it squelched in a muddy patch. The heat from the cooling vehicle and Gwen's body briefly melting the frozen earth. She banked round and landed neater than she had before some way behind the car so as not to flatten it. *At least I'm getting better at something* Gwen mused as she resumed her own form. Adopting the natural armored foliage look she had used earlier. Gwen caught up to the car just as Daniel and Tara were literally falling out of the abused vehicle, through doors that would barely open and definitely no longer close. They both saw her and as one, took an involuntary step back before they knew what they were doing. It was a small thing, but Gwen saw it. With that tiny gesture, another of the diaphanous threads that supported her heart tore irreparably. One more reminder that she was different now, more alone than she ever thought she would or could be. Feared.

'That was you wasn't it?' Daniel blurted, there was no need to explain the obvious of what *that* was. Gwen just nodded and looked at them both with sad eyes, assessing them for injury. They seemed fine, externally anyway.

'I wanted to believe so badly Gwen, honestly I did, but even with all that was going on, it was still hard.' Tara didn't know what to say as reality was so much more assertive 'It's the twenty first century isn't it? Nobody believes in anything anymore. I don't count religion,' she rambled 'that's just blind faith in the teachings of men. What I mean is the belief in the wonders of the world, the Universe...'

'Multiverse.' Gwen interrupted calmly, yet her voice carried such authority that Tara immediately stopped speaking 'There are more *verses* out there than just this one Tara, uni means one. I had it likened to grains of sand in a desert, except...' Gwen pointed upwards '...the desert is up there. And I don't mean to stop you Tara, I get where you're coming from, believe me, I had the same thoughts; it's just that it's not all wonderful and if you saw what I just did as we flew, you'll know it's about to get a lot worse. We are ants that have only just glimpsed what's beyond our cozy little environment. There is far more out there than can be imagined on heaven and earth, or something like that, and trust me when I say you don't want to meet the majority of it. In fact, it looks like the majority of it is actually heading this way. I'd say by this time tomorrow, where we're standing will be nothing but black, dead ash. Us too unless we get our collective ass's in gear'

'Bloody hell, you lose your happy thoughts on the journey here?' Daniel asked 'What have you done with Gwen? She at least had a little optimism. I liked that idea you're scaring and depressing me in equal measure and I assure you gal, *that* I really don't need, I've got enough scary and depressing of me own already thanks without you adding to them with your cheerful philosophizing. And what happened up there anyway? We nearly fried! You didn't pissing well warn us about *that*.' Gwen looked apologetic but said nothing, instead she turned away from the siblings and began walking around the stone circle, studying small rocks that protruded from the soil, finishing her lap at the dolmen in the middle. The entire time Gwen was doing this, Tara was watching Daniel thoughtfully, as though she was seeing him for the first time as he ranted on. Usually, when faced with insurmountable odds and things beyond his comprehension, Daniel had a tendency to glaze over. Resembling the proverbial rabbit caught in the headlights of the oncoming and very imminent future, but here he was; Taking the prospect of a giant green dragon, an invading army of nothing short of monsters and after having blown his best friends head into vapor, holding what was almost a sensible and coherent conversation. Her brother had done more than just sober up, he had grown up and she hadn't noticed. Tara felt an overwhelming urge to smother him and protect the little brother she had taken for granted for so long. A wave of guilt washed over her like so much arctic water. He had been going through such torment with his illness and he had not felt he could share it with her, what had she done to engender such secrecy from her own brother? Tara wanted nothing more now than to shield him from the horrors they faced, but most of all, to rid him of the terrible disease that promised to steal him away from her without a moment's notice. This was *her* brother, *her* flesh and blood. The only living family she had left in the entire world and Tara vowed there and then, to do everything in her power. Wait, Tara amended, her newly inherited powers - however that may turn out and Gwen or no Gwen, to save Daniel from his fate.

# TRINITY

Gwen stood at the central dolmen, eyes closed and one delicate hand placed reverently upon its rough, weathered cold stone surface. She was momentarily lost in the pulse and flow of power that permeated from the rock, fed from deep within the earth much like a natural spring; only in this case, it wasn't water that gushed forth, but power. The unnatural storm that had blown out Tara's home had failed in its mission to destroy all the sacred circles. She didn't know how, nor did she particularly care at this point, she was just thankful that it had survived at all. Gwen had no way of knowing that her presence empowered the land just enough to help withstand the malevolent tempests and the Lissivigeen circle stood also. Perhaps those behind the dark storm considered them too inconsequential. Those with power have a tendency to be arrogant that way, when in reality, nothing at all is inconsequential. Everything had a purpose. That was why it was there in the first place. Even in the largest machine man had ever made, the tiny sprung washer, or miniscule screw was there, serving its purpose. But unfortunately, such is the way with those who rise swiftly to power or have it handed to them with no understanding, they become blinkered and blinded to small things and all they see are the massive cogs and main moving parts; the headlines not the details. One day maybe, Gwen stood and silently meditated to herself as she absorbed the power of the dolmen, that humanity would learn to appreciate the smaller details of those they considered lesser in their world, maybe then they would be richer for it. Getting back to the reason they were there though, Gwen snapped back to reality and focused on bringing the power of the circle up where Tara could access it, but she suddenly hit a wall. Not in the power, but in her own mind. How did she do it? Her rational mind was supplanting her intuition and in doing so brought her up cold and empty. What was it precisely she was required to do? She needed to talk to Tara. Gwen lifted her hand off the stone and immediately felt the difference. It was akin to taking a bare hand out of warm water when you were standing naked in the snow, freezing. A part of Gwen instantly missed that connection like a child misses the connection to its mother. The sense of safety, security and invulnerability bestowed by that bond left Gwen bereft and momentarily sad as she severed the connection and turned towards Tara and Daniel. But before she could utter a word, her eyes were instantly drawn to the sky where the two siblings were now staring in horror. Something, or some things were plummeting out of the clouds at a phenomenal speed. And just to add insult to their already injurious predicament, it looked as though it was aimed directly at the spot they currently occupied. Each of the trio offered their own variation on their end. Tara thought plane, Daniel considered a missile or drone and Gwen instantly plumped for more deminions. But as the rapidly descending shape drew ever closer, four individual shapes could be distinguished instead of just the one. Closer still and Gwen could see they were humanoids on horseback. A fact Gwen could appreciate a little better than her companions were likely to as her supernatural Drakarim sight aided her. But there was only one group of individuals that came to her mind who fit that description and her stomach knotted in dread anticipation. Moments later, her suspicions were realized as the riders alighted expertly in the adjacent field and ghosted their way across to the periphery of the circle, where one of the riders; A large, heavily built and cowled figure, clad in midnight hued plate armor, complete with steel, full faced helm with the face plate carved into the visage of a grinning skull. A shield of what appeared to be a conglomeration of interlocking, metallic and viciously spiked bones on the arm holding the reins and an impressively huge, ebony and silver scythe with a fantastically carved and what looked to be razor sharp blade at its tip in the other hand, bowed his head in acknowledgement, the way a king would to another ruler. Then in a voice that made Daniel instantly moan and drop to the ground and Tara slam her hands over her ears, greeted Gwen in a most courteous fashion.

'*Well met Avatar. The Four Horsemen of the Apocalypse offer you and your companions whatever assistance we may be in your time of need. For as I suspect you have seen, we too have seen the wrath of the Adversary in the form of his legions descending on this location with all possible haste. It seems you have upset the Dread Lord somehow.*' Death paused briefly and before Gwen could formulate any sort of response, he added with an almost tinge of satisfaction to his concussive voice, a pleased full stop.

'*Well done.*'

'For what?' Gwen asked, genuinely surprised by the compliment. 'I don't have the tree; I still don't even know where it is, let alone be any closer to finding it.'

'*No, that seems true enough, but you do seem to have found something.*' Daniel moaned some more, a little louder this time. This caught the Reapers attention and he looked straight at Daniel. His indomitable gaze lingered on the fetal positioned human before moving to gaze at Tara. It was impossible to gauge what he thought, if anything, beyond the steel mask that hid him within the inky cowl, but he did seem to be taking a disturbing amount of interest in the siblings. When Death next spoke, his voice began softening to that of mortal tolerance, and firstly he addressed Daniel.

*'Get up Daniel, I apologize for any distress I may have caused you by my presence. We have been in battle constantly these past few weeks and I have become accustomed to having to utilize more power than I would like to overwhelm the lesser creatures, much as you experienced. I forget that you mortals also suffer from the effects of too powerful an aura.* This should be more acceptable.' Daniel expressed his gratitude by rolling over and groaning some more and clutching his head. Death looked closer.

'Ah I see the cause of your concern now, allow me.' Death waved a hand and Daniel immediately stopped groaning and sat up. A look of wonder and relief fleetingly crossed his features until his rolling eyes focused on the root cause of his problem. He back peddled away from the figure so fast he slammed back first into one of the standing stones, driving the wind from his lungs with such an Ooof that it made Gwen flinch and causing Daniel topple once more.

'Famine!' Death called to his own companions. 'Help the poor fellow will you before he hurts himself. I need to speak with the Avatar.' Famine, for his part, tossed his head and harrumphed. Muttering himself as he too dismounted.

'Just what did your last slave die from?' Famine jibed as he made his way across to Daniel.

'Disobeying an instruction I believe' Death retorted razor fast 'Now will you stop sulking and help the mortal. You know very well why we had to leave the battle when we did, you'll get another chance I have no doubt.' For all Famine's petulance at being ordered like a mere squire, he was smiling as he arrived at Daniels side and helped him to sit up. The banter of the Horsemen being a millennia long familiarity, like family.

'Are you well young sir?' His clipped accent reached Gwen and she detected a hint of the Spanish about it. Musical and cultured. She got the impression that if he walked into a room and started talking, the atmosphere would turn jovial and he would be the center of attention. Daniels eyes were still out on crab stalks as he looked at the four armored figures. Realization of who they were fought toe to toe with his religious upbringing. Possessed were one thing, that could be passed off as some infection Daniel reasoned...at a push, even Gwen was another simpler acceptance as dragons were mythological, a bit like dinosaurs he reasoned; but these four were straight out of the good Book of Revelation and that drove things home to Daniel in ways Gwen sympathized with, recalling her mother's own devout faith. It put the question into the very core of his soul, the foundations of his upbringing were standing over him…talking to him. Daniel struggled to grasp any of it.

'Th…Th…That's…That's…' Famine smiled and helped him out.

'Yes, that's Death. But don't go on like that, it'll just go to his head and he's enough of a handful already, dishing out orders left right and center like he's some big cheese. Honestly, I've lost count of the number of helmets we have had to have made for him as keeps outgrowing them.' Death shot Famine such a look it would have stopped a stampeding Rhino in its tracks. But Famine just smiled back the easy smile of one who's been through this many, many times before. Ignoring Death, he returned his attention back to Daniel. As he did so, the coldly beautiful oriental woman, who the other three knew as Pestilence had also dismounted and almost glided over to join Famine, her economy of movement would have had ballet dancers crying. Only one rider now remained in his saddle. Gwen opted for process of elimination that it was War. An easy call as much by his vast array of armamentaria distributed all over him and his equally massive warhorse than by any other less obvious reasoning. He kept vigil it seemed.

Tara, for all the initial conversation and byplay, simply stood and watched everything after Death modified his voice, though her head was still ringing her ears stopped bleeding. Her eyes however were darting between the mystical figures, watching every movement, expecting them to vanish any second. But as soon as two of the Horsemen converged on Daniel, she galvanized herself and went to him also, kneeling the other side of him. With Famine kneeling on the other and Pestilence standing above, legs braced before him looking down on the trio coolly.

'There is nothing to be done Famine.' She almost whispered, so quiet was her voice in comparison to Deaths booming baritone. 'It is a miracle he still lives at all. He is too far beyond the balance to recall him now. The coup de grace would be the kindest thing for him now. I will administer it if you do not have the stomach Famine?' Tara leapt up and planted herself squarely before the small, wiry oriental just as he pulled one of her wickedly curved swords up from over one shoulder where they were secured.

'*Don't you dare!*' Tara hissed in a voice that was colder than the surrounding countryside. One of the Horsemen of the Apocalypse she may be, but that wouldn't be enough to get her through Tara to lay even a finger on Daniel. Tara could be fiery and intimidating when she put her mind to it and was duly motivated. She was motivated now and unbeknownst to even Tara herself, she was almost glowing having summoned power unconsciously in Daniel's defense. Silver fire erupted from her palms and rolled around her hands waiting for the moment Tara unleashed it. To a spectator, she looked scarily impressive. The prospect of them even *suggesting* they put her brother down like he was a sick dog incensed her almost beyond reason...almost. An unseen and unfelt wind lifted Tara's hair and it flowed about her like a living thing as power ebbed and flowed around her. Having no weapon didn't deter her either. Tara's hands bunched into claws and the fire there grew larger and brighter. Tara knew she would have tackled the heavily armed woman before her, bare handed if that was what it took. Gwen glanced back at the scene, alerted by a subtle shift in the power of the circle, to see the two woman standing off from one another and Tara looking positively explosive. Pestilence hadn't sheathed her blade yet as she stared down the angry sorceress before her and imminent violence hung in the air. Their gazes locked and Gwen was convinced that nothing could have lived had it stepped between them into that void. But Gwen could see that Tara was livid and on the verge of doing something really, really stupid.

'Excuse me a moment my Lord Death.' Gwen felt it was the right thing to say as she excused herself and stepped back to see what was occurring with her companions.

'What the bloody hell is going on here?' Gwen commanded 'We are supposed to be on the same side!' Gwen demanded an answer of anyone who would face her, she didn't care who at that point. But Pestilence had only eyes for Tara and Tara likewise. Famine watched them both with casual interest, curious what might happen next. But Daniel was nearly apoplectic. What with all he had been through, now his sister wanted to fight one of the fabled horsemen to stop her from putting him out of his misery and she was glowing and on fire? It was all too much for him and his overtaxed brain, complete with its cerebellum cuckoo, so it sought a dark place where it could hide blissfully dragging Daniel into oblivion with it. He groaned and slid bonelessly down the rock, ignobly falling against Famine, who seeing the whole thing as one big joke, just smiled and gently propped him back up.

'I would have thought you, Lady Gwendoline, being the Avatar of Nature, of all beings on this world understood the natural order of things.' Pestilence spoke without taking her eyes off Tara. Gwen just arched an eyebrow and folded her arms over her chest, index finger tapping against her bicep. 'I'm new. Enlighten me!' This time Pestilence did look away, feeling the sorceress was the least of the threats if she annoyed the Avatar.

'I trust you know what this human has inside his head?' Pestilence asked.

'This human has a name I'll have you know' Tara snapped back 'It's Daniel you cold hearted bi…' Gwen stopped Tara before she put her other foot in the place currently occupied by one foot already as well as her teeth.

'Enough Tara.' Gwen said firmly, she knew Tara was stressed. 'No-one will be harming Daniel today, nor any other day and you have my word.' Tara turned to glare at Gwen then back to Pestilence as though she couldn't believe what she was hearing.

'That's all very well and bloody good. But not one of you has offered to heal him have you! Why not? I've heard your feeble excuse Gwen and I can't believe that, you're Nature for fucks sake, cancer surely works against nature, why wouldn't you want to free people from its insidious poison? I don't understand, I'm just a *mere mortal*.' the contempt in her words made Gwen flinch inwardly, she had a point but what could she say? How could she make Tara see that even cancer had its place in the natural order. Gwen didn't yet understand how or where but in her heart she knew the things purpose. It was a great equalizer, one that was all the more fearsome for humanities lack of understanding about its nature and inability to halt its ravages. Like any riddle, once humans had learnt all the lessons it had to impart, much the way Bubonic plague did, maybe it wouldn't be so terrible...maybe, then again maybe not. True, Gwen had never lost anyone close to the filthy disease, but she believed it had a place in the world. Man was top of his alleged food chain and had no natural predator to cull his ever expanding numbers. Yes, it was a terrible ailment and it caused great pain and suffering to those it left behind, but so did being run over by a bus. Humanity didn't abolish public transport. She had gone through this very argument several times with her friend back home, Dolores, Jen and Maddy. It was a complex and emotive subject and certainly not a suitable exercise to be entertaining considering their dire circumstance and the horde of minions just over the horizon but there is always a balance.

'There is far too much to even try to understand right now Tara' Gwen tried pacification 'and I'm in no way condoning the blasé attitude of Pestilence here…' Gwen turned then her own now indomitable gaze upon the still expressionless face of Pestilence, who in turn locked her unblinking eyes with Gwen's. '...however. Euthanasia is not an option here, call it whatever you will. Nor is this a battlefield...'

'Not yet anyway.' Famine interjected serenely, eliciting further scowls from everyone. 'Give it a little while and that'll be academic.'

'As I was saying' Gwen reiterated, casting a baleful eye on the still irritatingly smiling Famine before she continued 'Nor is this a battlefield where the sick and wounded are just a burden. Should I find the fabled First Tree, then maybe the fruit from that will decide who lives and who dies and of what. Until then, he is in my care and no-one is to lay a hostile finger on him. If you can't or won't help, back off.' Pestilence moved her cherry shaped lips in order to say something but Gwen forestalled her.

'No, don't even bother. I don't need to be the Avatar of Nature to understand the natural order, nor the balance between who dies and why, and who lives, but answer me this. You're Pestilence, to my mind that makes you responsible for all disease and associated ailments. Why can't you of all people heal him?' Pestilence looked at the group assembled around her, then she glanced at Death, who nodded almost imperceptibly.

'I can't. It is as simple as that, not anymore. Maybe once, before all this war began. There is a point where any ailment or disease or poison progresses to far in the organism, in this case, human. Since the Adversary rose to power, we have become weaker.' Gwen harrumphed at that prospect looking at them exuding power 'At least here on this world.' Pestilence added 'Our powers are restricted in the Domain and upon the homeworlds of the Drakarim and the Children of Thought, though we are not without power I hasten to add. As I said before, it is a miracle he even breathes with the amount of cellular degeneration and sheer size of the tumor within his brain. He could die at any moment.' Gwen glared harder if that was at all possible. Though apparently it was for even Pestilence blanched ever so slightly under her steely gaze. Pestilence finally released her sword and let it slip back into its scabbard and lowered her own almond shaped eyes and cast an unreadable expression over the unconscious Daniel. 'Very well. As the human...' Pestilence turned to Tara. '...Daniel, means so much to you, I will slow the growth and shield the remainder of his brain from the disease, he will feel no pain at least, it is as much as I can do. It has only delayed the inevitable, but as you say Lady Gwendoline, perhaps you will find the Tree in time to save us all.' With that, faster than Gwen could have thought possible, Pestilence side stepped her and with a squeal from Tara as she watched helplessly, plunged all four fingers straight into Daniels forehead, right up to the knuckles. In the time it took for her to blink, she withdrew them again, turned and strode back to her horse. Over her shoulder Gwen heard in her mind, *it is done*. But Tara wasn't. She rounded on the gathering of impossible entities and planting her hands on her hips, addressed them all, irrespective of rank or stature.

'Is that your lot? There is supposedly five of the most powerful entities I've ever bloody heard of standing before me and not one of you can do anything helpful about my brother's ailment? I can't believe it. Exactly how fucking useless are you?' Death stepped forward, though nothing about his manner said placating. He merely stepped before the furious red-head and looked down at her. To Tara's credit, she simply looked back up and locked her own steely, indomitable Irish and emerald green gaze on to the two sparkling, sapphire blue lights that shone within Death's armored helm which passed for his eyes, waiting for him to say whatever it was he wanted to say.

'My Lady Tara, why can you not accept that all things must die eventually, even us? We who may seem beyond immortal to you, yet it only means that we measure time differently. Daniel will die in due course, for that is his destiny to do so. Much the same way it was the fate of your Mother and Father to die when they did. In the cosmos balance must always be maintained and that is our primary role, to maintain that which is already set in motion, we do not instigate it.'

'What do you know of my parents?' Tara was too angry to realize the irony of her question considering who she was talking to and ignoring Death's attempt at explanation. 'What have their deaths got to do with why you can't save Daniel? They didn't die of Cancer, there was no curing what killed them.' Death stood impassive against her wrath and responded coolly.

'What do you know of their deaths?' The Reaper asked. It was a simple question but it seemed to deflate Tara considerably. It forced her to dredge up memories long buried, and the doing so obviously pained her. That pain taking the heat from her fury and the color from her face.

'I don't know much. I was too young, only eleven and Daniel was just a toddler when my ma died. My da told us it was a drowning accident but her body was never recovered and his death shortly after was just as empty. We had no body to mourn over cos the authorities wouldn't tell me much and my da's brother, when he came to take care of us never spoke of it neither.' Death watched the Tara as she cast her mind back into the soul wrenching part of her past that set her on her present path. 'Do you know what happened to your father, exactly?' Death asked and Tara nodded slowly as images filled her mind.

'He didn't want to tell us, but when our uncle eventually left us to fend for ourselves, his work finally took him to Europe somewhere, and he just never came back, dirty, pervy, miserable old fucker. I hope he's dead in a ditch somewhere, riddled with some foul sexual disease that has rotted his scrawny bollocks. Anyway…' Tara had fired up again as the thoughts of her child molesting uncle coalesced. '…before he left he told us that da had died when his boat blew up. I've hated the water ever since, can't imagine why hey?' Tara spat bitterly.

'It is understandable Tara,' Gwen thought it odd Death exhibiting sympathy 'the sea doesn't appear to have been too kind to you and your family. Your father wasn't a well man. Early stage prostate cancer. His illness could have been treated, but he chose to ignore it. Instead, recklessly he took up a career that ended his life even sooner. He supplied weapons for some very unpleasant people. Weapons that were used against the wrong people. He was caught in the backlash of retaliation and his vessel, along with its cargo and its crew were destroyed. It was not in the nature of those who carried this out to publicize their activities, so it was glossed over. It…' Death stopped talking suddenly and took a step back from Tara. Still watching her intently though.

'What is it? What's wrong?' Tara was so caught up in the recount of her father's death, hearing for the first time the facts surrounding his demise that Deaths sudden halt left her hanging in mid-air, momentarily forgetting her earlier outburst. Death continued to stare at Tara, then he turned his cowled head to run his cobalt gaze over Gwen. Gwen saw it lower slightly and she saw him shake his head ever so slightly from side to side as though he suddenly knew something he wished he hadn't. What on earth could he have seen to make *Death* react so?' The icy fingers of prescience all bar throttled Gwen's spine as she got the very distinct feeling that whatever it was boded ill.

'*What?*' Tara shouted a little louder when nobody responded to her the first time. Death answered her finally, but his tone had changed imperceptibly, it was as though he no longer wanted to explain anything and even wished he hadn't started talking in the first place.

'It is not that I am omnipotent Tara and know all there is to know about everyone who has died, I do not; but the blood-lines allow me to connect deeply to the past and those who lived within it. Through you I can connect to your entire familial history, and at this moment I can honestly say it is not an ability that has proved useful. You have some very colorful individuals in your bloodline Tara and I can only hope you do not live up to their expectations, though it seems recent events have conspired to challenge you on that front sorceress.' Something had changed, the energy of the group had shifted away from their inability to cure Daniel to something infinitely more dangerous. Gwen, who had been present at Tara's initiation, for there was little else to describe the ritual she had performed on the altar stone of her mantelpiece, made the assumption that Death had seen it too now and recognized it. Maybe he had seen the dark woman with the sickle from her vision or even knew who she was. That and more maybe. The skein was tangling rapidly since she had left the relative tranquility of her life in Santa Fe. A life that seemed suddenly so distant, almost dreamlike. Did she really do that? Gwen thought of the painting in Tara's back bedroom almost prophesying her arrival. How was that even possible? It was fast becoming a paranormal dot the dot. With some cosmic pencil slowly connecting people and events together in ways she didn't even begin to understand. Though at this moment in time, Gwen was blissfully unaware of just how relevant and potentially devastating her observation would be.

'There is no more time for this Tara,' Death said with a note of finality to it 'just accept that this is how it must be. Daniel has. Perhaps you should ask him before you say and do something you or the rest of the group may regret! We are in a war where the rules of the cosmos are in flux, powers are waxing and waning while the balance shifts. We all could die at any time Tara, be grateful for the time you do have with your brother and do not dwell more on the dark thoughts I sense are building within you about the futility of saving him, nor the lengths you feel you will go to. It simply cannot be done the way matters stand presently. Gwen is quite possibly our only hope, certainly she is Daniels. I suggest you channel your energies into helping her rather than harboring resentment to those who would aid you but are presently unable to do so.' Tara blanched and what color she had left in her already pale skin, fled. Gwen thought that it was a look of guilt that flitted over her companion's features, but it was gone before she could be sure. Either way, it seemed the fight had gone out of Tara at Deaths pertinent and somewhat on the money observation. Death then stalked away from Tara before she could say anything else, but it didn't look as though she even wanted to, she simply and silently moved to kneel by Daniels still unconscious form. As she did so, Famine stood too and backed away respectively, only stopping to deftly leap upon the dolmen in the circles center. He glanced at War who held up three fingers. Famine nodded and looked to Death. Death in turn glanced back then to Pestilence and Gwen realized they were communicating mentally between themselves and excluding her.

'Hey! That's a bit rude you know.' Gwen said simply, guessing they would figure out what she was referring to. Famine did and winked at Gwen almost cheekily.

'Good to see you're sharp Avatar, but you are right, it was rude and we apologize. Old habits but you have a right to know and it wasn't anything personal, only War letting us know the enemy are a mere three miles away and approaching fast. And it is with some regret that they are going to be here before Ezekiel and his celestial host arrive. And that means we will have to hold them ourselves until they turn up, oh well.' He sounded jovially resigned to the fact that he would be outnumbered roughly a few hundred thousand to one. Gwen was staggered how he could be so off hand about it. Even though he was a principle power in the Multiverse, even he could die it seemed if what Death was saying had any bearing on them. Beings considered previously immortal were now vulnerable and in danger of annihilation. They were still powerful, but against an enemy such as The Adversary, his generals and the other demonic creatures set against this world, they had their work cut out for them. Famine watched Gwen and knew she knew that much of what he said was bravado to maintain some sort of morale. It wouldn't do for lesser creatures to see the fabled Apocalyptic Horsemen waver in the face of seemingly insurmountable odds. They needed to appear invincible and as indomitable as ever. Gwen looked at Famine and thought he was doing a pretty good job of it too. Leaving Tara to take care of Daniel. Pestilence mounted and once more rejoined War and they both drew weapons, turning their steeds they silently cantered away in the direction of encroaching horde.

'They go to dispose of any scouts that may have ventured too close.' Famine offered 'Being so few, we need the element of surprise.' Gwen laughed at the idea.

'There only being four of you I think they'll be surprised all right.' Famine saw her point and he too laughed out loud. A rich and achingly infectious sound.

'You are full of observations my Lady Gwendoline.' Famine remarked when his mirth had subsided. 'But that surprise will lead them to arrogance believing us to be merely four. Arrogance as you surely know, then slips smartly into the realm of stupidity, and stupid enemies are much easier to dispatch. Weaker we may be, but we are not without a few surprises of our own.'

'True enough Famine, though I am loathe to employ them on this rabble.' Death commented as calmly yet deliberately moved across the circle to end up next to Famine and Gwen.

'You wanted to talk to me earlier?' Gwen prompted and the Reaper nodded.

'I did. We came because we sensed an extraordinary channeling of energy towards this isle. It had to hold some significance. We arrive to find yourself here and these humans fleeing more possessed than we have seen together in a long time and added to that an army of the Adversary's deminions large enough to raze this entire island. There is something here that he wants badly. Either to possess or to stop, we don't know which, but we can't allow either to happen. What did you intend Avatar? I ask because I'm curious as to how you are even here. This land is enchanted with an ancient and powerful incantation that is anathema to all your kind. Though more so the Drakareth but still, you seem to be holding up well against it.' The question threw Gwen because she didn't actually have an answer. Their imperative had been to get to the circle, based on the letter from Tara's mother. And Tara's insistence that they get to a stone circle, this being the closest of any significance, but beyond that she had no idea. How much protection was it going to be? Was it going to keep out a hundred thousand slavering demons? There were again more questions arising from her actions than she could fathom answers for and set her head spinning again.

'Honestly. I've no idea. Maybe the Earth herself shields me as I've only been here barely two days, I'd not given it any thought until now.' Famine accepted that and nodded to Death 'Our plan...' Gwen answered with a note of embarrassment '...which was a hasty one at best, mainly due to hundreds of bloody possessed screaming after our blood only got us this far. I was hoping for some respite or at least a clue as to our next move. Let's face it, fate hasn't been slow in presenting situations. I feel like a bloody pinball, bounced from pillar to post. I was hoping that something would manifest itself once we got here, but other than you, nothing has yet.' Gwen frowned, as an errant thought popped into her head. 'Unless it is you, you know, you're what's supposed to happen next?' Death paced back and forth, obviously agitated about something. His scythe had mysteriously vanished and he had clasped both heavily gauntleted hands behind his back as he did so. Looking so much like a military general, and less like the iconic Grim Reaper that it seemed to humanize him slightly in Gwen's eyes. More of a powerful ally than a principle power to be revered and feared.

'Tell me what you have learnt so far then Gwendoline and we shall see if we are indeed a part of your puzzle. But I suggest you be quick about it, I fear our time is short.'

Gwen took a second to reorganize her thoughts, then she told Death and Famine all she had experienced since arriving upon the Emerald Isle. She omitted nothing and waited with baited breath after she had finished as both Famine and Death weighed her account and sifted through it for anything pertinent. Long minutes seemed to stretch by.

'Dilmun.' Famine said suddenly. 'What?' was all Gwen could manage at the random word. 'That's so un lady like Gwen, you should say pardon me, or I'm sorry could you repeat that. Not what. Remember your station my lady.' Famine clucked at her.

'What?' she said again, more on purpose this time 'we're about to overrun by an army of demons who are baying for blood and all you are concerned about is my bloody etiquette? I'm really beginning to worry about your sanity.' Famine just smiled his ingratiating smile, one that he no doubt employed against the senoritas of history, and simply replied.

'Just because all about you is losing its way, there's no need to lower one's self to their level, but in response to your eloquent request that I repeat myself; Dilmun. Or that is what it used to be called. As I recall, the one place that sticks out geographically where four heads of water meet. Which is the merging of four mighty rivers, was at the area you now know as the Persian Gulf. That little sea never used to be the size it is now you know. It wasn't much bigger than a large river itself, and the land of Dilmun existed on its banks. Prior to that even, it was a lush and fertile land, a true garden of paradise.' Gwen and Death both looked at Famine as though he had sprouted a second head.

'What?' he asked innocently looking back, alternating his gaze between the two.

'Don't what me either.' Gwen snapped 'Is there anything connecting the bits inside your head or do they all free float around each other like orbiting planets?'

'I'm sure I don't understand what you are implying Lady Gwendoline, I have a very complex mental process I'll have you know.' Gwen just raised her eyebrows as though she had serious misgivings about that statement.

'I've been beating myself senseless trying to figure out the possible locations and likely countries where this tree could be. I've even entertained mythical countries like Atlantis or Avalon, not that I have any idea where they are either, but it bore consideration. Of course, the

Garden of Eden was my first choice, but like the other two, where the hell do you start looking for that? Then along you come, like it's a matter of inconsequence and just blurt it out like it's just occurred to you. Do you realize how much time you might have saved me if you had given someone that little bit of news just a tad sooner?' Famine stood from where he leant and raised a knowing finger and winked annoyingly again at her.

'Aha, but if you knew that from the get go, you would have gone straight there and not arrived here. From what you said, you were expected, so maybe it is just as well you detoured. For even after the millennia I've been around, it still amazes me how the fates weave their threads of destiny and there are days when I really wonder if they know what they are doing, if they did, I mean, would we be in the dire straits we currently find ourselves?' Death interrupted any further conjecture on the state of the cosmos.

'Now is not the time for philosophizing Famine, War and Pestilence have already taken out sixteen scouts and they have seen evidence of more in the vicinity.' A groan from behind them made them all turn. Daniel had come to and was sitting up and rubbing his head with a curious expression on his face. Tara was fussing over him as though he were ten and just had a close call, trying to make him drink water from a bottle she kept stabbing at his lips. He took some to mollify her then batted it away gently saying he was fine.

'My headaches gone.' they heard him say. 'Jeez, I didn't even realize I had one until...well, until I haven't. I must have gotten so used to it being there that I shut it out.' It was at that moment that it all came flooding back as to where he was and in whose company he found himself. He locked his gaze on the Grim Reaper as though seeing him for the first time instead of again.

'You're real aren't you? I mean you're actually Death.' They weren't so much questions as much as they were affirmations for the sake of his own sanity.

'I am.' The cowled and now winged and scythe bearing Reaper answered.

'I can't say I'm pleased to meet you, though I guessed I would sooner rather than later, presumably you know why.' Death nodded. 'We all know why now.'

'I don't want to die, not so young anyway.' Daniel blurted desperately 'It's not fair! Do you have to?' He didn't need to say what he would have to do, it was blatantly apparent.

'In answer to all those Daniel; No. it probably isn't fair, though fairness is entirely a matter of perspective, for whether it is fair or not, it is necessary. Though it is truly nothing to be as fearful of as your species seems to be. In all the time you have lived as a race, you still cannot accept death as a spiritual and natural process, to be embraced and celebrated. Consider it graduation. Your soul has learnt enough in this life to move on.' Daniel looked unconvinced. Death saw this one as a hard sell, but still gave it a go.

'If you believe nothing else Daniel Haden Fitzgerald, believe me, for I can offer you assurances that no mortal religious organization can even begin to match, if you catch my drift.' Daniel nodded. 'They have built an empire based on what they *believe* exists beyond this realm, unfortunately, it is based only on what *they* think and have come to believe exists, not what *really* exists. You have a phrase which says that they have built a mountain from a termite mound. The truth is not for them to know, it never was. Were they secure in the knowledge of what awaited them, they would not strive in this life. Which is what they need to do. Would a student strive to gain knowledge if it knew it would pass whatever it did? Probably not.' Daniel was trying desperately to hear what he was being told, but the expression on his face said he was struggling. Death continued all the same. 'But the one constant is that every human will die; at some point. What the Adversary is proposing will bring that about far too soon. He will eradicate both the present and the future, even to eradicating us.' Death gestured to himself and his comrades. 'That is a prospect that must *not* be considered, however appealing it may sound to short lived creatures such as yourselves, the implications would simply be catastrophic.' Death was trying, he really was. But Daniels mental sponge had absorbed all it could and the excess was dribbling away as fast as Death was pouring words in. But Tara had picked up on a few vital bits.

'That's all well and good...' Daniel said as though Death had not spoken at all. '...But you must have missed the bit where I said I didn't want to die!' Death just shook his massive armored and cowled head at the futility of what he was attempting. And Gwen noted a hint of annoyance in his voice as he spoke.

'You won't, not just yet anyway. You have as much of a chance at life as your sister, maybe you'll outlive her after all. Pestilence has stilled your disease for now and removed the pain, as you may have felt and I have boosted your own life force as much as I can. I suggest you make something of what life remains to you, for if the enemy wins, you'll be

354

praying for me with a fervor you never knew even existed.' Death turned away from Daniel and endeavored to talk to Gwen once more, there was obviously something he wanted to tell her, but again, he had no opportunity as Tara rose and strode across the clearing to join them. Death had time for two words only before Tara joined them.

*Watch her.*

## TRINITY

'I can feel it Gwen, the power in these stones.' Tara seemed excited for the first time since Gwen had – in Tara's mind - declined to heal Daniel. Though she couldn't get it through to Tara that it wasn't a declination for Gwen really did want to actually heal him. It was simply that she knew that in her present neophytic state, she'd probably kill him before curing him. It would take a precision she didn't have, as right now she was a supernatural blunt instrument. Tara took that admission badly, as though Gwen was doing it on purpose, she had seemed sullen ever since and her eyes had lost the earlier sparkle only to be replaced with something more guarded and Gwen didn't like to add sinister, but there was a definite mood there now that wasn't there before. Like a pair of embers, smoldering white hot below a dark ashen surface, just waiting to ignite into a conflagration. It hadn't helped either when Pestilence and the Horsemen abstained from healing her little brother either. That just poured more fuel on her already barely contained incendiary. Death stood aside and regarded the two women silently as Tara grew more animated around the Dolmen. Gwen was worried about just what might be burnt should she actually explode, what with her newly inherited powers and all. Gwen internalized all this in a split second as Tara rushed up and interrupted her and Death by slapping her hands up and down on the rock as if trying to find the sweet spot to activate it. Death was right about one thing it seemed, as Gwen regarded this new behavioral trait, she did indeed need careful watching. Gwen had to accept for all they had just gone through, she didn't know Tara at all, forty eight hours of mayhem and mystery was all she had and clearly that wasn't enough.

'What do you feel Tara?' Gwen asked carefully, for she too had felt the resonant thrum of the stones but she didn't want to give away what that felt like before hearing it from Tara. *Good grief, I'm turning into a suspicious and cynical old cow already. Is this how I'm going to see everyone from here on? That they all have some ulterior motive? I don't know if I like the sound of myself having to be like that, gotta watch that; don't want it getting the better of me, last thing I want is to go through eternity bitter and twisted.*

'It's hard to describe' Tara almost whispered 'but it's a little like standing on something with its engine running, only it seems to be running to some sort of melody. I know it sounds strange, but that's how it feels.' It didn't, not to Gwen anyway. She sensed a harmony to the resonance too but it felt more like a band tuning and warming up than actually playing a song. The music was there, but not quite.

'You're right,' Gwen agreed cautiously 'it's there, but it seems to be discordant at present. I get the impression that it has just awoken from a long sleep and isn't quite in tune with itself yet. The storm may have done that, or it might have been us.' Tara gave this some thought.

'You might have something there Gwen,' Tara eventually said after several minutes listening to the rocks. 'This is known as the Druids circle and I allegedly have some affinity to that particular branch, if you pardon the pun, of magical practice. Daniel used to rib me about my witchyness, but I don't feel as strongly about that side of the craft as I do about the Druidic aspect, the more natural, earthy side.' Gwen agreed, from what she had seen so far, that made sense but she kept her thoughts to herself seeing where this went.

'And you with a brand of a sickle on your arse,' Gwen tried a little levity in the hope it lightened an increasing heavy mood 'that goes some way to validating your thought.' Gwen smiled at her own remark, and she got a strained smile back as though it fought against Tara's annoyance. Neither seemed to have dominance at the moment and Tara was lost in between currently. Gwen hoped she had the strength to fight against the dark thoughts that could creep up on a person if they weren't careful. Anger and resentment could fester and turn into something destructive if left unchecked, and in the current climate, that was likely to leave that person open and vulnerable to malignant influence. It looked for doorways just like that, ways to permeate and insidiously corrupt bright souls.

'Yeah, that does seem to give it away doesn't it, but you might be right too, it wasn't this strong when we first got here, I'm sure of it and its getting stronger as we speak.' Tara glanced around, half convinced the stones would start glowing like her mantle any second now. Gwen looked thoughtful as she too studied the phenomena.

'We seem to be a nexus for a myriad of forces.' Death stated as he too began to look around warily. 'I imagine this site hasn't had such a gathering of powerful entities such as we represent for some considerable time, and, War says the demon army is closing in from our opposite side and to make matters worse, there seems to be a horde of possessed heading this way too. Yet from the West, there is another energy, one I haven't felt for a very long time, though it does not feel evil in its intent, I caution you to be prepared all the same, these are unpredictable times. You should be safe from direct diabolical influence in here, but I suggest you complete whatever it is you need to do soon before both the army and the possessed arrive.' Death looked faraway all of a sudden and Gwen knew he was being silently communicated to by one of the other three 'I will take my leave of you now Avatar' Death suddenly said 'for we must hold the rabble back to buy time for Ezekiel to arrive. He comes with haste, but will not be here before the enemy. Fare well Avatar, Lady Tara and you too master Daniel. On behalf of the Multiverse, I pray you succeed in this quest, sooner rather than later would be preferable if you could manage it.' With no other word or gesture, Death turned and with a down beat of his massive raven's wings, he glided the distance to his magnificent and ghostly pale stallion followed by a swift move that saw him almost fly, he swooped up to his saddle, spun his hypernatural mount and was galloping away before Gwen had even drawn her next breath. During their conversation, Famine had mounted and was galloping away with Death and Gwen wasn't entirely sure, for it could have been the wind, but she thought she heard laughter from the outrageous and oddly exuberant Spanish looking Horseman. *The world is turning into a very strange place.* Gwen spoke to herself as she spared a few seconds to watch them gallop away.

Gwen turned then to face Tara and for a few seconds before speaking, she looked directly at the fiery red head. She wasn't sure what she was looking for or expected to see, but the woman before her had somehow transformed in the brief time she had known her. Of course, her own arrival in the Irish woman's life hadn't exactly been uneventful. Her shoulders sagged almost imperceptibly as she accepted the fact that she was responsible for yet another life having its world inverted in ways they didn't exactly expect or invariably want. The same went for Daniel. How many more lives was she going to ruin as she *saved* the rest of humanity? But her self-pity wasn't going to help them right now; Gwen sloughed her somber mood like a discarded coat and addressed the other woman.

'So, Tara, what is it exactly we need to do here? Death implied we were here for a reason other than safety. And what is it with that sound? I take it that it has as much to do with you as it does with me?' Gwen left the question hanging and folded her arms. For some reason that escaped her, when she adopted that stance she seemed to become more imposing to those before her, more authoritative. Jen had told her once that it was her electromagnetic field. Her mind demanded a response, one that she thought she should get, and her own bodies generated field expanded out accordingly to swamp those before her, encouraging them to answer her and show due respect. Apparently this was the same practice unconsciously applied to those people termed *born leaders* and *charismatic*. Few people had it and even fewer actually knew what it was they had. Gwen believed these people would be very dangerous indeed if they understood what it was they did and how they did it.

'Whatever it is Gwen,' Tara was looking away at a distant spot as she spoke 'a part of me is saying that we can't do it until the wee hours. Between two and four in the morning. I'm at my strongest then I sense.' Gwen raised an eyebrow provocatively, as if she expected further information.

'Since that…that thing back at the house and I blacked out' Tara continued 'well I've been seeing stuff in my head. Images crash in every now and again in a rushed jumble.'

'Stuff?' Gwen reiterated as though by repeating the word it would prompt Tara to expand on her vague description.

'Yeah, stuff; images and people and animals and all manner of weird shit just flying through my head like a DVD on fast forward. Some keep repeating themselves but since we got here, I've managed to slow a few of them down and get a handle on one or two. There is another woman there, she looks a bit like me, but I know it isn't me and it's her I can hear talking.' Tara nodded knowingly and smiled a crooked smile, one that would have had men dribbling at her feet. It spoke of mischievousness and recklessness, and was firmly embedded in a morass of sultry earthiness. She ran her hands into her thick mane of flaming hair and tossed it casually over one shoulder as she spoke where it fell into place in such a way that it only enhanced her natural beauty.

'Sounds crazy doesn't it.' Tara continued, starting to pace back and forth as she did so, fiddling with her clothes; straightening her skirt and adjusting her top and coat. 'But it seems to be making some sort of sense. It is as though she is reminding me of things I already knew but had forgotten and one of those things Gwen, is how to use these ancient rings to travel great distances.' Tara let that bit of information sink in before carrying on. She saw the reaction on Gwen's face. One of barely contained surprise and even a little awe.

358

'I know, incredible isn't it? It has something to do with this tone, this harmonic that the stones generate. There is a way to harness it and something like tuning a radio in to channel it to create a link with other circles or sacred sites. Sounds fantastic doesn't it?'

'It does.' Gwen said warily. 'Is this all from the woman in your mind?' Gwen asked this as the image she had seen of the woman with the sickle, came to hers. The woman who had beheaded the other on the altar. There was something about her that pricked at Gwen's consciousness, even her newly expanded consciousness. There was a feeling of cruelty and selfishness. A sense of treachery and murder that emanated from her like maggots crawling from a corpse. It made Gwen's flesh creep at the mere memory of her. She couldn't comprehend how she might have felt should she have found herself before the woman in the flesh. But she kept her features impassive though and waited for Tara to explain further, if she would. Turns out she didn't. For at that moment, Daniel decided to get himself up off the damp grass and complaining about soggy pants as he did so, he walked jarringly over to Tara and Gwen. Moving with the distinctive walk of one who has wet underwear. He stopped and tried to crane his head round to see and at the same time pull his jeans around so he could see the extent of the wet patch.

'Will you feckin look at that! It looks like I've wet meself. Who thought it would be a good idea to park me on the wet grass? Thanks a feckin bunch.' Daniel stopped abruptly as he felt the gaze of the two women upon him. He was oblivious to the fact he had interrupted their probably very important conversation with abject trivia. He was also unaware of the annoyance levelled at him by Gwen for cutting short her questioning of Tara whilst she was so forthcoming.

'What? Where did Dea...you know who mean, where did he...they go?' He couldn't bring himself to say the names of the beings who had appeared before him, his mind had slipped into defensive denial mode. A natural safety zone for the majority of humanity.

'They've gone Daniel, you can relax now.' Tara tried to reassure him. Gwen thought she was pleased at the interruption and was happy to change the subject.

'*Relax?*' Daniel blurted, teetering on the edge of hysteria again. 'Relax? I don't think I'm ever going to relax again. Speaking of ever again, what do we do now? I take it going home isn't an option seeing as there is little left of it thanks too...thanks too...' He fought for the words, and failed. 'Thanks to you know who I mean.'

'We have to wait Dan.' Tara said calmly and coercively, using her past techniques to help put her brother's mind at rest. 'We will be leaving here, but we can't do anything until much later.' Tara put an encouraging hand on his fore arm, reinforcing her calming words.

'How much later? Other than a wet arse, I'm starting to feel a bit exposed here. The town is just over there, it's pretty open here and what is to stop any more of those damned possessed from getting us here? It's just a stone circle, it's not a bloody fortress.'

'Death and the other horsemen are taking care of those Daniel.' Gwen saw the boy flinch as Tara mentioned the Horsemen. 'And the demon army.' He grimaced more.

'Thanks! Did you really have to mention *all* of that? Couldn't you have just said don't worry, we'll be alright.' They all wondered then, in the privacy of their own minds, whether they would actually be alright ever again. It seemed doubtful right at that moment.

Their momentary reverie was brought to an abrupt halt as Daniel asked a very pertinent question. One they had all seemingly avoided thinking about until now.

'So what are we going to do until two in the morning then? It isn't exactly a social hot spot in case you hadn't noticed, nor is there a bar…' Gwen shot him a look so venomous, Daniel stalled and sputtered to a semi silence. 'Old habits and all that, I was just saying, no need to get tetchy.' he added submissively. The three of them moved about the circle for about fifteen minutes, each avoiding the other and only regarding their companions in a sullen silence. No one had any answer. Gwen didn't want to leave the apparent protection of the circle, but she was curious as to how the Horsemen were faring. Her Drakarim hearing could pick up the distant sounds of combat and it was slowly shredding her already taut and frayed nerves. Tara was lost in her own thoughts, alternating between her visions and the awakening of her newly found powers. Blossoming between the two was the beginnings of a plan to save her brother along with the realization that when she had said she would do whatever it takes to save Daniel, she meant it on levels so profound, her desire had transcended time; gaining momentum with every refusal to help him she received, and another had not only heard, but responded, setting events in motion that would – if she had her way - reverberate throughout history.

Daniel however, was simply misery incarnate. For although the interior of the circle seemed immune to the winter weather that was building on the outside, it didn't really stop the wind and he still shivered.

Not helped by his moist bottom and the lack of centrally heating spirits that his bloodstream was usually full of by now. His shivers were part weather, part fear and part shock. Though he didn't like to admit it, he was terrified and his drinking had increased proportionally to his diagnosis and ever depressing situation. The thing was, he probably had more concerns with his livers health than that of his tender brain with the sudden and vast quantities of alcohol being poured into it, but neither of the organs concerned him now. The Grim Reaper had intimated that his future was somehow connected to Gwen's quest, and not only his immediate future, but his long term one too. Whatever it was she was up to could cure him. Pure and simple. That fact alone had endeared her to him in ways he hadn't considered before, along with the monumental events that were going on around him too. He felt small and insignificant in the face of what he was witnessing, but amidst his personal maelstrom, he now had the one thing that had eluded him before. Hope. He really did want to live after all was said and done.

Gwen's thoughts drifted without direction. There were so many things flitting through her mind, she couldn't focus on any one of them with the intensity they deserved. One of her errant thoughts touched upon the music that was still emanating from the stones and she wondered if anyone other than herself and Tara and Daniel could hear it, or whether it was restricted to their immediate proximity.

*We hear it Avatar!* Came a thousand voices that resounded in Gwen's mind like the rumble of orchestrated thunder. A pure sound that she felt through to her bones and it resonated down the marrow within. The nearest Gwen had felt to the stunning sound was the day she had put her head phones on and switched on the power, totally forgetting she had used her stereo the previous day and had the volume up on high as she listened to Carmina Burana. The Carl Orff opera was one of her favorites, and she hadn't noticed the volume at first as the first part of the track had been quiet, until the choir had kicked in full pelt. Gwen was half convinced her ears were bleeding when she whipped the head phones off, certainly her head was ringing slightly and her nerve endings were jangling. But even that didn't compare to the voices as they bounced off the inside of her skull like her head was the inside of the Albert Hall.

'*We hear them Avatar as we hear you, and see you. We come!*' Gwen was rapidly becoming accustomed to the voice come voices and true enough, they did seem to be drawing closer. They were more distinct and clearer than the first hail. That or her head had stopped tingling.

'*Who are you?*' Gwen spoke in her mind, so as not to alarm Tara and Daniel, though when she looked at them they had a bemused expression and they were looking about them as though they had heard something, but couldn't fathom its source.

'What's going on Gwen?' Tara asked but Gwen hushed her with a finger to her lips. Tara and Daniel moved to the center of the circle, and stood by the dolmen.

'That's what I'm trying to figure out,' Gwen whispered. 'I think it's the other power Death mentioned was heading this way and they seem to know me.' *Who are you, answer me!* Gwen demanded again in her thoughts as she switched back her minds attention.

'*One amongst us comes Avatar, she speaks for us all.*' Gwen waited, though not as patiently as she would have liked. She felt her body tense and fidget with nervous energy as she awaited the arrival of the voices spokesperson.

Something in her minds newly wired capability engaged and with a thought, Gwen reached out and somehow parted a translucent curtain of reality. It was as though the terrain and view that surrounded them was painted onto canvas and she just pulled it back like a curtain. Beyond the veil was a panorama that vaguely resembled the one before it, only this was brighter. The colors more vivid and alive. Gwen was put in mind of The Wizard of Oz, how it went from black and white to glaring color. Here was the black and white by comparison. But what made her gasp was the profusion of figures milling about and moving in an agitated manner all around them. Some sitting upon the stones that encircled them and others massed in the fields beyond. Some even flitted through the air like massive darting dragonflies. Sparkling and diaphanous wings buzzing and thrumming as they dived, soared and hovered. At first glance, it resembled a hazy dream of Shakespearean fairies and sprites or cast from some Pre-Raphaelite canvas. But as her own supernatural sight began to assert itself, she saw that reality of the dream. She saw thousands of faces and bodies, in as many colors and anatomical configurations. To the ignorant, many of these creatures would be considered ugly or terrifying and others aesthetically beautiful. But to Gwen, she just saw fear and horror etched upon all of their faces. There was pain carved on to every one of their otherworldly expressions. They had experienced some terrifying ordeal for sure and they were fleeing it as best they could, much like animals will flee a wild fire. These were refugee elementals. *My god what has happened to set these beings on the run?* The thought hammered through Gwen with the sheer horror of what such an event

362

implied. In her instinctive response, born of her need to protect these spirits of the wild, Gwen pushed the energy that was pulsing from the stones and expanded its sphere of influence. She saw it grow and shimmer as it encapsulated the elementals nearest and still it expanded outwards. Those suddenly finding themselves within seemed to deflate almost, the tension of fear and what passed for adrenaline within them fled like bad air out of a balloon. Those elementals discovering themselves now within the incandescent bubble settled down on the rocks and on the ground, calmer and visibly relaxed. They sat silently now and watched Gwen with an almost animal intensity. Vivid multi-hued eyes swirling and dilating as they focused on the small, slightly green blonde woman before them. Then they started singing. Their song fused with the shield Gwen was expanding and if she thought about what she had done, rather than act on instinct again, she would have known how little effort it took to do what her will instructed, but even that tiny exertion evaporated like morning dew when the music started. At that moment Gwen knew that what she was hearing was none other than the song of life. The song that pervades every living thing, in the case of what she was hearing at that moment, it was solely for life on this planet, but songs such as she was now a part of were sung throughout the Multiverse, each symbiotically attuned to its own planet or star and the life forms that dwelt therein. What earth scientists called cosmic energy was nothing in fact but music. A harmonizing galactic and Multiversal orchestra, made up the interwoven songs of all worlds spanning the vast tracts of space; And all humanity sees in their limited capacity is just so many waves, frequencies, miscellaneous and unidentifiable signals, not the music. And from macrocosm to microcosm, Gwen saw that every spark of life, from every solitary blade of grass, every individual ant and insect and even down to a single tiny pebble on a beach, all that and more contributed to the song. As she felt this, Gwen was humbled, even shamed for her prior ignorance of her place in the weave. It affected her in such a manner that she had no way to express herself other than to simply cry. It was all she could do, so Gwen wept where she stood, caught up in the rapturous expansion of her awareness and the acceptance of her place within the cosmic harmonic, and flowers sprang up at her feet born from her tears, knowing now she had become the weaver.

'*Well met Avatar, you have our thanks and our gratitude for your shelter.*' A female voice separated itself from the song and spoke directly to Gwen. '*Too long has it been since your kind and ours sang the songs of power together. Though I am saddened by the reasons they are being sung this day. We do however, need to talk. And with some urgency if I may enter into your presence?'* Gwen couldn't argue with their need to talk, something had driven these beings from their homes and she wanted to know what or who it was that was capable of such a thing and how they had the audacity to do it in *her world*. Someone-Gwen promised coldly- was going to pay dearly for this.

The more rational and clear thinking part of Gwen responded to the silky and honey coated voice that requested her permission as though she were some sort of royalty to grant an audience to anyone.

'Of course you can you silly thing, you don't need my permission for that. Get yourself within the barrier as fast as you can, I don't want to push this out too far in case I'm giving too much away to the enemy about the level of power here and draw any more danger to us.' Gwen could see shapes flitting so fast across the country side that no mortal eye would have been able to track them. And even if they could, Gwen knew these beings existed in a realm so close, but so infinitely far from ours that they could stand on and around a mortal and they would never even know they were there. They lived in a world just beyond our capabilities to perceive, like the light beyond infra-red or ultra violet; we know it's there but can't interact with it without special equipment. Humans didn't possess the knowledge to devise such equipment that would expose this realm, yet; Firstly they had to accept it was even there in order to go looking and with the memories of past encounters with closed minded scientists, she knew they were safe enough for now. Though obviously, something *had* found them.

Like a harpist, Gwen reached out and touched every strand of the musical tapestry, feeling its origins and filling her with wonder as she felt the myriad of contributions from plants and animals, each offering a tiny aspect of itself to the song, each reinforcing the sphere of energy. As Gwen strummed the amorphous strings, one suddenly stood out. Brighter, stronger and clearer than the rest. Gwen withdrew her awareness and focused on this new thread. Materializing out of thin air, cloaked in starburst radiance stepped a lithe and willowy figure who proceeded to glide then the more Gwen watched it became a walk across the field, passing through the fence and eventually entering the druids circle, stopping several feet shy of Gwen. The figure then promptly knelt and lowered what Gwen took for its head.

'Stand up please, there's no need for that.' Gwen said as she blushed with the embarrassment of it. It had even taken her several months to get used to being called ma'am by the overly polite Americans she had first encountered upon arriving on their shores all those years earlier. She had never really gotten used to that and had been uncomfortable with excessive formality, recent events had only made her more self-conscious about it. What was expected of her now? She was Drakarim, highly esteemed too but she still didn't really know what that meant. Nor would she Gwen mused until this war was won and she had time to breathe. And of course always assuming they won it and she survived it.

The being of light stood and nodded an acquiescence to Gwen, then turned her dazzling gaze upon the other two souls who inhabited the circle and who were staring at her with wide eyed amazement. To Tara and Daniel who hadn't moved from their earlier positions, it seemed as though Gwen was talking to a ball of light. Gwen had - to Tara's way of seeing things - forgotten about her and Daniel as Gwen's eyes had glazed over slightly and a faraway expression had descended upon her delicate features. Gwen stared off into an unknown distance and as Tara watched. Her skin began to tingle and gooseflesh up. Daniels did the same and what looked to them at first like a heat haze that began to lift up from the rocks and gradually move away from them. Tiny motes of light started to fill the air then as though some invisible fire was sending smoldering embers aloft to skip and chase in the charged air above them. Tara and Daniel both thought little of them at first, rendering them a side effect of the highly charged stones of the druids circle. But it was only after several minutes of Gwen muttering to herself that Tara saw a particular large ember expand into a ball of light, drift across the field towards Gwen, enter the circle and hang immobile before her, perfectly still though pulsing slightly just hovering in mid-air.

'Wait here Dan, I'll be back in a moment.' Tara instructed her brother who for his part, hadn't planned on moving anyway. Not waiting for any kind of response, positive or negative or other, Tara walked steadily over to where Gwen stood and positioned herself beside her, fixing her own emerald gaze upon the gravity defying sparkle.

'What is it?' Tara asked Gwen in a conspiratorial tone, inclining her head and letting the words trail from the corner of her mouth.

'Why are you whispering?' Gwen answered in the same melodramatic manner.

'I don't know. Can it hear us?' Tara nodded ever so slightly towards the phenomena to indicate she meant the gently bobbing light. Gwen smiled, though she knew the being before her could see and hear all that transpired, she played along with Tara, half hoping that it would allay some of the shock she was due to experience when she discovered the truth.

'I believe so Tara. Tell me, what exactly can you see?' Tara told her.

'I see,' Gwen said, 'I suppose that's something, yet it is more. Try tapping into your new abilities, or letting your mind *unfocus* from the logical, if that makes any sense. Let your intuition and instincts take over. That might help.' Gwen reviewed what she had just said and grimaced. 'Bloody hell, I sound like one of those freakin' new age yo-yos. You know what I mean anyway. Trust me when I tell you there's more here than just a floating ball of light.' Gwen sensed humor from the entity as it seemed to enjoy the charade the way its head or what Gwen took for its head moved slightly between the two women.

'Allow me to assist.' the entity said and Tara almost leapt out of her skin when a glowing finger of light prodded her on the forehead. Tara's sight was suddenly opened to the realm before her and if her eyes lids had gone any wider, they would have slipped over the back of her eyes and vanished into her head.

'*Oh - my - good - god!*' was about all Tara could manage as she took in the vast array of beings who had seemingly materialized out of nowhere. Her exclamation all bar fell from her wide open and slack mouth as she gawped at the glowing figure before her. Apparently there was nothing like a truly enigmatic, magical and internally illuminated - to the point of absolute incandescence - being to over awe the rational mind. But Tara was never one to be slow coming forward and she regained her composure fast. Though Gwen did reach out and slip one finger beneath her jaw to afford the surprised Irish woman some dignity.

'Do close your mouth Tara, Its rude to drool I imagine in any realm my dear.' But before either of them could do or say anything further, the being had skipped past them and danced off around Daniel, who was bemused at first by the little light and kept reaching out to touch it, but when she reached out and smacked him on the forehead, much the same way it did with Tara, he yelped suddenly like dog when it's tail is stood upon and let out a strangled cry as his eyes suddenly focused upon the ghostly apparition capering in front of him.

'Arrgghh! Don't hurt me, I'm with them.' Her laugh was musical and reminded Gwen of a thousand tiny bells as rainfall cascaded over them.

'I have no intention of hurting you mortal,' she said musically 'quite the opposite in fact.' It was then that Gwen noticed how the figures form shifted 'Do you not find me appealing?' it asked hypnotically and Daniels gaze was drawn almost against his will to fall upon the glowing

366

elementals new shape. But apparently he saw something that neither Gwen nor Tara saw and he screamed, collapsing to the ground and curling up into a ball. His hands flying to his groin as though he had just been horse kicked there. Gwen and Tara raced to his side and Gwen shot a disapproving stare at the entity.

'What did you do to him?' The rage in Gwen's voice reverberated and the entity recoiled in fear, sensing the power inherent beneath it.

'I am sorry Avatar, long has it been since I have been before a mortal man, I merely gave him a glimpse of my true self.' Gwen knew little about the elementals, but some of the folk lore she did know was that many varieties of nymph, from whence the word nymphomaniac arises, used to lure men astray, promising carnal pleasures the likes they could only imagine. These unlucky souls would follow these mischievous sprites until they either died of starvation and thirst, so enraptured would they be by the nymph. Or, they would be spirited away to forever roam the other realms, lost and alone, unable to die but beset by the agonies of desire for the nymph that led them there and forever unquenched. Daniel groan brought Gwen's thoughts back to the present as he moaned and writhed on the ground.

'Stop it now! Whatever you are doing to him, stop it this instant.' Gwen demanded and as though a dimmer switch had been turned, the being faded noticeably. Her inner illumination giving rise to a silvery green toned skin not unlike Gwen's and the biggest, darkest orange eyes she had ever seen. She had only ever seen eyes similar to hers once before, and that was on deer, though they weren't orange. Huge, watery amber pools with enormous lashes. On a deer they would be amazing enough, but on this creature, well, Gwen saw how easy it would be to drown in them and be lost forever, and she was Natures Avatar. Poor old Daniel stood no chance whatsoever.

Gwen watched Daniel try and pull himself together, shrugging off all offers of help as he recovered gradually after taking both barrels of the elementals sexual energy. It was the same power Sirens and nymphs used in the legends Gwen presumed, except this one had been out of practice and turned it on full for Daniel. The effect was embarrassingly obvious for those watching and sheer agony for him. So now he sat apart from the rest of them, embarrassed after having cleaned himself up from the spontaneous, orgasmic effect the elemental had manifested in him. Feeling decidedly outnumbered by three females to one relentlessly battered male, he sat outstretched and glowered at them from time to time as the three of them got to know each other. He watched as the elemental made a few physical adjustments on Gwen's advisement and groaned just loud enough for the women to hear him as he saw what she did. She didn't look any better in his eyes. Though *better* wasn't the right term he knew. But she had just gone from the ultimate supernatural love honey who could sexually vaporize a man with a glance to something more companionable by trying to emulate her two new examples. She – for that was definitely the form it adopted, had toned herself down to a five foot nothing super, supermodel look-a-like that would stop traffic and be the death countless men as they crashed cars while gawping like idiots at her. Diminutive she may be, but there were no doubts whatsoever that she wasn't perfectly formed. Gwen had given her some things from Tara's pack, which caused Tara to scowl slightly. What was it with women and sharing their clothes thought Daniel but he had his answer soon enough, because the way she wrapped the old shirt around her chest, leaving her midriff exposed and the way the skirt, which she tore several ragged inches off the bottom - which only enhanced its look - hung on her hips perfectly, just leaving her bare feet poking out and in that rough guise, she made Tara look positively dowdy. To all intents and purposes, she looked like a regular girl about nineteen to twenty five, that is except those eyes. She turned them once in his direction as though she sought some kind of approval from her unwilling victim by way of an apology perhaps. She smiled and did a little turn, but Daniel just scowled all the more and turned away, though not before catching sight of her strikingly orange eyes scowling slightly at him in annoyance. That wasn't helped by the vertical pupil that slashed downwards through the middles giving that alien take to them. He was instantly put in mind of some alien-feline hybrid. That she is what big cats would look like if they could adopt human form.

'Finally.' Gwen announced, satisfied with her work 'Now that we've made you something close to presentable to mortal kind, mainly so you don't inadvertently do any more harm to Tara's brother there really, I think it would be nice if we knew your name. Mine isn't Avatar,' Gwen smiled to lessen the reproach. 'It's Gwen and this is…well as you might have heard me say, Tara and that poor soul there is Daniel, her brother. And you are..?' What came out, no human was going to pronounce.

'I see!' Gwen looked puzzled and frustrated as she tried and ran it through her mind and gave up 'Well I'm not even going to try saying that, I'd have my lips and teeth tied into so many knots, not even my dentist would be able to unravel them. Try again if you will and see if you can simplify it or at least say it a little slower perhaps.'

'AmberBiethsalamVasCorinamber. How's that? I've taken the linguistic nuances out and translated what was left as best I can.' Gwen tried it and so did Tara; both managed it fairly well, though it was still something of a mouthful.

'Nice, better. It's got a lovely ring to it, almost musical. Does it mean anything?' Gwen asked while at the same time shooting a reproachful glance at Daniel who muttered not quite under his breath. *Yeah, it means hello, I'm a vicious, spiteful orange eyed thing.* The elemental heard him apparently and turned swiftly in his direction, hissing and spitting. Her amber eyes flaring, and revealing at the same time, a mouthful of translucent, razor sharp, needle like teeth that any piranha would have gladly swapped its own for. Wicked talons extended from her finger just like cats claws only longer, which she brandished at him and Daniel recoiled fearfully, but only as far as one of the stones again, slamming into it brought him up short and knocked the wind from him. The elemental was all for leaping at him and inflicting even more horrible things on his tortured frame, but Gwen's icy voice chilled the flame of the elementals response and made Daniel turn away guiltily, desperately sucking in air. Tara mumbled something about how Gwen now knew how *she* felt, just wait until she had twenty four years of it like she had.

'Simmer down children' Gwen commanded in her most motherly tone 'or you're going to make mommy cross. And mommy doesn't like pulling rank…' Gwen waggled her finger at them threateningly and several roots popped out of the ground and began waving menacingly in sync with Gwen.'…But in case it has escaped the attention of either of you, I am the Avatar of Nature. Believe me when I tell you that should I be pushed too far, and unless you both behave and play nice, you will spend the rest of your lives as dung beetles and I assure you, there will be plenty of filthy, putrid, smelly dung for you to play in until you learn to get along. *Do I make myself clear?'* Gwen only raised her voice at the end, but the Drakarim in it had the desired effect. Their tenuous peace resumed as the elemental smartly turned her back on Daniel and smiled winsomely at Gwen, teeth and claws vanishing as though they were never there. Daniel just glowered, drew in several further ragged breaths where he had knocked his own out and muttered incomprehensible curses about women and demons.

'That's better.' Gwen continued in that same patronizing voice that makes any rational person want to heave repeatedly as though overdosing on verbal sugar. Gwen was good at it too. She made a Stepford Wife look like a howling barbarian. Of course she had no idea if she could turn them into dung beetles but the threat sounded good to them.

'Now, you were about to tell us what your name means.' Gwen reiterated sweetly, as though nothing untoward had just occurred. Daniel obediently stayed silent, though his expression was petulant. The elemental ignored him, much the way a big cat would ignore a maggot. Or, as the little group discovered, the way royalty ignore those beneath them.

'It means, in a round a bout sort of way, the royal living flame of the ancient and noble Birch, Daughter of Silvaraphim Corinamber and guardian of the crescent, keeper of the wilds, master of the hunt and father of the People. Or something like that, it is very long winded and somewhat pretentious and I never really had to use it before, let alone explain it. You however, may simply call me Amber if that helps.'

Gwen's eyes widened slightly in surprise at the revelation that Amber was elemental nobility, though she found that she was getting a little numb to these mind staggering discoveries she kept coming across. After all, just how much more fantastic could her life get? So! She was talking to a being that no-one had seen for centuries and was only documented in myth and legend. Not how she was expecting her day to go. Though if she gave it any real thought, she would have had to admit that she had no idea what to expect from anything, let alone one of the fey folk. They were apparently- considering the multitude she had witnessed arriving at the circle- as diverse and anomalous as birds in the sky and fish in the sea. And that wasn't including the carthy woodland and fire elementals. They were all as individual as humans and their various cultural nuances, shapes forms and colors. She sighed wearily and this drew concerned looks from everyone, even the sulking Daniel was caught by that sound; Gwen felt suddenly burdened all over again by how much she had to learn about this new world around her and the ancient world that had remained hidden from view for so long and that was joining this one now.

'You are a Dryade yes?' Amber asked Tara quite out of the blue, catching the Irish woman on the back foot, and who was not expecting to be embroiled in Gwen's conversation with the Sidhe woman. For Tara had no allusion as to what she was. One of the fey folk, faery, a wood nymph perhaps. Though not of the malevolent banshee type, but they were all tricksy right enough though Tara reasoned. Just not as evil and spiteful as some, but still more than others and Tara's instinct was to be wary of talking to her kind, lest she become trapped in some dangerous word game with her. They were renowned for having silver tongues and could talk a person right out of their skin if they had a will to. Now Gwen, Tara expected she could handle herself in a confrontation with these beasties, as she was proving with this one. But she wasn't so sure about getting involved herself, she had enough to worry about with the stuff swirling in her mind without having to contend with this.

'No, good grief no, I'm not one of you, I'm a human.' Tara answered to the question. Amber laughed then. A rich throaty and still musical sound, one that made Tara blush and Daniel squirm with the recollection of recent events. But she shook her mane of flowing auburn locks and leapt inhumanly up onto the dolmen and with one swift move, spun and folded her legs beneath her to sit cross legged on the rock. She propped her head into her hands and her fingers tapped lightly on her cheeks to some invisible tune that only she could hear. Daniel tried not to look as her skirt was pulled up over her now bare knees, exposing too much flesh for his liking. He was comedic to watch as he tried to stare at everything else *except* her.

'Not anymore you're not.' Amber responded not taking her eyes off Tara 'Not entirely anyway. You have the color and the frequency of the priestesses. Those that sought harmony with the elemental realms and the mundane world you live in and defended the forests and the wild places, the holy wells and sacred groves and rings, like this one. I believe you called them *Druids*?'

'Druids? Yes I know what they are.' Tara responded, somewhat relieved about the direction of conversation, though still cautious as to where it might be heading. 'But I'm not one of them either, they're a bunch white robed and bearded old men aren't they?' This time both Gwen and Amber laughed and Tara scowled at both of them in response to their joviality at her expense. She didn't like being laughed at.

'What's so funny?' Tara asked hotly. 'Well the ones I've seen are anyway, what's wrong with that?' Gwen found it ironic that a woman brought up in the land that probably had more famous druidic characters than anywhere else, should know so little about them. She wondered in light of her recent discovery whether or not her mother intentionally kept her in the dark about druids. Gwen quickly filled in some blanks for her with what she had learnt herself. There were some advantages to running a new age store; she got to read all the books for free. *Well, not entirely free I suppose. I did have to buy the damn things in the first place. And speaking of the store, I wonder how Dolores is getting on.* Gwen mentally digressed as Tara absorbed what she had just heard.

'But you called me a Dryade? Isn't that one of your kind?'

'It's an old word and often misused, but don't you see the similarity? We are both forces of nature who contend to see that the natural order remains the way it should. Some of us rather than just remain passive, choose to defend that balance in varying ways depending upon capability. Amongst our kind, much the same as in yours, there are those who perpetually extol the merits of peaceful resolution and the avoidance of conflict even in the face of certain destruction.' A dark cloud passed over Amber's expression fleetingly at that thought but it passed as swiftly as it had come. 'Choosing rather to run and hide than stand and fight for our right to exist.' It was clear Amber disagreed with this particular way of thinking. Tara was nodding as the undercurrent of what Amber was saying resonated through much of humanities troubles. Both recent and past. She recalled her father's tales and much of the bitter infighting of the days of the IRA, long before Al-Queada and the bloody Taliban and all those other religion based zealots kicked off and muddied the world's waters all the more. 'It is a shame we no longer have the wolves, they would be an invaluable asset right about now.' Amber looked away thoughtful for a moment before continuing as though recalling something lost, and Tara turned a confused glance her way, slowly walking towards her as she didn't want to raise her voice too much as the night crept slowly upon them and the darkness descended. She pulled her sweater and coat tighter around her, hugging herself as the bitter chill beyond the ring still managed to permeate her too few layers and she shivered involuntarily.

'How can a pack of wolves be of any use?' Tara asked Amber, looking up slightly at her 'they're just animals, to be fair though, bloody big animals with serious teeth but from what I've seen so far, even they'd be ripped to bits. We had a tough enough job, with Gwen, a shotgun and a car.' But Amber was shaking her head as Tara spoke.

'No Tara, the wolves were Dryades, like you and like me. More like me in any case if you get my drift, but they were a special caste of Dryade. These were warriors. Peace only went so far and when it failed. There were the wolves. Their purpose was not offensive mind, but defensive. Though early in their existence they were divisive about this and a faction split from their order and followed another path.' Gwen was listening and knew then where the Kore-Megara originated. 'Our kind never had any reason to attack another, not ourselves nor the world of men.' Amber continued, her eyes took on a reflective expression as though she wandered the paths of a different time as she spoke. 'Peaceful co-existence is much more preferable but even our history tells of skirmishes, minor arguments that got out of hand, then again whose doesn't. Your realm and ours clashed several hundred years ago and a fraction of it has been transcribed in to your legends, though much of it is incomplete and inaccurate. Your druids as you came to call them were terrible at writing anything down and they were supposed to be the intelligent ones?' Amber chuckled at the thought, though not in a maligning, detrimental way, but it was more of a pitying, regretful sound. 'The wolves Tara, were a fighting force to be reckoned with. They combined magic with martial prowess as well as being shape shifters. They were experts with bow, knife and sword, but their weapon of preference was their Scarta - sickle swords for want of a better translation. It was from their enchanted and mystical curved blades that humanity drew many of their designs. In this case, the druid sickle which is now more an agricultural implement drew its origin from this blade for this in turn drew its origins from the arcane and curved blade of the fabled Horseman, Death and his scythe. It is imagery that is prevalent throughout your history did you but understand your roots and it is perhaps because you don't this war has come about.

'I'm sorry Amber, but I really have no idea what you are talking about, though it sounds wonderful and all. It's not me I'm afraid. I can manage to cut myself peeling vegetables, let alone swinging some bloody curved sword, I'd do meself a mischief.'

'No one is asking you too Tara, I'm just saying that was what they did and who they were, and though you are Dryade, its clear your power is more sorceress than warrioress.' Amber looked at Gwen as though seeking some sort of confirmation. Gwen joined the duo with a few slow steps towards them and with a nod from Tara, a subtle permission giving, Gwen went through her tale again. Amber was a good listener and sat stock still until Gwen finished. Finally, when she was sure Gwen had finished speaking, Amber sat and absorbed her words for a few moments before speaking again herself.

'So it begins again then.' Amber's softly glowing eyes settled on Tara with a mixture of pity and reluctance. 'You bear the mark I presume?' The question could have related to anything, but Tara knew in her bones that the mark in question was the sickle brand, the scar that tied her by blood ritual to the legacy her mother had bequeathed her. Albeit reluctantly. Tara nodded. 'You don't seem too happy about it?' Amber noted 'Perhaps that is a good thing. Maybe you will not be seduced by the power as many before you were. It colors perceptions until the worst deed seems rational and justified. We have seen the ashen remains of cities and cultures, the smoking ruins and debris of peoples whose thirst for power blinded them to the consequences of their actions. Oddly how much of your world looks like this now.'

'My ma didn't want me to have this, but as Gwen said, my choices were limited at the time and my hand was forced. What was I to do? I didn't have a Scooby as to what was going on, all I saw was thunder and lightning and my fucking world collapsing around my ears. After twenty odd years, I find a letter from my Ma almost *predicting* what was taking place and she implied that I wasn't going to survive without embracing the legacy she sought to deny me, what would you have done?' Tara's voice had risen as the emotional level rose, elevated by the fact her memories were still fresh and poignant. Amber nodded sagely and reached out a delicate hand to place on Tara's shoulder. Tara didn't flinch, though her mind wanted too under the elementals alien touch.

'True enough, you did what you had to. It is all any of us can do. It seems your Rite of passage is turning into a baptism of fire.' Amber said safely and Tara started. 'My what?' concern coloring her question. 'Rite of passage.' Amber repeated and Tara blinked still not fully grasping the implications and even Gwen was curious as to the context.

'But isn't that some kind of initiation?' Tara found the presence of mind to ask 'sort of girl to woman and boy to man kind of stuff. I'm a little old for all that shit now surely, though not probably by your standards.' Tara recalled from legends how old these creatures got to be.

'Not at all. It's not like that at all. It's another example of how you humans change the meanings of many words to suit your own ends and the original is lost to time. The Rite of Passage originally and exclusively was for the Dryades and the priests and priestesses who connected to the Natural order. They existed all over this world then, some still do as we feel their interference, but we have not seen or heard from them for a long time now, until recently there was an upsurge of power we had not felt for aeons. It coincided with the attacks upon our kind and we knew then a tide had turned and we needed to act.'

'So what is this rite then if it's not what we think?' Tara was getting irritated, Gwen could sense it in her manner and the discordant tones of her voice. A look at her aura told Gwen that she was in conflict with herself and the colors oscillated around her like a cuttlefish on speed. What Gwen didn't know was that Tara was being bombarded with images and words, chants and songs, faces and names; all coming at her in tsunami of voices straight out of the past. They swamped her and surrounded her, filling her and carrying her along. It was all she could do to hang on to her identity amidst the cacophony and deluge filling her mind. It was why Tara was quizzing Amber, in a futile attempt to retain herself. It was an exercise in concentration. Whether Amber knew this was another matter, she gave no outward sign that she was aware of the inner struggle taking place before her, even though her senses were acute to the power flows and lines of energy given off by living matter. She carried on her explanation regardless.

'When humanity was closer to us and the Natural Order of the world, they sought the assistance and approval of those whose realm it was, those who were elevated beyond this land. Like students and supplicants, they endeavored to honor those beings and sang songs of power, gave offerings and gifts and the greatest of all, displayed a selflessness and devotion to others that opened their hearts and minds. When they sang the songs and completed the ceremony, they would be able to cross over to the adjacent realms. Ours being the closest, known by you now I believe as the *In-between*. By this crossing over, they could traverse the dragon lines of the world and cover vast distances in the blink of an eye, some could even slip through the holes in time and see possible futures. They learnt many great things from us and the Ch'drnOmThophilim who regularly visited our realm. What we granted to these seekers, was what was known then as the Rite of Passage. Some of your shaman call it Vision Quest now or Dreamtime. There are more names, but it equates to the same thing.' Tara frowned at the unfamiliar name and Gwen realized she hadn't mentioned them, though Jen and Maddy had explained to her who they were and who they embodied.

'The chdn...topilim. What? Tara belatedly asked. Who are they or what are they. I've never heard that word before and I sure as hell can't say it.'

'Simply Tara, they are the Children of Thought. Your kind came to know them as Angels, but before that, they were the old gods. They resumed whatever form was necessary to guide and steer humanity. But you all lost your way and the Children of Thought slipped away too, arrogantly believing that you as a race had failed and were doomed to self-destruct. But you didn't fade away as quickly as they thought you would, and their absence let the rot take hold and fester. We tried to encourage them to return but they paid us little heed for we are not as powerful as they and we are tied to this world unlike them. For they exist primarily upon a world of their own, they only held a stewardship over this one. We too then drifted away from this realm more, taking refuge in our own and the wild places here where humanity could no longer find us. But something else found us instead. That is part of the reason I am here Avatar.' Gwen knew by the serious use of her new title, Amber had something important to say.

'Avatar, we need your help. As the demon army pushes across this land, more and more of my kin are driven from their trees and rivers. Even the rocks tremble before the onslaught. It seems the Adversary is hell bent on wiping out *all* life before him, in every realm. We suffer Avatar and unless these elementals find new homes soon, they will wither and die, we are too tied to this world to take refuge in the *In-between* for too long.' Amber gestured around them and a thousand thousand faces appeared. Gwen heard Tara and even Daniel gasp as they finally saw what they were surrounded by. 'Were it not for the beacon you sent up by activating this ancient Dryade circle' Amber concluded with sadness in her voice 'we would have been lost, doomed to extinction for although we exist in an adjacent realm, without this one and its trees and wildlife, ours - along with my people - faces annihilation.'

'Sorry to throw a wet squib on your girly chat of doom and gloom,' Daniel piped up 'but is it my ears or is that sound getting nearer?' Daniel was sitting close to the edge of the circle so heard more what was happening outside of it. Gwen suddenly perked up, so enraptured had she been in the brief lesson and conversation with Tara and Amber that she had somehow forgotten the battles taking place just beyond them. She didn't even know if Ezekiel had arrived to support the Horsemen, but now with Daniels comment, she heard. Carried supernaturally to her by the horrible screams and the clash of a vast number of weapons, sounding more like the crash of thunder or waves against rocks than steel against steel, but it still said that someone had arrived and engaged the enemy. The disturbing thing though was that Daniel was right, it was closer now. Much closer.

'What time is it Dan?' Dan rolled his wrist and squinted at his timepiece.

'Two thirty five in the morning. Well, I think it is anyway, always assuming my watch hasn't stopped again.' he shrugged and looked guiltily embarrassed.

'Doesn't anything of yours work?' Gwen asked exasperation evident in her voice. Though the moment she said the words, she saw the potential for a double entendre and a smart arse remark from Daniel. But to his credit, he was still out of sorts from Amber's arrival and having his body pushed to limits he didn't even know he had, so he answered simply.

'Not all of the time, but it isn't my fault.' Daniel whined 'it's just leccy stuff, and leccy stuff always goes on the fritz around me don't know why, it just does - sorry.'

'No problem Daniel, it can't be helped now. Tara?' Gwen sighed resignedly as she turned to the other woman and asked if she was good to try out her new ability. Tara just pulled a face that said anytime was as good as any other.

'I can help Avatar.' Amber chimed in excitedly 'I know the Rite of travel if you know the destination. Tara will supply the power and the incantation as she is the Dryade, can we take every one?'

'I don't see that we have much choice in the matter.' Gwen answered as she took in the myriad of faces beyond them 'If we can get everyone in the sphere, or even better, in the circle we'll do our best. I think the most suitable place would be my grove back home. It is in the heart of a National Park and considering my new role I'm guessing it'll constitute as a sacred grove, and there should be enough trees and wildlife there to transplant the entirety of this island if needs be.' Amber looked pleased and Tara looked reticent. Still unsure of the enormity of everything happening to her and expected of her.

'What is it Tara, you can do it can't you?' Tara blanched and the color left her face. She was pale already and her skin looked almost translucent, putting her red lips and green eyes in stark relief. She looked worried. 'Tara, you're starting to scare me, talk to me, what's up?' Gwen asked with real concern.

'The images, the ones in my head. They have started to slow down and organize themselves as Amber spoke. As you've been talking about certain subjects, images and words relating to them have slowed and appeared to me.' Tara wrung her hands and looked between the elemental and Gwen.

'Go on Tara, for the love of god, say what's bothering you, we don't have all night. Really!' Tara flinched at Gwen's words as though the limited time they had just added salt to her wounds.

'This Rite of Travel you spoke of, for me to use it, I need the Athame, my Athame I suppose.' Gwen knew the word, it was a ceremonial tool used by contemporary witches, wiccans and pagans, as part of their magical practices, and it was more often than not represented by a small dagger. Gwen reiterated her thoughts aloud for Tara, who shook her head.

'No, it's not that Gwen, this is special. It has been handed down through the ages and my ma had it last, it's THE Athame, the original one apparently and more known as the Artavus.' Gwen had not heard this.

Neither Jen, nor Maddy had ever mentioned this reference when the subject came up, and it did. Tara popped Gwen's bubble of thought as she continued hotly 'But I've never seen it. I hope it's not still back at the house.' Gwen's frustration was getting the better of her and she snapped back at the pale woman as her heart sank and her stomach flipped at the prospect of so many problems and her over-thinking mind was trying to resolve them as she spoke.

'Well give us a bloody clue will you,' Gwen snapped 'what does this Artavus look like. We've got no more than one and bit hours before your window closes and god only knows how much time before the demon army break through or the possessed descend on us, if I have to, I'll fly back and search the house for it, but I need to know what I'd be looking for.'

'It's a sickle Gwen, but unlike any other. For its origin was as a quill sharpener and believed to start around the time of King Solomon the sorcerer. The blade sharpened the quills he used to write the first spell books of power, the blade became an integral part of the magical workings from there on.' Gwen's mind instantly replayed the woman from the reading she got from Tara. The woman with her back to them wielding the sickle that decapitated the helpless woman on the altar.

'Describe it!' Both Amber and Gwen commanded simultaneously. They looked at each other, questions in both their eyes. Seconds passed and they turned back to Tara.

'It is longer than most, and the handle is jet black, ebony perhaps or jet. It is warm.' Tara closed her eyes and drifted in the memory. 'The blade is a dull silver and sharper than any man made metal. It was forged from the ore from space, that which falls to Earth. The blade made molten by the breath of dragons and shaped by the first Dryade. Grave runes and sigils adorn its blade and in the hilt, there is a moonstone the size of a heart. It bears a name that should never be spoken, and its soul is vengeance.' This time it was Ambers turn to pale. And Gwen was really concerned now, it didn't sound like the type of object that she even wanted to see, let alone find. And she sure as hell didn't want it in the hands of Tara, another Dryade, who now she thought about it, bore a striking resemblance to the woman from her vision. Especially not when she said that a Dryade had been a part of the forging of this Athame, sickle or whatever it really was, it seemed somehow prudent to keep Tara away from it. In fact to keep everyone away from it. But as Gwen was distracted by the memory, Amber had turned and was reaching a hand through a glowing tear in the veil between this reality and hers, and was speaking rapidly to something beyond. Before Gwen could ask what she was up to, her eyes locked on the object that Amber was pulling through the tear. Gwen was thunderstruck. So much so, she found herself unable to move, to think or to make a cohesive decision. It was only a second or two, no more, but it was all the time needed for Amber to pass the object to Tara and for Tara's eager hand to snake out and grasp it like a striking cobra. Gripped with the same determination of a drowning man clinging to a life ring. As though her very existence depended on her possessing the object, Tara's face lit up with a joy and unhealthy exultation as she cradled the sickle to her breast. Gwen was sure that even a mother reunited with a lost child wouldn't have looked as joyous.

'Amber?' Gwen asked the elemental in a strained and subdued voice. Gwen felt the very air change within the circle with the arrival of the artefact. Amber turned her lightly glowing, dull orange eyes on Gwen and they held the question of *what did I do wrong?* It was the look of an innocent, or one fulfilling a charge. 'What have you done?' Gwen whispered but with no less gravity and Amber seemed conflicted.

'It is hers.' Amber stated flatly 'She described it perfectly and I have carried it with me since it was left to my care by my mother before me when I ascended to my royal duties. I was told to not speak of it unless it was spoken of to me, nor was I to show it to anyone unless it was described to me. But Tara described it perfectly and when she said she needed it for the rite, I was honor bound to return to her what was rightfully hers by birth.' Gwen was gob smacked 'She is her mother's daughter, whether her mother wished it for her or not destiny and events transpire to send us in whatever direction it sees fit and we are but flotsam upon its river.' Gwen watched Tara cuddle and coo to the artefact, talking to it as though it actually were a long lost child. A dull moist sheen had formed upon her brow as though she were suddenly feverish and her eyes, when they opened, were distant and a little glazed. Having dropped to her knees with the blade, Tara was rocking gently back and forth and muttering incomprehensible words to the sickle, or so Gwen presumed. Gwen was reluctant to disturb her for the moment, liking her predicament to that of waking a sleepwalker, not a recommended course. But she kept an eye on her.

'Amber! How is it that you even had *that*!' Gwen thumbed at the artefact, as she realized she had a distinct repulsion to the item. It wasn't something she could define but it made her flesh creep just talking about it. Heaven forbid she had to touch it, she felt that would tip her over to full blown vomiting.

'My mother and under the command of my father, the King Corinamber, ruler of the woodland elementals it was entrusted to me as next high priestess of our realm should I become queen, and who am I to gainsay the words of my mother the existing high priestess and that of my father and my King?' Amber seemed a little testy at being questioned so harshly about her charge, and Gwen grimaced, she had to move cautiously here, tread softly. The last thing she wanted to do was in one foul swoop alienate everyone around her and set them against each other. This was something that would just have to play itself out. Her main priority, in fact her only priority was the First Tree. All other matters had to be secondary, but that didn't mean they weren't worth watching and being aware of.

'I'm not saying that Amber, but all I am asking, is how your people came to have it in the first place if it was in the hands of Tara's mother, who I hasten to add, left a note saying that if Tara was reading it, she was dead. Do you know how she died?' This last question snapped Tara back to her senses and she bounded to her feet and rushed forward to where Gwen and Amber stood. She almost bowled them over with her eagerness to get to them and hear what Amber had to say.

'Easy girl.' Gwen put her arm out as a barrier and Tara all bar bounced off it, inches from Amber.

'Tell me Amber, tell me how she really died. I think all I've had so far are lies and I'm getting tired of those.' Tara's voice seemed calm as she asked the question, but Gwen sensed the barely restrained emotion roiling beneath her cool exterior. But Daniel, who had watched events unfold before him, wide eyed and stunned as though he was watching something on some trashy television show, seemed to be the only one who had any sort of grasp on the perils of the immediate and wasn't slow in voicing them.

'As much as I would love to know how my dear ma died,' Daniel almost shouted 'she at this moment in time is already dead and nothing we say will change that; we however are not, and if we don't get our collective arses out of here, and now me sis has her thingamabob, as I understand it we can do just that? Move first, chat later? Does that sound like a sensible plan to anyone but me?'

All eyes turned to him. Three varying, but equally intense stares couldn't have pinned him to the spot any better than had three spears could have nailed him to the ground. Gwen's emerald gaze, beneficent and cool; Amber's fiery, orange stare, all alien and dangerous, yet so full of invitation he felt like a moth before a flame. And his sisters. That one scared him the most now, for it had a faraway look to it and he felt akin to a mouse, trapped and held before a very wild cat as he caught sight of Tara's feral and terrifying expression scrutinizing him, disassembling him where he stood as though she was seeing him for the first time. What he didn't know was that a part of Tara, a part even she was unaware of, *was* actually seeing for the first time; the first time in several hundred years through eyes that weren't her own.

Daniel held up his hands in supplication and tried to take a step back. It took a concerted effort of will to do just that, but he did. And he felt better for it.

'Easy ladies, it was only a thought. I didn't want to interrupt anything or such but that sound is getting closer and I can make out voices now. Sorry to say but they are shredding my nerves a bit. It's like finger nails on a chalk board, or tin foil on your teeth. I'd really like to get out of here if it's alright with you, just don't hurt me, please?'

Daniels pleading dispelled the moment and Gwen nodded as the imperative returned along with her common sense. Even Tara seemed to return to herself briefly as she glanced away and muttered her agreement, though it didn't stop a brief arrow shot glance at Amber that said she wasn't finished with the elemental yet.

'Gather everything that's coming.' Tara spoke loudly and with a force that hadn't been there before. Gwen narrowed her vision to study Tara as she mentally summoned the elementals closer. Amber did the same and soon enough, the energy shield as well as the circle were both full to almost spilling out with the wispy and wild eyed creatures. Daniel came to stand beside Gwen and he gripped her hand. Hard enough to earn a curious glance from Gwen, it was then she saw the fear in his eyes, but not of what he was fearful of. She put it down to everything that was happening to him and she smiled a smile of reassurance. Gripping his hand in return to emphasize her smile.

'Let's do this Tara.' As Gwen spoke her eye was drawn to three figure riding towards them. It was the Horsemen except War who apparently was single handedly holding the horde back but even his prodigious capabilities would not hold for much longer. Ezekiel had arrived but with fewer forces than was hoped for. Famine advised the group to be gone before the horde broke the line and if they did, they would swarm this circle.

'Very well. Elemental?' Tara turned to the elemental. 'You heard the Horseman, begin your song I will attempt to leave the portal open allowing for everyone to pass through, but they must hurry, I don't know

381

how long I'll be able to do that for and we can't run the risk of any of those...things out there getting through.' As Amber began to sing, picked up by many of the elementals who knew the song too, Tara began to chant. The music that sprang up would have moved riots to peace, stampedes to a standstill and storms to calm. It rose in a spiraling vortex, twisting up into the night sky and unfolding above them like an umbrella of light and sound, cascading back down onto them to recirculate and rise again. Faster and faster it spun and twisted, rising and falling, with everyone at its center within the druids circle, the sound escalated to a crescendo of unimaginable sound and sensation that with a concussive boom that sent a shockwave rolling out across the land for a hundred yards in every direction, the power imploded on the group in a shower of incandescent lights and time stretched as the portal opened. Outside, it lasted a heartbeat, but inside it allowed time for every elemental to make it through, the last to leave were Daniel, then Amber, Gwen and lastly Tara who with a last backward glance to the land that was her home, stepped through the rift and disappeared. Tara, Gwen, Amber, Daniel passed through, and Tara fought the Athame to hold the gate open upon the other side to allow as many of the Elementals through as possible. Barely five hundred remained inside the stone circle when the horde punched through the line, finding the weakest link and that was Ezekiel's forces, they swarmed across the field and slammed into the now weakened shield. The first hundred possessed died instantaneously as they immolated themselves upon the magical barrier but it weakened it enough, what with Gwen and Tara and Amber being half a continent away, the magic only had the portal to flow through and it broke. The horde of deminions and possessed fell upon the remnants of the Elementals and their death cries were terrible. The portal was still open though and that was all the opportunity they needed. They had no idea Tara was struggling with the ancient artefact to control its outpouring and her own inner conflict shredded her concentration, all of which meant she couldn't close what she had opened. Gwen and Daniel began dragging her away from it in the hopes that distance would sever the link. Amber was busy dispersing her people and had moved a few hundred yards away from the rift so nobody saw the deminions pour out into Gwen's grove hot on the heels of the last fleeing elementals and it was their screams of pain and horror that stopped the group in their tracks and with stomach wrenching dread realize they had seconds to decide what they would do next or become victims of the horde as more and more poured through the rift, the cries and screams chilling the blood of all who heard it. Daniel turned suddenly at the sound of something large crashing through foliage, though it was more like a lot of large somethings crashing through the trees right behind him. He turned to expect his doom at the savage hands of the possessed and almost closed his eyes, were it not for the thousand yellow eyes looking back at him that held them transfixed open as the first of the possessed horde broke cover and ran towards him.

# The End of Book 3 Trinity
## Look for the next installment

# BOOK 4 REBELLION

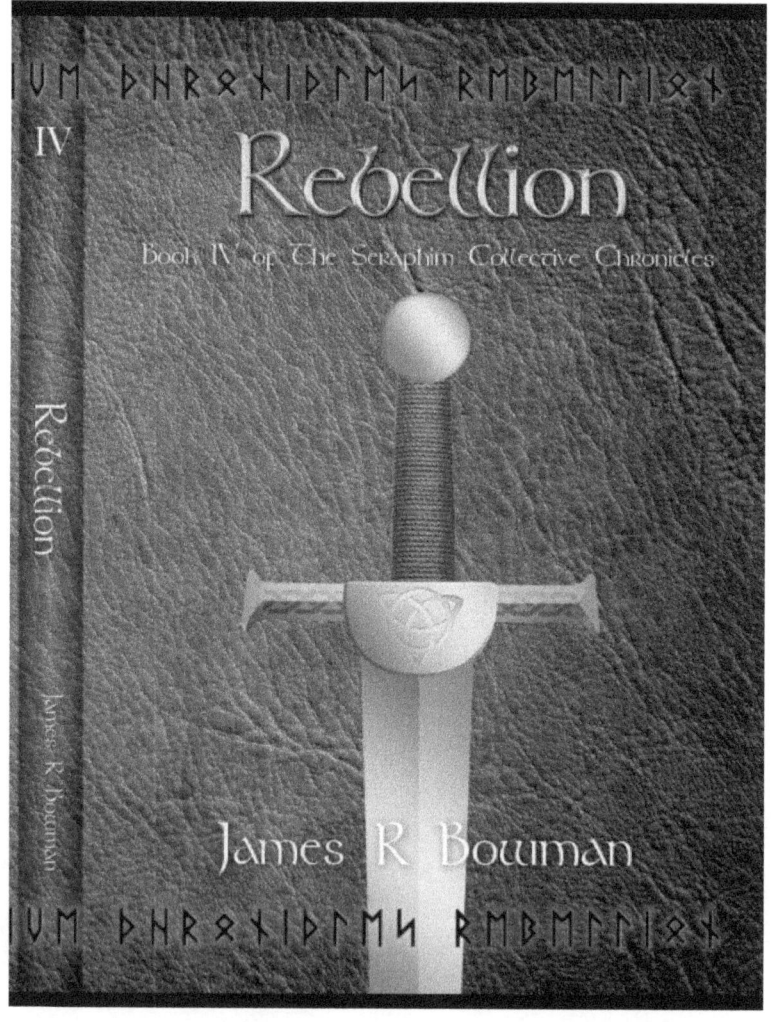

# Glossary

**Absolutes** – These are the four beings whose governance of this part of the cosmos have come to be known by humanity as the Four Horsemen of the Apocalypse. Written into scripture, but truth be told, they have existed for countless Millennia. Ensuring the planets move as they should, the evolved species evolved as they should and the great balance is maintained. DEATH, WAR, FAMINE and PESTILENCE are their more familiar names.

**Azaroth** – An arch demon who left Ellysia with Lucifer when the Covenant was formed.

**Asmodeus** – An arch demon who also left Ellysia with Lucifer at the Covenants formation.

**Avatar** – A physical manifestation of a deity or greater power operating through a medium in the gross material form. In this case, the Drakarim are the conduits for the planet to express her will. Every planet will have their Avatars as their language and communication is too vast and powerful for any resident of the planet to comprehend except in the occasional dream or intuition.

**Alfar** – Elves. Who are as diverse in their kingdoms as humans are on Erithia. Self-appointed keepers of the balance, Guardians of the Boundary and Wardens of the Marsh. All these lands exist within the In-between. When Kalith established her Empire on Erithia, the Elves-Alfar were ancient, having vast kingdoms in the wildlands. As the Empire encroached, clashed were inevitable but against the Drakareth, they were outmatched. They took to slowly moving their kingdoms through rifts to the In-between whereupon they flourished but kept tenuous affiliations to Erithia which was what early humanity interacted with until even we became too much for them and they made their move almost permanent…almost.

**Azazel** – Desolation. An arch demon who defied the Covenant to set foot upon the earth for her own agenda and not that of The Adversary and wanted Gwen's soul.

**Angel** – last name given to the celestials by humanity. Known to themselves and the other    races as Chdrn'OmThophilim – Children of Thought. Angel is derived from amongst others the Greek word Angelos, meaning messenger. This is a job not a species.

**Athame** – Long before Gerald Gardner appropriated the Athame on behalf of Wicca the ceremonial dagger had a convoluted origin, passing through black handled knife to black knife but heralded back to the time of Solomon as a blade for sharpening quills with which to write magical or Enochian enchantments. The Artavus became an integral part of the rites as its use grew more frequent. There are many Athame secreted around the world that hold incredible power but are lost to time.

**Bringer of Endless Night** – another name or title the Adversary goes under.

**Ballinskelligs** ( Baile 'n Sceilg ) - Homestead of the Rocks. Is an area that abuts the wild Atlantic, forms the Skellig Ring between Valentia Island and Waterville. Lending the area its name from the Skellig Michael (Sceilg Mhichil) an ancient monastery on the larger of the islands off the coast and there is a smaller island known as Little Skellig (Sceilg Bheag) But for all its history, what most don't know that deep within the larger Skellig Michael lies the ARCHIVE. The depository of the Collective and runs many, many miles deep beneath both the rock and the Atlantic Ocean floor. In fact few who live know the extent of the ARCHIVE. Excavated by ancient magics that burrowed through the stone during the time of the Kalithine Empire and may have been a covert sanctuary for those who did not believe in the Empire any longer if at all.

**Chthonian Forest** – We understand chthonian as relating to the underworld or inhabiting that realm, but the Greeks adopted that word after being introduced to it early in their civilisation when they adopted practices for sacrifice and worship of those they called their gods. The Chthonian Forest is the largest in the Domain and even the Demon lords give areas of it a wide berth for what dwells within.

**Covenant** – Shortly after the Kalithine Wars ended and humanity began to disperse and exercise it's newly granted 'freewill' it soon became clear there were massive flaws in the fledgling species that humanity was and it was also clear that many were not suitable to evolve and needed more time within the wheel. It was so decided by unanimous votes by the Absolutes and Triumvirate Council of Drakarim of Esolaria as well as the ruling Lords of Ellyssia that one planet back from Erithia (Earth) a new colony would be formed to take these corrupt or volatile souls and rehabilitate them sufficiently they could eventually re-join the Erithians for the great conjunction when all the planets move up a place and the closest planet fuels the Sun for another turn. There was no fall as recounted in modern texts, instead a contingent of upper echelon Ellysians would take charge and emigrate there. Lucifer was the first to volunteer, along with Lily who changed her name to Lillith, as did many who supported Lucifer in this great undertaking, they named their new home Nescaria and so the Covenant was formed. Part of this Covenant was non-intervention between worlds. The divide was to remain sacrosanct. Clearly until the Adversary took over then that went right out of the window.

**Density** – Now modern day science measures many things and many of these have a spectrum. Light and sound for the two most prevalent. But mass too has a spectrum range. We see everything in this range within our parameters to react too, from rocks to gas. Greater density to lighter density. Then we measure according to depth, or distance from the core. Closer to the core, the greater the density or mass, further away less dense. Then we consider the spectrum range from the Sun. The closer to the Sun, the greater the density, further away, less so, hence the gas giants are behind us, less dense. The same then applies to whatever dwells upon those worlds. Now here is the tricky part. Residents of whatever world, unless they have mastered density manipulation can only see what fall within the range of that world. Our eyes here on earth – made of the earth – are only made to see what is here. When we look beyond this world, we see only that which fall within our density spectrum. Our understanding of the universe is based upon our comparison to this world and what we can see or hear. Vast percentages of the multiverse, is lost on us and does not look how we think.

**Deminion** – in the hierarchy of the Domain, lesser demons are sent essentially illegally through portals to Erithia to foment chaos and gather willing or unwilling subjects. The only way these deminions can over-come the density difference is by inhabiting a human or living thing upon this world – it has been known for the odd animal to suffice in an absence of a human.

**Drakarim** – Dragon ( considered good by comparison, few remaining on Earth as most remain on Esolaria – their world - hidden deep within the heart of our Sun (as we call it).

**Drakareth** – Dragon (considered NOT so good.) These are the banished. Many still travel through space in their iron gaols but a vast number were pulled to earth and even after the great wars, many remain still. These are the Reversion afflicted and it is the name they adopted to differentiate themselves.

**Dolmen** – A megalithic tomb with a large flat stone atop upright stones. Mostly found in Britain, Ireland and France.

**Dryade** – What may seem a name for a tree spirit, Dryad – a nymph who were normally shy Oak spirits but were known to lure men to their doom and where we derive nymphomania. But this Dryade expands upon that and is the name for a female Druid. She who bridges the gap between the natural order and the sorceress. Using magic to protect nature. These powerful women were taught the arts by the Children of Thought to help them against the Kalithine Tyranny and the forthcoming revolution that would set humanity upon its path of freedom. But they were divided about their purpose and in conflict, the order split. See Kore-Megara.

**Drakel**  Basically non afflicted offspring of Drakareth here on Earth who choose to live in harmony with this world and some even help it, though they are still burdened by their nature they do what they can to assimilate.

**Drakul** – As above except they afflicted and have no moral compass. They do what they can to sow discord and chaos, many working for the Drakareth, most part of the Legion and all immensely dangerous.

**Drakeesh.** – Of the Drakel and Drakul, only Drakul have the ability to pass their disease along, a lingering curse of the Reversion. These creatures are as good as dead, nearly impossible to kill unless extreme measure employed. Many are mindless killers, some have a bit more control but nonetheless are violent and unstable. These were the cause of the earliest Vampire legends before humanity was sufficiently evolved to understand anything beyond superstition and folklore.

**Erithia** – actual name for what we call Earth. We derived it from other names of Gods – those we thought of as gods – the Children of thought – who freed humanity from bondage from the Drakareth Empire. So humans used what they could for a name.

**Esolaria** – The Drakarim home world – where we derive the word Solar from for the Sun.

**Ellysia** – The Children of thoughts home world – what we call Venus (after another goddess) but it's where our earliest humans heard the concept of Ellysian fields as a paradise in the after- life, why early Christians called their messiah - he of the bright morning star - which we know to be Venus and source of this persons home world.

**Elemental** – every living thing in nature possesses a life force, from rocks to trees to fish even the rivers themselves. Ancient and persecuted, they eventually withdrew themselves to a realm adjacent to this and every other realm – the In-Between. Possessing a complex royal lineage and great families that hearken back, they are as vast as the stars and as diverse. The majority want peace and prosperity, but there are some who would watch the world burn just for the fun of it. These are to be avoided at all costs.

**Fenris** – The Great Wolf, spawn of the Ellysians but imbued with an almost untapped strength, matched as it was by a wild ferocity. Fenris had ambitions that grew too great to manage so he was 'contained'. Bound by a magic so powerful, even he could not break free. A magic fetter created by the dwarves so long ago, none now live who can re-create it. This did not stop the devious sorcery of The Adversary who is a master of loopholes, found a way to free Fenris without having to break the chain, he simply replaced him with another.

**Gleipnir** – The third chain to bind Fenris, Thor forged the first two but they failed so the prowess of the Dwarves was called upon and a great magical undertaking was set in motion to gather 6 impossible things: the sound of a cats footfall, the roots of a mountain, the beard of a woman, the sinews of a bear, the spittle of a bird and the breath of a fish. The sons of Ivaldi created this and it's still going strong…it's just not holding Fenris any longer.

**Hadestria** – the last planet we have come to know at the edge of our solar system, humanity in its arrogance don't consider it a planet anymore – no-one thought to ask it of course. We called it Pluto (again, after yet another god) but it is known as Hadestria, where we learnt the word Hades from as a depository of what we thought of as the underworld. It is no such thing, instead it is the origin world of the beings who we only in the last few hundred years have come to recognise as the Four Horsemen of the Apocalypse. To the rest of our universe, they are the Absolutes. Caretakers if you will of the evolution of our part of the cosmos and they will exist until the last planet fuels the sun and even that winks out of existence to forge a new purpose.

**Hound of Fenris** – The great wolf was uncontrollable, even as a pup and it was then that it was discovered that his bite had a terrible side effect. One not all survived. The strongest survivor was turned and adopted many of the traits of Fenris. These early Hounds were powerful and pure and did not suffer the agony more diluted victims suffer. A Hound is a cross between wolf and man, the earliest references to what we now call a werewolf. In some parts of the cosmos, such a gift was revered but Fenris abused his as he grew, bringing a violent and vicious nature to the gift, so the Hounds of Fenris were brutal, savage and incredibly powerful. Created for war and battle and carnage and were totally loyal to Fenris. They could never regain human form and lived a life in agony due to the transition - assuming they survived it. The only way to assuage the pain was to feed but it was short lived. Another was to gain power, this was granted for service, more power gave less pain and more control until they too might regain their human form and manage the change at will. Many of the earliest Hounds who were more pure and mastered their condition grew disenchanted with their lot and many went into exile and hermitage, living apart from whatever world they inhabited. Many still do.

**In-Between** – where to begin for this is a place, a construct and a realm as old as this world and invariably older, and it existed at the beginning of this universe and grows and expands as the worlds evolve and shift even now. The Norse construct may help explain it more as theirs is contained within Yggdrasil, the world tree – just see this as way bigger. Where the nine realms are located upon its branches, trunk and roots. The realms are traversable if one knows the ways and the paths and possesses enough power to activate them. Because of density and the multi-dimensional structure of space and time, like interlocking rings the In-between connects the realms and spreads father and vast beyond these confines to accommodate species and kingdoms only ever dreamt of and it is a type of magic that many from our realm have made the trip, survived it and returned to tell us tales and fanciful stories of wonder and disbelief. Humanity has a great knack-to their detriment- of depleting whatever they do not understand or fear, making it small and harmless. Much of what we feared and rightly so resides there still and the veil between there and here is thinning, where it tears horror spills through – or if we're unlucky enough to encounter it. It is a place accessed via water as water is a conduit, bridges, the space you cross whenever you make a doorway from one place to another, the astral realm, and of course – magic can take us there. The In-between is as deadly as it is beautiful, lethal as it is lovely for such is the balance of the cosmos. Travel there at your peril.

**Kore-Megara** – an ancient sect of women, versed in the sacred arts of sorcery, necromancy many arts arcane. When mortal kind were first taught these gifts by those we considered gods and beings of power and protection, all was well. But division soon grew, and the Dryades split with the Kore-Megara leaving for the wilderness, communing deep within the earth and gathering in Kaverns, as they named their disparate groups. Usually fifteen to twenty but no less than nine, a tight hierarchy and strict regime. They became skilled in weapons and undertook assassinations, murders and toppled kingdoms. They were feared and as their legend grew so too did the fanciful tales surrounding their reputations. Much we see today is attributed to the Dryades, the benevolent side of the Matriarchy but in reality, the Kore-Megara are responsible for many of the stone circles and Barrows we see today lost to time.

**Kul fire** – an innate ability possessed a few Drakul to utilise a mystical breath weapon, sometimes magically induced as proficiency is an art form. It is vastly hotter than regular fire being magically enhanced, with the Drakul because of Reversion it burns black and very little can stand against it.

**Kel fire** – as above but even rarer amongst the Drakel. Just as hot and dangerous except it burns blue.

**Kalithine Empire** – A whole appendix is required alone for this vast and sprawling Empire. In summation though, As Reversion swept the cosmos and many of the Drakarim were afflicted, hideous numbers succumbed to this terrible malady; being of superior magical skill, many could contain the disease but this had a side effect of warping the mind and causing them to commit terrible acts. The Drakarim did not believe in death as a punishment so they exiled their afflicted out into the cold abyss of space. One such victim was none other than the mate of the head of the Triumvirate Council – one Kalith Sal Malkuth. Her crime is another story but suffice it was sufficient to remove her wings and banish her. As a paramount sorceress, when she arrived partly by accident, partly by the design of another, her status as former royalty (as such) elevated her swiftly amongst the exiles, over time she built her Empire to spread over the many nations we know today and the ruins of those outposts can still be found. Her capital was however one place prominent in human mythology – and for good reason, also another story – Atlantys. Kalith's seat of power and naval of the Empire. It was more than just destroyed at the ending of the Kalithine War, a fact that will be revealed as this Chronicle expands.

**Kachina** – Katsina or Tihu. They are essentially the spirit form of everything the world has to offer, though primarily to the People of the Mesas and the ancient Puebloans. Foremost amongst them we have the Hopi but we also have the many others such as the Zuni, Acoma and Laguna, though there are many more. These Tihu embody everything the People understand from the stars, to squash, to beans to gourds and corn. The animals are represented, the Crow Mother, Bear, Mountain Lion, Wolf, Eagle and so many more. But they are part of a balance and when the People left Tokpela, the First World, the Kachinas kept the people safe and helped them flee. So it went through Tokpa, the second world and Kuskurza the third world until the People ended up here with their last Emergence into Túrwaqachi – this fourth world. Because of this duality, this balance, what is not spoken of is the vacuum left behind, the void that was lost and alone, a shadow realm that drew forth Dark Tihu, the opposite to those that helped and fled with the People. The Dark Tihu have followed and searched and have finally found their counterparts and they draw closer.

**Nescaria** – After the creation of the Covenant, a contingent of Children of Thought left their world to take up residence one planet back from

Erithia – earth. We call that Mars (yes, after another god) but due to the flaw in humanity many had to be tempered and await the next planetary evolution. These damaged souls were contained one planet back and governed by these select few celestials. Over millennia humanity has become aware of this place, known to those who dwell there affectionately as the Domain, It is a word we mistakenly created the word Demon from, so those residents became demons, the Domain became known as Hell. Aeons of Chinese whispers have done us no good at all.

**Revenant / Possessed** – much like it sounds, except unlike current beliefs it cannot be removed. Once a Deminion takes possession, they ruin the body from the inside out, mutilating that outside too in varying degrees depending the inhabitant. Some possessions are subtle and others blatant and short lived as the mutilation is too much for the still aware person it was to cope with. A Deminion can keep a body moving for a short time after the body dies before needing to find a new host. These are very dangerous too and more prevalent than we would like to admit.

**Reversion** – An ancient affliction brought into being to forestall the increasing power and reach of the ascended races. A few died out because of this disease but the strongest – The Dragon kind and the Children of Thought learnt if not to cure it, certainly live with it. There were however those who could not contain its affliction and it did what its name implies. It erodes the mind and body, destroying any moral compass until those who fall victim to it suffer deformities, mental breakdowns that are an aberration of insanity, turning the victim not so much into a gibbering wreck but more into an evil psychopath fully aware and uncaring of consequence or outcome. Surviving Reversion became worse than dying from it and as the numbers of survivors grew so did the level of atrocities committed. To date there is no cure.

**Valkyrie** – Our own mythology tells us they are the Shield maidens of Odin and the Aesir whose role it was to collect the fallen and transport them to Valhalla where they feast for eternity in the great hall as the Einherjar – The Heroic Dead. Reality is a little different for the Valkyrie are the royal guard of the Aesir as well as elite shock troops being airborne upon the great flying steeds they are responsible for breeding and maintaining. They guarded Ellysia and were a force to be reckoned with. Humans encountered these majestic warrior maidens and in humanities latter years we sought to emulate them and so the Amazons were born, fierce and powerful in their own right who broke free of the Kalithine tyranny centuries before the last Kalithine Battle that brought down the Empire and there is record of the Valkyrie and the Amazons fighting side by side but that record is lost to history and is a story for another time.

Lightning Source UK Ltd.
Milton Keynes UK
UKHW011810080722
405587UK00002B/404

9 781803 690841